THE MANDEVILLE SECRET

CALLIE LANGRIDGE

Storm
PUBLISHING

Ebook ISBN: 978-1-80508-249-1
Paperback ISBN: 978-1-80508-251-4

Cover design by: Eileen Carey
Cover images by: Shutterstock, Midjourney

Published by Storm Publishing.
For further information, visit:
www.stormpublishing.co

ALSO BY CALLIE LANGRIDGE

The Mandevilles Series

A Time to Change

The Mandeville Secret

To the little girl in the green dress. This one's for you x

ONE

24TH JULY, 1924

HAD HOPED TO SPEAK BEFORE YOU LEFT STOP
TRUST HOLIDAY WILL PROVIDE INSPIRATION
STOP
ANTICIPATING SIX CHAPTERS WITHIN THE
MONTH . . . STOP
RA

Nell folded the telegram and slipped it back inside her handbag. In an attempt to silence her editor's words, she snapped the clasp shut. It was an exercise in futility. The three dots of the ellipsis boomed louder than any words spoken in the bombastic voice of Robert Amos ever could.

'We're holding a spot for you in the spring schedule,' Robert had said when, against her better judgement, she had joined him for lunch at *The Criterion* the week before. He had half-smiled, half-grimaced as the waiter refilled their glasses. 'Yesterday alone, I received a dozen manuscripts in my postbag. You wouldn't want an ambitious, young pretender knocking you from your perch now, would you?'

Crossing her fingers beneath the table and resisting the urge to down the entire glass, Nell had taken a sip of her champagne, promising Robert that he would have the first six chapters by the end of the month. A week away in the country was just what she needed to get the creative juices flowing.

The train lurched as it went over the points. Robert was nobody's fool; he must have known that she was ignoring the urgent ring of the telephone in the hall that morning, anticipating that it was him calling to remind her of the deadline. The telegram arrived as she left to jump on the bus to take her to Euston – Robert's way of ensuring that he had the last word.

Holiday. Had he selected that word particularly to goad her? Of course he had. Words were his business; he never used them by chance. She envied him that. His unfailing capacity to find words when, for the last two months, they had forsaken her. Each morning she had risen in the hope that, overnight, an idea had formed in her brain, yet within minutes she found herself gazing out of her window. She was now on intimate terms with the schedule of each of the nannies pushing their perambulators along the pavement or holding the hands of their charges as they guided them up the steps of the British Museum opposite. She often abandoned her small flat to spend hours roaming the halls of Greek marbles and Egyptian sarcophagi, fruitlessly clinging to the hope that the ancient plants on the hieroglyphs would somehow inspire an idea to take root in her mind.

Outside the train the seemingly endless fields of green rolled by. The leaves were full of their summer colour and plumpness, so unlike the barren wasteland inside her head.

The guard slid the door open and leant into the compartment. Nell showed him her ticket and, when he left, glanced at her fellow travelling companions. Often inspiration for characters came through chance encounters: an interesting nose here, an original turn of phrase there. She consulted the features of the middle-aged man who sat opposite. He had fallen asleep, head resting against the window, an empty seat separating him from a young woman who appeared to be deeply involved in a magazine. From her fresh complexion and fashionable clothes, Nell put her at twenty-three, perhaps twenty-two. At least a full half decade younger than herself. As she watched the young woman, Nell became aware that, every so often, the magazine dipped, and the woman peered at her over the top of the pages. Nell looked at the cover of the publication and held in a groan. It was the latest edition of *Tatler*. A photographer from their staff had been at a party she had attended the previous week.

The woman lowered the magazine. 'It is you, isn't it?' she said, turning a page for Nell to see herself captured in black and white. She was on the periphery of a group, her head turned to the side. On finding herself in the line of sight of the photographer, she had taken evasive action. But the manoeuvre hadn't been quick enough to hide her face.

'Yes, I rather suppose it is,' Nell said. She was rarely recognised, being something of an also-ran in the publishing world and notoriously camera shy.

'I hope you don't mind me saying, but I adore your books. I mean, I really do adore them.' The woman smiled.

'That's very kind.' Nell gave the woman her well-rehearsed smile.

'You wouldn't mind, would you?' The woman slipped a book and pen from her bag. 'I brought it to lend to my friend, Betty. Can you make it out to Gladys? That's me,' she added almost shyly.

Nell took the book – *Miss Derbyshire's Conundrum*. It was her second book and Miss Derbyshire of the title was a society 'gal', her conundrum being that she had been entrusted with delivering a diamond necklace to a cousin in Boston in order that she might wear it on her wedding day. Miss Derbyshire's plans had come perilously close to being thwarted by a dastardly and light-fingered head waiter on a transatlantic voyage until a dashing American hero stepped in to save the day. He was the heir to an oil fortune and the owner of a square jaw and an aquiline nose. There was a dashing hero in both of Nell's books and in her handful of short stories. They were not always American; they could just as easily be a French duke, a Prussian count or, at a pinch, an English gentleman farmer – just the type of man her mother would be happy for her to settle down with so that she might give up "this silly writing lark".

Nell unscrewed the lid of the pen. Her family would certainly not have approved of the most recent candidate for the role of her leading man – an artist recently graduated from the Slade whom she had met at the book launch for another of Robert's authors. In their final, terse conversation at the *Café Royal*, he had accused her of being spiky, like a conker in its shell, so desperate to protect whatever was beneath that she used her barbs to repel any man who dared get too close.

Nell bent the spine of Gladys' book and scraped some words onto the title page. With a final jab, she added a full stop to the signature: Margot Evangeline. Her real Christian name was too pedestrian for her publisher and her surname – Potter – too reminiscent of that worthy lady in the Lake District with a penchant for rabbits and squirrels and ducks in bonnets.

'I've read both of your books. And all of your short stories,' Gladys said and smiled when Nell handed Miss Derbyshire and her conundrum back to her.

'Really?' Nell had to resist the urge to grab Gladys by the shoulders and shake her, instructing her to take herself immediately to the nearest library to borrow some Hardy or Dickens, even Fielding would do.

Gladys glanced at the typewriter in the luggage rack above Nell's head. 'Are you writing a new book?' she asked.

Nell smiled again, attempting to look as friendly as possible.

It was eager young readers like Gladys who paid for her London lifestyle, such as it was.

'I'm hoping to find an idea soon,' she said.

'They say it comes in the strangest places,' Gladys smiled. 'Inspiration.'

The brakes heaved and the train slowed as it pulled into a station.

After prising her fingers free of Gladys' enthusiastic handshake, Nell stepped down from the train. She placed her luggage on the platform and a cloud of steam swirled about her as the shrill shriek of the guard's whistle screeched in her ears. The joints and pistons driving the wheels of the train began to churn, labouring like arthritic elbows, heaving the train into movement. It lumbered away up the track. The final swirls of steam dispersed, and Nell found herself alone on the platform of a small station. She pulled her collar away from her neck. It was warm enough to believe she had stepped from an oven directly into a broiler.

A man dressed in a chauffeur's uniform emerged from the ticket office. 'Miss Potter?' he asked and touched the peak of his cap. He looked around her, clearly expecting to see a trunk or valise.

'I travel rather light,' Nell said, laughing too gaily. The chauffer plucked her small suitcase and the battered case containing her typewriter from the platform.

Outside the station, the chauffeur placed her luggage on the ground before opening the backdoor of a cream-coloured Rolls Royce. Nell slipped inside. He closed the door with a satisfying thud and placed Nell's luggage in the boot.

Nell was no stranger to the inside of a private car or taxicab, but this car was something quite different, with luxury oozing from the hand-stitched, well-waxed expanse of fawn-coloured leather upholstery.

'M'lady,' the chauffeur said as he got into the driver's seat, touching the peak of his cap once again. 'If you're ready, we should be there in ten minutes.'

'Very good,' Nell said and smiled. *M'lady*. Her mother would burst with pride if she could hear her daughter addressed in such a manner.

The very thought of her mother, back in her parents' semi-detached house in Cheam, made Nell sink into the leather. Nell was attempting to make a life for herself in the very environment that girls like good old Gladys would have considered her natural habitat. But it came at a cost. The landlord was breathing down her neck for the next six months' rent on her postage stamp of a Bloomsbury flat, and, without the co-operation of her typewriter, mere pennies remained to rattle around in her bank account.

An image of her childhood bedroom in her parents' house appeared in her mind's eye. A London lifestyle was expensive. She lived as frugally as she was able, but she had to eat, didn't she? She had to have at least a few lumps of coal in the winter to keep warm. The handful of frocks hanging in her wardrobe had seen the needle of a talented (and cheap) seamstress in Whitechapel; stitching a hem here, adding a string of glass beads there. The quirky fashion for which Nell had become known – and which was attributed to her artistic inclinations – was a result of having to pay the rent rather than any skill at besting the fashion editors of the stylish magazines crowding the newsstands. But all these things would be for nothing if she could not find a story to write. And if she could not pay her rent, she had only one option.

In her mind, the Rolls Royce transformed into the small black car her father kept in his garage; the car he polished every weekend, and which emerged every other Sunday to drive her mother to see the sights of south-eastern England. The coast of Worthing, the Seven Sisters, The Devil's Punch Bowl. If Nell moved back into her parents' house, would she be expected to accompany them on those day trips, sitting in the back seat with the picnic hamper containing a thermos of sweet tea and a lunch of ham sandwiches wrapped in wax paper? She was used to lunching at *The Criterion*, for heaven's sake! Drinking at the *Café de Paris*. With the exception of when Robert was footing the bill, she paid for her meal in every restaurant. She would not – could not – accept anything that smacked of a handout or charity. But, unlike the circles in which she moved, she had no rich parent bankrolling her living expenses. What she had earned from her two books and handful of short stories had been chipped away. At least she knew her way around a type-writer. Perhaps that would stand her in good stead for a job in a typing pool. It would be of more use than all the literature and science she had studied at Cambridge. At least her mother would now have the chance to say, 'I told you so'. In spite of the heat of the day, Nell shivered.

She looked out the window as they drove past a small village with a post office, a public house and neat rows of cottages. 'Almost there, M'lady,' the chauffeur said.

Nell thanked him. There was something about his deep voice with its unrefined northern accent that intrigued her. It was the type of voice that had a story to tell.

They passed an old church, its weathervane perfectly still up on its steeple, and continued along the road with a high redbrick wall to their right. Just a little further on, the chauffeur turned the car through a set of gates with two golden lions atop, holding a globe between them. The tyres crunched through the gravel of a long drive, flanked on each side by neatly trimmed lawns and surrounded by woodland and parkland.

Nell fought an impulse to press her nose to the glass to take it all in. She was well aware that her friend and ex-roommate at

Cambridge was the daughter of a member of parliament and a minor aristocrat, so unlikely to live in a modest cottage in the Northamptonshire countryside, or a modern semi-detached house like Nell's own mother and father. But she had imagined Charlotte living in a respectable Tudor country pad or a reasonably sized villa, not this gleaming Portland stone Palladian manor, circled by hills rolling away into the distance. Nell pictured her small suitcase in the boot. She had packed sparely for what had promised to be a week of writing. The skirt, few dresses, trouser suit, and a blouse or two were unlikely to pass muster here.

TWO

The car pulled up to a portico held up by two columns, each as wide as a tree trunk. Almost before the chauffeur got out, the great front door of the house opened and Charlotte ran out, waving wildly, her blonde hair escaping its clasp and tumbling to her shoulders. She pushed it away from her face. Nell smiled. It was impossible not to smile in the presence of Charlotte Mandeville. 'Nell,' Charlotte called and waved through the window. Dispensing with formality, Charlotte opened the car door. Nell had barely placed one foot on the gravel when Charlotte swept her into a warm embrace.

'I'm so pleased to see you,' Charlotte beamed.

'If I'd known you lived in a mansion like this, I should have visited sooner,' Nell said. Taking a step back, she shielded her eyes and looked up at the pale stone and the windows gleaming in the midday sunshine.

Charlotte's nose wrinkled. 'A mansion? Hill House? I suppose I don't think of it like that. The old place is just home. Besides, if you'd accepted any one of my invitations before, you *would* have seen it sooner.'

'Fair point,' Nell said. Charlotte might appear to some as a soppy young girl, but after three years sharing a room, Nell knew Charlotte to be pin sharp. It had been two years since they left Newnham, but Nell had yet to meet anyone to match Charlotte's brains. Or her skill at bridge.

The chauffeur emerged from the back of the car, bearing Nell's embarrassingly small amount of luggage.

'You can take that in through the front door, Elliot,' Charlotte said. 'Since Mother's not at home, there's no need to stand on ceremony.'

'Very good, Miss Charlotte,' the chauffeur said.

'Do you have a trunk coming from London?' Charlotte asked Nell. 'Should we send someone to collect it from the station later?'

'There's no trunk,' Nell said, rolling a stone beneath the sole of her shoe. 'I didn't realise I was to be a guest somewhere so grand. I suppose we'll be expected to dress for dinner.'

'Not if we can help it,' Charlotte said. 'If my mother were home, it would be a different story. But she's on a trip to the Isle of Wight with my father and aunt. It's just me here with Edward and his family. And do you know, we sometimes even eat dinner from trays on our laps in the drawing room.' She lowered her voice and nudged Nell. 'And if we do happen to have a more formal evening while you are here, you will be more than welcome to borrow any frock from my wardrobe. It'll be like old times at college when we shared everything, won't it?'

'If you say so,' Nell said. 'Although I don't imagine you'll want to borrow either of my blouses.'

'You never know, I might just take a look at them in case.' Charlotte slipped her arm through Nell's. 'Do you know,' she said, 'I truly believe that our days at Newnham were the happiest of my life. Not to mention the most fun.' Charlotte gave Nell's arm a squeeze. Moving in closer, she said, 'Do you remember the secret midnight feasts in Millicent McCarthy's room?'

Nell pictured the bottles of gin and canapés Millicent had delivered from a local French restaurant. Her father was a top-flight barrister and his only daughter had not been at all shy in spending her generous monthly allowance on entertaining. All that Millicent asked was that the company at her legendary midnight soirées be stimulating and interesting. Nell smiled. 'I haven't thought about those parties in ever such a long time.'

'They were terrific fun, weren't they?' Charlotte said. 'And you always had us in stitches with your jokes and parlour games.'

'I suppose I did.'

Before Nell had the chance to think further on Millicent's parties, Charlotte said, 'Now come along inside. Edward's longing to see you. I've told his wife and children all about you and they can't wait to meet you.'

'You must have been spinning some yarns,' Nell said. 'Making me sound more interesting than I am.'

'Don't be so modest,' Charlotte said.

'You're confusing modesty with honesty.'

Charlotte shook her head and laughed. 'Even if you weren't a famous author, my family would want to meet my very dear friend.'

'Your very dear friend? Really? Even after all this time, and my abandonment of you?'

Charlotte flashed Nell a wicked sort of grin. 'We all have our cross to bear,' she said.

Nell smiled. Her friend was as adept at the art of sarcasm as her.

Arm-in-arm they made their way through the large front door and into a vestibule. They crossed the threshold of Hill House and Nell felt her mouth fall open. Before them was a grand hall panelled in pale wood. A vast staircase decorated with intricately carved animals and plants swept down the centre, its newel posts each topped with a carved pineapple. The bluest of skies was visible through a glass dome high in the ceiling and sunlight flooded through, picking out the mosaic floor tiles of tulip-like bronze flowers on a background of white. The mantelpiece of a great fireplace rested on the shoulders of two carved fauns – one playing a flute, the other a lyre. Above them, a stone relief on the chimneybreast bore the same coat of arms as that which adorned the gates at the end of the drive – two lions holding aloft a globe.

'When I think of that pokey room we used to share,' Nell said, craning to look up at the cloudless sky through the glass dome, her soles squeaking on the floor.

'It's the people that make a place, not the building,' Charlotte said, giving Nell's arm a squeeze. 'You should have seen this hall before the war. It was full of paintings and statues and Mother's collection of vases. They were all moved up into the attic when my aunt turned Hill House into a hospital for the wounded men. You remember my aunt, don't you?'

'Nobody could forget meeting Leonora Hart!' Nell said, picturing the woman wafting through the streets of Cambridge in a kaftan-affair of a dress in jewelled colours when she visited her niece. With the scent of jasmine about her, it was as though some exotic creature had landed from another planet into the drab greys and browns of students and dons. Nell had always thought that her given name suited her, since Leonora Hart had the presence of a lion.

'Aunt Leo does rather leave an impression wherever she goes,' Charlotte smiled. 'And normally, she gets her own way with everything. But after the war, even she couldn't convince Mother to return the paintings and decorations to the hall. Mother just didn't seem to have the enthusiasm for the house she once had. After she lost... After we all lost...'

It was Nell's turn to squeeze Charlotte's arm. Charlotte

never used a single word when half a dozen would do, and Nell knew any silence or pause to be a sign that her friend was upset or troubled.

'I still feel Tom here, you know,' Charlotte said. 'It's silly, isn't it? But sometimes when I'm alone in a room I imagine him coming in with his newspaper. I can almost smell his cigarette smoke and hear his jokes, always at my expense. He was the very best of brothers. So kind and generous. And such a part of this house. I don't think Mother will ever come to terms with losing him. Of course, we all lost someone, didn't we?'

Nell nodded. She had met Charlotte the year after the war ended. But while Charlotte had talked of the loss of her eldest brother, Nell had never given voice to her loss, no matter how many times Charlotte had pressed her.

She felt Charlotte squeeze her arm again. 'We decided that if Mother can't face it, we will. We all rolled up our sleeves last week to clean the walls and gave the panelling a fresh coat of wax. We brought all the paintings and statues and decorations down from the lumber room. They're locked away in the ballroom for now.'

'The ballroom?' Nell said.

'Yes.' Charlotte pointed to a set of double doors beside the fireplace.

'Oh, I see.' Nell decided against telling Charlotte that she was expressing surprise that her friend lived in a house with a ballroom, rather than asking where it was.

'The last party was Mother's Christmas Eve Ball the year before the war,' Charlotte said. 'I wish I'd known you then and you could have seen it, Nell. That time feels like a lifetime ago now, doesn't it?'

'You will have a party again, one day,' Nell said.

Charlotte managed a smile. 'I'm sure you're right. By the time Mother returns from the Isle of Wight, we'll have everything reinstated in the hall. So that's something to be happy about. I hope she realises we're doing it to please her and not to upset her. Now, do you fancy some tea? I could do with a cup. Let's go into the morning room. It's so bright and jolly when the sun is out.'

Charlotte let her arm slip from Nell's and stepped away. Nell was about to follow when a movement at the top of the stairs made her pause and look up. It was a fast movement, like someone running on the landing, accompanied by something that sounded like a laugh. Nell looked for a moment longer. The noise and movement stopped as abruptly as it had started. It was no doubt one of the children Charlotte had mentioned.

Nell followed Charlotte into a light room furnished with dusky pink sofas, floral rugs and green curtains at the vast windows looking out onto the drive. They sat in two pink armchairs and Charlotte pulled a cord beside the fire. She asked the maid who answered for tea.

'This really is a beautiful room,' Nell said.

'Mother would be delighted to hear you say so. Those little animals in the cabinet are her favourites.'

'Lovely,' Nell said, although she had never been a particular fan of chintzy china ornaments behind glass. 'I really am very grateful that you invited me to come and stay. And to your family for having me.'

'I'm sorry,' Charlotte said. 'I completely forgot to ask about your writing. Do you think you might find inspiration while you're here?'

'Let's hope so,' Nell said.

The door to the morning room opened. The maid entered again and placed a tray of tea things on a low table. She left, but as she closed the door, it opened again. Charlotte paused in pouring the tea. 'Hello there, poppet,' she said to a young boy peeking around the door. Charlotte placed the teapot back on the tray. 'This is my friend, Miss Potter. I told you she was coming to stay. Come in and say hello.'

The little boy pushed the door wide and charged into the room, coming to a stop by the side of Charlotte's chair.

'Is this Miss Potter?' he asked, speaking to Charlotte, but staring at Nell.

Charlotte stroked the boy's red curls. 'Yes, Tommy,' she said, 'this is my friend, Miss Potter. Go and introduce yourself properly to Miss Potter. And mind your manners.'

At a slightly slower pace than that which he had entered the room, he crossed to stand before Nell, and stood for a moment considering her from beneath his fringe of red curls. Nell wouldn't have minded if the child had decided to keep his distance. Save for her observations of the activities of the nannies outside her flat, her encounters with children were mercifully infrequent to non-existent.

'Good afternoon, Miss Potter,' he said confidently. 'I'm Tommy Mandeville. It's a pleasure to make your acquaintance.'

'And yours, Master Mandeville,' Nell said.

The child looked at her from beneath his fringe again. She felt compelled to fill the silence.

'How old are you?' she asked.

'Eight and three quarters.'

He offered her his hand. She could hardly refuse the gesture, so lifted her hand to shake the child's.

Charlotte busied herself with pouring the tea and the child leant in close to Nell. Still holding her hand, he moved in closer and, in a much softer voice said, 'Your name is Nell, isn't it?'

'That's right.'

His pupils widened, as though he had just come inside from the sun. 'Marbles and mummies,' he said softly.

'Sorry?' Nell said.

Without blinking, he said, 'Prams and nannies.' He freed his hand from Nell's and ran his fingers through his curls, staring intently at Nell.

Charlotte looked at him and laughed, as she stirred milk into the tea. 'Do you like Miss Potter's hair, Tommy?'

In an instant, the child's demeanour altered. He took a step away from Nell, cocked his head to one side, and said in a loud voice, 'It's short.' He studied Nell's hair. 'Not as short as a man's hair. It's very fetching.'

Nell stared back at him at a loss for how to respond.

Reaching into the pocket of his shorts, Tommy pulled out a doll, of the type that lived in a dolls' house. It was the figure of a lady, with her hair styled short. He ran his thumb over the doll's face before looking at Nell's cheek. He tried to peer beneath the hair that sat straight from the outside edge of her eye to just above her jaw. If she had tucked that hair behind her ear, she would have revealed a scar normally hidden from view. It ran from her temple to her cheekbone. It had been there for so long that Nell rarely thought of it. It matched a mark Nell could see on the doll's cheek.

Before Nell could say anything about the peculiar coincidence, the door flew open. A man with a small child on his shoulders and a woman holding the hand of a young girl entered.

'There you are, Tommy,' the woman said. 'Whatever made you run off like that? We were worried. One minute we were picking bilberries and the next you had vanished.'

'I came to see Nell,' Tommy said.

As Nell made to stand, Tommy placed his hand on her wrist. 'It wasn't me, you know,' he whispered. 'Up on the landing.'

She stared at the child. Once again lost for words. The man took a step towards them, and Nell stood; it would have been rude to remain seated and she couldn't very well interrogate the child about what he meant.

'Nell,' the man said, 'how wonderful to see you. You look magnificent, if a little pale. Our fresh country air will put the colour in your cheeks before you return to London.' He kissed her on both cheeks while still holding onto the legs of the child sitting on his shoulders. Edward's skin on Nell's cheek felt warm.

'It's lovely to see you again, Edward,' Nell said.

'And this,' Edward said, pushing his spectacles further up his nose, 'is my wife, Alice. Alice, darling, this is Nell, Charlotte's old roommate from Cambridge. I told you all about her. I used to take these devilish girls out for tea on my way to visit Father in town. How long has it been, Nell, two years?'

'Something like that.'

'It's a pleasure to meet you finally,' Alice said with a warm smile. Her beautiful auburn hair was swept up and held in place by clips. 'I so wanted to visit Cambridge with Edward, but I always seemed to have my hands full with small children. I see our eldest has made himself known already.' She smiled at the Tommy. 'This is Daphne,' she said, presenting the little girl who grasped a wicker basket. 'And this little monkey is Charlie,' she said, pointing to the little boy still on his father's shoulders, now gripping a clump of Edward's strawberry blonde hair while he attempted to prise it from the baby's grasp. 'I have both of your books,' Alice said. 'But I'm afraid,' she said, smiling at her children with a little raise of her eyebrow, 'I don't have much time to read, or do much at all. I know I will enjoy them when I finally get a minute to myself.'

Nell smiled. 'You really aren't missing much.'

'Don't be so silly,' Charlotte said. 'Your books are a real hoot. Don't forget the pleasure you give to your readers. Giving people joy is the greatest gift of all.'

Nell smiled at her friend. 'If you say so.'

'I jolly well do say so!'

When Charlotte and Alice fell into a conversation about arrangements for that evening's dinner, Nell used the opportunity to study them all. They seemed a relaxed family. Edward wore casual trousers and a shirt open at the neck, his sleeves rolled up. Alice was dressed in a simple pale blue cotton dress, with short sleeves and a round collar. They both wore sensible walking brogues. Their children were similarly dressed: Tommy in shorts and a cotton shirt; Daphne in a yellow dress and the baby in a one-piece bibbed suit.

Their casual appearance could be put down to the hot weather, making them shed their normal formality. But Nell felt formality wasn't something that Edward, Alice and their children would wear well. The three children – as well as their parents – had ruddy cheeks. As a family, they radiated sunshine, their hair ranging from the white blonde of the baby to the flaming auburn of Alice's tresses. They were a family of light and colour, down to the children's grass-stained knees and the tell-tale signs of bilberry juice smeared on their clothes and hands.

While Charlotte and Alice spoke, Daphne placed her basket on the floor and raised her arms to her mother. Alice bent to scoop her little girl into her arms, as automatically, Nell thought, as drawing breath. Alice held her daughter and kissed her cheek and Charlotte, who had joined them, rubbed the little girl's knee. All the while, Edward bobbed up and down, keeping the baby on his shoulders amused by singing a little song.

As hard as she tried not to, Nell experienced a sense of loss. She thought again of the house in Cheam. From when she had been a tiny thing, she had spent hours in the care of Mrs Nevin – Mother's 'woman who did' – sitting on a rug on the kitchen floor, playing with pots and pans, because her mother didn't want a mess or any noise in the drawing room. Any disturbance to Mother's routine played havoc with her nerves. After Mrs Nevin left her mother's employ, Nell was relegated to spending every day sitting at the dining table, in silence, playing with jigsaw puzzles until she was old enough to join Esme at school.

Now, as ever, any thought of Mrs Nevin was followed by a pang of guilt.

Nell felt her hand given a little squeeze. She had almost forgotten that Tommy was beside her. She looked down and he beckoned. She knelt beside him.

'You have nothing to be sorry for,' he whispered.

Before Nell could ask how on Earth Tommy knew what she was thinking, Edward said, 'It looks like you've made a friend there, Nell.'

Nell got to her feet. But this time, instead of taking her hand, Tommy ran to his family. He grabbed the fattest berry from his little sister's basket, popped it in his mouth, and stuck his tongue out at her. Daphne squirmed in her mother's arms, objecting. Nell looked on. He was now behaving like the type of boy she often saw running rings around their nanny at the British Museum. And what the devil had he meant when he said she had nothing to be sorry for?

'You'll have to excuse us,' Alice said, making a grab for Tommy's hand while keeping a wriggling Daphne balanced on her hip. 'Someone has had a little too much fun today and, perhaps, a little too much sun,' she said, firmly taking Tommy's hand in hers. 'I think it's bath time, then teatime, then bedtime.'

'But after that, it's time for the grown-ups,' Edward said. 'Would cocktails on the terrace at seven suit you, Nell?'

'That sounds wonderful,' Nell said, still perplexed by Tommy's behaviour.

'Wilco plans to arrive at about five o'clock, providing he can get away from town,' Edward said to Alice.

Charlotte let out a loud groan.

'Don't be like that, sis,' Edward said. 'Wilco is a good sort.'

'To you, perhaps,' Charlotte said.

'You know he doesn't mean most of what he says,' Edward said. 'It's all just sport to him.'

While still balancing Daphne on her hip and with Tommy

tugging at her dress, Alice said, 'I'll make sure to always sit between you and Wilco and see to it that you are never alone with him, if that would make you feel better.'

Charlotte sighed. 'No, it's all right. I know I'm probably overreacting. He's harmless really, but I find it all a bit wearing. Sit him next to me if you think it will do any good. I promise to be on my best behaviour.'

Edward smiled at his sister. 'Atta girl, Charlotte.'

'Yes, yes, yes, I know,' Charlotte said.

'Right,' Alice said, as Tommy dug his hand into the basket and pulled out a handful of berries. 'I think we'd best get on. We'll see you later for cocktails then, Nell. I can't wait to hear all about your writing.' Alice placed the basket on a table and shooed Tommy from the room.

'See you later, Nell,' Edward called as he bounced the baby on his shoulders and trotted out of the room.

Charlotte blew out a puff of air. She flopped into her chair and Nell retook her seat. Charlotte took a sip of her tea. 'There's never a quiet moment with those little monsters around!' she said with a laugh. 'They are darlings, really. It's so lovely to have them about the house, they fill it with life.'

'They don't have a nanny?' Nell asked, taking a sip of her tea.

Charlotte shook her head. 'Mother tried to talk Alice and Edward into hiring someone, but they wouldn't hear of it. They want to raise their children themselves. Wherever Edward and Alice go, the children go, too. Even on trips to check on the tenant farmers. It took Mother a while to get used to them having free run of the house rather than being confined to the nursery. She may not always admit it but secretly she adores having them around. I know my aunt does. She absolutely dotes on them.'

'That's a very modern arrangement,' Nell said.

'You'll see that many of Alice's ideas are very modern. I

adore her. She has been a breath of fresh air to the family. She's given us the shake-up we needed.'

Suddenly the penny dropped. 'Oh,' Nell said. 'She was a maid, wasn't she? I remember you telling me about her.'

'That's right. And she's absolutely marvellous. It took Mother a while to reconcile with Edward and Alice marrying. There could have been a huge scandal but what with the war, people – even Mother's society friends – had other, more important things on their minds.'

Nell tried not to wince at the casual mention of the war.

'I mean,' Charlotte continued, 'since Edward is now in line to inherit Father's title, Alice will become a Lady. I think it's fantastic. It's socialism in action, don't you think? It's what we all fought for. Not only did we win the right to vote but the future Lady Mandeville will be an ex-maid! And little Tommy will be the heir. He was quite taken with you, wasn't he?'

'If you say so. I'm not familiar with how children behave around adults.' Thinking for a moment, Nell said, 'Did you tell him my Christian name before I arrived?'

'I don't think so. He may have overheard it in conversation.'

'Yes, I should imagine he did.'

'Right-o, I think it's time to show you to your room so you can settle in.' Charlotte pulled the cord beside the fireplace. 'The staff is somewhat depleted these days,' she said. 'We have a handful in the kitchen and to help with the upkeep of the house. A few maids and father's groom live in, but the others all live in the village. We are particularly short on ladies' maids. Sally, who usually does for us all, is away with my mother, father and Aunt Leo. We rather tend to fend for ourselves these days. I hope that won't be a bother.'

'A bother! Really Charlotte, I think you know I have only ever fended for myself. I wouldn't expect anybody to fetch and carry after me.'

The door opened and the young maid who had brought

them tea entered again. She bobbed a curtsy. 'Nell, this is Mary. Mary has been with us off and on since she was a young girl. Mary, tell Miss Potter what you are doing now.'

Mary looked to the floor. 'I'm studying to be a teacher, Miss. I go to the college. In the holidays I come to work here.'

'Mary earned a scholarship, Nell. She's ever so bright. And when she's qualified, she's going to work in the village school. That's right isn't it, Mary?'

'Yes, Miss Charlotte.'

'Anyway,' Charlotte said, rising from her chair. 'I should let you go and freshen up, Nell. Mary will show you to your room.' Nell got to her feet and Charlotte kissed her on both cheeks. 'Perhaps you can start work on your next bestseller this afternoon! Mind you, I can't imagine anything at Hill House inspiring you. Nothing remotely exciting ever happens here.'

THREE

Nell followed Mary out into the hallway and up the stairs. She ran her fingers along the dark wooden handrail and over the exquisite carvings of fruit and tiny birds and animals. Looking down at the scarlet stair carpet, she saw some of the pale backing strands poking around the edges. The carpet might be a little frayed but it was still quite stunning.

At the top of the stairs, Mary led Nell along a corridor and into a room at the front of the house. Between the two windows overlooking the drive sat a pale wooden dressing table, with a matching wardrobe along the opposite wall. The bedspread and the curtains were a jolly sunshine yellow.

'Your case has already been brought up, Miss,' Mary said. 'I've hung your things in the wardrobe and put your bits in the drawers.'

'There was no need. I could have seen to it myself. But thank you.' Nell thought of the twice darned stockings and had to hold back a grimace.

'You'll find some other dresses and bits and pieces in the wardrobe,' Mary said. 'Miss Charlotte asked me to put them in there for you. She thought you might only be able to travel light, what with you coming alone on the train. And Elliot set up your typewriter here.'

A desk had indeed been created on a small table placed in front of one of the windows, with a neat pile of paper stacked on one side of Nell's typewriter and a tray containing a pen and a pencil, a bottle of ink, and even a notebook.

'It's a lovely room,' Nell said, taking in all the details.

'The family saves it for their favourite guests,' Mary said. 'Will you let me know if there's anything else you need, Miss? Just ring the bell by your bed.'

'Thank you, Mary. I will.'

Mary was about to leave but Nell called out after her. 'Mary, I don't suppose you know whether there is anything particular I should wear for dinner tonight?'

'The blue dress is a favourite of Miss Charlotte's, if that helps.'

'Yes, Mary, it does. Thank you.'

Mary left and Nell used the opportunity to explore. She looked into the bathroom leading from the bedroom. The tiles on the walls and floor were white marble, shot through with blue veins, rather like a ripe Stilton. She looked in the wardrobe. There were evening dresses and cocktail dresses and clothes for the day and for sporting activities. Nell smiled. Charlotte truly had no idea just how lovely she was. And this room she had chosen for Nell was by far the grandest she had ever had the good fortune to stay in. Nell thought again of the house in Cheam and her childhood bedroom. And with the picture came thoughts of her mother. She tried to silence her mother's voice by picturing the bedroom in her Bloomsbury flat. That made it worse, somehow. Her mother had never been a woman to be silenced when she had something to say. And she had had a lot to say about Nell's move to Bloomsbury.

'A single girl alone in the city, whoever heard of such a thing?' her mother had said when Nell announced that she would be moving permanently out of her parents' house to take a flat in London. It was after dinner one Tuesday evening. Mother was sitting before the fire with some magazine and Father had been smoking his pipe behind his evening newspaper.

'You went away to university, isn't that enough?' Mother bustled.

'No Mother, it's not.'

'I thought you had got that silliness out of your system. Girls and continuing education. I knew it wasn't a good idea. I told your father as much. And why your aunt left you that money, I shall never know. I'm sure she meant you to put it to good use. Into buying a property, perhaps. And you go and squander it on a couple of years at university.'

'Squander!' Nell said. 'Would you say that if I had been a son? Would you have seen it as a waste if a son had gone to university?'

Ignoring Nell, her mother said, 'You wouldn't be told. And look where it's got you now.'

Nell sat forward, primed for the fight. 'A career as an author,' she said.

'An author,' Mother laughed. 'You write one silly story and you let that publishing man fill your head with fanciful ideas. What is he about in any case? A man, taking an interest in a young girl. It's not... seemly.'

'He's my editor, Mother. I can't see what is more seemly than that. *He* has my best interests at heart.'

'Oh, I see.' Mother threw her hands in the air. 'And I don't? What will our friends and family say when they hear about this latest episode?'

'It's not an episode. It's my life. I'm of age and if I choose to move to London permanently, then it is nobody's business but my own.'

'Don't you have anything to say to your daughter, Harold?'

Nell's father looked around his newspaper. 'I hardly think anything I have to say on the matter will have any bearing on Helen's decision. As she says, she is of age.' He retreated behind his newspaper.

'I see.' Mother took up her magazine. 'Then I am the only one who cares at all about my daughter. About her reputation. About what everyone will think. But what do I know? You spent four years at the War Office before that silliness at college and for what? Can't you put that experience to use now? If you found a position somewhere you might meet a nice young man and settle down.' She flicked furiously at the pages of the magazine before slapping it down on the arm of the sofa. 'Very well. Have it your way. But don't think you can come back here, my girl, every five minutes, cap in hand when you find you can't look after yourself. What do you know about keeping a house and its accounts? Precious little, that's what. Don't think your father will be there with his cheque book every few minutes. Oh no, if you go, as you seem determined to, then you are responsible for yourself. I give it one month. Two at the most.'

It had taken two years, but her mother's words had come true. And wouldn't she be oh-so pleased with herself. On her bi-monthly trips home, Nell had hoped that Esme's impending nuptials to a most suitable man – a clerk in the branch of the bank their father managed – would direct their mother's attention away from her younger daughter. But even the talk of flowers and wedding breakfasts hadn't been enough to put her mother off the scent. Nell could practically see the words 'I told you so' perched on the tip of her mother's tongue, waiting for the day they could take flight.

Nell dug her fingernails into her palms. If she didn't come up with a story soon, she would let her publisher and editor down. She would let her readers down. The only person she wouldn't let down was her mother.

Nell sat down on the edge of the bed and fanned her face.

Edward's cocktails. Yes, she would think about Edward's cocktails. A few ice-cold drinks would certainly provide a welcome relief from the heat of the day. He was a nice chap, Edward. Charlotte loved him dearly, just as she had loved her older brother, Tom. Charlotte had spoken of Tom endlessly at Cambridge. She been thrilled to attend his old university and read the books in the library that perhaps he had; walk the halls Tom had; take tea in the tearooms her brother had. Charlotte had spoken so often and so freely of her brother that Nell felt she knew him. But he had been six years dead by the time Nell met Charlotte when they both arrived at Cambridge. He had died in the opening weeks of the war. Nell had no idea what Tom looked like. Charlotte wouldn't keep a photograph of him, preferring to recall the vibrant memories of her beloved brother moving, speaking and laughing, rather than a frozen version of him, drained of colour. But so successful was Charlotte in summoning Tom, that Nell could almost feel his presence in the small room they shared. He had seemed as alive to Nell as any of the young men who roamed and ran along the corridors of Cambridge. It was those men that Nell found herself resenting more and more with each passing day. She resented the breath in their chests. Resented their lusty voices singing out from the chapels, their ruddy cheeks in the winter months when they stamped along the pavements. Each one, each man, full of life, was a reminder of what she had lost. The loss she had never given voice to, not even to Charlotte.

A rivulet of sweat dripped down Nell's face. She would never share her memories, no matter how hard Charlotte tried to prise them from her.

Nell swiped at her cheek. Story ideas. She was here for inspiration, not to rake over the past. She stood, but before she could pull out the chair at the desk, there came a gentle rap at the bedroom door. Nell cleared her throat. 'Come in!' she called. The door stayed closed. Crossing the room, Nell opened the door. There was not another soul to be seen out in the corridor. She was about to return to her pressing appointment with the typewriter when a movement stopped her. At the far end of the landing, a door stood ever so slightly ajar.

'Hello,' Nell called.

Receiving no response, she made her way along the corridor and to the landing. The open door was smaller and narrower than those leading to the bedrooms, the bottom half panelled and the top decorated with paper to mimic the wall. Nell opened the door to a stone stairwell lit only by an unshaded bulb. She was met with a blast of cold air and a smell like damp clay. She took a step inside. It was so cold that she shivered. She placed her hands on the wooden handrail. 'Mary,' she called, 'did you want me for something? Mary?' A noise like shoes slapping on stone came rapidly from above. Nell looked over her shoulder. She was a guest here. The staff would quite rightly not take kindly to her sneaking around their domain. She took a step back into the carpeted heat of the landing. But as she began to close the door, the footsteps stopped. The sound changed. Someone was now running down the stairs. Nell expected to see Mary turn the corner but the footsteps stopped and headed away, higher into the house.

Nell brought her palms down on the wooden handrail. Even as a child, she hadn't enjoyed the frenzied uncertainty and unpredictability of games such as Hide and Seek. As an adult, she liked being led on a wild goose chase even less. She craned her neck, listening. When the footsteps seemed to reach the very top of the stairs and disappeared, she couldn't help herself. Hitching up her skirt, Nell ran up the steep staircase as it twisted its way to the very top of the house.

The steps eventually gave out onto a landing where Nell paused to catch her breath. She looked around. She was in an attic space consisting of a single long narrow corridor. Windows in the slanted ceiling let in daylight so that it was quite bright.

Nell made her way slowly, the bare floorboards creaking frequently as they took her weight. Doors to a series of rooms opposite the slanted windows stood open. Each small room was empty save for items of modest furniture piled neatly in the centre: bedsteads; chests of drawers; rugs rolled and secured with twine. There were other items: jugs and wash bowls; a book or two; a framed print standing on the mantelshelf. One or two of the rooms showed signs of damp with peeling wallpaper and buckets positioned beneath dark patches blooming in the ceiling. It was clear that the only occupants of these rooms in quite some time had been the spiders who had set up home in the webs at each window.

'Hello?' Nell tried again. The only response was the creak of floorboards. She looked further along the empty corridor. 'Look here,' she called. 'If you want me, tell me where you are, otherwise I intend to go back downstairs.'

No sound. 'Have it your way,' Nell said. She spun around but had taken only one step away when the sound of creaking came from directly behind her. She stopped. Held her breath. A floorboard creaked again, closer, as though someone was walking towards her. It was accompanied by a blast of cold air that whipped about Nell, making the hair on her arms stand on end.

Nell's brain performed a sequence of mental gymnastics. A door had opened, causing a draught. Yes, that was it. Breathing deeply – and ready to face Mary, who it was sure to be – Nell turned sharply on her heels and came face to face with... nobody. The corridor was empty, just as it had been when she entered. Squares of daylight from the windows lit the floorboards and fine dust particles swirled in the air. She let out a sigh and laughed softly, thinking she had read one too many books set in creepy old houses. There was nothing remotely sinister about Hill House. It was a warm house, full of love. Of course, it was prone to creaks and strange noises. It had stood on this spot for more than a century. Didn't the bones of an old man creak when he rose from his chair?

Nell shook her head. She was about to head for the stairs when the sound of footsteps started up in a room further along the corridor. But these footsteps sounded like someone was running. Stamping.

'For heaven's sake,' Nell said. She ran towards the racket and stopped in the doorway of a room in darkness. The footsteps stopped. Nell felt along the wall inside and flicked the light switch. A series of bare bulbs lit a room far larger than the other rooms but with no windows. Cases and trunks were stacked from floor almost to the ceiling. Furniture and ornaments were piled high: armchairs, dining tables, side tables, bureaus, lamps and stacks of paintings. This was clearly the lumber room Charlotte had spoken of. Like a loft in a normal house, it was where the family stored furniture or possessions that had fallen out of fashion or favour.

'Is anyone in here?' Nell called. No answer. 'Hello?' she called again. No response.

In the back corner of the room, she spotted a colourful shawl, its vibrant colours of purples, pinks and greens rather out of place in the room of dark leather and faded tapestry. Nell eased her way along a path through the valises and crates and cases. She came to the shawl and found that it was suspended across the backs of four chairs, giving the impression of a tent. Sinking to her knees, Nell looked under the shawl.

Nestled beneath its tented sky was a dolls' house: a replica of Hill House. The front stood open revealing beautiful miniature interiors. A staircase ran up the centre of the hall, just as it did in the life-sized version. Rooms spanned four floors, from kitchens in the basement to tiny bedrooms in the attic. Inside an open cigar box on the floor lay a household of residents, including animals and children. Nell looked from room to room. Each was empty of inhabitants, save for one. From the dusky pinks and pale greens, she recognised it as the morning room. A lady with blonde hair sat in an armchair with tea things laid out on the table before her. In the armchair beside her sat a woman. And standing beside that woman was a small child. The woman had short hair and the child – a boy – a shock of red curls.

The footsteps started up again. This time they were accompanied by the sound of a child giggling.

Nell leapt to her feet. 'Tommy! It's you, isn't it! You are playing a trick on me! I shall tell your mother.'

The footsteps ran out of the room, the laughter faded, and Nell felt more relieved than she had reason to.

Back in the heat of the bedroom, Nell sat at the desk. She breathed in deeply, staring at the keys of the typewriter. She had been here only a few hours and already there were too many distractions. Resting her elbows on the desk, she cupped her chin in her palms and looked out of the window at the view towards the gates at the end of the drive. What had she gathered by way of inspiration since her arrival? A rather unexpected encounter with a child – who was by turns beastly and then angelic and, frankly, a little odd – who revelled in playing tricks and saying bizarre things before leading guests on a merry dance into the depths of a grand old house in need of a spot of love and attention. Tommy's behaviour and the slightly sorry state of Hill House were no more than random pieces of a jigsaw. And not a particularly interesting jigsaw at that. There were more pieces missing than there were pieces present.

Nell took up a sheet of paper and wound it into the typewriter. She did what she knew how to do best: she began typing furiously at the keys, punching out something, anything, until a whole army of quick brown foxes appeared on the page, jumping over a lazy dog.

FOUR

After a less than productive afternoon, Nell eventually abandoned the foxes and dogs to take a bath in the coldest water she could bear.

At just after six o'clock, she left her room, made her way down the sweeping staircase, and stepped through the front door. Outside, a perfect shadow of Hill House was cast on the drive and lawn, creating a chill which provided welcome relief from the early evening sun still blazing in the west. Nell was tempted to linger in the shade but even more tempted to head off to explore the grounds before dinner.

Taking a left, Nell headed along the path running parallel to Hill House. She came to a stable yard. Parked up on the cobbles was the Rolls Royce. Elliot, the chauffeur, sleeves rolled to his elbows, was washing the windscreen of the car. He paused to wipe the sweat from his brow on the shoulder of his shirt. Nell judged him to be a man in his late fifties. He was physically fit and clearly a man not shy of labour. As though eavesdropping on Nell's thoughts and finding them directed at him, Elliot stood up straight and spun on his heels to face her. He gave a deferential nod.

Nell waved. 'It's a hot afternoon to be working outside,' she said.

'That it is,' Elliot answered.

That it is, Nell thought, enjoying his unconventional turn of phrase. It was very northern. A dog appeared in the doorway of the stables, a beautiful golden Labrador. He trotted directly to Nell and stopped at her feet. 'What's his name?' she asked, stroking the dog's silky ears.

'Ben. Ben, come away now.'

'Don't worry,' Nell said, still stroking the dog's ears. 'I like all animals.' She looked toward Elliot. 'You're not from around here originally, are you?' she said, trying him. Some people flinched from the direct line of questioning she used as a yard-stick with which to judge a person's potential for usefulness in her writing.

Rather than flinching, Elliot answered her directly. 'I was born in Yorkshire. Sheffield. But this is home now. For as long as the family will have me.'

'Have you worked here long?'

'Twenty years.'

'And do you enjoy it? Your work?'

'I do.'

'How did you come to work here?'

'I was Sir Charles' orderly in the regiment. He liked how I cared for his horse so asked me to come and work for him here.'

'Are there still horses in the stables?' Nell asked.

'Only the two. Sir Charles' favourite hunter and another a bit too old to ride now.'

'That's rather sentimental. Keeping a horse which has no purpose.'

'Some might say that.'

'But not you.'

'It's not for me to judge.'

Nell smiled. She liked this man's directness. 'Where would you recommend I walk if I have half an hour to kill?' she asked.

'You could do worse than carrying on down the path and seeing the lake. There might be a breeze what's welcome in this heat.' Elliot bent to collect his cloth from the bucket.

Sensing that he wanted to return to his work, Nell said, 'Thank you for the tip. I'm sure I'll enjoy the walk.'

'Aye, like as maybe.'

Nell smiled again. She turned and continued down the path. Ben followed her for a short while until a sharp whistle from Elliot sent him back to the stable yard.

Like as maybe. Nell smiled.

Passing the open gates of a walled garden, she saw that the beds and glasshouses inside were a riot of colour. Tomato vines reached to the glass ceilings of the greenhouses, their boughs full of ripe juicy fruit. The leaves of plants in the beds reached to touch the leaves of plants in neighbouring beds. At a strawberry patch, two young girls knelt, picking fruit. Nell judged the older girl to be no more than thirteen, fourteen at most, and the smaller girl perhaps a year or two younger. They wore black dresses and white aprons. Both had long dark hair pulled back into plaits and the older girl wore a pair of round spectacles. They bore enough of a resemblance to see they were sisters. When the younger girl made to pop a strawberry in her mouth rather than in the truckle, her sister smacked her hand away.

'How many times, Rosemary?' the older girl said. 'They're for the basket, not your belly.'

The younger girl folded her arms across her chest. 'You're not my mistress, Audrey. It's not for you to tell me what to do.'

'I'm older, so it is. Do you want to keep coming here every day rather than going to that factory?'

'You know I do.'

'Well then, Mrs Mandeville won't have us back if you steal the fruit, will she? No,' she said in the manner of a cross headmistress, 'she won't. Keep taking what's not yours and it will be tanning leather in the shoe factory for you.'

Audrey stooped to collect the truckle, giving Rosemary the opportunity to pop another strawberry she had been hiding in her mouth. She chewed, staring at the back of Audrey's head. Just before Audrey turned around, Rosemary stuck out her tongue.

Leaving the two girls to their fruit picking, Nell continued down the path. To her right, and just beyond the trees in a woodland, she saw the church they had passed earlier in the car, its weathervane motionless up above the spire.

Walking west, Nell had to shield her eyes from the sun, which had slipped lower in the sky but lost little of its brightness. A patchwork of fields stretched into the distance and the woodland to Nell's right eventually gave way to open ground with Elliot's promised lake spreading out before her. It lay a little lower than the pathway and reached all the way to the horizon, each gentle wave shimmering blue, green or silver in the evening sun. Further along, a small boathouse sat on the edge of the lake and a little further still, a jetty on stilts extended over the water. Nell looked longingly at the clear waves lapping at the water's edge where a patch had been cleared in the thick rushes to reveal a sandy strip of shoreline. Perhaps tomorrow she could borrow a bathing costume from Charlotte. She was a proficient swimmer, even if she did say so herself, and never missed her weekly trip to the ladies' pond on Hampstead Heath, even on frosty winter mornings. As her mind drifted away to the pond a few hundred miles from Northampton, the fine hairs on Nell's arms stood on end. Snapping to her senses, she looked this way and that. Feeling as though she was being watched, Nell's intuition drew her to the wood and the dark thicket of trees. She peered into the dense foliage and was sure she saw movement. A chill raced down her spine.

'Hello,' an unexpected voice said from the direction of the boathouse. Nell clutched her chest, her nerves teetering on a knife edge since she had neither heard nor sensed the approach of another person. She spun around.

A man stood before her but, with the sun behind him, he was nothing more than a dark shape with a halo of the sun's rays seeming to emanate from him.

'Sorry,' he said, taking a step to one side so that the shade of the boathouse blocked at least some of the sun. Blinking to clear her dappled vision, Nell took in the details of the man. He was tall and broad, with dark hair swept away from his face. He wore a white shirt, with the sleeves rolled up to his elbows, and the type of trousers one might wear for a leisurely Saturday tending the borders in one's garden. His skin was tanned and creased about the eyes, although Nell would have put him at no more than a few years older than herself.

'At least I can see who is sneaking up on me now,' Nell said, bringing her voice under control.

'I'm not sure whether that's better or worse for you.' The man spoke with a laugh in his voice. He smiled and his self-deprecating humour seemed entirely genuine. He was handsome in a very traditional square-jawed sort of way. 'Sorry if I gave you a scare,' he said.

'There's no call to apologise,' Nell said. 'I've had a few surprises today so I'm rather jumpy.'

The man smiled again. 'You must be the writer.'

Nell paused to consider her response. 'You have me at a disadvantage, sir,' she said. 'You know who I am, but I don't have the foggiest who you are. I'm presuming you work here.'

'On and off,' he said. 'When extra help is needed.'

'Oh, of course,' Nell said. 'Charlotte said that most of the staff live in the village now rather than at Hill House. It's a beautiful old place, isn't it?'

'There's nowhere I would rather be.'

Across the treetops, St Mary's clock chimed the three-quarters.

'I'm sorry to run off,' Nell said. 'But I promised to be back by seven.'

'Ah yes,' the man said, forcing his hands into the pockets of his trousers and rocking back on his heels. 'Cocktail hour.'

Nell smiled. 'Yes. And I can't very well be late. Not on my first evening. It was lovely to meet you, Mr... sorry, I don't know your name.'

'Townley,' he said.

'Well, it was lovely to meet you, Mr Townley.'

'Likewise, Miss Potter,' Mr Townley said. 'Have a wonderful evening.' He nodded before turning away. Nell watched him make his way back up the bank and blinked as the sun shone about him once again.

FIVE

'Don't you look a picture!' Charlotte clapped with delight as Nell appeared.

On arriving back at the house, Nell had followed the sound of voices round to the terrace. With its south-facing aspect, the lawn was flooded with sunlight glinting in the crystal glasses, decanters, bowls, and jugs arranged on a dining table brought out onto the grass.

'What,' Nell said, 'in this old thing?' She pinched the strap of the blue dress she had found hanging in the wardrobe.

Charlotte tutted and smiled. 'It looks far better on you than it ever did on me. You're all tall and willowy.'

'Scrawny, you mean.'

'Fashionably slender.'

'Hardly!' Nell laughed.

Charlotte patted the chair beside her, and Nell took a seat. A beautiful arrangement of flowers in pinks, lilacs and blues stood in a vase on the white tablecloth. Charlotte was busy adding a few stems of roses to the display. 'It really is wonderful to have you here,' Charlotte said, using her secateurs to snip the end from a stem before placing it in the vase. In her pretty loose-fitting lilac-coloured dress with her fair hair pulled back from her face, Charlotte might have been mistaken for a girl of eighteen or nineteen rather than a woman in her late twenties.

'I've missed you,' Nell said. 'A year really is too long.'

'Then don't leave it so long next time,' Charlotte said. 'You know I don't get to London much, and I hope I have made it clear that you are always welcome here. My home – wherever that may be – will always be your home.'

Nell tried to think of something witty to say. A joke to crack. After all, that was her adopted role in company – coming up with something funny to cut through anything that smacked of emotion or sentimentality. But sitting beside Charlotte she could find no quip to make.

'Thank you,' was all she could say.

Charlotte looked at Nell, her wide blue eyes seemingly attempting to look beneath the surface. 'Are you all right?' she asked. 'You don't seem yourself.'

'I'm fine. Really. It's just so good to see you.'

'Good evening, one and all!' Edward emerged through a set of double doors at the back of the house, bearing a tray of what looked like cocktail ingredients. He set it down on the table and Nell looked over the intriguing array – bilberries, gin, sugar, strawberries, all sorts of bottles that gave no clue to their contents.

'You look splendid this evening, Nell,' he said. 'If a little pale.'

'Edward!' Charlotte chided. 'Stop saying that.'

'Well, it's true. Nell needs a bit of sun on her skin. London does nobody any favours, the wretched place. We'll make sure she sees plenty of the outdoors while she's with us.'

'I am here,' Nell laughed. 'Feel free to bring me into the conversation anytime you like.'

'Sorry,' Edward said, as he arranged the glasses.

'I'm teasing,' Nell said and patted his hand. She had grown

to know Edward well enough on his visits to Cambridge to
know this intimacy would be appreciated. Like his sister,
Edward wore his heart very much on his sleeve.

'Wilco arrived an hour ago,' Edward said. Holding up one of
the bottles, he shook the cloudy unidentifiable liquid. 'He's
freshening up. And then he's going to make some telephone
calls from Father's office. He has some business that needs his
attention. He'll join us presently.'

'Wonderful,' Charlotte said, in a voice that said she didn't
think it wonderful at all.

'Charlotte,' Edward frowned. 'Please.'

'I know. I know,' Charlotte said.

Nell looked from brother to sister. 'Is there something I
should know about this Wilco chap?' she asked.

Edward looked towards the upstairs windows. He lowered
his voice. 'Wilco is thinking of investing in some parcels of land
we have on the market. His father is a top man in the construction trade and they're looking at building some rather fine
houses on the land over towards Huntingdean. They have an
idea to set up a small town on the principles of the Arts and
Crafts movement. Artisan sort of thing. Beautiful houses and
cottages with gardens for the normal man.'

'If the *normal man* has a small fortune to spend on buying a
property,' Charlotte snorted. 'Don't fall for Wilco's patter, Nell.
This is no philanthropic endeavour on his father's part. I'd
rather we kept the land and built houses for the working man.
And woman.'

Edward pressed his finger to his lips before pointing to the
windows open upstairs. 'Did you know, Nell,' he said quietly.
'Charlotte has rather had her head turned by this new Labour
government. She is something of a socialist these days.'

'And what if I am,' Charlotte said. 'Wheatley has the right
idea with his Housing Act. Reasonably priced houses for workers. Our land would be better used for that purpose than fancy

homes for clerks and bank managers. Sorry,' she said turning briefly to Nell.

'That's quite all right,' Nell said. She felt no need to rush to the defence of her father's profession. Instead, she sat forward in anticipation, a little swell of excitement at seeing Charlotte with the bit between her teeth. She had quite forgotten how adept Charlotte was at fighting her corner, taking on any of the doe-eyed boys at Cambridge in a head-to-head debate. She had always won. Always.

'Yes,' Edward said. 'But the local council can't pay us what Wilco's father can.'

'Maybe not, but don't we have a moral obligation to put our land to use for the greater good? The council would build houses that those on a low wage can afford. They would be able to rent a decent home with a bathroom – imagine!'

'You know I don't disagree, Charlotte,' Edward said. 'But we've spoken about this. We need to make as much as we can from that land. If we can convince Wilco to pay handsomely then we can look to perhaps selling another parcel of land to the council.'

'A less attractive piece of land. With worse views and further from the village.'

'Charlotte,' Edward said, the hint of a frustration in his voice. 'The roof won't see out another winter without some serious patching up. And if we get a good price from Wilco, we might be able to see to those gutters too.'

Charlotte let her hands fall into her lap. 'I know, I know,' she said.

'Oh, don't look so dejected, please,' Edward said. 'I can't bear to see you sad. But you will be nice to Wilco, won't you? If only for me. We might even be able to get him to sign on the dotted line before Father and Mother return. Now wouldn't that make a splendid homecoming? Put everyone's minds at rest.'

'Yes, all right,' Charlotte sighed. 'I'll be pleasant. But only for you.'

'Thank you.'

Nell looked from Edward to Charlotte. She felt a bit sad that the tussle over this Wilco chap had come to an end. There was something so very exciting about seeing her old friend with fire in her belly.

'But don't forget, Edward Mandeville, that you owe me,' Charlotte said. 'And I won't forget it.'

'Don't I know it,' Edward said.

Charlotte took up the discarded stem of one of the roses and snapped off a thorn. She turned away and, when she turned back, the thorn was stuck to her nose, looking for all the world like she had sprouted a miniature rhinoceros's horn.

Edward laughed. Nell laughed too. There was more than fire in Charlotte's belly, there was the flame of mischief licking in her eyes.

'You really are quite ridiculous,' Edward said, still laughing.

'Who's ridiculous?' Alice stepped through the doors. She placed a pile of plates on the table and slipped her arm though Edward's.

'My ridiculous sister,' Edward said. He turned and kissed his wife on the cheek. It was so brief. So natural. So tender. Nell turned her attention to clearing away the discarded stems of the roses.

Charlotte brushed the thorn from her nose and helped Alice lay five places at the table. Nell busied herself with the tray of cutlery.

'Thank you.' Alice smiled at Nell as she folded a napkin and placed it beside a plate. A long tendril of her auburn hair had worked its way free of the clip holding it back from her face. She tucked it behind her ear.

'How are the children this evening?' Nell asked. It seemed the polite thing to say and she had already decided against alerting Alice to her son's earlier prank in the attic. The child seemed capable of getting himself into bother without any help from her.

'They're very well, thank you,' Alice said. She smiled in that way Nell had noticed mothers did whenever one enquired after their children. 'They are a bit fractious with the heat. Tommy was threatening to run down to the lake and jump in. But I managed to talk him out of it. I'm afraid I told a fib and said there were eels living in the deeper water. He's not a fan of snakes.' She smiled again. 'Mary is sitting with the children this evening. She's ever so good with them. They feel so far away when they are in the upstairs nursery without us. I don't like to leave them on their own. They seem so small in a house this size.'

'I explained to Nell that we don't have quite as many staff as we once had,' Charlotte said, without a hint of any kind of embarrassment at their reduced circumstances. 'After the war, it seemed prudent to cut our cloth rather better. Most of the help we do still have are in the Isle of Wight with Mother, Father and Aunt Leo.'

Alice smiled, tucking the wayward strand behind her ear again, as she arranged another napkin. 'We quite like it this way. It makes us feel a bit more normal. More relaxed.'

'We're very used to fending for ourselves, aren't we Nell?' Charlotte said, adjusting a side plate. 'Do you remember the marvellous cheese on toast we used to make over the fire in our room? I don't think I've tasted anything as wonderful since.'

'No, nothing,' Nell said. She could have gone on to say that she still resorted to a diet of almost exclusively toasted bread when cash was tight, but thought better of it.

'Keep your voices down, can't you?' Edward said, tilting his head and nodding towards the upstairs windows. 'We don't want to appear as though we are on our uppers.'

'We should be taken as we are,' Charlotte said. 'Why should we put on airs and graces?'

'Because, little sis, I've said to Wilco that we are light on staff because they've all gone for a trip across the Solent with Ma and Pa. I explained that our current casual living arrangements are a result of much of the house being closed for the summer. I think I've done a rather good job of convincing him. He's quite excited at the prospect of a relaxing time. And if the rain holds off, he'll never need to know that the roof is a tad sieve-like. Besides, most of the offending rooms are in the unoccupied male quarters in the attic. Although the rain does sometimes have a habit of finding its way down into the odd guest room.' Edward scratched his chin and looked up at the row of windows in the very top of the house.

'And is Wilco too good for a bucket?' Charlotte said, placing a fork beside a plate.

'Yes, he is. The first rule of negotiations, sis, is making a chap think you don't need to sell. We need to show Hill House in her best finery this week. If you have the upper hand—'

'You can push the price up,' Alice said.

'Precisely,' Edward said. 'Which is why, Charlotte, you need to be on your very best behaviour.'

'I'm not a dog!' Charlotte objected.

'I know, otherwise you might be a bit more obedient.'

'You cheeky so-and-so!' Charlotte laughed and chucked a napkin at her brother. Edward and Alice laughed with her. Nell watched them all, observing their pleasure in each other's company.

'You're such a tease,' Charlotte said.

'Who's a tease?' A man stepped through the double doors. He was tall, with a strong jaw and shoulders to match. He had a modest paunch – no doubt from good living – and wore a crisp white shirt, open at the neck, with sharply creased brown trousers and highly polished brown brogues. His hair was parted to one side – not a hair out of place – and his full moustache neatly trimmed and waxed so that it looked to Nell like an exquisitely coiffed broom head.

'Good evening, old chap,' Edward made hastily to the man. His voice was full of something Nell couldn't quite place. It was a tad loud and – she hated to think it – sounded a bit desperate to please. 'Did you find everything you needed in my father's office? Did you manage to make all your telephone calls?'

'I did indeed.' Placing his hands on his hips, the man closed his eyes, puffed out his chest, and took a breath so deep that Nell thought his intention might be to suck all the air from the world, leaving the rest of them gasping for oxygen. He opened his eyes and looked around the landscape; at the hills rolling to the horizon, resplendent in their summer greenery. 'What a splendid evening,' he said.

'It is rather,' Edward said. 'If you like, we could take a walk down to the Huntingdean plots this eve—'

The man held up his hand and shook his head. 'No business talk tonight, Ed. There's a time and place for that. And it's not in the company of these gorgeous creatures.' He turned to look at Alice, Charlotte, and Nell. Nell couldn't help bristling.

'Wilco,' Alice said, stepping forward. 'It's so lovely to have you here.'

'I can't tell you how wonderful it is to see *you*,' Wilco said. He took hold of Alice's shoulders and planted a kiss on both of her cheeks. Alice smiled, somewhat graciously, Nell thought. But it was a smile which did not extend to her eyes.

Charlotte stepped forward next. 'Hullo, Wilco,' she said. There was definitely no smile in her voice and her lips were tight when Wilco planted a kiss on each of her cheeks. When he stepped back, he looked her up and down.

'Stunning. Radiant,' he said. 'A Greek goddess if ever I saw one.'

Charlotte gave another smile. This time, she showed her

teeth. But it looked to Nell more like she was baring them, as a cornered dog might.

'Please let me introduce you to our guest,' Edward said, in the unfamiliar showy voice again. 'This is Miss Nell Potter. Nell is an author, Wilco. You might know her as Margot Evangeline.'

It was Nell's turn now to come under Wilco's scrutiny. He looked her up and down. 'No time to read,' he said. 'Shame. If the books are anything like this beauty I see before me then I must be missing out on something quite special.'

Nell felt her lips curl away from her teeth. She had to be nice to this Wilco, didn't she? She couldn't respond in the way her nature intended. Now that really would have scuppered Edward's plans.

Wilco leant in and kissed Nell on both cheeks. He smelled like the expensive barbershops along Piccadilly where men went to be denuded and primped and buffed. Passing by the open doors of those establishments with their jars in the windows and heavily wooded exteriors, a person could almost be knocked off their feet by the heady scents emanating from within.

'It's nice to meet you, Mr Wilco,' Nell said, attempting to keep up the pretence of being polite. She was shocked when his response was to lean back and laugh.

'It's Mr Wilkinson, Nell,' Edward said quickly. 'Mr Anthony Wilkinson.'

'No harm done,' Wilco said through a laugh. 'I've been called far worse, believe me. You call me what you please, Miss Potter, I'll answer to pretty much anything.'

Nell smiled. Perhaps she had misjudged him. A man who laughed so easily and with so much gusto – especially at his own expense – was generally a man who could be trusted, in her experience. She had spent so much time in the company of artistic types who carefully crafted their personalities that she had almost forgotten that some people could simply be genuine with no intentionally hidden edge. 'Thank you,' she said. 'I think I'll stick to Wilco.'

'Jolly good, jolly good,' he smiled.

Alice approached and slipped her arm through Wilco's. 'Now Wilco,' she said, 'come and have a look at what Edward's preparing. He's going to treat us to cocktails this evening. And all his own recipes.'

'Lummy,' Wilco said, as Alice led him away. 'If they're as strong as the drinks Ed concocted for us in our younger days, then we could be in for an interesting evening.'

Nell stayed at the open door in the shade, watching Alice and Edward talk Wilco through the ingredients on the table, Alice explaining that the fruit they were about to enjoy grew so well thanks to the fertile land at Hill House. If Edward was the chief salesman in the hoped-for deal with Wilco's father, then he had a very skilful business partner in Alice. Her relaxed subtlety and charm provided the perfect counterpoint to Edward's overenthusiasm.

Charlotte joined Nell. 'He's a bit of an oaf, don't you think?' she said quietly as they looked towards the table, the hills beyond bathed in evening sunlight. 'He makes love to every woman he meets. He doesn't seem able to stop himself.'

'Perhaps you could be his redemption.'

Charlotte laughed. 'I am nobody's saviour. Certainly not Anthony Wilkinson's. I know I must be friendly to him for the sake of the leaking roof. It wouldn't be the other way around, you know. No man would be expected to flirt with a woman for the sake of a business transaction. We may have fought for the vote but there's a longer fight to be had to reach parity with men.'

'You rebellious woman, you,' Nell said. 'How dare you presume to be the equal of men.'

Charlotte nudged Nell's arm. 'You're no different. With

your London life and your publishing career. You've achieved everything on your own merit, through your own hard work. I am in awe of you, you know. What do I do here but help Mother with the house and Alice with the children?'

'You needn't be in awe of me,' Nell said, thinking about the trite stories she pedalled and her precarious finances.

'In the war I had a purpose,' Charlotte said, her brain clearly on a course from which it would not be diverted. 'I was a nurse. I helped Aunt Leo care for men in the very rooms where we dine and take afternoon tea once again. That mattered. And then we had Cambridge. I really believed that would be the beginning of whatever it was that my life is supposed to be. Now, I just don't know.'

'You need to find out what that is,' Nell said. 'Have you ever thought about going into politics? You would make a spectacular advocate for the underprivileged. And taking a seat at Westminster is rather your family business.'

Charlotte laughed. 'For the men, perhaps. I can't see a time when the wealthy landowners hereabouts would put a cross in the box for a Mandeville woman.'

Nell shrugged. 'You've said yourself: times are changing.'

'Changing but not being turned on their head.'

'Someone has to be the first,' Nell said. 'And you know I will support you in whatever it is you decide to do. Whether it's politics or something else entirely.'

Charlotte slipped her arm through Nell's. 'You really are my most dear friend, you know that, don't you?'

Nell smiled at Charlotte. 'Ditto.'

'You sound just like a guest of my aunt's who stayed with us before the war,' Charlotte said. 'She tried to make me believe that I could be anything I wanted to be. I'm sure she was behind convincing my father to let me go to university. She was only here a week. She lived in India, you see, and had to return. She was very close to my brother, Tom. It felt like there had never been a time when she wasn't a part of Hill House. Have you ever felt that? That you've known someone your whole life when in fact you've only just met?'

Nell was saved having to answer by Edward calling to them.

'What are you two doing over there in the shade?' he said. 'Come and have a drink.'

Charlotte and Nell joined the small party at the table. Edward entertained them with the preparation of his drinks. The pulping of the fruit and the mixing of the spirits was like alchemy to Nell. She sipped the rather-too-strong drink and joined in the conversation. Wilco was quite keen to talk about his new-found love of jazz music, which he indulged in various clubs in London – many of which Nell had frequented but decided against saying so. She left it to Wilco to fill the others in on the thrilling details of the dark basement bars, where people met to drink and dance and laugh. Charlotte hung on his every word, pressing for details of each venue and the music, and what people wore and how they behaved. Wilco went so far as to offer to take her to one of the clubs when she was next in town. After a while, Alice skilfully directed conversation to the production of food and the ever-increasing demand for fertile land to produce crops. Wilco listened intently, his chin pinched between his thumb and forefinger. Alice hadn't once mentioned the land around Hill House, although its presence was very much part of the conversation, as they were dining al fresco. Had it been Alice's idea to bring the table outside? Clever Alice.

A noise from inside the house caught their collected attention. A girl, who Nell recognised as the older of the sisters from the walled garden, stepped through the double doors.

'Mrs Mandeville,' she said softly and with a curtsy.

'Yes, Audrey,' Alice said, smiling her encouragement.

'Mrs Randal says the food is ready. Will we bring it out?'

'Please do. And thank you, Audrey.'

The girl smiled shyly and bobbed another curtsy before heading back inside.

'You start them young here,' Wilco said, a note of surprise in his voice.

Edward looked a little alarmed as though unsure of what to say. Alice touched Wilco's arm. 'Remember, most of the staff have gone to the Isle of Wight with Sir Charles and Lady Mandeville. We're using it as an opportunity to train up some younger people from the village. Audrey and her sister, Rosemary, will be waiting on us tonight. Call it work experience, if you like.'

Wilco nodded. '"Work experience",' he repeated 'What a jolly good idea. Training them up for a trade. I approve. My father is a self-made man. Started off with nothing but took all the opportunities offered. And look at him now! Running some of the largest construction contracts in the country. I say, "good luck" to young Audrey and her sister.'

Nell looked at Charlotte who seemed more that a little surprised at this nod to socialism. Edward looked relieved and smiled at his wife.

'Please,' Alice said, 'won't you all take your seats? Wilco, I've put you between Nell and me. I trust that's to your liking.'

'Absolutely,' he said. 'As long as I get my scran, I don't mind where I sit. Should I consider myself the rose between two thorns, I wonder?' He laughed and they all laughed with him. He was just a bit of a harmless buffoon, and Nell had been forced to sit beside worse men (and women!) before, making polite conversation.

Charlotte sat opposite Nell and beside Edward. As soon as he was in his seat, Wilco took his napkin and wiped a trail of perspiration inching down the side of his face. He took up the glass of water that had already been poured and downed it in one. Alice picked up the jug and refilled Wilco's glass. 'As we serve ourselves, I'll keep your glass topped up,' she said.

'The most attentive hostess, the most attentive hostess,' Wilco said and took another gulp of his water.

Nell watched Edward smile at his wife across the table.

Audrey returned with a tray of chicken already carved. When Rosemary followed bearing a bowl of potato salad, Wilco said that he had never seen such a young lady working quite so hard or quite so well. Both girls returned with more trays and bowls of salads. Audrey asked whether they should stay to serve the food, but Alice sent the girls away kindly, telling Audrey she would ring the bell in the billiard room when they were next needed.

The food was passed around the table, from person to person, as were the bottles of wine and the jugs of water. Everyone helped themselves and Wilco, in particular, seemed enamoured with the arrangement. 'Gives one the chance to fill one's plate rather than suffer the meagre rations that some of the help dish up,' he said, taking a chicken leg from the plate as it passed him on the way around the table.

'There's always plenty of food here at Hill House,' Alice said. 'Lady Mandeville is very particular about ensuring that each guest receives the hospitality that pleases them.'

Wilco took a bite of the chicken leg and waved it as he spoke. 'And her daughter-in-law is doing her proud tonight. I am enjoying Hill House,' he said. 'Enjoying it very much. I hope this isn't to be my last visit here.' He dabbed the grease from his lips with his napkin. 'So, Ed, tell me more about these plots of land you have on offer. I could also be tempted into hearing about some of the farming that goes on around here.'

Edward launched into an animated description of the land and farming at Hill House. He didn't mention the sale but spoke of the history of the land and the area, of the fact that Hill House had been built by an ancestor in the eighteenth century following his judicious marriage to the daughter of the Earl of Caxton, who lived across the valley. With the marriage came great wealth so that he was able to commission the finest archi-tect to build his Palladian idyll. By virtue of his marriage, their ancestor also had a baronetcy bestowed on him by the king. Alice and Charlotte joined in every so often with a titbit of information, each new detail building to a wonderful – perhaps irresistible – proposition of the area and the lifestyle it could provide.

Nell sat back and watched them all. She didn't feel the need to be drawn into the conversation. She had precious little to add. The Mandevilles were a formidable team. They conducted the conversation as though undertaking a pincer manoeuvre with Wilco as their unwitting prey. Observation rather than participation was the way of a writer. Watching. Waiting. And it was what Nell liked – putting some distance between her and the world. She felt herself relax. The meal, the company – they were easy, charming. Quite unlike dinners and parties in London where one was always on one's guard or had the very real feeling that the person talking to you was, in fact, looking over your shoulder, looking for a more important person with whom to talk. There was none of that shallowness here. Just honest hospitality. There was also no hint of a story idea. But she didn't mind that so much. As she relaxed she began to hope it would come. Eventually.

SIX

When the sun slipped behind the hills and the moon began to show its face, Edward took matches from his pocket and lit the many candles arranged along the table. The air had cooled slightly so that it was warm rather than oppressive. The chirp of crickets filled the air and was joined by the occasional hoot from an owl and the odd distant screech of a fox. Nell smiled when the two young maids returned to clear away dinner and bring a dessert of strawberries and cream – the strawberries from the walled garden, Alice said, and the cream from the productive dairy herd managed by one of the tenant farmers, Charlotte added. The other adults were so busy talking that they didn't see the girls bickering and pushing each other.

The table having been cleared of dessert, and the coffee served, Edward had just begun to pour the port and brandy when there came an almighty scream from the direction of the house. Edward slammed the decanter down on the table. Nell joined everyone else in jumping to their feet. Wilco nearly sent the table flying in his haste to get from his seat.

'That was no vixen,' Charlotte said.

As one, they headed for the double doors and made their

way through the billiard room and out into the hall. Not
knowing her way, Nell followed the others through a smaller
door at the very end of the hall and into a long corridor with
whitewashed walls, similar in design to the stone stairwell.
There were no windows and a welcome coolness surrounded
them as they passed the servant bells high on the wall. But the
coolness didn't last long. As they took a well-worn stone
stairway down, a waft of hot air raced up to meet them. They
made their way along a corridor and soon arrived in the vast
kitchen, with a table in the centre and a huge range running
along the far wall that was belching heat. The remnants of their
dinner sat on the table beside trays holding pale, uncooked
loaves.

'I saw him, I did. He was evil looking,' Rosemary half
screamed, and half spoke. Audrey stood on one side of her
sister, holding her hand, and an older woman Nell hadn't seen
before stood on the other side.

'There, there, Rosemary,' the older woman said, 'there's no
call to fuss.'

'What's going on?' Edward asked.

'Oh, sorry you've had the trouble of it, Mr Edward,' the
woman said. 'But Rosemary here's had a nasty turn.'

'There was a man... In the door... he was going to come in,'
Rosemary said, a look of utter fear in her eyes.

'Don't talk so, Rosemary,' the woman said, wiping her hands
on her apron.

'It's all right, Mrs Randal,' Edward said. 'Let her speak.'

The young girl's bottom lip began to tremble. She tried to
look up at Edward but immediately looked down. At the sight
of a fat tear slipping down her cheek, Alice and Charlotte raced
to her side. They cooed and stroked the girl's hair. 'There,
there,' Alice said. 'Whatever has got you into such a state?'

The young girl looked to her sister.

'Mrs Mandeville,' Audrey said, taking a step forward, 'Mrs

Randal asked Rosemary to go and open the door to the outside to let some air in. It's been fierce hot in here all day and was getting worse, what with wanting to get the bread in the oven for the breakfast in the morning.' She nodded to the pale dough proving on the table. 'Rosemary was unlocking the door that leads up to the gardens when she saw a man. She says he was lurking at the bottom of the steps. When he saw her, he—'

'He growled!' Rosemary yelled, before burying her face in Alice's dress.

'Pay her no mind,' Audrey said. 'She gets spooked sometimes.'

'It's true! He growled and then he ran back up the steps!' Rosemary sobbed.

'And what did he look like?' Edward asked softly.

'Like, like... A monster! A big dark monster,' Rosemary managed to say before she wailed again. Alice pulled the girl close to her.

'Edward,' Alice said. 'I think Rosemary has had quite enough excitement for one evening.' Alice knelt before the girl. Strands of hair clung to Rosemary's damp cheeks and Alice brushed them back. 'I'm sure the man meant no harm,' she said. 'I'm sure he had just lost his way.'

'I don't doubt that he was more scared of you than you were of him,' Charlotte added. 'He was probably terribly surprised when you opened the door.'

'And what you took for a growl was probably him howling in terror,' Wilco said. He threw back his head and let out a comical howl. 'There, that's what it sounded like, isn't it?' he said.

Rosemary nodded. 'I think so.'

The sound of shoes slapping on the flagstones in the corridor made everyone look to the door. A young chap ran into the kitchen, his face aglow. 'I... I... couldn't see anything,' he panted, resting his hands on his knees as he caught his breath.

Charlotte hurried to his side. 'You went after him?' she said. 'Oh, Bertie, what if he had been dangerous? What would your mother have said if you were hurt? I promised Sally I would look after you.'

The young chap scooped his fringe from his face. 'I'm fine. Honestly.'

'And did you see anything, Bertie? Anything at all?' Edward asked.

'No, Mr Edward. If there was anyone then he is long gone.'

'Good,' Edward said. 'And it was brave of you to go after him.'

The boy's face was already flushed, but it grew redder. 'Thank you, sir,' he said from beneath his fringe.

'Promise me you won't do that again,' Charlotte said, taking his hand and patting it.

'You can't ask a chap to make a promise like that,' Wilco said. 'When a young buck's blood is up, it's up.' He took a step towards Bertie and thrust out his hand. 'Wilco,' he said. 'And you are?'

The teenage boy was tall, taller than Charlotte, but he was barely half the width of Wilco. Even so, he took the hand offered and shook it assuredly. 'Albert Morrison, sir,' he said. 'But everyone here calls me Bertie.'

'Bertie is our maid, Sally's, son and Mrs Randal, here, is his grandmother,' Charlotte said. 'He's home from school for the holidays and is helping around the house while Sally's on the Isle of Wight with our parents.'

'I see,' Wilco smiled. 'So, they are keeping you gainfully employed? And are you part of this "Work Experience" scheme the divine Alice has in operation for the young people of the village?'

'Something like that, sir.'

'Jolly good. Jolly good.'

And with that, the incident came to an end. Charlotte and

Alice made sure that Rosemary and Audrey were settled and that they were still happy to stay at Hill House for the night as arranged, rather than return to the village. Mrs Randal said that she would see to it that they both had a mug of warm milk before bed.

Edward dispatched Bertie to ask Elliot to take a turn around the grounds to check for any intruders. With the household settled, the guests all retreated to the billiard room.

'Well,' Wilco said as he sat in a chair before the fireplace. 'That was a bit of excitement for the evening.' He took a handkerchief from his pocket and wiped his brow.

Alice returned from checking on Mary and the children and sat on the sofa with Charlotte and Nell. 'I feel terrible about it,' Alice said. 'No doubt that poor man was homeless, looking for a place to stay for the evening or something to eat. I wish I could have given him a plate of food.'

'Homeless?' Wilco said, raising his eyebrow. 'Do you mean a down and out?'

'Alice has an unusual turn of phrase sometimes,' Charlotte said. 'You'll get used to it. It's because she's not local. She's from Truro.'

'Cornwall!' Wilco said. 'I have friends down there. Do you know the Agar-Robartes from Lanhydrock? A lovely family. I used to enjoy going to stay at—'

'I left Cornwall when I was very young,' Alice said. 'I'm afraid I don't remember much about it.'

Nell felt Alice shift beside her.

'I say,' Nell said. 'This brandy is delicious. Might I have another drop?' She really didn't want to drink anymore but could feel Alice's discomfort at the path the conversation was taking.

Edward topped up Nell's glass.

All talk of the mystery man came to an end and conversation turned to the impending rehanging of the paintings in the hall as a surprise for Sir Charles and Lady Mandeville on their return. Nell felt Alice physically relax beside her and she re-joined the conversation.

After another half an hour, there was a knock at the billiard room door. Edward left briefly. When he returned, he said, 'Elliot's done a circuit of the land with his dog.' He paused to collect the decanter to refresh glasses. 'He found nothing apart from the scent of a fox or two. So, there we are. We can all sleep soundly in our beds tonight with no fear of strange men lurking in the shadows.'

Soon after the reassuring message was delivered, the party began to disperse. Nell was first to leave, thanking Alice and Charlotte profusely for their hospitality.

In her room, Nell turned out the light, drew back the curtains, and threw open every window. She stepped out of the blue dress and draped it over the back of the chair at the dressing table. In just her slip, she glanced at her typewriter. She had to write another book. She absolutely had to. She simply could not face the prospect of handing over her money at the station to buy a one-way ticket to Cheam. Or worse still, have her father drive up to the pavement in Bloomsbury to cram her few belongings into his car. Her father would not like her standard lamp sticking out from his back window. He did not like anything that drew attention to himself or his family.

Nell looked out at the dark night sky. In the daylight, she could distance herself from the doubt she would ever write another word worthy of publication. But in the solitude of night, there was nowhere to hide from the truth that a wall was building itself around her imagination. Brick by brick it was rising to cut her off. And the wall didn't just dam her creativity, it separated her from the joy in life. Because writing was her joy. Her only joy. For years, creating worlds for characters to inhabit had been her single reason to get out of bed in the morning. It wasn't great fiction. It wasn't worthy to sit beside those authors she had studied. But the worlds she created gave her somewhere to retreat to.

Without the diversion of her writing, a sensation crept in to fill its place. It was always there, biding its time, waiting to fill any void that might appear. And it was as far from joy as it was possible to be.

Nell looked down at the moonlit drive, to the lawn at the front of the house and toward the lake. It had been a good day. And on a good day, it was difficult to comprehend the depths to which something within her was able sink. Something that she was utterly powerless to control. When the inner darkness came, it found a natural ally in night. During the day, and surrounded by people, there was distraction. At the bawdy London clubs and parties in the evenings, she could drink and be loud and gregarious; she could be the devil-may-care author, always ready with a quip or a joke. The first to accept any invitation. The first to dance and the first to suggest they try a new club or restaurant. She could pull on her costume of unconventional clothes and transform into Margot Evangeline. In certain circles in London, she was known as the life and soul of the party, and she did her utmost never to disappoint.

And sometimes, she did enjoy it. Sometimes she *was* the life and soul of the party. But when the darkness descended, it found its way into every part of her, every fibre and sinew. Its ferocity took her by surprise every time; the desire to scream into an abyss, tear at her skin and cry out from the centre of her soul. Instead, she would curl up in her bed and shrink away from the world. As skilled as she was at hiding her feelings from others, on those days, there was nowhere to hide from herself. To hide from what she had done. And what would haunt her for the rest of her life. All she could do was wait until the darkness slipped away, going to wherever it hid when it had temporarily done with her. She had always bartered with herself, convincing herself that as long as the darkness didn't outweigh the light, as long as there was enough light in life to act as a counterbalance, it would be all right. She could cope. If she could laugh genuinely and freely and have fun and dance and sing with joy sometimes, and hide inside her writing, then life was worth living. But the darkness had begun to descend with greater frequency, its visits lasting longer.

Nell pushed the sash windows up as far as they would go. There was no movement to the air, not even the briefest whisper of a breeze. The darkness hadn't descended today. There had been only light with the distraction of the Mandevilles. Even without an idea for her writing, she had escaped. For now.

Leaving the window, Nell took a thin robe from a hook on the back of the bathroom door and put it on over her slip. She lay down on the bed and stared up at the ceiling. So many souls she now knew slept beneath this roof in need of repair. For once, she was not alone in a building of strangers. And in a house where the children ran almost feral, it was more than likely that she would cross paths with Charlotte's nephew again. So far as she could tell, nobody had noticed whether her interactions with him had been unusual. But it would certainly be thought odd if she avoided him. She would have to do her best to be polite. He had every right to roam the house. She was the interloper, not he. She was the one who had constructed her life to avoid the presence of other people's children.

A knot of discomfort twisted in Nell's chest. It was followed by a familiar pang of longing. Closing her eyes, she breathed in the scent of the lavender in the bowl on the nightstand. Edward's strong cocktails began to work their way through her system. The one saving grace was that she knew sleep would come quickly. It always did.

SEVEN

25TH JULY 1924

Morning sunshine streamed through the windows unchecked and Nell blinked, then sat up and stretched. She paused at the open window to breathe in a lungful of the clean morning air. In the bathroom, she drew a cool bath, poured in a splash of rose water, and stepped in. She slid beneath the water so that only her face was above the surface. As she ran her fingers through her hair, she remembered that once or twice in the night she had woken to the sensation of someone stroking her hair. It had felt reassuring rather than alarming. She had put it down to a breeze blowing in through the open window, and had drifted back to sleep.

After her bath, Nell brushed her hair so that it would sit straight, then dressed in a frock she had brought with her, a sort of loose tennis-style dress with a dropped waist and a small bow at its neck. It was unlikely that it would grace a tennis court any time soon. The last time she had reluctantly agreed to participate in a game of doubles, she had almost taken a chap's teeth out with a frantic and misjudged swipe at the ball, which ended with the borrowed racket flying over the net and just missing her opponent's face.

.   .   .

'Here she is,' Charlotte said when Nell stepped into the dining room. 'Sleep well?' She folded her newspaper and placed it on the table.

Nell took the seat beside Charlotte where a place had been laid. 'The best night's sleep I've had for as long as I can remember,' Nell said. 'It's so peaceful here, and that bed is ridiculously comfortable.'

'Good,' Charlotte said. She covered Nell's hand with hers and gave it a squeeze. 'Edward and Wilco breakfasted early and have gone out to visit one of the farmers. Alice is having her breakfast in the nursery with the children. Mother may have made many concessions to Alice regarding the children's upbringing, but she has drawn the line at having them in the dining room! Alice did try it once, but the carpets paid a terrible price in terms of spilled milk and dropped boiled eggs. For the sake of Mother's nerves, she didn't try it a second time.' Charlotte grinned and lifted the lid on a serving dish, releasing the delicious scent of bacon. 'Tuck in,' she said.

Nell helped herself to a rasher of bacon and a sausage. She plucked a slice of toast from the rack and buttered it. The fresh country air had given her an appetite and a breakfast of bacon and sausage was a rare treat. Charlotte lifted the lid on another dish and Nell took a scoop of scrambled egg. Nell carved into her bacon and Charlotte filled a cup with coffee from a pot.

'Thank you,' Nell said after swallowing her bacon. 'You really are looking after me. I'm not sure what I have done to deserve this attentiveness.'

'Nonsense,' Charlotte said, 'you seem like you need a bit of care and I'm happy to oblige. Here,' she said, dabbing a spoon of jam onto Nell's side plate beside the toast. 'Mrs Randal makes it from the raspberries in the garden.'

'I'm not Wilco,' Nell grinned. 'You don't need to extol the

delights of Hill House to me. I'm sold already.' She had expected Charlotte to laugh.

Instead, Charlotte fiddled with the napkin in her lap before looking at Nell. 'You can tell me to keep my sticky beak out,' she said. 'But are you all right, really?'

'Of course—'

'Because I've been your friend long enough to know when something might be a bit off. You don't need to say anything if you don't want to. I just wanted to say that I am always here for you. Always here with an ear if you need it. I would hate to think you felt blue but thought you couldn't talk to anyone. There, I've said it. And now we don't need to mention it again if you'd rather not.'

Nell swallowed. She picked up her napkin and dabbed her lips. 'Thank you,' she said quietly.

Charlotte smiled at her. 'Now that's out of the way, let's talk about other things,' she said brightly. She babbled on about what Nell might like to see in the grounds, pausing only to heap more bacon onto Nell's plate.

'And if you don't want to write in your bedroom,' Charlotte said, 'you're more than welcome to use Father's office. He has a typewriter on his desk that rarely gets used. Or we could arrange to have your typewriter taken anywhere on the estate if you'd prefer to be outdoors. I know you artistic types need to go where the inspiration strikes. Perhaps you'd like to read the newspaper? There might be something in there to spark your imagination.'

Her stomach fuller than it had been in a long time, Nell sat back in her chair, and took a sip of coffee. 'Why don't you fill me in on the highlights?'

'There's not a great deal. Apart from the Olympics. You should probably know that Bertie – Mrs Randal's grandson, you met him last night – well, he has become a bit obsessed with running since he read about Harold Abrahams and Eric

Liddell. He's always been a sporty boy but now he can take himself off and run for hours. Don't be surprised if you bump into him anywhere on the estate, running like the wind.'

Nell was vaguely aware that the Olympics were taking place in Paris. The man selling newspapers outside her flat had shouted about it every afternoon for a few weeks, including the news that some British chaps had won important medals.

'Good for him,' Nell said. 'But you know me and sports,' she grimaced.

'Indeed, I do! I won't be suggesting we crack out the croquet set while you're around. I think we all value our shins too much.'

'How dare you!' Nell laughed. And then, remembering the lake, she added, 'I did wonder – and only if it's no trouble – but I walked down to the lake last night before dinner and it looked rather inviting. You don't have a bathing costume I could borrow, do you?'

'Already done,' Charlotte said. 'I took the liberty of putting a costume in the chest of drawers in your room. You'll find it in the top drawer. The water can be such a relief from this heat. And now,' Charlotte said, 'I shouldn't keep you. You need to write, don't you? I should let you go.'

Nell twisted her cup in its saucer. 'I suppose you should.'

'You don't sound very enthusiastic.'

'It's just that I don't really have an idea for a story at the moment.'

'And you can't write until inspiration strikes?'

'Having an idea makes it a lot easier.'

Charlotte smiled brightly. 'If you want my advice, I'd say don't try so hard. Take a walk. Go for a swim. Sit under a tree for a few hours. Let the ideas come to you. Maybe your brain just needs a bit of a break.'

Nell released the cup. 'When did you become so profound?'

'I always have been. You just rarely listen to me,' Charlotte laughed.

Nell smiled. But a sudden sense of dread stopped her short. 'There aren't really eels in the lake are there?'

'No! That's just what Alice tells the children to keep them away from the water. There's nothing to fear anywhere on the estate. You'll be safe wherever you go. You're not in London now. We don't have criminals hiding around the corner to club you on the head and pick your pocket!'

'No, only intruders lurking at the bottom of the stairs to frighten young maids!' Nell laughed.

'I wouldn't take any notice of Rosemary,' Charlotte said. 'She's quite highly strung. I wouldn't be surprised if it wasn't her own shadow that alarmed her. Audrey is the sensible one.'

'They are rather young, aren't they? Where are their parents?'

'They don't have any. They're orphans. Alice is on the Board of the local orphanage. She has a passion for giving opportunities to the disadvantaged. She's had a whole string of children coming through the doors of Hill House to learn a trade or give them experience so they're better equipped to find employment when they leave the orphanage. She's had great successes. Many have gone on to find good jobs. She even brings home some of the poorly children to nurse them back to health. Or if there's a particularly sad child, she might invite them to spend a weekend as a guest.'

'She sounds like she has a wonderful social conscience.'

'I'm often humbled by her. I talk socialism but Alice puts it into action. She asks no thanks for it either. She simply wants to improve the lot of those less fortunate than us. It seems to be her calling. But anyway, that's enough talk of politics for one morning. I won't keep you any longer.'

Nell drained her coffee cup. 'Do you have plans for the day?' she asked.

Charlotte pushed the newspaper away. 'I need to pop into town,' she said. 'I have to see Father's solicitor for a bit of business. I should warn you that lunch is a bit of a come-as-you-are affair while Mother's away. Feel free to ring for anything you like. But you would be equally welcome to go down to the kitchen to grab something or even ask Mrs Randal to wrap up a sandwich to take out with you. Alice and Edward often spend the whole day away from the house. We just all make sure we're back to meet up for dinner at seven.'

EIGHT

Wearing Charlotte's bathing costume with her dress over the top, Nell stepped out of the front door of Hill House. With a towel draped over her arm and a bag over her shoulder containing a swimming cap, her notebook, and a flask of iced lemonade that Charlotte had asked Mrs Randal to prepare, Nell walked down the path in the direction of the lake.

Today, there was no Elliot or car in the stable yard and no quarrelsome sisters in the walled garden. The only sound as Nell passed the church and wood to her right, was the sound of her soft-soled pumps on the gravel path and the symphony of gentle birdsong. Actually, it was too lovely to be a symphony, it was more akin to a Medieval madrigal.

Smiling at her apt simile, Nell arrived at the lake and slid down the sandy bank to the water's edge. She placed her bag on the ground and laid out the towel. With her hands on her hips, she looked around the landscape. A cooling dip really should be a reward for getting some words down on paper rather than the only reason for visiting the lake.

Reluctantly, she abandoned the towel and her bag, climbed back up the bank and slowly traced the path around the lake.

With nowhere to hide from the blazing sun, perspiration dripped down her neck and onto her chest. She pulled at her collar, trying to waft air onto her skin, but only succeeded in moving the warm air about her. She continued to walk until she came to the small boathouse. Resting with her back against the side of the building in the shade, Nell breathed in deeply. There was the hint of some oily preservative – creosote perhaps – it smelled like the fences in the back garden in Cheam when heated by the summer sun.

Nell kicked at a stone in the dried earth and slammed down the shutters on the memory of her father's garden. She chivvied her thoughts along and tried to focus on creating a new story. There might be something in the Olympics that seemed to have captured public interest. Perhaps she could take inspiration from young Bertie and write about a chap obsessed with running. He could be inspired by an older athlete to train to compete to represent his country. Perhaps there could be a femme fatale who was after getting her hands on the athlete's gold medals more than the man, wanting to melt down the gold. The irony of her writing about sport was not lost on Nell. But casting the woman as the villain would be a refreshing twist on her usual stories. The trope of the femme fatale might be as old as the hills, but it was not one about which she had ever written.

With the idea percolating, Nell made her way back to her towel. She kicked off her pumps, sat down, took out her notebook, and scribbled some plot notes and character descriptions. Before she knew it, she had filled almost half a dozen pages. That wasn't to be sniffed at. She had achieved more in six minutes than she had in the previous six months!

Grabbing the flask from her bag, she unscrewed the lid and downed half the lemonade to toast her breakthrough. To seal the celebration, Nell jumped to her feet, pulled her dress over her head, and made a beeline for the water. She ran into the waves, the water splashing her legs, and was already up to her waist when she remembered the swimming cap in her bag. Oh well, her hair was short, it would dry. She held her breath and submerged her head under the water. After a few seconds, she emerged, laughing at the shock of the cold. She bobbed up and down, treading water. She had almost forgotten the absolute thrill of coming up with the idea for a story.

Nell kicked up her legs and lay on her back in the water. With a flick of her feet and moving her hands gently to and fro, she floated, the water sparkling about her. With her head back and her ears beneath the surface, the only sound was the swish of the water as she floated further from the shore. Her hands and feet moving beneath the surface to keep her afloat made no sound at all. As she floated, she thought about her characters. And it came to her. Mr Townley! Perhaps he could be the basis for her hero. He was tall and broad and handsome. Yes, that was a splendid idea. Flipping on to her front, Nell began to perform a gentle breaststroke. She had swum almost to the far side of the lake when, with a kick of her legs, she turned around and performed a rapid crawl back. Her fingers twitched. They wanted to get to the typewriter to take flight. Perhaps this was how the athletes in her book would feel; the muscles in their legs itching for the crack of the starter's pistol.

Nell grabbed the towel and rubbed her body and hair quickly and roughly. Draining the lemonade, she popped the flask back in her bag before wrapping the towel around her body and securing it with a twist at her chest. What she had failed to dry, the sun would remedy soon enough.

Shielding her eyes, Nell looked along the path. There had been nobody about to see her walk down to the lake; her journey back to Hill House would no doubt be as solitary. Pushing her feet into her pumps and her dress into her bag, Nell headed back up the bank, squinting into the sky. From the position of the sun, she judged it to be just after midday. As though in confirmation her stomach growled. She began to walk rapidly, her feet squidging inside her shoes, thinking longingly of a cheese sandwich and a cup of tea, hoping that Mrs Randal wouldn't mind her invading the kitchen. As the path drew alongside the wood, Nell wiped the back of her hand across her forehead. Her hair was already almost dry, and perspiration rather than water inched between her breasts. She looked into the trees. They seemed to be beckoning for her to take a shady detour. It would be a safer route anyway. She was far less likely to bump into anyone, and in her state of undress that would be no bad thing.

The instant Nell left the path and stepped into the woods, the heat of the day eased. Keeping the path to her right, she made her way carefully, avoiding the gnarled roots breaking through the ground, twigs cracking underfoot. Names for the characters in her new story began to run through her head: Carlos, Nero... Perhaps her hero was to be Greek or Italian or Spanish. Oh, yes! A Spanish prince might make a fun leading man for her femme fatale to toy with. Nell's fingers began to twitch again. 'Hold your horses,' she said to her hands. 'We'll be at the typewriter soon enough.'

High above Nell's head, birds sang and called to each other. Steadying herself against a tree, she looked up into the branches and smiled. From someway off came the sound of a twig cracking. The fine hairs on Nell's arms stood on end. She looked around at the trees and patches of course undergrowth. She shook her head. 'Get a grip, Potter,' she said under her breath. But as she said the words, she recalled the sensation of eyes watching her from the woods yesterday before she had spoken to Mr Townley. Perhaps she hadn't imagined it after all. Her breathing grew more rapid. Taking a step, Nell was reassured to hear just a single crack. But it was a short-lived reprieve. Before she moved again, there came another crack. Louder this time. She stopped and spun around.

'Who's there?' she called. No answer. 'Who's there?' she

called again. 'You don't scare me.' Although the quiver in her voice said otherwise, she pulled herself up to her full five feet eight inches. Life had taught her that to appear afraid was almost as dangerous as being afraid. As a young woman and fledgling member of the WSPU, she had been tutored in jiu-jitsu to protect her fellow suffragettes should they find themselves under attack from the police. The skills may have been learned a decade earlier, but her muscles still recalled the manoeuvres to turn an attacker's energy back on him. If necessary, she could also instigate an attack.

In the few seconds it took Nell to consider this and to wonder whether the creature making the noise was an unsuspecting person out for a walk, a man dressed in dark clothes and a long black coat emerged from the trees before her. He wore a hat pulled down so that it was impossible to see his features. He was a large man, huge in fact. He approached with assurance. He didn't run. He didn't say anything. Almost before she knew it, the man was a few paces away, his head down. Nell tried to make out his features again but was still unable to see beneath his broad-brimmed hat. He raised his fist in readiness to attack. Her heart hammering at her ribs, Nell prepared to take up her stance but, as he reached her, another noise came crashing through the trees from behind.

The man stopped short. He seemed to hesitate briefly before turning and running away through the trees. Within a second, another man, in a tweed jacket, ran past Nell. It was Elliot, and he passed so close that she felt the air around her disturbed.

'Stop or I'll shoot!' Elliot called. He stopped, raised a shotgun to his shoulder, and took aim. But the man in the hat didn't stop. With a speed and nimbleness at odds with his size, he leapt over branches, dodging trees, and smashing through the wood until he disappeared. Elliot lowered his gun. He muttered under his breath. He turned around and ran back to Nell.

'Are you hurt?' he asked, looking Nell over. It was only then that Nell realised her towel had slipped and she was standing before Elliot in just Charlotte's bathing costume. He surveyed her as he might an injured sheep or cow.

'I'm all right,' she said. Her heart was pounding fit to burst free of her chest, but she would not let anyone see her anything but composed.

Elliot stooped to collect her towel and handed it to her. Nell wrapped it around her body and secured it at her chest. Elliot slipped off his jacket and tried to hand it to her.

'There's really no need,' Nell started. But Elliot placed the jacket around her shoulders anyway.

'If I'd had the dog, he wouldn't have got away,' Elliot said. 'Are you able to walk? I'd rather not leave you here alone to go and fetch the car.'

'Who was he?' Nell asked.

Elliot paused before he looked past her. 'Nobody. A poacher, I should imagine.' It seemed to Nell that it was taking a great effort for Elliot to tell a lie.

'A poacher?' Nell said.

'P'raps. We should go.'

'Why? Do you think he'll come back? Surely a poacher would take you for a gamekeeper and steer clear.'

'Like I said, we should go.'

As bold as Nell was attempting to be, she was in no mood to stay in the woods alone.

'This way,' Elliot said and stepped aside, pointing to the best way through the trees. Back out on the path, Elliot said, 'I'll walk you back to the house.'

'Thank you, but there's no need.'

'I'll see you back to the house,' he said again without looking at her.

They walked along the path, Elliot watching the trees then looking forward. Every so often, he looked behind them.

The only sound was Nell's pumps squelching and the birdsong.

'If that happens again,' Elliot said. 'Shout out. And I'll come.'

'Were you following me?' Nell asked.

Elliot looked straight ahead. 'It's my job to keep a watch on the house and everyone here.'

Nell shook her head. 'Aren't you the chauffeur?'

'I am.'

'Then why were you following me?'

'Running away would be best. Next time don't try to stand your ground.'

'You were following me. You were watching me.' Nell stopped and looked at him. 'And what do you mean "next time"?'

'If there is a next time.'

'That's not what you said. And why were you following me?'

'Like I said, I'm always in the woods.'

Had it been another man evading her questions, she would have taken him to task. 'I thought initially it might be Mr Townley in the woods,' Nell said.

'Mr Townley?' Elliot said. Nell was sure she detected a question in his voice.

'You do know Mr Townley, don't you?' she said. 'I understand he works here sometimes.'

'Of course, I know Mr Townley,' Elliot said.

'Then why did you sound unsure when I said his name?'

'Because you won't find Mr Townley in the woods. You'll see him in the gardens or by the lake. Sometimes around the stable yard. Not in the woods.'

They had reached the kitchen garden and a scuffle just beyond the wall made Nell turn, just in time to see Tommy run through the open gates. Before she knew what was happening, he ran to her. He gripped her hand and pressed his face to the towel around her middle. Nell stared down at his red curls for a moment, lost for how to respond. She could hardly ignore a child so clearly in distress, especially since he had attached himself to her.

'What has happened?' she said. Gathering up the towel with her free hand, she crouched on her haunches. Tommy released his grip and placed his warm little hands on either side of her face. He looked her directly in the eyes. 'Are you all right?' he said, searching her face, his own eyes full of concern, and his pupils once again larger than they ought to be.

'Yes, yes, I'm quite all right.'

He pushed her hair away from her cheeks and stared at the scar running down the side of her face. 'Trees can be so very dangerous,' he said softly. 'Oh, don't be afraid. I am here.' He wrapped his arms around her neck and placed his head on her shoulder, holding her tight. 'I am here,' he repeated. 'But please, do not go into the woods alone again. It might not be safe.'

As he clung to her, Nell looked around. There was no sign of his mother, Mary or Charlotte.

'Are you alone?' she said to Tommy.

'I am never alone when I am with you.'

Nell shifted, feeling the light weight of his arms around her. 'You barely know me. It mightn't be such a good idea to trust a stranger so very much.'

'You are not a stranger. I know you very well. Very well indeed.'

Nell looked up at Elliot. 'Isn't he young to be playing out here with nobody around?'

'The boy is fine,' Elliot said. And then added somewhat brusquely, 'Come on Master Thomas, let's get you back to yer mother.'

He prised Tommy away from Nell. Tommy reached out to her, tears welling in his eyes as though the parting was painful.

Stooping, Elliot whispered something to the boy. And then, in a louder voice that Nell could hear, said, 'Hop on board, young 'un.'

In an instant Tommy's tears dried. He launched himself onto Elliot's back in the manner of the child who had thrown bilberries at his sister. Elliot set off walking again. His gait did not alter, neither did his pace as Tommy bobbed up and down, playing at being Wellington at full charge. He shouted out lustily, his red curls bobbing as he bounced on Elliot's back.

Nell collected her bag, which had fallen to the ground, and hurried to catch up with them. Surely Tommy's behaviour was not that of a normal child. But how would she know what normal was?

Just past the stable yard, Elliot stopped. He deposited Tommy on the ground.

'Hey,' Tommy said, 'I wasn't finished having my fun. Let me back on.'

Ignoring him, Elliot turned to Nell. 'I'll take my leave here. I've my work to be getting on with.'

And with that, he departed as quickly as he had arrived, disappearing into the stables, leaving Nell no time to call after him to say that she hadn't asked him to leave his work to rescue her. She was no damsel in distress. But as she thought it, she pictured the man in the woods. He had meant to do her harm, hadn't he? She could have thrown him to the ground had the situation called for it but still...

She took hold of Tommy's hand. 'Come on,' she said. 'Let's go and find your mother.'

Tommy tried to yank his hand free. 'That's not fair,' he whined. 'I want to play.'

'Like yesterday in the attic,' Nell said. 'I know it was you.'

'I don't know what you're talking about,' Tommy said. He tried to pull his hand free of her grasp again. 'I want to go into the woods. I have a den, you know, but I shan't tell you where it is.'

'I didn't ask,' Nell said under her breath, not caring for this boisterous version of Tommy. The version that also told fibs about playing tricks on unsuspecting visitors. The kind and gentle version of Tommy, though strange, was easier to bear. And she hadn't asked for the responsibility of looking after another woman's child. She gripped his hand tighter, and Tommy dug his heels into the gravel to try to stop her. Once or twice, as they made their way back to the house, he attempted to yank his hand free of Nell's again. As tempted as she was to set him free, picturing the man in the woods, she kept a tight grip.

'Thomas!' Alice said. 'How many times do I have to tell you not to run away?' She was standing in the kitchen, looking down at her son and scowling while Tommy made a grab for a sandwich on the table.

Alice had handed a bowl to Mrs Randal and the cook had taken over the job of feeding an unidentifiable mush to the baby, who was in a highchair at the table. He smacked his lips joyfully as the food was spooned in. Little Daphne sat quietly beside Mrs Randal, eating an apple that had been peeled and cored. It seemed to Nell as though they were quite used to scenes such as this playing out before them. After another few minutes where Tommy had to accept his scolding and Alice forced him to make a begrudging apology, he was finally allowed to sit at the table to tuck into his sandwich.

'He sometimes runs off on his own,' Alice said to Nell, 'but these last few days have been worse than ever. Where were you this time?' Alice said to her son.

'Playing in the walled garden,' he said through a mouthful of sandwich. 'And then Miss Potter caught me and brought me back. Although I didn't want to come. I wanted to go down to the lake and the woods.'

'How many times?' Alice said. 'You're not to wander off alone.'

He shrugged his shoulders and carried on eating.

'Thank you so much for bringing him back,' Alice said, reaching to stroke her son's hair.

'It's really not a problem,' Nell said. She was just glad that she had managed to pull on her dress in the vestibule. She had stuffed Elliot's jacket and her towel in her large bag and left it beneath a table in the corner of the hall.

Nell accepted Mrs Randal's offer of making her a sandwich. She thanked Alice for the kind offer of joining them for lunch but explained that she would rather eat alone as she had work to do. On her way up to her bedroom with a sandwich and glass of lemonade, she collected her bag. Something, and she wasn't sure what, had stopped her from telling Alice about the man in the woods. What was the point when it would alarm her unnecessarily? Nell told herself it was likely he was just a poacher, as Elliot had said. Nothing to worry about.

NINE

Nell ate her sandwich looking out of the window. There was no sign at all of anything or anyone that didn't belong there. As she ate, she thought about Elliot and his behaviour towards Tommy. What had he whispered as he knelt that she was unable to hear? One minute Tommy was clinging to her affectionately, whispering as though he had seen the man in the woods, and the next, he was a naughty little boy again.

Whatever Elliot had said to the child, it was as if it had broken a spell. And why had Tommy focused on her scar again? How could he know that it had anything to do with a tree? Nell dabbed at the crumbs left on her plate. She licked them from her finger. He didn't know. Tommy was simply toying with her. From what she remembered of her very first school, it was what small boys did. They teased. They tormented spiders and mice and flies. Well, if he tried any of his nonsense again, she would take him by the shoulders and shake it out of him. Or she would tell Alice; that would probably be the most sensible course of action.

Abandoning her plate on the dressing table, Nell sat at the desk. She grabbed her bag and removed the towel. Pushing

Elliot's coat aside, she pulled out her notepad. But her thoughts returned again to the man in the woods. Something like irritation bristled in her. Why had Elliot felt the need to jump in to protect her? She had been alone in London for long enough to know how to look after herself. She didn't need a man to play the hero.

Nell flicked through the notepad, but as she attempted to reconnect with the characters, her mind's eye kept being drawn back to the man pushing through the trees, head down, hand balled in to a fist. Her pulse quickened. How dare he try to attack her? If it was the same man Rosemary had seen, then it seemed likely that he was not beyond attacking a young girl. If Rosemary hadn't screamed, bringing the whole household to her, what might he have done?

Nell closed the notepad and pushed it away.

TEN

Nell headed down to the hall. Opposite the billiard room and beneath the sweeping staircase, she pushed open a door and found the corridor she was looking for. She made her way along it, with its low ceilings and small rooms crowded together. The first room she came to had a door leading to the grounds at the back of the house. It was the type of room where a guest's luggage might be stored before being taken up to the rooms on the floors above. A long wooden bench ran along one wall, and hooks held all manner of coats and jackets and hats. There was even a ceramic stick stand, fashioned in the form of a rather comical, turquoise-coloured monkey. Further along the corridor, she peered into a room full of boots and an array of garden games and sporting equipment.

At the very end of the corridor, a door stood open. Nell made her way along and was relieved to find the person she was hoping to speak to sitting behind a desk.

'Hello,' she said from the doorway.

Edward, who had been consulting a ledger, his fingers dug into his hair, looked up. He rose from his chair. 'Nell,' he said. 'How nice to see you, I hope you've had a good day.'

'Very good, thank you.'

'And to what do I owe this pleasure?' Edward said, pushing his spectacles further up his nose.

'I wanted to speak to you. On a little matter.'

Edward stepped from behind the desk. He pulled out the chair on the opposite side to his. 'Please,' he said.

Nell sat down and Edward retook his seat.

Nell looked around the room. There was a fireplace behind Edward. A few paintings hung on the walls, all of London. There was a street scene of the Houses of Parliament with Big Ben looking down from the sky on a rainy day with a carriage passing by. And there was a scene Nell recognised as the view from the top of Primrose Hill. Nestled amongst the paintings were some of the most amazing artworks Nell had seen in a private house. Tribal masks, carvings of faces and animals in wood, tapestries in the brightest colours.

'Ah,' Edward said. 'I can see you're admiring Father's collection. As a young man, he travelled extensively in South America. He amassed quite a collection of art. It's far more cheerful than the usual paintings one finds in an office, don't you think? You must explore the conservatory. It houses Father's collection of orchids. He developed quite a passion for them during his travels. It's the far door leading out from the billiard room, if you're interested.'

'I am, thank you, I shall have to take a look.'

'So?' Edward said. 'What is it you wanted to speak to me about?'

Nell shifted in her seat. 'Well, Edward. This is a bit odd... It's just that... I went down to the lake today for a swim—'

'Oh, it's lovely, isn't it? Just the tonic in this heat.'

'Yes, yes, it is. But Edward, that's not what I wanted to talk to you about. There was a man. After I went swimming. In the woods. I wouldn't normally say anything, only, with the children, I thought you ought to know.'

Edward placed his elbows on the desk. Knitting his fingers together, he rested his chin on his hands. 'Have you seen anyone else unexpected since you arrived?'

'I bumped into a man down by the lake yesterday evening. Mr Townley. He said he's working here. For Mr Elliot.'

'Yes,' Edward said. 'Elliot brings men in from the village when he needs help around the house and in the garden and such like. Anybody else?'

'Well, I wasn't expecting Elliot to come charging through the woods to scare the stranger off.'

Edward sighed. 'Elliot was there. Good. That's good.'

'Is it?' Nell sat forward. 'Edward, is something going on? It feels like there's more to this than meets the eye. And I had the very real feeling that Elliot was watching me, perhaps even following me, which was why he appeared so quickly. Edward, do you know something about this strange man? Did you get Elliot to follow me?' She had never been one to mince her words and wasn't about to start now. But when she saw the look in Edward's eyes, she almost wanted to swallow the words back down.

'Please, Nell,' he said, a note of panic in his voice. 'I'm sorry that you've been caught up in this... in this... oh, gosh.' He covered his face with his hands.

'Edward, Edward,' Nell coaxed. 'What is it? What's happening?'

Finally, he looked at her. 'It's gone too far,' he said. 'I can't deal with this alone.'

'Deal with what? Edward, tell me and I can try to help.'

Edward laughed sadly. 'I'm not sure anyone can help.' He removed his spectacles and rubbed his eyes.

'Is it the land? Do you need money. Is it something to do with the deal you are planning with Wilco?'

Edward shook his head. 'No. But the timing couldn't be worse what with Wilco in the house. He's in Northampton for the afternoon doing some business. I'd hoped that all of this had come to an end.'

Nell frowned. 'Edward you are going to have to speak more plainly if you want me to understand.'

Edward wiped his eyes again before replacing his spectacles. 'Nell,' he said. 'We have had a bit of a problem with an intruder. There's nothing to worry about really. I've had Elliot keeping an eye on everything, which is why he probably seemed to appear as if from nowhere today. I had hoped to keep it quiet. But I can see that the cat is rather out of the bag.'

'And do you know who the intruder is?'

'No.'

'But you think he's the man who Rosemary saw, although you all made her believe she was mistaken?'

'Nothing much gets past you, does it?' Edward laughed sadly again. 'I didn't like to do that to poor young Rosemary, but I didn't want to worry anyone. And with Wilco here, I had to make him believe... May I ask you a question?'

'Of course.'

'Did this man threaten you. Did he try to harm you?'

'He raised his fist to me. But I would have seen him off. I know how to defend myself.'

'Oh no! It has gone too far by a long way.' Edward ran his fingers through his fringe, making it stand up almost straight.

'What will you do?'

'Would you mind awfully if I give it some thought... I would rather we kept this to ourselves for the moment, if you wouldn't mind.'

'Of course.'

'I'll be sure to let you know what I decide.'

'And do you think this intruder is a poacher, as Elliot seems to think?'

'I hope so, Nell. Really, I do.'

ELEVEN

Nell returned to her room and sat at the desk. It was time to work. The Mandevilles were Edward's responsibility, and this was his house. It was clear that there was more to events than a poacher hoping to bag a stray pheasant or snare a rabbit, but Edward seemed to be attempting to deal with the situation. As much as her profession made her an expert observer, it was sometimes better to slip into the background and let others take charge of their own problems.

Nell pulled the yellow curtain across the window to avoid the distraction of any comings and goings outside. She took up a sheet of paper and fed it into the typewriter, rolling it into place and lining it up. It was enough to have responsibility for herself and for her contract with her publisher, as well as her obligation to her landlord. She flipped open her notepad and began typing. Keeping her focus on the page before her, she punched at the keys, pulling each completed page from the typewriter's grasp, placing it in the tray, and winding in a fresh page. Whenever any thought of the man in the wood, Elliot following her, or Tommy's strange behaviour, attempted to elbow its way in, she silenced it with an increased *tip tap* of the keys and a *ting* of the bell as she began a new paragraph.

After an hour or so, Nell sat back and looked at the pile of papers in the tray. It was nowhere near sufficient to get Robert off her back, but it was a respectable beginning of a story of an athlete called Carlos – a prince from a fictional European country suspiciously like Spain, and who looked remarkably like Mr Townley – and his athletic prowess. The opening chapter looked at his determination to represent his country at the Olympics in Paris, which put him in conflict with his father – the king – who wanted him to concentrate on the responsibilities of his royal future. It was an interesting set up, which Margot Evangeline's readers would find familiar enough to be intriguing. Nell was mulling whether the femme fatale would masquerade as a fellow athlete and what country she might be from when there was a knock at the door. She sat back. 'Come in,' she called.

The door opened and Mary entered, carrying a tray containing a glass. 'Mrs Mandeville asked that I bring this up for you,' she said. 'She thought you might like a glass of lemonade, what with it being so warm.' The ice in the glass chinked as she crossed the room to place it on the dressing table.

'Thank you,' Nell said. 'That was very kind of Alice.'

'Miss Alice is a very kind person. And she said that you might want to choose one of Miss Charlotte's dresses to wear this evening. She has a surprise for Miss Charlotte and is asking everyone to come a bit more formal. Drinks will be in the drawing room at seven sharp.'

'Sounds intriguing.'

'If I know Miss Charlotte, I think she will be very pleased with her surprise,' Mary said. She looked past Nell to the typewriter. Her eyes lit up when she saw the papers in the tray.

'Do you like books, Mary?'

'Oh, I love them, I really do.' It was as though a switch had been flicked in Mary. A passion flared in her eyes. 'And your books are so good, they really are. My mother loves them. And my sisters. We borrow them from the library. I mean, I like the books I read for college, but they're not fun like your books. Your books make us laugh and cry too and... sorry, am I talking too much? Sally, the lady's maid who usually does for the family, says that the ladies mightn't like to hear me go on so... sorry.'

'There's no call to apologise,' Nell laughed. 'I'm not a very formal person. And it's always a pleasure to meet someone who likes my books. But are you sure you wouldn't rather read something more serious and sensible?'

'Oh, no,' Mary said, shaking her head. 'When I read your books, it's like you know me. I know the ladies in your books are fine and grand, but they are like me, too. Underneath their fine clothes and jewels. I wouldn't mind going on some of their adventures! Like on an ocean liner or travelling across Siberia on a train. But at least I can imagine it when I read your books. What are you writing now? Sorry, I probably shouldn't ask.'

Nell laughed again. 'You can ask, but I shan't tell.' She tapped the side of her nose. 'We wouldn't want to spoil the surprise, would we? But I'll be sure to send you a copy just as soon as it's published.'

Mary put her hand to her chest. 'Really, you would do that for me?'

'It would be my pleasure,' Nell smiled.

Fresh from a bath, Nell combed her hair before collecting the dress Mary had laid out on the bed. It was a loose-fitting sleeveless dress, white with a blue pinstripe. Nell had just slipped it over her head when there came a knock at the door. 'Hello,' she called from inside the folds of cotton. No response. 'Not this again,' Nell muttered as she emerged from the neck and slipped the dress down her body. 'Mary, is that you?' No response. Nell already had her hand on the door handle when she heard the soft thud of footsteps on carpet. She yanked open the door and peered out into the corridor. As she had suspected, the 'hidden' door on the landing stood open. 'I know that's you, Tommy Mandeville!' she called and heard the distant sound of a child giggling and the slap of shoes on stone steps.

TWELVE

'Hello,' Alice said when Nell entered the drawing room. Edward and Wilco were already there, dressed in dark suits rather than slacks and shirts. They both rose when Nell entered. She wondered whether Edward might have something to say about their earlier conversation. But he and Wilco retook their seats and almost immediately fell back into conversation.

'How was your afternoon?' Alice asked. 'Productive, I hope.'

'The best I've had in a while,' Nell said. Once again, she had decided against alerting Alice to her son's mischief. It was harmless really. 'I do love your frock,' she said. 'That pink voile goes perfectly with your hair.' She sat on the sofa beside Alice, who handed her a glass of a green liquid.

'Another of Edward's concoctions?' Nell said quietly.

'There's sherry if you'd prefer,' Alice said just as quietly.

'No, this is fine, thank you. Here goes nothing.' Nell held her breath briefly before taking a sip. She held in a cough and Alice laughed.

'Evening one and all,' Charlotte said as she swept into the room. She wore a peach-coloured dress of taffeta over a silk under-dress. 'Oh dear, she said, looking at the tray on the side table. 'You haven't been at it again, have you, Edward? What do we have this evening?'

'Try it and see,' Edward said.

Charlotte plucked a glass from the tray. She took a sip and spluttered. 'He's trying to kill us all!' she said.

'I think it's rather good,' Wilco said. 'Here, pass us another, young Charlotte.'

Charlotte handed Wilco another drink. He thanked her and almost immediately fell back into conversation with Edward. From the snatches Nell caught, it sounded as though they were discussing business. It would seem that businessman Wilco was a different beast to party Wilco. His focus was very much on Edward rather than teasing the women. He took a cigarette case from his pocket, offered it to Edward and lit one for himself while listening to Edward.

Charlotte sat in the chair close to Nell and Alice. 'It's all our cousin Emma's fault, you know,' she said, taking another sip of the green liquid and grimacing. 'It was Emma who introduced Edward to cocktails years ago and he hasn't looked back. It's a shame you won't meet her while you're here. She's taken her children to France for the summer. She closes up the house and her husband stays in their London house. He'll go out to join them next month. Imagine two months in Menton!'

'It is a pity,' Alice said, 'If Emma were at home, we could have paid a visit. Caxton Hall is so beautiful. So elegant and grand.'

'Grander than Hill House?' Nell asked.

Charlotte almost spat out her drink. 'You could fit Hill House into Caxton Hall five times over,' she laughed. 'But it is a shame. Emma is a hoot. You'd get on like a house on fire. Before she married, she lived in London and went to all the parties and plays, just like you. But that was almost a decade ago. She married during the war and moved back to Caxton Hall permanently. You'll just have to visit another time so we can introduce you.' She flashed Nell a wicked grin.

'Nell has had a productive writing afternoon,' Alice said to Charlotte.

'Oh, that's wonderful,' Charlotte said. 'I knew Hill House would do you good. Come on then, tell us what you're writing.'

Nell pretended to seal her lips. 'You'll have to wait and see. I don't want to jinx it.'

'Spoilsport.'

There was a gentle knock at the door. 'Come in,' Alice said.

Audrey entered. 'If you please, Mrs Mandeville, your visitor's here. Will I show him in?'

'Please, Audrey,' Alice said.

'A visitor?' Charlotte said. 'Who?'

'Wait and see,' Alice smiled.

Nell heard the door open. She was facing Charlotte and saw her face light up. 'Paul!' Charlotte said. 'Whatever are you doing here?'

Turning to see the new arrival, Nell tried her very hardest not to appear shocked by the sight that met her. The man smiled. Or rather half-smiled. The left-hand side of his face was perfect. Almost too perfect. His lips rose and the creases around his eye deepened just slightly. There was even a dimple in his cheek. That half of his face was tanned, shaved smooth, incredibly handsome, flawless even. And it was in stark contrast to the other side of his face. The geography of his features on the right-hand side was so altered that it was difficult to believe they were two halves of the same man. Scars ran the length of his face. Beginning at his temple, they ran all the way down to his chin. In appearance, the scars resembled the gnarled branches of an ancient tree, entwined and fighting for prominence in the same space. But in colour, they were at once fleshy pink or quite raw, some hard and others with the texture of tapioca or sago. His eye with its dark pupil sat amongst these scars. There was an eyebrow of sorts, but the sporadic hair sat at a steep angle, from the bridge of his nose down to the corner of his eye. The lips moved for him to speak but a smile seemed impossible to master. It could not fight with the tight scars. And there was no dimple in that cheek.

'I was invited,' the man said in what Nell recognised to be an American accent.

'I invited Paul,' Alice said. 'I bumped into him in the village today and said he must join us this evening. I thought that would please you, Charlotte.'

'In the village! What were you doing in the village? I thought you were still in New York with your family. At least that's what you said in your last letter.'

'I'm visiting.'

'Visiting? Who. When. How. *Why?* And why didn't you let us know you were coming?'

Edward laughed. 'Enough of the interrogation, Charlotte.' He got up and took the new arrival's hand, shaking it warmly. 'It's good to see you, Paul. Very good. May I introduce an old college friend of mine, Mr Anthony Wilkinson. He's visiting for a, for a...'

'It's quite all right, Ed.' Wilco said, getting to his feet. 'Tell it like it is. I'm here on a bit of potential business.' He reached to shake the man's hand. 'And who do I have the pleasure of meeting?'

'Paul,' the man said. 'Paul Kenmore. It's good to meet you Mr Wilkinson.'

'Call me Wilco. We're all friends here.'

'It's good to meet you, Wilco.'

'Looks like you took a bit of a pasting there,' Wilco said, pointing to Mr Kenmore's face.

'I stood a little too close to a shell,' he said. 'It did quite a good job of reconfiguring my features.'

'I'll say,' Wilco said. 'I bet that smarted.'

Nell breathed in sharply and only exhaled when Mr Kenmore laughed. 'It did a bit,' he said.

'I was in the Royal Field Artillery in France,' Wilco said. 'How about you?'

'East Surrey's,' Mr Kenmore said. 'A shell at Passchendaele saw to it that my posting to France was cut a little short.'

'But aren't you a Yank?' Wilco looked a tad confused.

'Only on my mother's side.'

'And you chose to fight with your father's fellow countrymen?' Wilco smiled and nodded. 'Bravo, good on you. Joining us rather than waiting for the late arrival into the conflict of your mother's countrymen.'

Edward and Wilco retreated to their seats and Alice took the few steps to Mr Kenmore. 'Paul,' she said. 'Let me introduce you to Miss Nell Potter.'

Mr Kenmore faced Nell. There was nowhere to hide, so Nell looked him directly in the eyes, trying to avoid the rest of his face. He took her hand and shook it. Nell glanced down at his hand. It was perfectly unscathed.

'Good evening, Miss Potter,' he said.

'Nell,' she said, 'call me Nell.'

'Then you must call me Paul. It's wonderful to meet you, Nell,' he said in a deep American drawl.

Focusing on the smooth side of his face, Nell was reminded of a matinee idol and realised too late that she hadn't responded. Paul smiled again. 'It is rather something, isn't it?' he said. 'Fritz did one hell of a job on me.'

'Sorry,' Nell said and felt the colour rise to her cheeks. 'I didn't mean to stare—'

'It's perfectly understandable,' Paul said. 'It's natural to be at once intrigued and repelled.'

'I'm not repelled,' she said, keeping her focus on his face to show that she wasn't at all shocked.

Paul leant in a little closer. 'You're very polite but I can see myself in the mirror when I shave in the morning.'

Nell couldn't help but laugh.

'I was lucky to be treated at Queen's in Kent. My surgeon, Gillies, did his best to rebuild what the shell did such a good job of destroying. He wasn't able to do as much for me as some of my fellow patients. But you should have seen my face before he got to work.' He raised his left eyebrow and the right eyebrow tried to follow.

'You'll have to excuse Paul,' Alice said, touching his arm. 'He is very American and speaks his mind.' She handed him one of the green drinks from the tray.

Paul laughed softly. 'I forget that you English prefer to dance around a subject. I should have gotten used to it after being here for over a year.' He took a handkerchief from his pocket. After taking a sip of the green liquid, he dabbed at his lips.

'Has Paul told you he was a patient here?' Charlotte asked Nell.

'I was just getting around to it,' Paul said, taking another sip of the green liquid and dabbing at his lips to mop up the moisture that sat in the lines etched into the damaged side of his mouth. 'I should have known that you would jump in to tell everyone.'

'Sorry,' Charlotte said and looked to the floor.

'I'm joking,' Paul smiled. 'Tell the rest of it and we'll see if you get it right.'

Charlotte smiled and picked up the thread of her story. 'After Paul's treatment in The Queen's Hospital in Kent, he was sent here to convalesce. He was too poorly to go home to his mother in New York. His father and my father were friends at Cambridge, so my father made particular arrangements for Paul to be brought here. Did I get that right?' Charlotte said, turning to Paul, a little pride in her voice.

'As always,' Paul said. 'Mrs Hart, Alice and Charlotte did a good job of patching me up before sending me back home on the boat. After a year, you couldn't wait to see the back of me, could you?'

Charlotte looked to the floor again. Her cheeks flushed. 'Don't be silly, Paul.'

Nell looked from Charlotte to Paul. He most certainly had a smile in his eyes when Charlotte kicked at the rose pattern decorating the rug, while still unable to look at him.

'Paul has visited us a number of times since,' Alice said and Nell detected a smile in her eyes as she looked from Paul to Charlotte.

'I like the countryside around here,' Paul said. 'And with my father's family in Norfolk, I figure there's no harm in stopping by whenever I'm around. The afternoon teas aren't too bad, either.'

Nell watched Paul. His eyes never once left Charlotte as he spoke. His visits to Hill House had nothing to do with the countryside, Nell was sure of that. She looked at Alice, who was watching Charlotte and Paul and now smiling with the air of a clucky hen.

'What line of business are you in?' Nell asked.

From the way he turned slowly from Charlotte, Nell had the distinct impression that Paul would rather have stayed staring at her friend without interruption.

'Medicine,' he said.

It was Charlotte's turn to look up now. 'Paul was at medical school before the war. He went back to New York to complete his studies. He's specialising in trauma surgery. Operating on people after accidents.'

'Top points for accuracy again,' Paul smiled. 'Perhaps I should always leave it to Charlotte to tell my story. She is far more entertaining. Tell me, Nell, have you noticed how enthusiastic she is about just about anything.'

He smiled at Nell and then at Charlotte. For the first time Nell briefly forgot to notice the altered geography of his face.

Charlotte opened her mouth to say something but was a silenced by a knock at the door.

'Dinner's not planned for another hour,' Alice said to everyone and no one. 'Come in,' she called.

The door opened and Audrey appeared. 'There's more visitors, Mrs Mandeville,' she said.

'Oh, I wasn't expecting anyone else.'

'Beg your pardon. But it's for Mr Edward.'

Edward jumped to his feet. 'Ah, yes. There's just somebody to see me. They've been a bit delayed. It's all right everyone, you go on and enjoy yourselves.' He was using the slightly high pitched and desperate voice that Nell didn't care for. 'If you'll excuse me,' he said, practically sprinting from the room.

'Well,' Wilco said. 'Old Ed was certainly in a rush.' He got up from his seat to join the others standing in front of the open window and the welcome breeze disturbing the curtains. He stared at the good side of Paul's face. 'I get the very real feeling that I know you,' he said.

'I don't think we've met,' Paul said.

'Are you a member of any clubs?'

'Not in London.'

'And what regiment were you in again?'

'The East Surrey's.'

Wilco shook his head. Nell noticed that he continued to stare at Paul's face while Paul explained that he was staying in a room above The White Lion pub in the village. Charlotte tried to convince him to come to stay at Hill House. They could make up one of the guest rooms for him.

Paul had just refused for the third time when Wilco shouted, 'I've got it! You're Percy Kenmore's cousin. I knew I recognised the face. Well, half of it, at least.'

Nell winced but Paul showed no sign of taking offence. 'You are very perceptive. And with not much to go on,' he said.

'How is good old Perce? I haven't seen him since Cowes last year.'

'He was fine when I saw him last week.'

'Good. That's good.' Wilco turned to the women. 'Did you know that Kenmore here is practically Yankee royalty? His mother's family owns half of New York.'

'I think it's closer to a quarter now,' Paul said. 'What with the Rockefellers elbowing their way in.'

Wilco threw back his head and roared with laughter. He slapped Paul on the back. 'Touché, old man. And tell me, isn't your father Prof Kenmore? My mother is fascinated by what he has to say on the subject of "the other side". She's quite the fan.'

'He is,' Paul said. 'But my interests are more focused on this side.'

Charlotte wrinkled her nose. 'The other side? What the devil are you talking about.'

Wilco laughed again. 'Good God, Mother would have a fit if Beelzebub popped up at one of her table tipping parties.'

Charlotte looked to Paul. 'I'm not sure I understand.'

Paul ran his fingers along his shirt collar. 'You know my father is a professor of philosophy at Harvard. Well, he's made a study recently of the popularity of the spiritualist movement.'

'Mother attended a lecture your father gave when he was last in town,' Wilco said. 'Whatever he said turned Ma's head. She's a convert.'

'I'm not sure my father would consider himself a proponent for the movement. He's simply studying it as a scientific endeavour.'

'Well, whatever he's doing, he's turned Mother onto it. A week hardly goes by that she isn't sitting in a darkened room with a bunch of people communing with "the other side". Pa said when he gets home for his dinner, he's never sure who he's going to bump into in the dining room. He likes his spirits but usually from a bottle.' Wilco roared with laughter again.

'Anyway,' Paul said. 'I'm sure the ladies aren't at all interested.'

'I am!' Charlotte said. 'It sounds absolutely fascinating.'

Edward had left the door to the drawing room open in his haste to leave and he returned to hover in the doorway. 'Nell,' he said. 'Might I have a word?'

'What have you been up to?' Wilco said to Nell, raising his eyebrows and laughing. 'Mischief, I shouldn't doubt, if I know you women!'

Nell was rather disappointed to leave the conversation. Charlotte was pressing Paul on his father's research and, almost reluctantly, it seemed, he began explaining the history of the spiritualist movement in America, beginning with two sisters from New York.

Nell followed Edward out into the hall, and he closed the door behind them.

'What is it?' Nell asked.

Edward beckoned for her to follow him. 'I'm so sorry you've had to become involved,' he said as he led the way to the doorway below the staircase. 'I telephoned...that's to say, I just wanted to be sure of what to do. With Wilco here, I'm trying to keep it under wraps but sometimes, well, you know, you need to call in the professionals.'

Nell followed him down the corridor. 'You've lost me,' she said.

'There's someone who wants to speak to you,' he said.

THIRTEEN

Edward stepped aside to let Nell into his father's office. Two strangers waited inside. The first, a police constable, stood beside the desk. He was young, with a fair moustache, his helmet tucked in the crook of his arm. The second man was taller. He had his back to them and was looking at the painting of the view from Primrose Hill. Edward closed the door and the man turned around. He wore a dark suit. His jacket was open, and he had his hands dug into the pockets of his trousers. When he saw Nell, he removed his hat – a dark brown homburg with a deep black band. He placed it on the desk and took a step towards her.

'Inspector Painter,' he said. 'And this is PC Atkinson. You must be Miss Potter.' He held out his hand and Nell took it. His grip was firm and reassuring, as a police inspector's should be.

Pulling her hand free, Nell glanced back at Edward. 'Sorry,' she said, 'but what's going on?'

Before Edward could reply, Inspector Painter spoke. 'Mr Mandeville telephoned this afternoon to report sightings of an intruder hereabouts. We've been sent from Northampton to look into the situation. And from what we have been given to believe, you have seen this "intruder" at the closest quarters. We have a few questions we'd like to ask you.'

Not particularly caring for the way he said 'intruder', as though there may be some doubt about her sighting of the man, Nell said, 'I'll answer any question you care to ask. But you should know that I didn't get a very good view of the "intruder". He was wearing a hat pulled down over his face.' She looked to the homburg on the desk. 'Not dissimilar to your hat, Inspector Painter.'

She glanced at PC Atkinson, who was already scribbling notes in a pad with his pencil.

'If you could focus your attention on answering the questions I put to you, it would be appreciated,' Inspector Painter said. He nodded to the chair for her to sit down.

'I'd rather stand, if it's all the same with you,' she said. There were not chairs enough for them all and she'd be damned if she would sit down so these men could hover over her.

'As you please,' Inspector Painter said. 'If you could tell us everything that happened to you in the woods today, please.'

Nell recounted the details of the encounter, beginning with her decision to take a detour through the woods rather than walk along the path and ending with Elliot escorting her back to the house and Tommy's appearance from the walled garden. PC Atkinson scribbled continually in his notepad. And, as Nell spoke, she noticed Inspector Painter force his hands into the pockets of his trousers again. The stifling heat that was making PC Atkinson pull at the collar of his uniform seemed to have no effect whatsoever on his superior officer.

When Nell came to the end of her account, Inspector Painter glanced at PC Atkinson, who nodded. 'Got it all, sir,' he said, holding up his pad.

'So, Miss Potter,' Inspector Painter said. 'You say you came back to the house and didn't see the man again?'

'I don't just say it. That's precisely what happened. He ran away through the woods when Elliot gave chase.'

'And you didn't see his face at all? No features whatsoever?'

'None.'

Inspector Painter began pacing and Nell watched him. As he thought, his head dipped. Inspector Painter seemed to be a man of around forty years of age. He was slim and tall with dark hair cut in a military fashion. His complexion was rather sallow, as though he spent little time out of doors. He looked like he might have been handsome once upon a time. Now he looked... weary. As though life had taken the spirit from him.

At last, he spoke again. 'Thank you, Miss Potter. You have been very thorough. But, if you will allow me, I have one more question. You say that you were prepared to defend yourself using jiu-jitsu?'

'That's correct.'

'And where did you learn such a skill?'

'Is that relevant?'

'Please, if you could answer the question.'

She thought for a moment. 'Can I ask you a question first?'

'That's not how this usually works.'

'But will you allow it?'

He studied her face. 'Very well.'

'Your accent,' Nell said. 'You don't sound like you're from around here.'

'I'm not.'

'Are you from London?'

'I am. Originally.'

'And were you a police officer in London?'

'That's two questions.'

'Please, if you could answer the question,' she said.

Inspector Painter looked at her. His eyes were grey. 'Yes,' he said, 'I was a police officer in London.'

'Before the war?'

'Before. And after,' he said.

Nell stood up straight. Her activities a decade earlier may have been reserved to learning jiu jitsu and painting rocks for other women to throw through windows, as she had been considered too young to take direct action., but along with every other member of the WSPU, she had promised, if ever she was arrested and questioned by a police officer, to confirm her allegiances and her actions. She wasn't under arrest now. But if this man had been a police officer in London, there was a chance he had been involved in arresting her fellow activists. 'Before the war, I was a member of the Women's Social and Political Union,' she said. 'I was training to become a bodyguard for the movement. That, Inspector Painter, is where I learned jiu-jitsu.'

PC Atkinson stopped writing and looked up from his pad. Edward, who hadn't uttered a word throughout the exchange, said, 'Heavens, Nell. I had no idea.'

Inspector Painter said nothing. He simply studied her face.

'I was good at it,' she added. 'And I have forgotten none of my training.' It was a little lie. She hadn't been tested for years. But these men surrounding her weren't to know that.

Inspector Painter nodded. 'I don't doubt it. But next time, I suggest you run, rather than stand and fight. This man may be dangerous. The fact that he was preparing to attack until he was scared away is a cause for concern. I mightn't normally say such a thing, but you are clearly a woman who likes to hear the truth.'

Inwardly, Nell shivered. Outwardly, she nodded. 'Thank you. I do. But who is he? What does he want?'

'There have been some thefts from large houses in the area in recent weeks. We think this man may be responsible. We don't know for sure, and I am keeping an open mind. But it's as well that you know so you resist putting yourself in harm's way.'

'I'll bear it in mind,' she said.

Inspector Painter removed a watch from the pocket of his waistcoat and consulted it. 'Thank you for your time,' he said.

His voice was soft and measured as it had been throughout their exchange. There had been no rise or fall to give any clue that anything Nell had said had affected him in the slightest. 'We'll leave through the back door so that we don't cause any alarm to your guests. I would suggest that we keep this to ourselves for the time being.'

'Very well,' Edward said. 'That's all right with you, Nell, isn't it?'

'If it helps with the investigation then I'm happy to say nothing.'

Inspector Painter collected his hat from the desk. 'We'll say goodnight,' he said. He headed for the door, PC Atkinson following him, bidding Edward and Nell, "Good evening".

From her position just inside the office, Nell watched Inspector Painter make his way up the corridor, placing his hat on his head and adjusting it as he walked. With his dark suit, hat and watch chain rather than a wristwatch, he seemed rather old fashioned. Like the world had continued to turn in the last ten years but he had somehow been left behind.

The clock out in the hall chimed eight. She and Edward made their way in the direction of the dining room, Edward concocting a story that he had called her into the office to show her a book for research to aid her writing and that the visitors had been travelling salesmen who had been very late for an appointment. He would instruct the staff later not to mention the police officers to any other members of the family.

While they walked, Nell thought about her behaviour toward Inspector Painter. She smiled. Even after all these years, little victories over the authorities put a spring in her step.

FOURTEEN

Dinner was a lively affair involving a fine Russian salad, a cold roast ham, and plenty of wine from Sir Charles' cellar. It was followed by cheese made from milk produced by the dairy herd over towards Buryton and Mrs Randal's spicy and sweet chutney made from the previous autumn's Hill House harvest.

They sat in the dining room with every door and window open. As with the previous evening, Nell managed to keep her interactions to a minimum. There was far more value in listening to everyone else. The subject of the table tipping and spiritualism was one that would not drop and Charlotte pressed both Paul and Wilco on all they knew. By the end of the meal, they were all aware of the Fox sisters in the middle of the previous century who had sparked a craze for spiritualism in Upstate New York when they reported noises in their family's farmhouse, which appeared to come from sentient creatures. Then there was the celebrated medium who had crossed the Atlantic to thrill the good ladies and gentlemen of fashionable London in their darkened parlours and drawing rooms.

The subject intrigued Nell. It might be of some use in this or a future book. But as much as she tried to focus on the conversations, she was drawn back to the image of the sallow-faced police officer, staring at a painting of Primrose Hill. As she recalled him, she saw how his shoulders slumped when his back was to her, as though the image was taking some of the life from him. When he turned around, he drew himself up to his full height. But there had been something so sad, so lost in those grey eyes.

Following dinner, they took their port into the drawing room, except for Wilco who departed to make some telephone calls in Sir Charles' office. Every so often, Edward looked sheepishly over his glass in Nell's direction. She would put his mind at rest later. She would let him know that she had no intention of sharing the secret of the police officers' visit to Hill House or the investigation of the intruder. His presence would not put her off exploring the land around Hill House.

Charlotte walked up and down the drawing room, fanning her face with her hand. 'Edward,' she said. 'Do you think we might have a medium visit here to give a demonstration of their skills? It sounds positively fascinating. Wilco even said that his mother saw Arthur Conan Doyle at a debate about spiritualism. He's a great believer. Arthur Conan Doyle,' she emphasised. 'You know, the creator of Sherlock Holmes, who you adore.'

'Thank you, Charlotte. I'm well aware who Conan Doyle is. But that doesn't mean we need to invite him – and his ghosts and ghouls – into the house.'

'There's something to be said for letting sleeping dogs lie,' Paul said, tapping the ash from his cigar into an ashtray on the arm of his chair.

'But your father studies the subject,' Charlotte said.

'He does,' Paul said. 'But it's a scientific study and I wouldn't say that he necessarily believes in it. Enough of the people purporting to commune with spirits have been shown to be charlatans. Using fake photography and becoming very dextrous with their feet to move objects out of sight.'

'Some,' Charlotte said. 'But not all. Have you ever been to a séance?'

'No, I have not.' Paul said. 'What about you, Nell? Do you believe in any of this?'

Nell didn't have to think. 'When you're dead, you're dead,' she said. 'And if you could come back, why would you bother wasting your time tipping a table in an old woman's parlour, rather than doing something meaningful?'

Paul nodded. 'My feelings exactly.'

'And mine,' Alice said. 'Let's change the subject before Wilco returns.'

The remainder of the evening passed pleasantly. When Nell returned to her room, she undressed and lay in her slip on the bed. Alice hadn't fully succeeded in quashing all talk of ghouls, but she had managed to stop Wilco and Charlotte from turning out all the lights to tell ghost stories.

Nell stared up into the darkness. There was no reason to be scared of the dead. What man was capable of doing to man was far more horrific than the prospect of coming face to face with a long-dead Mandeville roaming the rooms of Hill House.

With the darkness as a canvas, she pictured Paul's face. Another man had done that to him. It was a shell designed by man, loaded by man into a gun designed by man and fired by man. It was another man that had obliterated half of Paul's face, not a ghost. He was lucky to have been operated on by Gillies. Nell knew of Gillies but had decided against raising that when Paul mentioned him, since it was Paul's story to tell, not hers.

Many of the artists of her acquaintance had trained at the Slade under Henry Tonks, a towering giant of a man, with a face like a hawk, who scared all but the most determined away from an artistic career with his withering critiques of their attempts at art. Tonks had painted the faces of many of the men at the hospital in Kent both before and after Gillies' treatment of them. One of the men of Nell's acquaintance had acted as Tonks' assistant and travelled to Kent with him to mix paints and carry his canvases. He had tried to articulate in words what he had seen at those sittings, but until tonight, Nell hadn't fully appreciated the utter destruction a shell could wreak on a man's face.

Fortunately, for Paul, what remained of his face and his personality made him more attractive than most other men. Charlotte was clearly of that opinion. It would be good to see Charlotte happy. If anyone deserved happiness, it was Charlotte who, with every breath, tried to make the world around her a better place.

Nell turned onto her side and looked out of the window at the stars. The moon hung pale and low in the sky. There was another face from tonight that would not shift from her thoughts. A pale face, with cheeks slightly sunken. And grey eyes. Flat eyes. With no spark. What was the story of that face? What had the world done to it to make it so careworn?

Briefly, Nell felt guilty that she had goaded him about her WSPU activities. But it was a passing guilt. He seemed like a man capable of standing his ground.

Tiredness made her eyelids flutter. She prised them open. Once she closed them, she would fall almost immediately to sleep. It had always been that way, even as a child. And when she slept, she slept soundly, with no dreams. Not one. Even at her most troubled, she had slept deeply, undisturbed by her subconscious replaying events. And tonight, she had more to ponder. She hadn't quite finished her thinking for the day. Her eyelids fluttered again. And then... darkness.

FIFTEEN

26TH JULY 1924

Two cheese and pickle sandwiches wrapped in wax paper –
tick
An apple – tick
A flask of Mrs Randal's delicious homemade lemonade – tick

Nell pulled the large bag onto her shoulder. In a wide straw
sunhat and wearing a cotton blouse and a pair of culottes
borrowed from Charlotte's seemingly never-ending wardrobe of
loaned things, she opened the door of the small luggage room
next to Sir Charles' office and pushed a bicycle out through the
door to the path at the back of the house. When she had
mentioned over breakfast that she quite fancied the idea of
cycling out, Charlotte had asked Bertie to check the tyres, wipe
down the seat, and oil the chain so that it was ready for Nell to
leave at just after eleven o'clock.

Out on the main path, Nell squeezed her bag into the
wicker basket and settled onto the seat. It was early, but the heat
of the sun warmed her bare arms as she pedalled past the stable
yard and the walled garden. Passing the woods, she peered into
the trees. All looked calm. The intruder was no doubt long

gone, off to poach – if indeed, that is what he was up to – on a property where he could go about his nefarious business unmolested by screaming girls, half naked bathers, and brawling grooms.

Drawing up to the lake, Nell was tempted to stop, but she couldn't; she was on a research trip to see whether Caxton Hall might provide inspiration for some settings in her new story. The idea for the excursion had come to her in the middle of the night. Unlike the first night when she had been woken by the sensation of someone stroking her hair, in the wee small hours of this morning, it had been the sensation of someone touching her hand. She had woken quite naturally, without a start or fright. On looking around the room, she had found it to be empty and put the experience down once again to the gentle breeze coming in through the open window. As she remembered it now, it hadn't been at all unpleasant. Quite the opposite. It had made her feel as though someone she loved had been in the room with her, sitting on the bed, petting her as she slept. But in the bright light of day, she knew she had been alone in bed, just as she always was.

Passing the boathouse, the path began to rise. Nell frowned at the hill looming before her. The map she had consulted in the library had told her that her destination lay three miles away towards the east. It had given no indication that she would be expected to scale a mountain! She could turn back to take the alternative route through the villages and along the roads, but the thought of being outdone by a hill made her press on and begin the ascent of the dirt path that wound its way to the top.

Pedalling soon became hard, like attempting to wade through syrup. Nell fought against it for as long as she was able, pushing down on the pedals as they grew increasingly leaden. When she came to a point where the bike threatened to go into reverse and take her back down the hill, she reluctantly admitted defeat. Dismounting carefully, she kept hold of the handlebars and began pushing the bicycle. With no shade, she was at the mercy of the sun and paused every so often to swipe the sweat from her forehead.

At the summit, Nell paused to catch her breath. Her calf and thigh muscles on fire, she pushed on for the few feet remaining until her destination came into view. If her breath had been taken away on stepping through the doors of Hill House, the view opening up before her momentarily made her lose the power of speech. Below the hill on which Nell stood, was a vast valley. The grass shone in the sunshine, so green that it seemed every blade had its own source of light. Nature had created half an amphitheatre, circled on two sides by hills and, in the very bowl of the valley, in the very centre of this view, stood Caxton Hall.

'Bloody Hell,' Nell said. The home of the Mandevilles' cousins wasn't quite Buckingham Palace, but it wasn't far off. From her vantage point, she could see that Caxton Hall had a central frontage with wings running on either side. There were so many buildings on the far side of the main house that it could have been a village in its own right. Where the land flattened on the other side of the valley, a lake stretched out as far as the eye could see. Behind the house, formal terraced gardens gave way to woodland reaching into the distance. The driveway ran over the top of the hill to Nell's right, as though the intention was for the house to be obscured so the spectacular frontage of Caxton Hall might be gradually revealed to approaching visitors.

Of course, Nell had approached in a way that had never been intended for the Caxtons' normal guests. She had approached by the equivalent of what would have been the tradesmen's route and sweating like a person who had done a day's work. Nell smiled to herself. It was fitting; her mother might have pretentions to grandeur, but her Great Aunt Hilda – an aunt of her father's – had once told Nell that she was descended from a maid of all work on her mother's side and a long line of farm labourers on her father's. Over the years, her ancestors had managed to claw their way up the ladder of society with education and hard work but the blood running through Nell's veins was as far from blue as it was possible to be. "And you've nothing to be ashamed of in that," Hilda had said to Nell when she was still a small child. "Your family's money has always been honestly earned. More than can be said of some of those hoity-toity, lah-dee-dah ne'er-do-wells you read about in the newspapers. I see it on the front pages over my shop counter every day."

Nell laughed at the memory of Hilda, folding her arms aggressively across her ample chest while sitting in the parlour in Cheam. She may not have cared for Mother's snobbery, but she wasn't averse to the generous afternoon teas Mother served. Whenever her mother scolded her in front of Hilda, that most forceful of women would intervene to say that a child without spirit was like an egg without a yolk. Even as a very small child, Nell had been sure that Hilda had done it to goad her mother. Whatever Hilda's motivations, Nell had appreciated the glimmers of camaraderie. She'd also enjoyed the bags of barley sugar Hilda had brought from the newsagents she ran in Surbiton and smuggled to Nell when her mother wasn't watching, in defiance of Mother's no-sweet rule.

Nell looked down at the front wheel of the bicycle. It had been the profits from the sale of that newsagents that had funded Nell's years at Cambridge. She'd had no idea that Hilda intended to bypass her father to leave her great-niece the lion's share of her inheritance. She owed Aunt Hilda so much and had never been able to thank her.

Nell turned the handlebars so that the wheel was no longer parallel to the brow of the hill but facing straight down. Gingerly, she mounted the bicycle and slowly eased up on the brakes. The bicycle lurched forward. Nell lost her nerve and gripped the brakes again. She could traverse the slope, of course, which would be the sensible approach to tackling the descent. But winding her way gradually down would be the egg white's way, wouldn't it? The yolk would be bolder, brasher, more adventurous.

'You fool, Nell Potter,' she shouted. Before she could talk herself out of it, she released her grip on the brakes. Gravity took over instantly and the bicycle began flying down the hill at a rate of knots, with Nell holding onto the handlebars for dear life, bouncing this way and that as the tyres hit mounds in the grass, screaming and laughing at the same time.

Even if she'd wanted to, she couldn't stop. She held her legs perpendicular to the bicycle as the pedals span wildly. The wind whipped past. Her straw hat flew off. Whether the feeling was exhilaration or terror, Nell couldn't tell, but almost as soon as the wild journey had begun, it was coming rapidly to an end. For a fleeting second, Nell wondered whether she should throw herself from the bicycle, but, as the ground began to level off, she pulled on the brakes and brought the bicycle to a gradual, if rather precarious stop, saving her from flying over the handle-bars and landing face down in the grass.

Panting wildly, Nell laughed. 'That one's for you Aunt Hilda,' she called out to the sky, rubbing her hair wildly as she could only imagine how she might look.

With her legs trembling, Nell laid the bicycle down on the grass. She made her way back up the hill on foot, at some points almost on all fours, to collect her hat. Then she ran back down the hill stumbling and laughing. She crossed the grass, fanning her face with the hat as she joined a path that seemed to circle the entire estate.

Approaching the house, Nell felt like a minnow swimming beside a whale. Caxton Hall was vast, in height and scale and splendour. The largest windows Nell had ever seen stretched almost from floor to ceiling in each floor of the sandy stone. Standing back, Nell had to crane her neck to take in the spectacle. There were two floors that she could see but each floor appeared to be at least three storeys high. A balustrade ran the length of the roof, which itself was topped with a series of spires and domes, rather like smaller versions of the dome of St Paul's Cathedral.

Nell ran her fingers along the wall beside the steps leading up to the vast front door. She was no expert, but this house seemed older than Hill House, the stone more nibbled by the elements as though it had faced more hard winters than its neighbour over the hill. If she had been a betting woman, she would have put money on it being in the Baroque style. As a child, the weekend trips with Esme and their parents to see the sights of southern England often involved a visit to the gardens of a stately home. Her father had been at great pains to point out features, sharing his passion for all things architectural with his disinterested daughters. In another life, with money no object, Nell felt sure her father would have gone to university to study to become an architect. Perhaps that was why he had raised no objection to her spending the inheritance that should rightly have been his, on studying at Cambridge.

Nell turned to look at the fountain in the centre of the drive. Stone cherubs clung to each other, balancing at precarious angles, all blowing trumpets, their stone cheeks puffed out. The water sat motionless in the base of the fountain waiting for the family's return, just as the windows on the ground floor had been tightly shuttered so that Nell couldn't get so much as a glimpse inside, no matter how hard she tried.

Coming to the end of the house, Nell continued on the path running beside the wall and soon arrived at an archway with a gate. She pushed open the gate and walked across the lawn with its urns, stone figures and ornamental borders. It wasn't until she was halfway down the flight of stone steps on the second terrace that it occurred to her that she was trespassing. She stopped, looking around. The windows in the house stared back blankly. Nobody was home to care. Apart from some birds swooping low in the unbroken expanse of blue above, she was quite alone.

'Are you all right there, my dear?'

Nell turned around. An old chap stood before her, dressed in workwear and a flat cap, his heavy boots muddied, and the pocket of his jerkin stitched roughly at the side where it must have torn. His nose was red and bulbous from too much time spent outdoors and too many hours spent in a public bar. He looked surprised rather than cross at her intrusion. All of this Nell took in while he waited for her reply.

'I'm fine, thank you,' she said. 'I'm sorry if I shouldn't be here. I'm staying in the house across the valley—'

'You're a guest at Hill House?' The man's look of surprise turned to a crooked-toothed smile. 'Oh, well then, you are very welcome. Lady Caxton has told us we are always to welcome any guest of the Mandevilles as though they are her guest.'

'That's very kind,' Nell said. 'My friends at Hill House made Caxton Hall sound so wonderful that I just had to see it for myself.'

The man looked up at the house. 'It is quite the finest house in the county,' he said. 'Maybe three or four counties around. A Caxton house has stood on this land since the 1600s when the first Earl was given the title by King Charles II. It's been added to over the years according to fashion but parts of it date back over 300 years. It's a shame Mrs Wentworth, the housekeeper, is away with Her Ladyship. She would usually give a tour of the inside. But it's locked up with no way in.'

'You're doing a fine job of explaining the history of Caxton Hall,' Nell smiled. 'Have you worked here long?'

'Man, and boy,' he said. 'I was apprenticed to the head gardener at thirteen years of age and have been here ever since.'

'It's the most beautiful garden I have ever seen.'

'I don't know about that,' he said, barely hiding a smile. 'I think the parterre over at Huntingdean might pip it to the post.'

'Well, it is certainly the finest garden I have ever seen,' Nell said.

'Then you must feel free to see more,' he said. 'The gardens run for a mile or so down to the woodland and onto the deer park.' He pointed into the distance. 'Further along the path you came, you'll find Lady Caxton's walled garden. She is particularly interested in the growing of flowers for the table and decorating the hall. And then there's the kitchen garden and stables. The door to the orangery is kept unlocked.' He nodded to a vast stone and glass construction running parallel to the house. 'That was the current Ladyship's father's passion; God rest his soul. He had a passion for growing pineapples and exotics.'

'So, there is no current Earl? Was there no son?'

Nell had thought it an innocent enough question, but the man tugged at his collar and sniffed before responding. 'There was a son. But his father decided he didn't deserve to become Earl. His Lordship thought his daughter far more... suited to take on Caxton Hall. He went to India and never came back. Best thing that could have happened to this family is him going off. I say good riddance. And I'm not saying anything you won't hear from anybody else.'

'I see,' Nell said, her story antennae twitching. 'And what was his name?'

'George. George Caxton,' the man said as though he had taken a bite from an apple and found half a worm inside.

Nell stored the detail away in her mental filing cabinet. 'Is it all right to take a look around the garden?'

'Absolutely,' the man said, brightening. 'Roam wherever pleases you. If it takes your fancy, pick some fruit in the orangery. There's always so much and it all gets turned into marmalade anyway. Just say you've spoken to Sullivan, and nobody will give you any trouble. There's only a handful of us here, keeping things ticking along. Since the house is shut up, we're all staying above the stables or in the servants' wing.' He pointed to a part of the building connected to the main house by what looked like an enclosed corridor. 'Just knock on the door if you need anything.'

'Thank you, Mr Sullivan,' Nell said. 'That's most kind.'

Mr Sullivan tipped his hat. 'I'll be getting on then,' he said, pushing his wheelbarrow away.

With permission to roam, Nell wandered out through the gate and back onto the main path. In the walled garden she walked among the display of flowers in beds and up on trellises above her head. In the midsummer sun, it was a riot of colour. Next, she made her way to the vast kitchen garden, with its regimented lines of vegetables and fruit trees trained along the brick walls.

Following the path, Nell came to the stables. The buildings around the cobbled courtyard were so grand and on such a scale they would dwarf most London mansion blocks. A large clock above a door tall enough to admit a carriage chimed. It was almost one o'clock. In response, Nell's stomach growled, and she hurried back to the bicycle.

Crawling up the hill, she sat in the warm grass. With her hat pulled down to shield her eyes, she tucked into a cup of the lemonade and one of the sandwiches. From her vantage point, she was able to survey the Caxton land again. What a thing it must have been for the son and heir to all of this to have to give it up for his sister and her family to inherit. Nell wondered if she could ask Charlotte what was behind George Caxton's fall from grace. There might even be a role for a disgraced aristo in her book. She took a bite out of the apple and chewed slowly. No, that was probably a terrible idea. If Mr Sullivan had remained tight-lipped, then a member of George Caxton's family would be unlikely to want to discuss it.

Brushing crumbs from her culottes, Nell wrapped the

second sandwich back in its wax paper and pushed it into her bag. She dropped the apple core into the grass for the local wildlife to enjoy later before heading down the hill and placing her bag in the basket of the bicycle.

Retracing her steps along the path and through the archway, Nell walked along the top terrace at the back of Caxton Hall. She looked up at the shuttered windows. How odd that a house so large should be so empty. She was about to turn away when, for the briefest of seconds, she was sure she saw one of the shutters move in a room on the top floor. She shielded her eyes and looked up again. All was still. She shook her head and carried on.

Almost before Nell reached the orangery, she felt the heat radiating from the building. Stepping through the open door onto the tiled floor, she breathed in the heady aromas. Ripe fruit hung from the branches of trees. Oranges, lemons, limes, and many fruits she couldn't identify. Remembering Mr Sullivan's words, she reached up through the waxy leaves and plucked two oranges. She picked a fruit that looked a bit like a lime and a purple fruit that resembled a plum although it was far too hard. She pushed all the fruits into the deep pockets of her culottes.

SIXTEEN

The heat too much to bear, Nell left the glasshouse. She removed her hat and fanned her face. At a fountain in the middle of the lawn, she slipped off her shoes and stepped into the cold, still water. Before her stood stone figures of a naked man and woman entwined in an embrace. Their love had lasted so long that they bloomed with moss. Nature had decorated their unashamed union. The world around them meant nothing to them. They were oblivious to it. They were eternally in love and the actions of no man could part them. Nell felt her head droop.

A shadow crossed the water, casting an undulating reflection. 'Miss Potter?' a man said.

Nell recognised the voice. It was Inspector Painter.

'Miss Potter?' he said again. 'We met yesterday.'

She took a steadying breath, hoping the sun would dry the disobedient tear that had formed in the corner of her eye. 'I'm well aware that we met yesterday,' she said.

He didn't respond. After another second or so, Nell turned around, the water splashing about her legs.

She thought she detected a brief quizzical twitch in his

eyebrow, although she couldn't be sure as his face was in the shadow of the brim of his homburg. Even with the sun beating down, he wore his dark, old-fashioned suit with a tie fastened at the neck of his shirt.

'Good afternoon,' Inspector Painter said, never once taking his eyes from her. That was the way of a police officer, Nell thought, always watching. Always judging. She became aware of the ridiculousness of her situation, standing almost knee deep in a fountain. She raised her chin and sloshed to the edge. Inspector Painter stepped forward.

'I can manage, thank you,' Nell said as he made to hold out his hand. His questioning of her in Sir Charles' study still did not sit well with her. The WSPU training clearly ran deeper than she had realised. Stepping rather ungraciously from the fountain and ignoring the water dripping from her, Nell pulled back her shoulders. 'What are you doing here?' she asked.

'I might ask you the same thing,' Inspector Painter said.

'I'm visiting,' she said. 'That is allowed, isn't it? I'm not expected to curtail my experiences because a man decided to jump out on me from behind a tree, am I?'

'No. But you might want to be on your guard.'

Nell felt the hairs on her arms bristle. 'Are you following me?'

'No.'

'Then why are you here?'

'I'm conducting enquiries.'

'Into what?'

'You might not draw so much attention to yourself. Splashing around in a fountain is an unconventional activity.'

'Now listen here,' Nell said, 'am I under investigation in any way?'

'You are not.'

'Then I'll splash about wherever and whenever I please.' She had forgotten about the fruit in her pockets; one of the oranges worked its way free and fell, hitting her foot before thudding in the grass. She thought she saw a smile pass across the grey eyes of Inspector Painter.

'I didn't steal it if that's what you're thinking,' she said. 'The head gardener said I could take whatever fruit I wanted from the orangery.'

'I know,' Inspector Painter said, the faint smile still in his eyes. 'I saw Mr Sullivan out by the front of the house. He said you were down here, helping yourself.' He knelt and collected the orange from the ground.

Nell snatched it and forced it into her pocket. 'Thank you,' she said curtly. She bent to pull on her shoes.

'My car is at the front of the house,' Inspector Painter said. 'I'll drive you back to Hill House.'

'There's no need.' Nell said, slipping her feet into her pumps.

'How did you get here?'

'I cycled.'

'Through the villages?' he asked.

'Over the hill, actually.'

'Then you may want to reconsider my offer.'

'Why?'

'Because it would be virtually impossible to cycle back the way you came. It's too steep. You'd have to cycle back through the villages, and it might be further than you think.'

'You think I don't have the stamina? Or perhaps you think as a woman I am too feeble.' Even as she said it, she pictured the near sheer face of the hill she had hurtled down, and her legs threatened to tremble.

'From what I've seen,' Painter said, 'I would say you are likely to achieve anything you put your mind to.'

She looked him directly in the face. He looked back at her, his hands in the pockets of his trousers. He didn't appear to be mocking her.

'If I cycle through the villages, I might be late for dinner,' she said. 'And I wouldn't want to put Charlotte and Alice out.'

'No, you wouldn't want to do that.'

'But the bicycle?'

'Let's take a look at it.'

Nell followed Painter up the steps to the top level of the garden. He was really quite tall and very slim. Perhaps too slim. As though he existed only on air. It was a look she was familiar with since most of the male artists and actors and authors of her acquaintance made it their life's work to stay slender and fey. But a police inspector? She thought about offering him the sandwich in her bag.

Painter's car was parked on the verge near her bicycle. He opened the boot.

'Are you sure it will fit?' Nell said, looking uncertainly from the car to the bicycle.

Painter simply picked up the bicycle and carried it to the car. He lowered it into the boot. From wheel to wheel it was wider than the car, but somehow Painter managed to manoeuvre it so that it wedged in place.

He opened the passenger door and Nell slipped inside. Painter got in beside her, started the engine, and drove off up the drive. Nell looked at him from the corner of her eye as he navigated the car up the steep incline. How was he not melting inside his suit and hat? There was barely a bead of sweat on his face. Did nothing faze him? She focused on the view as Painter drove steadily and carefully over the crest of the hill and down the other side.

'So, what have you found out about the man in the woods?' Nell asked.

'Our investigations are continuing.'

'Isn't it your job to solve crimes rather than just investigate?'

'Crimes can't be solved without investigation. There are procedures to follow.'

Nell folded her arms across her chest. They were on a long flat drive now. The waist-high grass in the open parkland all around was bleached to a pale yellow. Soon they came to a set of grand gates. Painter brought the car to a stop and a man appeared from the gatehouse. He opened the gates and as the car passed through, the man gave a little salute. Painter nodded to him.

'Do you know him?' Nell asked.

Painter gave her a sideways glance. 'He opened the gates for me earlier.'

'Why did he salute you?'

'I didn't notice.'

Nell slumped back in her seat. He had noticed. He noticed everything.

Still progressing at a ridiculously sensible speed, they turned onto a meandering country road, so narrow that any car approaching from the opposite direction would have been unable to pass. At some points, the road dipped below the surface of the forest floor, so that the roots of the trees were exposed and visible in the hard earth like wizened fingers reaching out to snag them. Watching the road rise and fall through the undulating countryside, Nell was secretly relieved that Inspector Painter had offered to drive her. She glanced at him again. He appeared not to want any conversation. He stared ahead, his focus on the road. Slow and steady.

Nell wondered whether a man such as Painter could possibly possess enthusiasm for anything. Surely, he must have displayed a level of determination to have been promoted in the police force. But that had to have been some time ago, perhaps when he served with the police force in London, before retreating to the dozy Northamptonshire countryside. The spate of thefts was no doubt an unwanted disturbance to the millpond of the sedentary life of a rural police inspector. Had his harshness as a police constable in

London seen him rise through the ranks? Had he arrested more men than any other constable? Had he disrupted protests and tried to silence the voices with which his society did not agree?

'Did you arrest any members of the WSPU?' Nell said sharply.

'Why do you ask?' he said.

'Why do you think?'

He glanced at her. 'I always did my duty as directed.'

'That's not an answer.'

'What answer would you have me give?' he asked.

'The truth, of course.'

'Then that is what you have.'

'That you always did your duty? That's no answer.'

'We don't always get the answer we want,' he said.

'Why did you move to Northampton? Was it for promotion?'

'Something like that.'

'Couldn't you have been an Inspector in London?'

'Yes.'

'That man at the gatehouse saluted you. Were you in the military?'

Inspector Painter didn't answer immediately. A muscle flinched in his cheek. 'We'll be at Hill House soon.'

Nell sat as far back in her seat as she was able. She had pushed too far. If she pursued her questioning, Painter would probably never speak to her again. While he focused on the view through the windscreen, Nell stole glances at him, keeping her thoughts to herself. He was an incredibly neat man. His hair that she could see beneath his hat was cut with precision, his shoes highly polished. His clothes might be old-fashioned, but they were fastidiously clean and pressed. On the surface, at least, he was perfectly presented. And yet... something didn't sit quite right with Nell. She read people. It was what she did. She watched them, took in details, and worked out who they were and what made them tick.

Painter's words gave nothing away. His responses to her questions – even her goading – led nowhere. His replies were guarded. Curt, but never rude. He did not rise to her intentionally timed prods. And yet... his face spoke of something. It was as though he wore a mask. There was a story in the sad grey eyes and the flinch in his cheek when he didn't want to answer a question. And there was a heaviness to his bearing. Not physically, but in his essence. Nell studied his profile for a second longer before turning away to stare out of the window. His looks hadn't faded, they were hidden, and something about his sombre air touched a nerve in her that she would have rather remained buried.

Soon, Painter navigated the car through the village, around the pretty green with its public house and duck pond. They came to St Mary's and approached Hill House. Unlike Caxton Hall, the gates of Hill House were not staffed, standing permanently open for anyone who cared to arrive or depart. The car slowed as the tyres crunched up the drive, creeping to a halt outside the front door. Dispensing with formality, Nell opened the door for herself before the car had come to a complete stop. She leapt from the seat and went round to the back. Opening the boot, she took hold of the bicycle, one hand beneath the seat, the other beneath the handlebars. She tensed her muscles and pulled. But the blasted thing wouldn't budge. She heard the driver's door open and close. She tried again to move the bicycle. Painter appeared beside her. He leant into the boot and unhooked the seat from where it had become trapped. He stepped back. Said nothing. Nell pulled and this time the bicycle came free with little effort. She lifted it and placed it on the ground.

'Thank you,' Nell said quietly, still not looking at him.

'I just made a small adjustment. The effort was all yours.'

Nell paused. She felt she ought to say something else. 'Thank you anyway,' she said. 'For helping me and for driving me back.'

As she set off, she felt resistance on the bicycle. She looked down; Painter had placed his hand on the saddle. 'Miss Potter,' he said. 'I know you think you are capable of looking after yourself. And I'm sure in normal circumstances, you are. But for now, would you please be extra vigilant and take extra care.'

He sounded so serious. So solemn. What was going on?

'What is happening here?' she asked. 'Really?'

'I won't offend your intelligence by saying "nothing". You wouldn't believe me in any case.' Painter said. 'But please, be on your guard. And would you report back anything unusual you see directly to me.'

'Is someone in trouble? Is that why you were at Caxton Hall today, to check on thefts there?'

The muscle in Painter's cheek flinched again. 'I've possibly said too much already.'

'Not at all. And of course, I'll help. Anything for Charlotte and her family.'

Painter took his wallet from his breast pocket and removed a small card. He handed it to Nell. 'Telephone me. Any time, day, or night. If you see or suspect anything.'

Nell balanced the bicycle against her hip and placed the card in her bag. 'I will.'

'Thank you. Then I'll say good day.' After replacing his wallet, Inspector Painter clasped the top of his hat and lifted it briefly. He was about to leave when Nell remembered what was in her bag.

'I don't suppose you've had the chance to eat lunch today?' she said. 'It's just that I have a sandwich going begging. Mrs Randal is always too generous.'

Painter smiled. 'Thank you. But I ate lunch at The White Lion.'

He lifted his hat again and Nell watched him walk round to the driver's side. Once inside the car, Painter removed his hat. He took a handkerchief from his pocket and wiped his brow before starting the engine and driving away. Watching the car disappear through the gates, Nell realised that her desire to needle Painter to get a reaction had been replaced by wanting to know the story behind his grey eyes.

SEVENTEEN

Nell wheeled the bicycle to the back of the house and entered through the door into the small luggage room. The chill air from the bare stone walls and floors made her shiver as she balanced the bicycle against the wall beside the bench. She emptied the fruit from her pockets into her bag and looked back at the door to the outside. If there were burglars operating in the area, then Hill House was surely a veritable treasure chest just waiting to be plundered. Turning the key, she gave the door a push to make sure it was locked. Edward really should arrange to have all the doors secured.

Nell made her way through to the hall which, for once, was silent. She paused. She should probably go up to her room and sit at the typewriter. There were two projects demanding her attention now: her book and Inspector Painter's request for her help. From what he had shared with her, it was clear there was more to the presence of this intruder than was being let on. And if she was in any position to help the Mandevilles, she would.

Making her way slowly through the hall, Nell stopped at the fireplace. She looked up at the coat of arms hewn from gleaming stone: two lions holding aloft their globe. The beauty in this hall screamed of the wealth that generations of this family had enjoyed. At least their descendants were hanging on, looking for ways to fund overdue repairs. Not everyone had the grit and determination of the Mandevilles. It had been that war. The rising taxes imposed after peace was declared and the huge cost of keeping these places alive was too much for some to bear. Many a family had been forced to relinquish homes that had been in their families for centuries.

A wave of sadness made Nell close her eyes. Everything good in life had ended with that pointless conflict. Steadying herself, Nell took a moment before opening her eyes. She came face to face with her reflection in the mirror. It wasn't a sight she usually lingered on. Today, she looked a little changed. Her skin was tanned. A handful of freckles danced across her cheeks. But the eyes were the same hollow eyes that always looked out at her.

Sun streamed through the glass dome high in the ceiling and blazed in the mirror. Nell stared past her face into the hall. As she looked, something began to take shape. In a shaft of light behind her, she saw pinpricks of smaller, sharper light. The pinpricks twisted and turned in the light as dust might. But as they moved, they appeared to take on a shape. Gradually, they became flames, tiny flames, topping tiny candles, in the branches of a Christmas tree. It couldn't be. She was seeing things. But as hard as she tried to look away, to clear her vision and her thoughts, something stronger compelled her to keep watching, to look deeper. There was a movement. Behind her, Nell saw the reflection of a young woman. She was dressed in winter clothes. Old fashioned winter clothes, of the kind that might have been worn before the war. Nell wanted to move. But she found all she could do was stare at the scene unfolding around her. The woman looked past Nell, as though she did not see her. Side by side they stood at the mirror, the woman oblivious to Nell's presence. Her cheeks were nipped to a healthy pink as though she had just come in from the outside. She adjusted a silver clip in her hair and smiled, seemingly pleased about something. And then, as quickly as she had appeared, the woman disappeared. The light altered. Nell was once again alone in the hall with the sun streaming through the dome above. She spun around. There was no Christmas tree. No woman.

EIGHTEEN

The silence of the hall was disturbed by a scratching noise outside. Glad of the distraction, Nell rushed through to the vestibule and opened the front door.

Sitting on the ground beneath the portico was Tommy, quite alone except for two small dolls. He looked up at her. 'Hello,' he said, 'have you had a good day, Nell?' He spoke in a matter-of-fact way, as though he had been expecting her.

Nell recognised one of the dolls. It was the doll with short hair and the scar on its cheek. The second doll was dressed in a long tweed skirt with a high-necked blouse. It had what looked like a silver clip holding back its hair. Tommy placed the dolls side by side before rummaging in his pocket and producing a tiny Christmas tree, which he placed on the ground behind the dolls.

'What are those?' Nell said, doing her absolute best to stay calm.

Tommy adjusted the Christmas tree. 'They are dolls,' he said. 'My dolls.'

'But where did you get them?'

'Great Aunt Leo gave them to me for my birthday. I used to

try to play with Bertie's dolls in the dolls' house. But he doesn't like it. So, Aunt Leo gave me my own set.'

'To play with in the dolls' house in the attic?' Nell said.

Tommy shrugged and rearranged the branches of the tree.

'I know it was you,' Nell said, trying to still the shake in her voice.

Tommy paused in his play to look up at her. 'What's me?' he asked.

'Knocking on my door and running away.'

'Oh, that's not me,' he said and returned to his play.

Nell dipped to see his face. There was no trace of guilt. Of course, he would say it was not him who had been playing tricks on her. What fun was there to be had in mischief if the game was given away too soon? No doubt he had more tricks in store for her. Well, if he wanted to play at being evasive and dim, she would jolly well play him at it.

'I would have thought Bertie too old to play with a toy like a doll's house,' Nell said, a little triumphantly. 'That's what babies do. Not young men like Bertie.'

Any sense of one-upmanship evaporated in the look of disdain Tommy gave her. 'The dolls' house is not a toy,' he said. 'They live here.'

'Who lives here?'

Tommy sighed, as though attempting to explain something remarkably simple. He got to his feet. '*They* do,' he said, lifting the two dolls and holding them up to face her. He stared at her so intently that she felt she wanted to look away. Closing her eyes, she shook her head. She was the adult here. She was in charge of this situation, not this little boy. 'Tommy, where is your mother?' she demanded.

He shrugged.

'Why are you out here alone?'

'I'm not alone. *They* keep me company.'

They? Surely, he was not asking her to believe that the dolls were able to keep him company. A shiver raced down her back as she remembered Painter's warning and an altogether more sensible thought took shape. What if it was not imaginary friends that Tommy had been playing with? 'Have you seen someone, Tommy? Have you seen someone you don't know? A stranger?'

Tommy sighed. 'I know what a stranger is, Nell. You don't need to explain everything to me.'

He knelt on the ground again. Taking up the dolls, he positioned them as though they were talking. He leant in closer and began to whisper to them so that Nell couldn't hear what he said.

All Nell could do was look on. Was the child in some way unwell? A friend from her War Office days had gone on to study nursing and to work in a mental asylum in Hanwell. They met for tea every few months and Nell always listened in horror as her friend recounted the stories of the behaviour and suffering of the patients. She looked at Tommy's sweet little face as he chatted to the dolls, at his adorable red curls and the freckles across his nose. It wasn't uncommon for children to have imaginary friends, was it? Or to imbue inanimate objects and toys with human qualities, characteristics, and traits. Perhaps it was her who was delusional, not Tommy. She was the one who had seen a fantastical reflection in a mirror, which had seemed as real and as solid as the stone pillar beside which she now stood.

'They are real, you know, Nell.'

An icy blast chilled Nell's blood. Tommy's voice had altered. He spoke in the strange voice she had heard him use before. The faraway voice. How did he perform this trick of seeming to read her mind? He looked at her, his pupils enlarged.

'Or at least one is real now,' he said. 'And one was then.'

'I don't understand what you're saying, Tommy.'

He smiled. 'Yes, Nell. You do. And you will learn more in time. Time is all you need to be able to see. But remember, we don't always see with our eyes. Sometimes we have to trust in others to help us.'

'What if I don't need help?' she said.

Tommy smiled again. 'You do.' He laid his dolls down on the ground. Getting to his feet, he stood before Nell. He took her hands in his and looked up into her face. 'The pain you have suffered; I can feel it.' He closed his eyes. A tear crept down his cheek. 'One in, one out. It's the way it has always been. And you have seen one. Oh yes, you have seen one of our visitors. She will help if you let her. Listen to what she has to say. Please.'

Opening his eyes, Tommy put Nell's hands to his lips and kissed each one. She couldn't speak. What was happening here?

Tommy continued to look at her, his smile so gentle.

The sound of feet running on gravel made Nell snap back to her senses. Her hands slipped from Tommy's grasp. She turned to see a figure sprinting towards them. Nell was about to grab Tommy's hands again to drag him inside and away from any threat when she realised who the figure was.

Bertie came to a stop beneath the portico. His damp hair stuck to the sweat shining on his forehead. He wore white shorts and a white exercise vest, his long limbs boyishly slender. He placed his hands on his thighs and bent from his waist, catching his breath. 'Hello,' he said finally.

'Hello,' Nell said. She had to behave normally. She had to regain control of herself. 'Been for a run?'

Bertie nodded and gulped down another lungful of air.

'I don't suppose you know why Tommy is out here by himself?' Nell asked.

Bertie nodded, sweeping his fringe away from his face. 'He ran away from Mary. She's looking after the children as everyone's gone to call on the family at Huntingdean.'

'Mary let him escape? She should take greater care.'

'She said she'd taken the children out to pick flowers for their mother in the meadow. She turned her back for a second and Tommy was gone. I came across her looking for him. She's in ever such a state.'

'It's just that he's so small,' Nell said, knowing that Mary would never do anything to harm the children. She felt something squeeze her hand. She looked down.

'I'm sorry,' Tommy said, back to his normal self again. 'I wouldn't want to get Mary into trouble.'

'Then promise never to run away from her again,' Nell said.

'I promise,' he said and smiled up at her.

After arranging for Bertie to take Tommy to his grandmother who was cooking in the kitchen, Nell agreed that it would be a good idea for Bertie to run to find Mary to put her mind at rest. She avoided looking in the mirror as she ran up the stairs and the boys headed through the door at the back of the hall.

NINETEEN

Dropping her bag to the floor, Nell collapsed onto the bed. She stared up at the ceiling, the events of the day spinning around in her head. She waited for everything to fall back into some sense of order. It didn't. The events whipped around and around. Painter's warning. The mirage in the mirror. Tommy's strange behaviour. She searched her mind for other strange occurrences since arriving at Hill House and remembered the previous two nights when she had been woken by what felt like someone touching her.

None of this was normal. It wasn't normal for a police inspector to confide in a civilian and ask for help. It wasn't normal to see things in the mirror as though a long-forgotten Hill House Christmas was coming back to life. It wasn't normal for a small child to speak as though he could read her mind. It wasn't normal to be woken in the middle of the night, feeling the touch of another when you were quite alone.

It felt as though the moment she had stepped foot across the threshold of Hill House, a key had turned inside her, as if someone was trying to gain entrance to the room she kept firmly padlocked and bolted. She ran her finger along a ridge in the quilted bedspread, feeling its shape and the twists of thread. But try as hard as she might, she could not divert her thoughts. They fought her and dragged her to a place she feared more than any other. They took her to that little boy playing innocently with his dolls beneath the portico. When she had felt that Tommy might be in danger, a sensation had risen inside her that threatened to knock her off balance. The sensation of a connection to a child. Of concern. Of wanting to take care of him. Even now, she could feel it. And the sensation came with a memory on a dark wave. It lapped at her, wanting to catch her and drag her down. She sat up abruptly. Not today. She could not let that wave take her and drown her in the blackness. If she let that happen, she would be capable of nothing except curling into a ball behind a closed door for days.

Jumping from the bed, Nell sat at the desk. She ignored the typewriter that held a page of ramblings for her fledgling novel. The deadline and her promise to Robert loomed large, but she pushed them away, too. She hadn't imagined all that had happened to her since her arrival at Hill House. The experiences were real. They were tangible. Which meant a solution for why they were happening must be somewhere to be found. And the tool for how she dealt with everything sat beside her on the desk.

She pulled her notebook from her bag and began to write. Beginning with the moment she had arrived at Hill House, she recounted in as much detail as she could everything that had occurred since. What she needed now was to get this out of her head and into a form she could study and understand until there was some sense to be found. She would return to her work of fiction later.

TWENTY

'So,' Charlotte said as she sat on a chair in the back garden following dinner. 'It's decided. We're all going to the seaside tomorrow!'

Nell took a sip of her whisky and nodded. After much cajoling, she had agreed to join the Mandevilles and Wilco on an impromptu trip to their favourite seaside town in Norfolk. Paul had been unable to come for dinner but had been contacted by telephone and had agreed to join the charabanc to the coast. Even Mrs Randal, Mary, Bertie, Audrey, Rosemary and the little Mandevilles were to go. It had all been decided: Hill House was to be shut up for the day. Nell had tried to resist, using the excuse of her deadline, but the Mandevilles had pooled their persuasive powers. Edward had been particularly persistent, no doubt wanting more help in buttering up Wilco.

Charlotte began to reel off the things they would need to take, losing Nell somewhere between buckets and spades for the children and the extra wicker hamper, even if the flask had been smashed on their last trip. Nell nodded along but wasn't listening. Having spent the afternoon writing up her experiences, she was more convinced than ever that there were logical explanations for every one of her strange experiences. Each one could be explained by her being tired, having a highly active imagination or falling victim to a series of tricks played by a clever little boy.

Nell took another sip of whisky. She held the golden liquid in her mouth for a moment and when she swallowed, it warmed her throat, just as the evening air warmed the bare skin of her arms. The glow of light from inside the house lit the lawn and, on the horizon, the final pink flush of day smudged the outline of the hills. A day at the seaside might be just the ticket to clear her head so she could focus once again on her novel.

'I'm looking forward to it already,' Nell said. She looked past Charlotte to the billiard room door. 'Where have Alice and Wilco disappeared to? I thought they were going to join us for a drink.'

'Alice is checking on the children. She wanted to see how Mary is getting on with preparing everything they need for tomorrow. I give you one guess where Wilco is.'

Nell smiled. 'He wouldn't be making telephone calls in your father's office, would he?'

Charlotte let out an exaggerated sigh. 'Honestly, I have no idea who he has to talk to so often.'

'His father,' Edward said, stepping through the door and into the garden. 'They have lots of business to attend to.' Edward surveyed the contents of his makeshift cocktail bar, created on a trolley brought out into the garden. 'I say, these are rather exotic, Nell. I hardly know what to do with them.' He picked up the fruits Nell had collected from Caxton Hall and studied them. Holding up a green fruit, he shrugged his shoulders.

'It's a guava,' Charlotte said. 'Don't you remember the wonderful ice creams Monsieur Gotti used to make for Mother's parties? He favoured the shape of guavas for some reason.' Charlotte turned to Nell. 'Monsieur Gotti was Mother's Swiss chef before the war. He was quite a gruff man but made the most delightful dishes. Mother was heartbroken when he left us to take up a position in a London hotel. I don't think he was best pleased when he was called on to give up conjuring fine cuisine to prepare invalid food for the convalescing soldiers! Mrs Randal was far more suited to making hearty meals for the men. Aunt Leo said that it was Mrs Randal's food that cured many a wounded soldier. It made them feel at home and loved.'

'How is your aunt?' Nell asked.

'Very well. Just as energetic as ever! She is sorry to have missed you. She telephoned today and asked after you.'

Edward held up another fruit. 'Charlotte?'

She peered at it. 'Passion fruit,' she said. 'Cut it open and scoop out the insides. It's quite delicious.'

'As the name suggests!' Wilco called as he stepped out through the billiard room doors. 'Passion is always delicious. What do you say to that, Nell?'

Nell had grown quite used to Wilco's quips and taunting, and the need to keep him onside and play along for the sake of Hill House's roof and gutters. 'It's what life was made for,' she said.

Wilco laughed. 'Quite right, my dear. Quite right.'

He took a seat beside Charlotte and asked about the plans for the next day. He might have business to attend to and it would be useful to have access to a telephone from time to time. As Edward prepared the fruit, smashing it to a pulp in his mixing jug, he explained that there were a number of hotels on the seafront in Hunstanton that would be sure to let Wilco have use of their telephones.

Edward added his pulpy mixture to four glasses and poured in an array of spirits. Handing them around, he took Nell's empty whisky glass from her before sitting beside her.

'Down the hatch,' he said chinking his glass to hers. He took a sip and coughed. 'Blimey, that's a bit lively,' he said. 'Anyone want a splash of soda?'

'Good God no, old man,' Wilco said. 'We could all do with a few more hairs on our chests, I daresay.' He knocked back his drink in one and handed his glass to Edward. 'Capital! Any chance of a top up?'

'Of course. Glad you like it,' Edward said. He took Wilco's glass and went to his trolley. Nell placed her untouched drink on the grass and followed him. She had been waiting all evening for the opportunity to get him alone. She made a show of helping him prepare the fruit.

'Any news from the police on their investigation into the intruder?' she said.

Edward glanced towards Charlotte and Wilco. Charlotte was busy telling Wilco all about Hunstanton.

'Not really,' he said softly. 'Inspector Painter telephoned today to tell me there was nothing much to report. He's keeping an eye on all the houses in the area.'

'I know, I bumped into him at Caxton Hall today.' Nell cut one of the passion fruits in half and scooped the insides into the jug. It was quite odd, the flesh inside being orange and in complete contrast to the outer shell of purple.

'Did he say anything to you?' Edward asked.

'Such as?'

'I don't know, really. Just whether there have been any further thefts and whether they are closer to capturing the culprit.'

'No. Nothing like that.'

Nell was waiting for Edward to give some clue that he too had been warned by Painter about the increased threat. 'Do you have any clue who is responsible?'

'No,' Edward said, pouring some clear alcoholic beverage into his cocktail mix. 'But they are going after properties like ours. That's all I know. Listen,' he glanced at the others. 'You will continue to keep this under your hat, won't you? I don't want to go upsetting Alice and Charlotte and scaring Wilco off. And I really think we won't be bothered. Not now you scared the probable culprit off. No doubt he was watching the house looking for his opportunity. I'm sure he's moved on. I just wish you hadn't had to become involved. You are supposed to be writing your next bestseller, not being attacked by men in the woods. I'm sorry.'

'Don't be. I enjoy the excitement.'

Nell nudged Edward and he smiled. After helping hand around more drinks, Nell took her seat again.

So, Painter really hadn't said anything to Edward about an increased threat. She would have known if Edward was keeping something from her. He was as open and as incapable of perpetuating a falsehood as his sister. Painter must have had his reasons for keeping it from Edward while telling her. It was up to her then, to be on her guard. And to look out for any threat to the Mandevilles. Even more of a reason to accompany them on their trip to the seaside.

Nell drank some of the second cocktail but managed to pour most of it unnoticed onto the lawn. When a polite opportunity presented itself, she gave her thanks for another splendid evening, made her excuses, and headed to her room.

TWENTY-ONE

Nell was sitting at her desk, looking out of the window. It was after nine o'clock, but a line of pink light still clung to the horizon. She took up her notebook and picked up where she had left off. Beginning with leaving her room for dinner, she recorded every detail she could recall of the evening. The conversations, the delicious roast chicken and divine summer pudding. When people had entered a room and when they had left and roughly how long they had been away.

Satisfied that she had as much on paper as she could remember, Nell closed the notebook and lay her pen on top. Her work of the afternoon may not be the makings of a novel but getting the events out of her head and onto paper had made sense of it all. As she wrote, it became clear that she had let her imagination get the better of her. It was an occupational hazard for a writer. There was a perfectly rational explanation for everything she had experienced.

Nell picked up her pen and tapped it against her cheek. The only thing still to unpick was Painter. Naturally, he couldn't be at Hill House twenty-four hours a day. It made sense that if he would ask anyone to keep their eyes and ears open for him, it would be someone close enough to the family to observe them but at enough of a distance to retain some level of objectivity. It was also quite likely that he had recognised her inquisitive nature, making her a perfect candidate to report back on the comings and goings at Hill House. But it wasn't his request for help that had occupied her mind over dinner and during drinks on the terrace. It was him.

Nell put her pen down on the desk and placed her hand on the notebook. She pictured Painter's face. Of all the nuts she had ever attempted to crack, he had by far the toughest shell. He remained a conundrum. Perhaps, in Painter's case, she would need to take up a sledgehammer rather than a nutcracker. After all, he might prove useful for inspiration for a character in her book. The theft of Prince Carlos' medals would certainly call for the expertise of an experienced police inspector.

Nell glanced at the neglected pile of papers beside the typewriter as a schoolgirl might look at her unfinished Latin revision on a Sunday evening. Tomorrow. She would return to her work tomorrow.

Pushing the notebook into her bag, Nell removed the card Painter had handed to her. One side was blank. She turned it over. Printed on the other side were his details. His rank. His official telephone number and his name: Inspector James Painter. James. She pictured him and tried the name beside him. A single syllable. Traditional. Unfussy. James. It suited him. And beneath his name was a telephone number written in pencil, with the word 'Home' written above. She read the numbers then tucked the card safely back inside her bag.

As she pushed the bag beneath the desk, Nell became aware of the smell of cigarette smoke coming in through the open window. She got up from the chair and leant out. In the waning light, she recognised Mr Townley walking along the path, away from the house and in the direction of the lake. Nell glanced at her wristwatch. She was wide awake. If she were in London, it would be hours before she stumbled through the door of her flat and fell into bed.

Nell made her way through the vestibule and out through the front door. Joining the path, she headed away from the house, surrounded by the heady, warm evening scent of jasmine. Just as she came level with the stable yard, Mr Townley walked through the gates.

'Mr Townley,' she said.

He turned to her and smiled. 'Good evening, Miss Potter. Out for a constitutional?'

'It was too nice an evening to stay inside,' Nell said. 'But it's late to be working.'

He shrugged. 'I'm busy with a special restoration project. Sometimes you have to strike while the iron is hot. Besides, it's never a chore to spend time here.'

Nell looked back to the house. The Portland stone walls gleamed in the evening sunlight turning to moonlight. 'I've only been here a few days, but I've been made so welcome.'

'Hill House has that effect on visitors,' Mr Townley said. 'I was on my way to the kitchen garden. You're welcome to join me for the stroll.'

'Thank you. I'd like that.'

Nell fell into step beside him. She glanced up at him and smiled. He felt more familiar to her now since he was the unwitting inspiration for the athlete in her book and she found herself summoning his face frequently each day.

'How were the cocktails last night?' Mr Townley asked.

'Strong!' Nell laughed. 'As were the cocktails this evening.'

Mr Townley laughed. 'Glad to hear some things don't change.'

'I tipped half of the last one away in the grass,' Nell said.

'Probably for the best,' Mr Townley smiled. 'Otherwise, you'd be good for nothing in the morning.' He turned into the kitchen garden and Nell followed him.

'Are you working in here?' Nell asked, looking along the rows of vegetables.

'I'm helping out all over the house,' he said.

'Elliot's keeping you busy then?'

'Always! He's a hard taskmaster.' Mr Townley stopped before a white painted bench and pointed to it. Nell sat at one end, and he sat at the other.

'Do you mind if I ask you a question?' Nell said.

'Not at all,' Mr Townley said. 'Ask away.'

'Have you known Hill House long? You seem very fond of it. That's to say, have you always lived around here?'

'In the main,' he said, crossing his legs and resting back against the seat. 'Except when I've travelled abroad.'

'You've worked abroad?'

'You sound surprised!'

'Sorry. That must have sounded incredibly rude. I didn't mean it to.'

'No offence taken. And to answer your question, I've known Hill House all my life.'

'And what did you do overseas?'

'I was in the military.'

Nell felt her spine shrink as she leant forward ever so slightly. For a moment she had pictured Mr Townley as some dashing diplomat in the Colonial Office, adventuring to far-flung shores. In reality, his story was the story of all able-bodied young men, plucked from every community across the nation and packed off on a ship across the Channel. Mr Townley had no doubt marched off with the other men of the village just beyond the walls of Hill House. Many of his number would never again see the pub and the duckpond on the village green, or look longingly at a young woman further along the pew in St

Mary's who made his heart skip a beat whenever he so much as sensed her close by.

'Of course,' Nell said. 'Sorry.'

'For what?'

'The war...'

'You don't need to be. I did my duty and was proud to do it.'

'Of course, sorry. I didn't mean... It's just...' Nell hooked one of her legs around the wooden leg of the bench. She looked along the canes lined up in rows in the beds, tendrils of plants climbing through the netting.

The silence was disturbed by the hoot of an owl in the woods by the lake. Nell could sense Mr Townley looking at her. 'Listen,' he said. 'Let's not part on bad terms. I'm sorry if I've said anything to upset you. And before you try to let me off the hook, don't! I am quite skilled at putting my foot in my mouth. It's difficult not to when you have plates of meat as large as mine!'

Nell couldn't help but smile. 'Cockney rhyming slang,' she said. 'We're a little far from the sound of Bow bells here, aren't we?'

'I learned everything I know from a good friend from Whitechapel. The things he taught me would make you blush!' He gave Nell one of his smiles and this time raised his eyebrows.

His smile was one that most women would go weak for. They would find Mr Townley's traditional good looks appealing, with his broad shoulders, straight teeth, ruddy complexion, and thick, dark, auburn-tinged hair. He possessed all the qualities she wrote into her leading men. But she preferred her men more unorthodox. More unusual.

'What have I said now?' Mr Townley said.

'Pardon?'

'I can tell when I have upset a woman.'

'I'm not upset... I was just... thinking.'

'Would you mind if I give you one piece of advice to think about? It's advice that someone once gave me?' he said.

Nell nodded.

'You can only live the life you have,' Mr Townley said. 'Even when it's not the life you expected.'

Nell turned the words over in her mind. He was right. But saying the right thing and knowing it was right were never the same as being able to live by sensible words.

'Was it your friend from Whitechapel who shared that pearl of wisdom?' she asked.

'Good God, no,' Mr Townley laughed, his head thrown back. 'He was many things, but a philosopher wasn't one of them. He could swing a mean left hook and save me from getting my teeth knocked out in an East End brawl for teaching me insults masquerading as compliments. But nuanced subtlety and social niceties weren't his strong points.'

Nell couldn't help but laugh again. 'Thank you,' she said. 'For making me feel better.'

'Ah,' Mr Townley said. 'It's my life's work. I was the oldest son, so it was my role to be the good big brother to my younger siblings. Well, as good as I could be. Right,' he slapped his hands on his thighs. 'I shouldn't keep you. You need to be fresh for your trip to the seaside tomorrow.'

'How do you know about that?'

'Elliot. He's to drive you all to the station in the morning.'

Mr Townley rose, and Nell walked beside him out of the garden and along the path. He had such presence. She hadn't been able to put her finger on it before, but walking beside him now, she could feel it. It was the sense of someone who cared as much as they liked to joke.

At the stable yard, Mr Townley stopped. 'I'll take my leave here,' he said. 'I've to speak to Elliot about something. I'll watch you the rest of the way until you're at the front door.'

'There's really no need.'

His eyebrows rose. 'I'll make sure you get there safely anyway.'

Nell passed through the hall. The ceilings here were high and the rooms large, but there was an intimacy about Hill House. She felt safe here, somehow. Settled.

She looked in the mirror above the mantlepiece. Freckles still danced across her nose and her skin glowed, kissed as it had been by the sun. She smiled at the thought of Mr Townley. Had she been a normal woman, she might have been tempted to see where an attraction to him could take her. But it would end in the way of all her disastrous flirtations in recent years. Her barbs would repel him. As they repelled every man unfortunate enough to stumble into her path.

TWENTY-TWO

27TH JULY 1924

'Hurry up! We're going to miss the train!' Charlotte shouted.

Three cars – the Rolls Royce belonging to the Mandevilles and two borrowed from Caxton Hall – disgorged their passengers at the doors of Stevenage Railway station. It had seemed the sensible thing to travel by car to a station from where they could take the train to Kings Lynn and on to Hunstanton. But they were now facing the very real prospect of having to spend a good part of the day on the platform. The children's toileting needs having necessitated an unscheduled stop at a roadside tearoom, Charlotte had decided they couldn't possibly leave without buying something.

Elliot and the two Caxton Hall chauffeurs hurried to open the doors to free the occupants and wrestled from the boot many picnic hampers, blankets, and all manner of paraphernalia deemed essential for the children to spend a day away from home. Edward, Paul, and Wilco helped Elliot and the other men, while Bertie was sent to run at breakneck speed into the ticket hall, shouting for the station master and guard to hold the train, under instruction from Wilco to tell them that he would make it worth their while.

The brakes of the approaching train sighed as it pulled into the station and Nell helped Charlotte, Alice, Mary and Mrs Randal chivvy the children along, running as fast as their little legs would carry them, the baby squealing with delight as he was bounced about in his perambulator. Audrey and Rosemary were despatched to buy the tickets, brandishing handfuls of money.

Finally, everyone was on the platform. Wilco had telephoned ahead to secure three compartments for their exclusive use. As they climbed aboard, Edward, Paul and Bertie struggling to manhandle the baby's perambulator up and through the door, Nell saw Wilco hand some coins to the station master. They had just closed the doors to the compartment when the guard blew his whistle and the train heaved into motion.

There was much laughter and puffing and congratulating each other. Although they were all dressed in the loosest of dresses, shirts and slacks, the sudden heat was stifling, as though they were all sitting directly on top of the fire from the engine. Realising that they were squeezed into one compartment, it was decided that the women should all travel with the children while the men would occupy another compartment, so that they could read their newspapers in peace. The compartment separating them could be used by anyone who wanted to escape their travelling companions. When Bertie looked unsure of which compartment he was expected to travel in, Edward put his arm around the boy's shoulders. 'You'll travel with the men, of course,' he said.

Bertie blushed and scooped his fringe away from his face.

The men left with a flask of Mrs Randal's tea and a basin containing some sweet buns. Alice and Charlotte settled the children as well as they could. It was not easy when Audrey and Rosemary were so full of the thrill of seeing the sea for the very first time that they heaped coal onto the Mandeville children's excitement.

'We've never been outside of Northampton. Not in our whole lives,' Audrey said. Rosemary nodded her agreement while she tucked into one of Mrs Randal's sweet buns.

Nell watched Alice smile at the girls. That was precisely why Alice had brought them along: because they hadn't had or seen much of anything in life. They were even wearing pretty dresses that Charlotte had ordered for them from a department store in Northampton; Audrey's decorated in a pattern of small blue roses and Rosemary's in daisies. Both had long red ribbons tied at the back, which matched the red ribbons decorating the sisters' hair. When Mrs Randal moved as though to bring Audrey and Rosemary back into line, Alice touched her arm gently and shook her head.

The children watched the world rushing past the window with the baby's perambulator positioned so he too could see out of the window, chatting about what they would see at the seaside: the sand, the pier, the ices. Tommy filled them in on the details of what to expect in Hunstanton and Audrey and Rosemary sat enthralled.

The women – except Nell – took seats, and Mrs Randal and Mary began rifling through the hampers, producing flasks and more basins of buns. With four grown women seated, two older girls, two small children and a baby in the perambulator, there was hardly room to raise an arm to sip a cup of tea.

'If you don't mind,' Nell said, 'I think I'll go and sit in the free carriage.'

'Of course,' Alice said. 'You'll probably want to get on with your writing. You did bring your notebook, didn't you?'

Nell patted her bag. She refused a cup of tea, opened the door, and closed it behind her. She slipped into the empty compartment, slid down the window, and fell into the seat closest to the window so that the wind was in her face. Along with the sound of the train rushing through the countryside, it was possible to hear the murmur of the men talking in their carriage and the noises of the women and children in theirs, but none of the sounds was loud enough to be a distraction.

Nell took the notebook and pen from her bag. Twisting the cap from the pen, she opened the book, smoothed down a page and began to write, while the wind blowing in through the window kept her hair back from her face. She wrote about their journey and the Caxton employees who had delivered them to Stevenage and would be there to ferry them back when they arrived home at the end of the day. An extra car and driver would be sent from Caxton Hall as Elliot had a prior engagement that night. She recorded details of the journey they had taken, such as she could recall. She wrote about the employees of the station and even of the tearoom where they had stopped.

With everything recorded, Nell replaced the cap and slipped the pen and notebook into her bag. She settled back into the warmth of the cushioned seat. Mercifully, she had not been visited in the night by any odd occurrences. Of course she hadn't. Because nothing untoward had happened at all during her stay at Hill House. Aside from the appearance of the man in the wood. But he had been real; Elliot had seen him, too. The fact that she had passed the night unmolested just went to prove that everything else had been a figment of her imagination.

Nell closed her eyes. The smell of smuts from the engine blew in through the window, carried on the warm air. It was pleasant, as a roaring fire would be in a cold room on a winter's day. She let her thoughts drift to her fledgling novel, picturing an Olympic stadium such as she had seen in the newspapers, packed with cheering spectators. Prince Carlos was there, running on the spot, warming his muscles to compete in the race to represent his country and prove a point to his father, the king. She tried to picture the femme fatale. Nell wanted to see a woman with jet black hair cut severely at her angular chin, who was ravishing, intriguing and powerful. Instead, she saw a normal looking young woman with mousey, rather ordinary hair. She tried to picture the clothes a female athlete might wear, long shorts and some short-sleeved blouse. Instead, the woman insisted on appearing dressed in a high-necked blouse with a long serge skirt. It didn't suit her. She looked like the type of woman who should be free of such constraints.

Again, Nell tried to summon up the image of the female athlete. But again, she was presented with the other woman.

This time, she was not in a stadium but in a stable yard. Thick snow lay all about. Attempts had been made to clear it, but the falling snow covered the cleared cobbles. Nell became aware of movement inside the stable building. She stepped towards the window and, using her sleeve, she wiped ice from the glass. Inside, a woman was talking to a man. He was in a stall with an incredibly large horse; black, sleek, beautiful and powerful. The man had his back to the woman, but Nell could see from the line of his shoulders that he was not happy. The woman said something, but Nell could not hear the words. It was as though she was underwater, able only to observe rather than hear or interact. The man spun around, a bag of hay in his hand. He was devastatingly handsome but, from his expression, Nell could tell that he was fiercely angry. At the same time, he was also sad. When the woman wasn't looking at him, the man looked at her with such love in his eyes that Nell felt her breath catch in her chest. She didn't know how, but she knew that this was a good man. An honourable man. She looked from the woman to the man. They were in love. Deeply. Only neither was able to say this. Nell wanted to rush to them, to tell them that they should be together. The man stepped closer to the woman. Suddenly Nell realised she knew the woman. It was the woman from the mirror in the hall at Hill House. With the Christmas tree. And she knew the man. It was Mr Townley and...

'Do you mind if I join you?'

Nell snapped awake. 'What? Oh, of course. Please.'

'Did I wake you?' Mary asked as she took the seat opposite Nell.

'I was having a catnap,' Nell said. She must have been asleep, there could be no other explanation for the dream.

'It was a bit noisy in the carriage with the children,' Mary said. 'Mrs Mandeville said that I should come and sit in here with you. I've some books to read before I go back to college. Mr Hope, the schoolmaster, said I should read this so that I might be able to talk to the children about it when I go to practice some lessons on the class next term.' She turned the cover of the book to Nell.

'*Oliver Twist*,' Nell said, remembering the many Sundays she had spent in the nook of the dining room in Cheam with her father's leather-bound copy open in her lap. 'It's a wonderful story.'

'I haven't started it yet,' Mary said.

'Then you are in for a treat.'

'What's it about?'

'The downtrodden in society,' Nell said, glad for the distraction from the dream. It had left her with an odd sensation, knowing it to be a fiction but at the same time feeling it to be real. Very, very real.

'Oh.' Mary looked uncertainly at the cover.

'Don't be put off,' Nell said. 'You won't be disappointed. And I'm sure the children at your school will enjoy it. The characters come to life on the page. Did you know that Dickens' father was in a debtors' prison and Charles Dickens had to go out and work at a very young age?'

'I didn't,' Mary said, sitting forward.

'As an older man, when he was writing his books, Dickens would walk the streets of London all night in order to understand the people he wrote about. To see how they lived. He really wanted to inhabit the lives of those people so that he could be truthful in how he wrote about them. I think writing from experience gives a level of authenticity. It gives truth to your voice.' Nell looked at Mary and realised the young woman was hanging on her every word.

'Is that how you write your stories?' Mary asked. 'From your life?'

Nell pictured the many fey and fatuous creatures and characters existing only between the covers of her novels. Had she written the truth, from her own life, nobody would want to read it. Readers wanted excitement, and redemption or, at the very least, a promise of hope.

'Are you all right?' Mary asked. 'You were miles away there for a moment.'

'Sorry.' Nell quickly painted on her smile.

'I should like to read books about real women,' Mary said. 'Women like me, rather than people I don't know. Does that make sense? Don't get me wrong, I like to read thrilling books and the kind of books that show glamorous people in marvellous settings, like yours. But sometimes I feel like I want to read about people like me. That feel like me.'

'Perhaps you should write,' Nell said.

Mary laughed. 'I have no talent for that!'

'A bright and able young woman like you can do anything she puts her mind to.'

Mary smiled. 'You know, I could listen to you speak for hours. You have such a way with words. You make me feel like I could do anything.'

'That's because you can.'

Mary smiled again. 'You remind me of someone. A lady that stayed at Hill House before the war. She was so lovely. Everybody liked her. She said things such as you do. She made us all believe ourselves capable of whatever we wanted to do. And she wasn't afraid to stand up to the men in the house and stick up for the staff.'

'She sounds marvellous. Who was she?'

'A friend of Mrs Hart's. She was from India. The staff who were serving at dinner said that there was much talk of her being one of those suffragettes, just like Miss Charlotte and Mrs Hart.'

'Even better!' Nell said. 'I should like to have met this fellow campaigner.'

'You would have become great friends, I'm sure.' Mary said. 'Just like she and Miss Charlotte.'

'What was her name?'

'Miss Arnold. She was just about the kindest person I ever met. She was so good to me and my family. She was only at Hill House a week, but it felt like she had been a part of it forever.'

Nell wracked her brain but couldn't remember meeting a Miss Arnold. And then she recalled the conversation with Charlotte the evening of her arrival. 'I think Charlotte mentioned this good friend. What happened to her?'

'She left suddenly. She had to go back to her family. But – and I hope this isn't speaking out of turn – it was a comfort to everyone that she was able to make Captain Mandeville happy. He was sweet on her. Everyone downstairs knew it. When you do for people you get to know a great deal about them. I'm sure the family must have known how sweet they were on each other, too.'

A sadness swept over Nell. 'Captain Mandeville? Miss Charlotte's brother?'

Mary nodded.

Nell wanted to stick her fingers in her ears, guessing what was to come next.

'He died in the war, but you probably know that,' Mary said. 'He was in the army for years and never got a scratch. Then two weeks in France and he was gone. I've never seen a family so sad and for so long. They keep his room just as it was on the day that he left.'

Unseen hands twisted Nell's heart.

'It was a terrible time for everyone,' Mary said. 'Anyway, I should get on with reading this. And I shouldn't take up anymore of your time. You need to get back to your writing.'

'Yes,' Nell smiled, although she knew it to be a hollow smile. 'I suppose I should.'

Mary settled back and opened the book. She was soon engrossed. Nell tried to imagine the world of Oliver and Fagin and the Artful Dodger, but her disloyal imagination forsook her. It kept taking her back to the image in her head. Of those lovers torn asunder by that bloody war. She wanted to ask Mary what had happened to Miss Arnold since but couldn't find the words.

Nell took the notebook and pen from her bag. She opened the book in her lap but couldn't bring herself to write a single word. She glanced at Mary, who was so deep in the goings-on in the darkest parts of London that she didn't notice what Nell was or wasn't doing. Nell read through the notes she had made. Every so often her eyes closed. Each time, she was presented with the vivid dream that had ended the moment Mary entered the compartment. It had felt so real, so raw. Mr Townley's role in the dream was easily explainable since she had enjoyed his company only last night and he lived in her imagination as Prince Carlos. But who was the woman who kept appearing in her dreams?

Nell let her pen fall to her notebook. Perhaps she should give in and consult a doctor about these hallucinations and the strange occurrences her brain seemed intent on summoning up.

TWENTY-THREE

When the train pulled into Kings Lynn, Tommy and Daphne appeared at the compartment door. With some help from Nell, they were able to slide the door across. They said they had been sent by their mother to fetch Nell and Mary as it would soon be time to change trains.

Tommy ran back to his mother's carriage as soon as the message was delivered. Daphne loitered while Nell pulled her bag onto her shoulder and Mary collected up her book. As Nell was about to follow Mary from the compartment, she felt something brush her fingers. Looking down, she saw that Daphne had taken hold of her hand. The little girl blinked up at her and smiled. Nell gripped Daphne's hand and a tear sprang to her eye. 'Oh, dear me,' she said, wiping her eye with the side of free her hand. 'A smut must have blown in through the window and into my eye. It's a pickle when that happens, isn't it, Daphne?'

Daphne nodded, making her red waves bounce adorably. She smiled at Nell again before guiding her out of the compartment.

There was much activity in the corridor as the men made their way into the women's compartment. Soon they were all

clambering down onto the platform, transferring the paraphernalia to the next train, which would take them to the seaside.

The last leg of the journey was short and the train was
crowded. The Mandeville party squeezed into a carriage.
Neither they nor any of the other passengers seemed to mind
the crush. Everyone was too excited by the prospect of a day on
the coast. The anticipation grew as they travelled through the
Norfolk countryside, stopping at a few small stations. When
they passed through the pretty station at Wolferton, Paul
explained that it was the station used by the king and queen
when they holidayed at Sandringham. The small Mandevilles
were more interested in the buttery biscuit Mrs Randal broke in
half and handed to them, but Audrey and Rosemary pressed
their noses to the glass as though trying to soak in every detail.
Nell noticed many of the passengers looking at Paul. Some
stared, some looked then looked away, others appeared visibly
shaken or horrified. If Paul noticed the interest in his face, he
didn't react.

Soon, the train pulled into Hunstanton, and the Mandeville
party was swept along on a wave of people in the tremendous
rush to alight. All the adults carried something or held the hand
of a child. Nell tucked a blanket under her arm and followed
the others along the platform and to the doors of the station,
which gave immediately onto a green with an impressive hotel
and array of guesthouses, public houses and tea shops. Opposite
the green was the pier and then the sea, the peaks of the waves
glittering in the morning sunshine.

It was a little after eleven, but the promenade already
bustled with day visitors and holidaymakers. Nell breathed in
deeply. The tang of the sea. She would never tire of that smell.
Some of her happiest childhood memories involved the family's
seaside holidays to Dorset.

It was decided that they should go directly to the beach to
find a good spot to set up camp. The happy band made their

way across the promenade and laughed as they stumbled comically through the sand before settling on a position close to the pier and its amenities. Blankets were spread out, half a dozen deckchairs hired from a man further along the beach, and a cricket set wrestled from a bag. Since it was early, the beach was reasonably quiet, and a cricket pitch was established far enough from anyone for it not to be a bother.

Alice and Mrs Randal settled into their blue and white striped chairs, with the baby on the blanket filling a bucket with fistfuls of sand. Nell sat on another of the blankets. She kicked off her shoes and flicked the warm sand with her toes. Taking out her notepad, she added a few notes. Just a short distance away, the game of cricket was about to start.

Teams were established, captained by Edward and Wilco. Jackets, ties and even shoes and socks were removed. And so began a lively and determined game. Bertie proved himself to be an excellent bowler, and had the most successful run rate. Not to be outdone by the men, Charlotte proved that her overarm was something to be applauded and both Audrey and Rosemary ran with such determination that their faces glowed, and they had to constantly readjust the ribbons in their hair. Mary earned the nickname 'steady hands' for her ability to catch a ball mid-flight. For a time, the two small Mandevilles acted as spectators. When they tired of watching the grown-ups' game, they returned to the blanket to help their little brother construct a sandcastle.

Slipping her notebook back inside her bag, Nell joined Alice and Mrs Randal to sit in a deckchair. The sun had moved higher in the sky. She closed her eyes, feeling the warmth on her eyelids. She breathed in deeply. The waves shushed at the shore. The lure of the sea was great. She had packed Charlotte's bathing costume in her bag and had spotted what looked like bathing huts further along the beach in which she could change. There was the sound of thwack on willow and somebody shouted about being out of bounds. A chorus of voices either supported or objected to the call.

'How are you today, Nell?'

Nell opened her eyes, shielding them from the sun now overhead. 'I am very well, thank you Tommy. Are you enjoying your day?'

He nodded and held out his hand. 'I would like to paddle. Will you come with me? Mama says I mustn't go on my own as I can't swim. You can swim, can't you?'

'I can,' she said.

'Good.' Without further discussion, Tommy dragged Nell in the direction of the sea. Nell laughed and apologised to the other people on the beach as they accidentally kicked sand at them and only narrowly avoided standing on a few picnics. She was still laughing when, without breaking his pace, Tommy charged into the sea. Almost immediately, he was up to his knees in the water. But whereas Tommy wore a smart little bathing suit, Nell wore a dress. It was loose and of a thin cotton, but she didn't relish the prospect of getting soaked.

'Stop, Tommy,' she laughed as he tried to drag her further into the water. 'I shall get very wet indeed.'

'And?' Tommy said without looking back, wading deeper.

'And I have no change of clothes! I have only this to travel home in.'

'It will dry,' he shouted. Releasing her hand, he was suddenly moving at a very fast pace so that the water was up to his waist.

'Tommy, stop!' Nell called.

Then it was up to his chest.

'Tommy!'

He showed no sign of stopping and Nell could not wait to see the water up to his neck. She splashed through the waves and was waist-high when she reached out to take hold of him. But as her hand was on his shoulder, she slipped on the uneven seabed. Stumbling, she fell heavily on her knees, her head submerged beneath the murky waves. She emerged coughing and spluttering. Tommy had stopped. He was bobbing in the water directly in front of her, laughing as if he had just witnessed the funniest thing in the world.

Nell had no choice but to laugh, too. 'You little devil!' she said. 'That was your intention all along, wasn't it?'

He continued to bob. 'Yes!' he said.

'And is this fun for you?'

'Yes!'

When in Rome, Nell thought. She put both hands in the waves. Scooping up seawater, she splashed Tommy. He laughed uncontrollably. Like her, he was now wet from the top of his head to the tips of his toes. He splashed her back. She blinked away the water and laughed harder.

Tommy demanded that Nell give him a swimming lesson. She was already wet; she couldn't get any wetter. So, dutifully, she showed him how to lie flat in the water, holding up his head, while she took the weight of his slight body by placing one arm beneath his chest and the other beneath his thighs. He kicked and splashed and giggled as she moved him along so that he floated half below and half above the surface of the waves. By the end of the impromptu lesson, Tommy had improved so rapidly that they were able to progress to the point where Nell was able to hold only his hands as he lay flat, supporting his own bodyweight and kicking with his legs to stay afloat.

'That's wonderful,' Nell said, when Tommy finally let his body relax and his feet fall so that he could stand on the seabed. 'We'll have you swimming in the next Olympics, you just see if we don't.'

'What's the 'Lympics?' Tommy asked.

'A bit of a sporty thing.'

Something that Nell had been pondering during the lesson,

came back to her. 'Tommy, I'd like to ask you a question. Do you remember talking to me yesterday outside the house?'

Tommy studied her as though she had asked a preposterous question. 'Of course, I was playing with my dolls.'

'Do you remember what we talked about?'

Tommy shrugged.

'Do you remember you said something about not always seeing with your eyes and something about "one in, one out"? What did you mean?'

'I don't remember,' he said.

'You said that somebody wanted to help me. And that I should listen to them. Do you know who that is?'

Tommy shrugged again.

'Were you playing with me Tommy? Like your mischief with the attic? Was it a game? You can tell me if it was.'

He looked up at her and wrinkled his nose. 'No. I don't remember any of that.' He looked past her. 'I'm hungry.'

There was clearly nothing to be gained from pressing him further – either Tommy was playing with her, or he really didn't remember what he said sometimes – so, Nell took his hand. 'Come on then, let's see what Mrs Randal has for us.'

'I hope there's pork pie.'

'Me too.'

Together they waded through the sea. But once out of the water, Tommy released Nell's hand and ran ahead up the beach. She watched him kicking up sand, his red curls dark from the water. Did he really not remember what he said to her sometimes? He did seem to go into a different 'state'. That was the only way that she could think to describe it. Was this really all part of a little boy's mischief?

By the time Nell reached the blanket and deckchair camp, everyone else had descended to stage a raid on Mrs Randal's hampers. Tommy had already told them all about his swimming lesson.

'You're soaking,' Charlotte laughed.

Nell plucked the towel from her bag and rubbed roughly at her hair. 'Sometimes you have to do things just for fun.' Nell winked at Tommy and he giggled.

Sitting down on one of the blankets, Nell joined everyone in falling onto Mrs Randal's picnic. It was a fine meal with ham sandwiches, cheese sandwiches, boiled eggs, a seed cake, flasks of refreshing lemonade and Tommy's hoped-for pork pie. It took Alice and Mary to stop the baby from garnishing the sandwich clenched in his tiny fist with sand. After each mouthful of sandwich, little Daphne begged to be taken to ride on one of the donkeys further along the beach.

When the meal was finished, Wilco stood. 'A fine spread, Mrs Randal,' he said, brushing the sand from his trousers. 'Right chaps, what say we conduct some business up at the Sandringham Hotel? Bertie, you are welcome to join us.'

As the men got up and made to leave, Alice called after them, 'Just a shandy for Bertie.'

'Thank you, Mrs Mandeville,' Mrs Randal said. 'My daughter wouldn't be happy if Bertie was to get tight while he's in my care. Sally telephones every other day to make sure he's well and I shouldn't be able to keep it from her.'

With the men dispatched, the women cleared away the picnic, except for Mrs Randal who was excused as she had made such a splendid job of it. It was decided that Alice, Charlotte, and Nell should take a stroll while Mrs Randal and Mary remained in their encampment to take care of the children. Mrs Randal was most content with the arrangement and settled back in her chair with her hands clasped over her chest and her eyes closed. While the little Mandevilles set to fashioning a pirate galleon out of sand, stones and shells, Audrey and Rosemary were told that they may have an hour to enjoy themselves.

Alice took her purse from her handbag and pressed a coin

into each girl's hand. 'Go and explore. But be sure to be back here by two o'clock.'

Audrey and Rosemary looked at the coins as though Alice had presented them with the crown jewels.

'Thank you, Mrs Mandeville,' Audrey said and bobbed a curtsy.

Alice smiled. 'Have fun.'

Needing no further encouragement, the girls hitched up the skirts of their dresses and set off at a pace across the beach towards the promenade, their ribbons flying in their wake.

Alice gave Mary some coins too, telling her to feel free to take the little Mandevilles for a donkey ride if they tired of making their ship. 'There's a little shop on the promenade if you want to run the risk of ice creams. And if you see a souvenir that catches your fancy, don't be shy about getting it.'

Nell looked around as the party dispersed, attempting to take in the details of everybody on the beach. There were men asleep in deckchairs with newspapers over their faces; women sipping tea poured from flasks; children running and shrieking, chasing each other with handfuls of straggly seaweed and poking around in rock pools. Nobody made Nell immediately suspicious, but she committed each to memory as best she could. She would make a note in her journal as soon as she had the chance.

Nell joined Alice and Charlotte and they made their way up to the promenade. It had grown so busy that they had to negotiate a crowd gathered to watch a dance routine performed by three Pierrots in crisp white silk costumes with black pompoms and pointed hats. Another crowd had formed around a red and yellow striped Punch and Judy tent. Children sat on the ground and roared with laughter at the crocodile with sausages dangling from its mouth. Some of the children jumped to their feet, shrieking at Mrs Punch, telling her where she could find her baby. At the appearance of the police constable,

Nell thought about Inspector Painter. She pictured him in The White Lion, eating a slice of some disappointing pie; a mean meal compared to the feast she had just enjoyed. He really needed feeding up. He looked like a man in need of a good woman to take care of him. Nell shook her head. Who was she to presume what he wanted or needed, or indeed imagine that a woman should wait on him hand and foot? For all she knew, he had a wife at home making him fine meals when he returned to put his feet up in front of the fire after a day's detecting. Did he have a wife?

'Nell?' Charlotte called.

Charlotte and Alice were some yards ahead of Nell. She had stopped. The crowd threatened to swallow them but fortunately Nell managed to push her way through. 'Sorry,' she said as she caught up with them.

'We thought we might take a walk along the pier,' Alice said.

'That sounds like a splendid idea,' Nell said. Charlotte slipped one arm through Nell's and the other through Alice's and they walked, arm-in-arm, onto the pier. Pausing to look over the side, they spotted Tommy and Daphne sitting in the saddles of two donkeys. Nell was pleased to see Mrs Randal still holding the fort at their encampment with the baby on her knee.

'What-o, Tommy! Hey there, Daphne,' Charlotte called, waving madly, and leaning so far over the side of the pier that Nell and Alice had to grab her and hold on to her, laughing that she was about to fall over the edge. Even then, her niece and nephew couldn't hear her as they were too far away.

'You really don't mind taking your life in your hands, do you, Charlotte?' Alice laughed as they all tumbled onto the bench that ran the length of the pier.

'Life's for living,' Charlotte laughed as she caught her breath.

'If you'd leant any further over the side, you wouldn't have one to live!' Nell puffed.

'You can talk,' Charlotte said, still laughing. 'I'm not the one who went swimming in the sea fully clothed! You might have drowned.'

Alice leant against Charlotte's shoulder. 'Seeing you two together is a breath of fresh air, you know. Nell, you must promise to visit more often. Charlotte is a changed woman these last few days.'

Should she...? Nell couldn't resist. 'I fancy it's not my presence that has made Charlotte so happy—'

'What do you mean?' Charlotte said rather too abruptly.

Alice leant past Charlotte and winked at Nell. 'Do you mean the presence of a certain Yank—'

'Hey!' Charlotte said. 'Paul is my friend. Nothing more.'

'That doesn't mean she doesn't want it to be more.' Alice winked at Nell again.

'Now listen here—' Charlotte said.

Before Charlotte could finish her sentence, Alice was up from the seat and had hold of her hands. 'Come on, Charlotte. Let's walk. Your love life is so dull, anyway.'

Alice smiled at Nell, who jumped up too and helped drag Charlotte to her feet. The three women recommenced their promenade, pausing to look at the many stalls along the way selling postcards, small pieces of pottery emblazoned with the words *A Souvenir from Hunstanton*, and so many sweet treats, from bars of coconut ice to bags of liquorice and peppermint creams.

Alice and Charlotte fell into a deep debate over which piece of pottery to buy Mrs Randal as a 'thank you' for her hard work. While they rifled through the offerings, Nell considered Alice, her behaviour and demeanour. Alice had been quick to join Nell in teasing Charlotte about Paul. Nell had never imagined she would see that kind of impish behaviour in a county wife. Alice may look as though butter wouldn't melt but there was something different about her. And it wasn't just her strange turn of phrase. Now that she thought of it, Nell hadn't noticed a Cornish twang. She would have said that Alice's way of expressing herself was more modern than regional. Perhaps that's why Tommy said and did things that appeared odd; he had learned his strange ways from his mother.

Charlotte and Alice finally settled on a small plate for Mrs Randal, which the stallholder wrapped in a paper bag. With the task sorted, Charlotte pointed to an amusement further along the pier. It was a small hut draped in bright fabrics – pinks, greens and yellows – with rather odd paintings pinned to the material and a hand with an eye painted in the centre, and a crystal ball.

'Come on,' Charlotte said, taking off at a pace before Nell or Alice could object.

They had no choice but to follow and joined Charlotte outside the entrance. A sign hung on the hut announcing *Madame Zelda. The All-Seeing Eye. Enter now to have your future revealed.*

Charlotte looked at the sign, her eyes wide. 'Come on,' she said. 'It'll be fun.'

'No, it won't,' Nell said. 'It's poppycock.'

'If you don't believe it,' Charlotte said, 'then you will have nothing to fear.'

'Who said anything about being scared?'

'You've been spending too much time with Wilco,' Alice said to Charlotte. 'He's filled your head with a lot of mumbo jumbo.'

'Actually,' Charlotte said defiantly, 'I am more than capable of making up my own mind about what to believe in. Paul says his father—'

Nell and Alice laughed.

'What?' Charlotte demanded.

'"Paul says…"' Nell and Alice said in unison.

'You are both fools,' Charlotte said. 'And if you're too afraid, I shall go in to see Madame Zelda alone.'

Alice nudged Nell. 'What do you say? Shall we give Madame Zelda a whirl?'

'Don't tell me you believe in it, too?' Nell said.

'No. But if Charlotte wants to cross that woman's palm with silver, then I'm up for being a witness.'

Nell glanced down at her dress, still damp from the sea. 'If Madame doesn't mind my soggy draws on her upholstery, then I'm game, too.'

Charlotte tutted at her companions as she pushed the curtain aside, and the three women stepped into the dark interior of Madame Zelda's domain.

TWENTY-FOUR

With Alice and Charlotte pressed against her, Nell peered into the darkness. The whole interior was swathed in crimson fabric, just visible in the mean smudges of light provided by candles in what looked like ale bottles up on the shelves.

'Welcome,' a voice said from the darkness.

'Bloody hell!' Alice said. Charlotte shrieked and Nell grabbed her friend's arm, her heart pounding as though she had just taken a turn on a terrifying fairground ride. All three laughed hysterically and clung to each other.

As Nell's eyes adjusted to the darkness, she saw that there was in fact a person sitting at the small table. Like the interior of her hut, the woman was swathed in fabric, her face covered, so that she and her environment were one.

'Sit down,' the woman said. A hand emerged from beneath the fabric and pointed to a bench. Each movement the woman made was accompanied by a jingling sound. Still clinging to each other, Nell, Alice, and Charlotte obeyed the woman's instruction, squeezing onto the small bench. The woman held out her hand and the source of the jingling was revealed. She wore bangles and bracelets on each wrist that made the noise as they moved against each other.

Alice took her purse from her bag, removed a few coins, and placed them in the woman's palm. The hand disappeared. There was the sound of coins chinking before the hand appeared again and the woman pulled back the scarf covering her face.

For some reason, Nell had anticipated coming face to face with an old, gnarled woman, perhaps with a wart on her nose or her chin. What she hadn't expected was this young woman with jet black hair sitting before them. In the smudge of light, Nell could see that not only was she young, but incredibly beautiful, with wide eyes, lips coloured a bright scarlet and a little too much rouge on her cheeks.

The woman took down a candle and moved it from side to side, surveying the three women before her. Nell felt Charlotte's grip on her arm tighten whereas her own heart rate began to slow. The sudden shock of the woman's presence had caused a momentary blip and, as she settled, Nell could see the theatre of this situation. The dark interior, the red swathed fabric, the candlelight, the crystal ball, and deck of oversized cards on the table – these things were all designed to create an atmosphere.

The woman placed the candle on the table.

'I am Madame Zelda,' she said – although Nell fancied that she was more of a mademoiselle – 'Who is for a reading first?'

'Her,' Alice said, pushing Charlotte forward slightly. 'And only her.'

'But you have paid enough for three readings.'

'It's really just her,' Nell said.

'That would be bad luck. You've paid for three readings; you shall receive three readings.' Madame Zelda fixed her eyes on Charlotte. 'But you will be first. Tarot, crystal ball or mediumship?'

Madame Zelda waited, still staring at Charlotte.

'Sorry?' Charlotte said.

Unfazed by Charlotte's response, Madame Zelda said, 'Would you like me to read your tarot cards, or consult the crystal ball or read you?'

'Tarot cards?' Charlotte said uncertainly.

The woman took up the deck of cards. She moved them around and had Charlotte cut the deck several times. Madame Zelda fanned the cards on the table then stacked the cards again. Nell had to stifle a sigh as the woman finally began to lay some of the cards face down on the table. The remaining cards, she put to one side. She waved her hands, making her bangles jingle, then selected a card and turned it over. The image was of a man and woman entwined.

'The lovers,' the woman announced with what Nell felt to be an awful lot of ceremony for the simple act of turning over a card. She was doing nothing more than playing an elaborate game of Happy Families with her highly decorated deck.

'The lovers,' the woman repeated, 'Does not always signify two people in love. These cards hold deeper meaning than simply the picture painted on them.'

She began to turn over more cards. Nell watched on, raising her eyebrows as the woman announced that this turn of cards showed Charlotte's future to be with a man. That she was at this very moment in love with a man. He had come from afar. Yes, that was right, he had come from overseas. He was a professional man. A teacher? A professor? A lawyer? A doctor. Ah, yes, he was a doctor.

It was all Nell could do not to shout out that this woman was a charlatan and chuck her cards in the air. Really, it was a pantomime of the highest order. The woman had clearly watched them as they took their walk along the pier. From the lack of a queue forming to pull back the curtain to her crimson lair, it was quite obvious that she had not been busy. She would have heard them teasing Charlotte about Paul. And the rest was

a fishing expedition, until Charlotte was able to validate a fact
or turn red at the mention of her love. Nell looked at Charlotte,
who was lapping up every word. Every promise of marriage and
children. Nell would have to shake some sense into her friend
when they re-joined the real world. If Madame Zelda's predictions came true, then it would be by chance rather than through
any skill at seeing into the future.

It was Alice's turn next. Rather than waiting for Alice to
choose the manner of her reading, Madame Zelda cleared away
the cards and moved the crystal ball closer to her. She
performed some elaborate hand gestures over the ball, then
peered into the glass, apparently waiting for the mists to clear.
The method may have been different, but her predictions were
as asinine as before. It would be clear to anybody who cared to
look that Alice wore a wedding ring. It wouldn't take a professor
of mathematics to put two and two together to come up with the
conclusion that Alice was married and had children. And
anybody with even the most basic powers of observation would
notice her striking colouring and take a stab at the fact that her
children would take after their mother. How many children was
it that Madame Zelda could see taking shape in her crystal ball?
One, two, three – that's it; three. Three beautiful red-headed
children coming into view through the mist. If Madame Zelda
had been watching them from her hut before they entered, she
would have seen them waving to Tommy and Daphne as they
rode their donkeys on the beach below. Nell stifled the urge to
roll her eyes when Madame Zelda said that Alice had a good
soul. She was like a mother to all she met. No doubt Madame
Zelda had been hanging over the edge of the pier while they
picnicked earlier and had seen Alice hand coins to Rosemary,
Audrey and Mary. Madame Zelda probably spent all day on the
lookout for anybody who seemed like a potential customer so
she could observe them and collect clues to build into stories to
feed back to them with a gilded edge.

Nell was pleased to see that Alice was far more guarded in her responses to her reading than Charlotte. She was a practical woman, less likely to fall for this nonsense. But when Madame Zelda began to describe another person appearing in her crystal ball, Nell noticed Alice begin to worry the clasp of her handbag.

'It's a woman,' Madame Zelda said, peering into the crystal ball. Her hands hovered over the glass almost cupping it, but without touching it. 'Oh, and she was such a great friend to you. Her heart is almost too big. She cares so much about others. And your friendship, it was brief. She had to go far away. But her friendship has made you who you are. And she sacrificed her happiness so that you might—'

Alice leapt from the bench.

'That's enough,' she laughed. 'Surely it's Nell's turn now.'

'But she's coming through clearly now,' Madame Zelda said. 'Is it L—'

'Nell, really,' Alice said. 'It is your turn now. We can't spend all day in here. We must get back to the children.'

'I'm not at all bothered,' Nell said. 'We can go now—'

'No,' Madame Zelda said. She brought her hands down with force on the table so that her bangles jangled furiously. 'You have paid for three readings; you must have three readings.'

'Go on,' Charlotte said. 'Take your turn, Nell.'

Alice settled back on the bench. Thinking that Alice was glad to be off the hook of hearing this codswallop, Nell said, 'Very well. If you insist.' The sooner this was over, the sooner they would be out in the sunshine again.

'Give me your hands,' Madame Zelda said. She rested her elbows on the table and reached out to Nell. Nell looked at Madame Zelda's open hands and the many silver bangles. With a sigh she couldn't contain, she placed her hands in the other woman's.

Madame Zelda's hands were warm and soft as she clasped

Nell's and her fingers closed to keep Nell in their grip. She traced lines on Nell's palms. Nell had expected this soothsayer to conduct some kind of palmistry trick, telling her that the lines on her hands predicted her future. On the contrary, Madame Zelda's focus was on Nell's face. Rather than consult the lines on Nell's palms, she looked her directly in the eyes. Beyond the thick line of kohl, Madame Zelda's eyes were so dark that it was impossible to see were the pupil ended and the iris began. She consulted Nell's eyes as she had consulted the cards and the crystal ball. It was ridiculous; she could no more divine Nell's past or predict her future by looking into her eyes than she could by staring at some scraps of thick paper or a ball of glass. But stare she did. At first benignly. And then Nell saw a flicker of Madame Zelda's eyelids.

'Water. Swimming. You like the water,' Madame Zelda said.

'Yes. I was in the sea earlier. Did you see me? My damp hair rather gives the game away, don't you think?'

Madame Zelda seemed not to hear Nell's words, dripping with sarcasm. 'It holds you up. It supports you. You need that support.'

'If you're swimming you do rather need the support of the water,' Nell said. Again, Madame Zelda seemed not to hear her.

'There was a man!' Madame Zelda gripped Nell's hands tight. 'He tried to harm you. In the trees.'

A shiver raced down Nell's spine. Madame Zelda may be on a fishing trip and may have hooked something by chance, but she couldn't give this away to Charlotte and Alice. She had promised Edward she wouldn't tell them. She had promised Inspector Painter too. She felt Madame Zelda's grip tighten. Before Nell could say anything, Madame Zelda leant forward.

'There's another man. Old-fashioned. In a hat.'

'I don't know what you're talking about,' Nell said, hoping for a dismissive laugh in her voice. She looked round, hoping too that Alice and Charlotte were giggling. She found them hanging on Madame Zelda's every word.

When she turned back, she found that Madame Zelda had closed her eyes. She was rocking backwards and forwards slightly.

'Oh, but what you have experienced,' Madame Zelda said softly. 'What you have lost.'

Nell tried to pull her hands free, but Madame Zelda's grip tightened still further. A tear slipped down her cheek.

'I can't bear it,' Madame Zelda said. 'I am so lost. I shall never be able to make right what I did. I should never have let him leave like that. I caused him such heartache. It's my fault. It's all my fault.' She was practically sobbing as she held Nell's hands in hers. 'But he wasn't all I lost.'

With every ounce of force she could muster, Nell yanked her hands free. 'This is a load of nonsense,' she said, springing from the bench, pushing past Charlotte and Alice.

'Please,' Madame Zelda, called after her. 'The water! Beware the water.'

Almost tripping over her friends' legs in her haste, Nell yanked the curtain from the entrance and stumbled out into the light.

TWENTY-FIVE

Squinting and taking gasps of salty air, Nell ran to the side of the pier and looked out over the deep water. She had only moments to compose herself before Alice and Charlotte were at her side.

'Nell, Nell, are you all right?' Charlotte said.

'What is it?' Alice asked. 'What did she say to upset you?'

'Nothing,' Nell said, still looking out over the dark water. 'It was all rubbish.'

'Then why take on so?' Charlotte asked.

'I don't like small spaces,' Nell said. 'I couldn't breathe. I needed air.' She couldn't say that every word that had come from Madame Zelda's mouth had struck a chord with her, like a hammer striking the largest bell made in any foundry. And the words rang in her ears as though she were standing beneath that bell as the hammer struck.

'I'm the same,' Alice said. 'I hate cramped spaces. And what she said was a lot of silliness.'

'I quite liked what she had to say,' Charlotte said.

'That's because it's what you wanted to hear,' Alice said.

'She was guessing at things she thought we might like to hear or might scare or alarm us. It was all for show. Isn't that right, Nell?'

'Yes,' Nell managed to say.

'It's a terrible trick to play on a person,' Alice said. 'Come along, Nell, let's walk to the end of the pier to clear your head.'

Nell had no strength to resist, and no fight left in her to argue. Alice linked arms with her. At that moment, she could have guided Nell anywhere. Her emotions felt like a rag doll in the hands of an angry child who had shaken her and thrown her into the air in a fit of pettishness.

Partway along the pier, Charlotte decided that she wanted to stop at a stall selling souvenirs made from shells. Alice said that she and Nell would carry on.

As they walked, Alice asked, 'Did some of what Madame Zelda said ring true?'

'A little.'

'Do you think she can actually read minds?'

Nell shook her head. 'I think it's a horrible magic trick.'

Alice stayed silent for a moment. Nell became aware of seagulls screeching in the sky. When Alice spoke, her voice was quiet. 'I won't pry. We've only known each other a few days. But I hope you think of me as a friend. If you ever need to talk, I'm here.'

Nell tried to smile. 'You're a friend to everyone.'

Alice gave her a real smile. 'I try.' She squeezed Nell's arm. 'But some of us have things we would rather keep to ourselves, haven't we?'

'One or two.'

'Then if you ever feel the need to sit in silence and just have someone there, I can do that, too.'

Nell wanted to ask Alice what it was that made her so understanding, as though she had the broadest shoulders for anyone and everyone to lean on. But Charlotte reappeared with a souvenir she had bought for her Aunt Leo. It was a mouse, fashioned from many tiny shells that she thought would tickle her aunt.

Charlotte chatted as they made their way back along the pier. She had a spring in her step and her cheeks were flushed a little pinker than usual.

Soon they were back at the encampment where they helped Mrs Randal and Mary pack up the blankets and hampers. The children were full of their donkey ride and how thrilling it had been to splash through the sea. Might they have a donkey at home? They would be sure to look after it very well and feed it carrots and brush its coat every day. They pestered Alice so much that she finally said she would ask their father for his thoughts on the subject. Audrey and Rosemary returned so happy with their excursion. They had watched the Punch and Judy and the Pierrots and had gifts for each of the Mandeville children. There was a yoyo for Tommy and a small ball for the baby. But it was Daphne's gift that received the most enthusiastic thanks. In honour of the donkeys she loved so much, they had bought her a postcard of two donkeys wearing pyjamas and tucked up in bed in a Hunstanton guesthouse. Daphne declared it the best thing she had ever seen. She was so thrilled that she would keep it by her bed always. When Alice asked the girls what they had bought for themselves, they produced a bag of peppermint creams and a bag of coconut ice, which they promptly shared with everyone.

Nell shook the sand from a blanket. She listened to the chatter and took great care in folding the blanket neatly, carefully. If she kept her brain engaged and her body occupied, there would be less opportunity to think back to what had been said on the pier.

With everything packed away, the party made their way to

the promenade where they stopped to watch a clown juggle and trip over his incredibly large shoes, before calling in at the Sandringham Hotel to round up the menfolk in time to catch the three o'clock back to Kings Lynn.

On the first train, Nell sat beside Mary and talked to her of Dickens. On the train from Kings Lynn to Stevenage she decided against sitting in the empty compartment, preferring the company of the other women and children.

The compartment was rather more subdued than on the outward journey. The children – including Audrey and Rosemary – fell asleep almost the instant the train left the platform. They all huddled together in only two seats, like kittens curled around each other in a basket before an open fire. Even the baby had been taken from his perambulator and was somewhere in the midst of the sleeping bundle. Mrs Randal closed her eyes and began to snore gently. Mary and Charlotte left to seek out the empty compartment, one to read her book, the other, no doubt, to gaze longingly from the window, reflecting on the promise of love made by Madame Zelda. Nell was glad when the sound of the door sliding open cut across her thoughts.

'Would you mind if I join you?' Bertie asked.

'Have the men grown tiresome?' Alice asked.

Bertie nodded. There were no free seats, so Alice shifted and patted the portion of the seat she had vacated. Bertie, being the slim boy he was, slipped in beside her. He rested his head on her shoulder and Alice stroked his blonde hair as though he were one of her own.

'Have you had a good day?' she asked softly.

Bertie murmured and nodded.

'And they didn't try to make you take a drink?'

Bertie shook his head. 'I had a shandy, a lemonade and a scotch egg.' His eyelids closed and soon his breathing grew deeper.

Alice smiled at him. 'I think this day has worn him out,' she said to Nell.

'He's a lovely young chap, isn't he?' Nell said. 'Very polite.'

'He's a credit to his mother, Sally,' Alice said. 'She's been in the service of the Mandevilles since she was a young woman. I think she's the best lady's maid they've had.'

'Where's his father?'

Alice looked down at Bertie, still resting on her shoulder, as though to check that he was still sleeping. 'The war,' she said quietly. 'He never came back.'

'Oh,' Nell said and looked down at her skirt.

'The Mandevilles took Bertie under their wing,' Alice said brightly, clearly trying to lift Nell's mood. 'Charlotte insists on paying for his education from money she inherited from her grandmother and Edward is something of a father figure.' She smoothed the sleeping youth's hair. 'He was such a little boy when I first arrived at Hill House. Only four years old. He was the first person to make me feel at home. He has a very special soul, and he is very precious to me. I love him very much.'

Nell wondered whether it would be the done thing to ask Alice about her first experiences at Hill House. The fact that she had arrived as a maid and was now married to the heir was the stuff of fairy stories. But it would be crass and rude to say anything. And if today had taught her anything, it was that some subjects were better left alone.

Nell felt her eyelids grow heavy. She was warm and full of food and... Her next awareness was of being shaken gently by Alice. 'We should be arriving in about ten minutes,' Alice said. 'I hate to disturb you, you were sleeping so soundly, but I could do with a hand rousing this lot.'

Nell looked around the compartment. Apart from Alice, everyone was fast asleep. Nell helped Alice bring everyone to life and Mary and Charlotte returned to collect everything in readiness for arriving at the station.

At Stevenage, the men appeared and conveyed the various children from the train into the cars that were waiting for them outside the station. They were soon on their way and pulled into the driveway at Hill House at just after seven o'clock in the evening.

TWENTY-SIX

'Well, that was quite the day,' Alice said when she appeared in the billiard room after putting the children to bed. 'They are all fast asleep for once.'

Nell sat with Charlotte in the chairs before the unlit fire while Paul and Edward played a game of billiards. Wilco was ensconced in Sir Charles' office, making telephone calls, and Mary and Mrs Randal had rustled up a dinner of cold meats and cheese, which was spread out on the sideboard.

Every window in the billiard room was open, as were the doors to the outside. A welcome breeze blew in, although the air in the room was still and hung like a curtain of heat. 'Mrs Randal thinks there'll be a storm tonight,' Alice said, plucking a grape from a plate of fruit.

Edward left the game to pour Alice a glass of wine. 'If you look out to the east,' he said, 'you can see the dark clouds rolling in. I'd say Mrs Randal is spot on.'

'Good,' Charlotte said, fanning her face with a fabric fan decorated with pagodas. 'I've had just about enough of this heat now. What we need is a good storm to clear the air.'

Edward returned the carafe to the sideboard. He made to

join the women, but Nell noticed Paul take him aside. She strained to hear their conversation.

'Is there something on your mind?' Paul asked Edward, his American drawl slow and measured as though stilted by the humidity.

'Why?' Edward said, somewhat defensively, Nell thought.

'Because you spent most of the last frame watching the door rather than the balls. And you've not been yourself all day. You've been wound tighter than a coiled spring.'

Edward gave one of his awkward laughs. 'There's nothing wrong with me,' he said and took a gulp of wine.

Nell watched them re-join the women. She had not spent enough time with Edward during the day to observe his behaviour, but the way in which he was attempting to shrug away Paul's comments made her think that, had she been on a jury, she would have convicted Edward of any charge on which he stood accused.

Edward took a handkerchief from his pocket and wiped his forehead. His cheeks were flushed so that they were almost as pink as Charlotte's, now that Paul was sitting beside her. Every other heartbeat, Charlotte stole a glance at Paul, who sipped his wine, seemingly oblivious to the fact that he was the sole focus of Charlotte's attention. Nell watched her friend. She was in the grip of an infatuation so deep and so all-consuming that her whole being rested in the hands of the man who sat beside her.

Paul looked up from his drink and caught Charlotte's eye. She looked down, her fair eyelashes shielding her blue eyes. As bold and as self-possessed as Charlotte was, she was as susceptible to the power of an infatuation as any woman. Thankfully, Paul smiled back at her. The scars running down his face meant it was limited to a half-smile. But it was completed by the smile in his eyes.

Take care of Charlotte's tender heart, Nell wanted to say. She sipped her wine. It wasn't her place to involve herself in this budding romance. But she hoped with all her heart that's what this was. Nell looked down into her wine. She swirled it around, watching it stick to the inside of the glass.

She felt something touch her hand. She looked down to find Alice's hand on hers. 'Are you all right?' Alice asked.

'I'm fine.'

'After today I thought...'

'Really, I'm very well. I think I just need a bit of air.'

Nell rose quickly from the chair, heading for the door open to the outside. As she was about to step into the garden, the first fat spots of rain darkened the paths. The prospect of traipsing her damp self and clothes across the carpets of Hill House made her take a detour. She left through another door leading from the billiard room and for the first time in her visit, stepped into the conservatory attached to the house.

Her senses were instantly overwhelmed by so many stimuli that she could hardly separate them out; the heady scents hung like a cloak in the air; the vibrant colours of lush greenery and tropical blooms from pinks to blues to yellows to oranges. Above her, vines trailed across the glass ceiling. Around her were multi-coloured plants arranged on shelves at waist height, each separated from their neighbour by pinkish gravel. Each gave off its own scent, combining to rival the perfume of the great glasshouses of Kew Gardens.

Nell sat down in one of two wicker chairs. This glasshouse was far smaller than the glasshouse at Caxton Hall, but it felt full of love for the plants rather than parading them for show. She traced the progress of a plant from its pot amongst the gravel, up the supportive canes to which it was tied, right up to its leaves arching across the glass ceiling. It was just like the tomato plants in her father's greenhouse. As a small child, her father had shown her how to gently press earth into pots containing tomato seeds and how to water the delicate seedlings as they developed, nipping out the side shoots to let the plants flourish. When she had been too small to reach her father's workbench, he had picked her up and held her so that she might reach.

The rhythmic drip, drip of light rain hit the glass roof. Nell closed her eyes. Her mind too occupied to rest, she replayed the events of the day. Try as she might, she was unable to explain away everything the clairvoyant had said. She had seen Nell swim in the sea and present herself in the dark hut still dripping seawater. Any comment about water was likely to hit its mark. As was the reference to being attacked by a man. That could easily be a symbolic attack. Hadn't every woman had to defend herself against a man or men in some way? And the man in the hat and the old-fashioned suit? There was nothing unusual in knowing a man in a hat, nothing at all. There was also nothing unusual in having lost someone. Take a ball and throw it into a crowd and it was likely to be caught by someone who had experienced grief. Nell blinked back tears. Her pain was not unique. But there was one remark Nell found more difficult to reconcile. That 'he' wasn't the only thing she had lost.

Nell let her head fall to one side, and looked past the plants to her colourless reflection in the window.

The door to the billiard room opened and admitted the sound of chatter into the conservatory. 'Hello there,' a voice said. Nell watched Paul's reflection in the glass as he joined her. He took the seat beside her before handing her a glass.

'Thank you,' she said, turning to face him.

'I've been sent to summon you,' Paul said. Taking a handkerchief from his pocket he took a careful sip of his wine and dabbed the damaged side of his mouth. He gave her one of his half smiles. 'Are you okay?' he said.

'I'm fine,' she said and took a sip of wine.

Paul paused a moment before he said, 'No, Nell, you're not.'

She smiled at him. 'Is that how you treat your patients when they answer you? If so, that's a very questionable bedside manner, Doctor Kenmore.'

'I am indeed a doctor. Which means I know when someone is not one hundred percent well. And I hope I know when I can detect an ailment. Otherwise, all my training has been for nothing.'

'I'm not ailing.'

Paul sat back and crossed his legs. He ran a finger along the good side of his mouth. 'I've seen a lot of men in the last few years who you would think are perfectly well,' he said. 'To anyone, they appear unscathed. Unlike me.' He turned squarely to look at her. Nell wanted to turn away but knew it would be rude. It would seem like she was afraid to look at his scars when in fact it was his directness she found off putting.

'I carry my scars for everyone to see,' he said, dabbing the moisture from the corner of his lips. 'I've had to come to terms with my wounds. I'm reconciled to them. I've learned to live with them.'

'Which is why you don't flinch when people stare at you,' Nell said.

'I'd be surprised if people didn't stare,' Paul said. 'But my scars are as much a part of me as the rather unfortunate possibility of baldness I've inherited from my mother's father. They are part of my history and I accept them.'

'That's a good way to be,' Nell said.

'My speciality is trauma surgery, but because of what I have been through, I have made an extracurricular study of psychology. My interest is in the rehabilitation of people who have experienced traumatic events.' Paul sat forward slightly. His good eyebrow dipped so that he frowned in a way that made him appear concerned. 'The patients I work with as part of my study of psychology may not have physical scars. In some ways, their wounds are worse. They are on the inside.'

'Their internal organs are damaged?' Nell asked, unsure of what Paul meant.

'You could say that,' Paul said. 'Their wounds affect the most important organ in their body.' He tapped the side of his head. 'I treat many men who saw action in the war. Their brains weren't damaged by a bullet or a shell but by what they saw, what they experienced. It has left them emotionally damaged. Scarred on the inside.'

Paul left the words there and Nell was reminded of her friend in Hanwell. 'Do you mean that you treat people who are insane?'

'The people who pass through my consulting room are anything but insane,' Paul said. 'Their "illness" if that's what we can call it, is the only logical – the only sane – response to what they saw and experienced. If a person weren't affected by witnessing such horror, I would be worried.'

Nell looked down into her wine. 'You talk about it in a way that people normally don't.'

'You mean the war?'

Nell nodded.

'We can't hide from it. It happened. A wall of silence helps nobody. I think this reluctance to talk may have something to do with your British reserve. But your stiff upper lip means that many of you are storing up problems for the future. Only once we bring our experiences out into the light can we begin to understand them and learn to cope with them.'

Nell shook her head. Was Paul's use of the word "you" a collective grouping of the British? Or was it directed at her? 'I don't know,' she said. This conversation was taking her too close to a destination she did not want to go.

'A person mustn't be rushed,' Paul said. 'They can only talk when they are ready.'

Nell could sense Paul trying to meet her eye. She continued to look into her wine.

'It's not only the men who went to war that I see in my consulting room,' Paul said. His voice was softer. 'Those left behind and those that lost someone can experience a trauma just as great.'

The surface of Nell's wine trembled.

Paul placed his glass on the floor before prising Nell's fingers from around the stem of her glass and setting it on the floor too. 'When you are ready, you just come to see me.'

Staring into her lap, Nell said, 'Has Charlotte said something to you?'

'As far as I know, there's nothing much to tell. You have kept it all inside. But Charlotte is your friend. She knows how you respond when she talks about the war. How you flinch and shut yourself away. She loves you dearly. She is worried about you. Worried that you may be retreating still further inside yourself.'

'You are very blunt,' Nell said, trying to laugh.

'It's the Yank in me,' Paul said. 'We don't have much in the way of reserve.'

'And has... has Charlotte spoken to you about her brother?'

'She has.'

Nell nodded. In little more than a whisper, she said, 'I'm not going insane, am I?'

'No,' Paul said. 'You're sad. But if that sadness goes on too long, it can make you unwell. I'm here to help. If you'll let me. But only when you're ready. And don't worry, I've taken the Hippocratic oath so anything we speak about goes no further than me. Okay?'

Nell nodded, still without looking at him. 'Okay.'

A silence fell, interrupted only by the pit-pat of the rain. Nell looked at Paul's hands. She took in the undamaged flesh. The perfect fine hairs at the base of each of his fingers. If she allowed her eyes to travel up, that perfectness would be replaced by visible, tangible, visceral evidence of the devastation of that filthy war. Paul wore his scars overtly. She knew he was right; hers were hidden, tucked away out of sight. Was that why her brain had begun to play tricks on her? Had six years of burying her pain proved injurious to her brain?

'May I ask you a question?' Nell ventured.

'Of course,' Paul said quietly.

'If...that's to say... if this sadness you speak of goes on too long, can it make you begin to see things?'

'You mean hallucinations?'

'I don't know.'

'What do you see, Nell?'

'I'm not sure. Just things that aren't really there.'

'And you couldn't be dreaming when you see these things?'

'No. I don't think so. I'm always awake. And these things I see, they are like shadows almost. I can't seem to interact with the people I see.'

'What are they doing?'

'Just going about their business.'

'And how many times has this happened?'

'Twice. And only since I've been here. The first time it happened I was in the house. Today it happened when I was on the train.'

'The brain is a wonderful and fascinating organ, Nell,' Paul said. 'In truth, we don't understand what it's really capable of. But imagine this: you are a creative person. You make stories out of what isn't really there. You summon up worlds and people. This isn't a diagnosis or anything close, but do you think it could be your subconscious being overstimulated somehow and that these things you see are in your imagination?'

Nell thought back. She had been trying to create a world for the novel she was meant to be writing. 'I suppose it's possible.'

'It is possible too that you're under pressure, which has caused these episodes. But let's not try to label them or make any kind of hasty diagnosis. Will you let me know if you experience any more? Then we can look at the circumstances around them and try to establish what is causing them. How does that sound?'

'Good.' Nell looked up and smiled at Paul.

He gave her one of his half smiles in return.

'Charlotte is a very lucky woman,' Nell said.

'I'm sure I don't know what you're talking about,' Paul said with a slight smirk.

'Oh, I think you do,' Nell said.

A knock at the door leading to the billiard room made Paul and Nell look up. The door opened gently. 'Everything okay in here?' Charlotte asked.

'Sorry,' Paul said. Rising to his feet he collected the glasses and handed Nell her wine. 'I was sent to summon Nell, wasn't I?'

Charlotte nodded over her shoulder. 'It's just that Wilco wants everyone in the dining room. He has a surprise that he's desperate to share. I think he might explode if we don't join him soon. Edward's in Father's office waiting for a telephone call and refuses to be moved.'

Paul looked down at Nell. 'Let's give Nell a minute or two,' he said. 'She's a bit tired after the long day we've had.' He placed his hand on Charlotte's waist and guided her back into the billiard room, closing the door behind them.

Nell took a sip of wine. Above her, the tip-tap of raindrops sounded on the glass roof like a thousand pins. She wrapped her free arm around her waist. For the first time someone had seen the darkness in her and acknowledged it. She took another sip of wine. Until now she had managed to fool everyone that she was a fully functioning human being and member of society. Until now, nobody had seen past the façade.

Swiping roughly at her eyes, she rose from her chair. The rain began to fall harder. She looked out to the grounds of Hill House and to the sky growing darker, the clouds heavier.

TWENTY-SEVEN

Nell decided to delay her entrance to the dining room. She wasn't ready to face everyone, not quite yet. Since Edward had separated himself from the group, it was as good a time as any to find out what, if anything, had been found out about the local thefts.

As soon as Nell entered the small corridor beneath the staircase, she heard Edward's voice. Stopping short of Sir Charles' office, she listened to the one-sided conversation.

'What do you mean, you think it was an attempt to distract you?' Edward said. 'You assured me you would be here all day.'

Pause.

'No, no, everything seems in order here. We came back and the house was locked up. Elliot has been patrolling the grounds. He must still be out there now.'

Pause.

'No, I haven't seen him since we got back. But I'm sure if there was anything to tell, he would have sought me out.'

Pause.

'No, I haven't seen PC Atkinson either. What do you mean

by leaving him here alone when you assured me that all of your men would be here?'

Pause.

'No, nobody suspects as far as I can tell. They all think the trip to the seaside was a day out. You do realise I am taking a very great risk to flush him out, don't you? Especially with Wilco here. I can't allow anything to get in the way of the deal.'

Pause.

'No. No time soon. He seems to be enjoying his visit and is in no hurry to leave.'

Pause.

'Very well. I will expect you tomorrow. Yes, goodbye, Inspector Painter.'

As the bell rang, signifying the return of the handset to its cradle, Nell retreated from the door. So many thoughts fought for space in her mind. The day out to the seaside had been some kind of diversion to get everyone away from the house. Elliot had been patrolling the grounds, but why? Had there been a further escalation in the threat to the Mandevilles? Or even a specific threat? Edward clearly knew more than he was letting on. And what was this about flushing someone out, and a distraction that had taken Inspector Painter and his men away?

This whole business about Painter asking that she record what she saw to report back to him might have been one of his tricks, just as the excursion to the seaside seemed to have been. By keeping her occupied, had he been trying to keep her away from his investigation, just as he had kept the Mandevilles and their guests away from home all day? While she had been running around, scribbling in her notebook, Painter had been free to get on with his real work. No doubt all she had taken the time to write would end up at the bottom of Painter's wastepaper basket.

Nell felt her cheeks flush. She had been so gullible. And she had wasted her time when she could have been working on her novel. She would give anything – anything – to help the Mandevilles. But to be tricked into having her loyalty cruelly taken advantage of. She should have trusted her instincts to never let a man dictate her actions.

The chair in Sir Charles' office creaked. Nell let herself into the small luggage room. Closing the door gently, she stood with her back to the wall. Through the glass panel in the door, she watched Edward pass.

TWENTY-EIGHT

'There she is!' Wilco said when Nell entered the dining room. She looked about. It took a moment for her eyes to grow accustomed to the gloom. The electric lights had been turned off and the curtains pulled to. The room was lit only by candles, placed about the available surfaces in all manner of candlesticks and holders. Around the table, she could make out the faces of Wilco, Paul, Alice and Charlotte.

'We're just waiting on Edward now,' Wilco said, consulting his wristwatch, moving it close to a flame so that he could read the face. 'Where the devil has he run off to this time? He keeps disappearing today. It's almost as though he is up to something.'

'I'm sure he's not up to anything,' Alice said. 'He said that he wanted to speak to his father.'

Wilco's response was an unintelligible grunt. He took a large slug of the drink in his hand.

Nell looked at the table. It had been reduced in size; leaves removed so that it was now a perfect circle rather than a long table with rounded edges. In the middle sat a board. It looked like a game. But it wasn't a game that Nell had come across before; it was no Snakes and Ladders or Ludo. Arranged in two rows in a semi-circle, and taking up half the board, was each letter of the alphabet. Beneath were the numbers zero to nine and a few basic words including *Yes* and *No*. There were no dice and no playing pieces. The only item on the board was an object that resembled an elongated heart, almost like a pointer.

'You're right to look confused,' Paul said to Nell. 'Whisky is not the only spirit Wilco intends to commune with tonight.'

Wilco brought his hands down to the table and let out a loud roar of laughter. 'Touché, Kenmore. I'll let you have that one.' He took up a case and removed a cigar, which he lit by the flame from the candle before him.

Charlotte patted the chair beside her. Nell took a seat.

'It's a spirit board,' Charlotte said to Nell. 'Wilco says that it is used to contact the spirit realm. Isn't that exciting?'

'I managed to procure it from a shop in Northampton,' Wilco said. 'I've seen one used at my mother's parties. It's terrific fun.'

'Fun?' Paul's good eyebrow rose. 'I'm not sure that an instrument for contacting spirits should be sold in a toy shop or that it should be used by an untrained person.'

Wilco laughed. 'I thought you didn't believe in this. What harm is there in us playing this game if you don't believe we are really contacting the dead?'

Paul took out his handkerchief and dabbed the corner of his mouth. 'I do not believe that this board can summon spirits. But I do believe in the power of the human mind. If it's not the case that people around these tables physically push the pointer, then it's quite possible that it is somehow moved through the power of the mind. We none of us know for sure what the human mind is capable of. And we should be wary of playing fast and loose with it.'

'Oh, Paul,' Charlotte said. 'It's just a bit of fun. Besides, with you at the table, I'm sure that whatever happens will be well controlled. Please say you will play.'

'Very well,' he said. 'But only because you asked me to. But I don't call this playing. I call it participating.'

'And you, Nell. You'll join in, won't you?' Charlotte said.

Nell looked about the table. She didn't care for this darkness or the long shadows moving across the faces of her friends and the candles throwing light where it ought not to be. Everyone looked odd. Not quite like themselves.

'You can count me out,' Nell said. She had had enough of things she did not understand for one day.

'Oh, please play, Nell,' Charlotte said. 'If it's because of what happened on the pier today—'

'It's not that,' Nell snapped. But on seeing Charlotte's alarm, added more kindly, 'It's because I don't believe in it.'

'Don't harangue Nell, Charlotte,' Alice said. 'Let her think about it. She may change her mind and if she doesn't, she's entitled to sit the game out.'

Nell picked up the glass of wine Wilco poured for her. While Charlotte quizzed Wilco on what he had seen when playing with the spirit board at his mother's parties, Nell took a sip. A few days ago, there would have been absolute truth in what she said about not believing in the spirit board. But what she had experienced in the past few days had introduced enough of a doubt for her not to want to meddle in something she did not understand.

'You do know that many of those spirit mediums have been discredited,' Paul said. 'They have accomplices who sit behind screens pretending to be the voice of a long-dead relative. And the ectoplasm they are seen to emit has been proven to be silk and they kick the tables—'

'Ah yes,' Wilco said, stabbing the air with his cigar. 'As you say, *some* have been discredited. Not all. As is the case with any profession. You get some wrong 'uns and some who are the very model of professionalism.' He blew out a plume of smoke. It hovered over the candle flame like a miniature phantom, before dissolving into the ether.

Nell watched Paul, waiting for a response. She saw him look to Alice who shook her head.

Like a man truly bested, Paul said, 'You're right, Wilco. That was a sweeping generalisation on my part.'

Wilco smiled and held up his glass while across the table, Alice mouthed the words 'Thank you,' to Paul. They had all spent so much time together that it would have been easy to assume each could say anything to the other. But ultimately, they all had to be on guard against offending Wilco.

'The wanderer returns!' Wilco said suddenly.

'Sorry,' Edward said, running his fingers through his hair. 'I was just dealing with a spot of business.' He looked toward the table.

'It's a spirit board,' Charlotte said, answering the questioning look on her brother's face. 'Wilco ordered it from Northampton.'

'Come on then, Ed.' Wilco said. 'Sit down.'

Edward sat in the empty chair beside Alice. He moved the chair closer to the table, the feet scraping along the floor.

'Now what?' Charlotte said to Wilco, her eyes gleaming in the candlelight. She looked to Nell like a little girl about to unwrap the largest present beneath the tree on Christmas Morning.

As Wilco explained that they should all place a finger on the pointer, Nell glanced at Edward. She was finding it difficult to bite her tongue to stop from asking what on Earth he and Painter were up to, concocting the seaside trip to get them away from the house. The police didn't surround a house to keep watch simply because a strange man was lurking at the bottom of the kitchen stairs or in the woods. A few burglaries wouldn't see such an elaborate ploy by the police to flush out a single thief, surely. There was something far more sinister going on here than was being admitted to. She was sure of it.

Everyone looked to Wilco. The candles flickered on the breeze coming in through the open doors and windows, casting strange light in the dark corners. Wilco looked at everyone in turn, the whites of his eyes bright in the candlelight. 'Are we ready?' he said, with an ominous tone to his voice, clearly put on for effect.

Charlotte nodded. Everyone else reluctantly murmured their agreement. Nell sat back in her chair and folded her arms.

'I've seen my mother and her friends do this enough times to know what to do,' Wilco said. He closed his eyes and let his head fall forward. The room was still, as everyone waited for what was to come next. They watched Wilco breathe in deeply and then exhale slowly. Once. Twice. On the third breath he threw back his head. 'Spirits!' he said so loudly and so suddenly that Nell felt her heart punch her ribs. 'Spirits,' he repeated, 'come forward and make yourselves known to us.'

Wilco looked at the pointer. Everyone looked from Wilco to the pointer.

Charlotte looked up. 'Is something supposed to happen?' she said.

'Shh,' Wilco answered sharply. 'We must give the spirits the chance to come through.' He closed his eyes again and breathed in deeply.

When, after what seemed like an eternity, nothing happened, Nell was about to excuse herself. She made to push back her chair but was halted in her movement by a scratchy sound coming from the table. The pointer was moving ever so slowly across the board.

'Who's moving it?' Alice whispered.

Everyone shook their heads. Nell stared at the pointer as it made a slow motion as though forming a circle.

'What's it supposed to do?' Charlotte whispered.

'Shh!' Wilco said firmly.

Slowly, the pointer moved towards the letters. Nell observed how the movement was smooth as though it were gliding somehow. As she wondered whether the board and pointer were somehow manipulated by magnets, the pointer stopped.

'H!' Wilco announced. Almost before the letter left his mouth, the pointer was on the move again.

'E!' Wilco announced when it stopped once more. He continued to reel off the letters – L L O. 'Well, hello to you too!' Wilco called out.

The pointer returned to the bottom of the board, but it constantly moved in a circular motion as though waiting.

'What shall we ask it?' Wilco said, looking around the table. 'Any questions from you, Kenmore? You seem the most familiar with this process.'

'No,' Paul shook his head. 'I have nothing to ask.'

'Do you want to speak to someone around this table?' Charlotte asked, directing her question to the pointer without invitation.

The pointer stopped its circular motion and set off across the board at such a pace that Edward and Charlotte's fingers were briefly left behind. They re-joined the pointer as it firmly pointed to the word 'YES'.

'Who?' Wilco asked.

This time the pointer made no circular motion. Instead, it set off across the board, spun around and pointed in Nell's direction.

'Nell?' Charlotte said. 'You want to speak to Nell?'

The pointer raced back across the table and pointed again to the word 'YES.'

'But she's not playing,' Charlotte said. 'Choose someone else.'

The pointer shot first to the opposite side of the board and pointed to the word 'NO'. Without stopping it shot once again to Nell.

Nell looked down at the pointer, its sharp end swaying slightly backwards and forwards on a level with her ribs.

'Someone wants to speak to you,' Wilco said, with a sense of fun in his voice.

A cold blast raced down Nell's back while simultaneously her cheeks blazed. 'Don't be ridiculous,' she said. But she couldn't take her eyes from the pointer swaying before her. It inched closer to her, everyone's fingers coming with it.

'Someone *really* wants to speak to you,' Charlotte said.

'This is a ridiculous party trick,' Nell laughed. She didn't care for the way her voice trembled.

'Ask who it is,' Charlotte said to Wilco.

'No. Don't,' Nell said. The pointer still swayed before her.

'Why?' Wilco demanded. 'If you don't believe in it, what harm is there?'

Paul coughed. 'Nell said she didn't want to participate. I think we should leave her out of it.'

'Perhaps we should start again,' Edward said, pushing his spectacles up his nose.

Wilco let out an exaggerated sigh. 'Very well,' he said. Grabbing the pointer, he returned it to the centre of the board. 'Fingers,' he demanded. Everyone placed a finger on the pointer but before Wilco could issue a command, the pointer shot across the board again and only just stopped before flying from the table.

'It really does want you,' Alice said to Nell.

Nell stared at the pointer again.

'Who are you?' Wilco demanded.

Nell wanted to shout at him to stop. But she had said that she didn't believe in this. 'It's nobody,' she said, trying to laugh. The pointer flew across the board. It stopped at various letters with Wilco announcing each one. I T pause I S.

'It is?' Wilco said. 'What the devil is that supposed to mean?'

'I think it's answering Nell,' Charlotte said. 'Nell said that it's nobody. The spirit is saying it is someone.'

The pointer flew across the board and stopped at the word 'YES.'

Wilco laughed. 'You're getting good at this, Charlotte. Perhaps you should take over the questions.'

It was clear that he didn't mean it, but Charlotte took him at his word. 'Who are you?' she asked. The look in her friend's eyes made Nell want to turn away. It was manic somehow, made even more sinister by the shadows cast by the candles.

The pointer moved off at pace. It went first to the letter P. Then to the letter H. Then to the letter I. When it raced to L, Nell jumped to her feet. She heard nothing but the blood thudding in her ears. Turning from the table, she tried to race away, but the door to the dining room slammed. She took hold of the handle and tried to turn it. It refused to move. She tried with two hands. Still, the door would not open.

Trying with all her might to turn the handle, Nell became aware of Alice and Charlotte by her side. 'Nell. Nell!' Alice said. Nell couldn't find the voice to form any words. She was afraid of the sound that might come out – afraid it would be the guttural cry of animal pain she had once made in response to the name forming on the table.

'Edward, a brandy, please,' she heard Alice say.

Before Edward could leave the table, Wilco called out, 'Good God!'

The women all turned back.

Edward, Wilco and Paul remained seated. Their hands were nowhere near the table. And yet... and yet, the pointer moved.

'Wilco, what's happening?' Charlotte said. 'Is this part of the game?'

For once, Wilco looked unsure. 'No,' he said. 'No, I've never seen this happen before. Do you know what's happening, Kenmore?'

Paul shook his head. 'I've no idea.'

While they spoke, the pointer continued to move. This time it made small zig-zag movements.

'Wilco,' Charlotte said. 'I think it might need energy to move. Put your finger back on it.'

Without argument, Wilco did as Charlotte said. As much as she wanted to turn away, Nell felt compelled to watch. The pointer began to move towards the letters. Slowly now, as though having lost some of its power, the pointer began to spell out words. It still seemed to float somehow, not in a way that it might if somebody had been pushing it. When the pointer stopped, it was Charlotte who announced what it had said.

'"He is gone",' she said. '"He would never scare you. We love you."'

The words cut like a blade to Nell's heart. 'I can't,' she whispered. 'Please make it stop.' She tried the door handle. Still, it would not move. She let go and her hands fell to her sides.

The rain lashed against the windows.

'I think we've had enough of this,' Paul said. But as he reached for the pointer, it flew across the table away from him. Every window in the room slid shut. The resulting draught made the curtains billow. The candles guttered and were snuffed out and the room was plunged into darkness. Charlotte screamed. The door flew open. Light flooded into the dark dining room from the hallway and a shadow lengthened on the dining room floor. Charlotte screamed again.

TWENTY-NINE

Edward jumped to his feet. 'What in hell's...'

The little figure from the doorway ran towards the women. Nell sank to her knees and took Tommy in her arms. She heard adult voices about them while she clung to Tommy, his little body warm through his cotton pyjamas.

'How very much he loves you. He didn't mean to alarm you,' he whispered in her ear, his face resting on her shoulder.

Nell felt an attempt to pull Tommy away, but he clung to her.

'Listen to this house,' Tommy said urgently. 'It wants to help you.' Again, someone tried to pull him away. Again, Tommy clung to Nell, his arms tight around her neck. 'He loves you too much to think that you will never be loved again.'

Nell relinquished her hold on Tommy. She clutched her mouth to hold in a cry and Tommy was snatched from her. Alice's face swam into Nell's view. She was kneeling on the floor beside her. She took hold of Nell's arms.

'Nell,' Alice said. 'Nell, are you all right? Nell, you're shaking.'

Nell stared ahead. Rain still lashed at the windows and a

rumble of thunder sounded in the distance. She could hear Charlotte talking to her nephew. Tommy was telling her he had no idea why he was in the room. The last thing he remembered was being asleep in bed.

'He has started walking in his sleep recently,' Alice said. And then more quietly, 'If he has shocked you, Nell, I am sorry. Has he said things...? About—'

Before Alice could finish, another person appeared in the doorway. Bertie raced across the room to Alice. He was soaking, and water pooled on the floor about him. He tried to talk to Alice quietly, but they were close enough for Nell to hear.

'I was at my grandmother's cottage,' he said. 'I felt... Has Tommy...? Something's happening, isn't it? I should have been here with him. To guide him.'

Alice helped Nell to stand before releasing her to put her hand to Bertie's cheek. 'It's not your fault. Let's talk about this away from here.' Alice smiled at him. 'Okay?'

Bertie nodded.

The electric lights came on. Nell blinked. Paul approached her. He placed his palm on her forehead and bobbed his head, trying to make her focus on his eyes.

'Is Miss Potter all right?' Wilco asked. 'I didn't mean for anyone to take a turn.'

'We know that,' Edward said. 'We know you didn't mean for this to happen.'

'I think Nell's tired,' Paul said. And then added quietly, 'Alice, I think Nell might be in shock. Will you help me take her to her room?'

Nell let herself be guided from the dining room into the hall, Paul on one side of her and Alice on the other.

'Charlotte,' Alice said, 'would you arrange a cup of warm milk for Tommy and Bertie? I'll be back as soon as we've taken Nell to her room.'

They crossed the hall, Paul gently holding Nell's elbow to

guide her. 'Why in hell's name did Edward let Wilco bring that thing into the house?' he whispered.

'Don't be so hard on Edward,' Alice whispered back. 'You know he's trying to humour Wilco.'

'I shouldn't have let it happen. I know enough of my father's research to know that this is not a game. Look what this meddling with the unknown has done to Nell. What's going on here, Alice?'

'I don't know what you mean,' Alice said. Even in her troubled state, Nell was unconvinced by the tone in Alice's voice.

Reaching the bottom of the stairs, Nell was about to place a foot on the scarlet carpet when a shout came from the dining room. Tommy ran into the hall with Bertie at his heels.

'They are there,' Tommy shouted. Bertie caught him before he could cross the hall. He held Tommy tight as he squirmed to be freed.

'In there,' Tommy pointed to the ballroom.

Charlotte caught up with Bertie and Tommy. 'There's nobody in there, darling,' she soothed. 'Come along,' she said, holding out her hand to Tommy. 'Let's go down to the kitchen and warm some milk for you. There might even be a biscuit if you're a very good boy.'

'No!' Tommy shouted. But as Bertie held him, a transformation now familiar to Nell occurred in the child. He stopped squirming. He looked Bertie in the eye and, in a quiet, calm voice said, 'Feel it, Bertie. Feel it.'

The younger boy and older boy stared at each other.

Charlotte looked from them to Alice. 'What is happening?' she said.

And then Bertie burst into life. Jumping to his feet, he ran to the ballroom. He grabbed the handles. But the double doors were locked.

'Where's the key?' he demanded, looking over his shoulder to Alice as Edward and Wilco joined them in the hall.

'What's going on?' Edward asked.

'The key,' Bertie demanded. 'I need the key.'

'A spare is kept in the drawer there,' Charlotte said.

Bertie ran to the hallstand, yanked open the drawer and took out a key. He ran back to the ballroom, turned the key in the lock and pushed open the double doors.

'Oh no!' he called out. And without pausing, he ran into the room.

THIRTY

The cry Bertie made when he entered the ballroom was enough to take all attention from Nell. Paul let his hand slip from her elbow and ran to join him. Alice, Edward, Charlotte, and Wilco followed, so that Nell was left alone in the hall. She knew that she was not in shock as Paul had suggested. She was confused. Nothing happening tonight made any sense. It could not *be* happening. Nell looked into the dining room. The abandoned spirit board looked like what it was. A piece of thick card covered in letters. It was not a portal to another realm. It was a game. A cruel parlour game. But as Nell looked, she was sure for a second that she saw the pointer move. She was about to run away up the stairs when voices from the ballroom stopped her short.

The familiar voices of the day were joined by another voice. And then another. Nell crossed to the ballroom and stopped in the doorway. She gasped at the sight before her.

The room was quite possibly one of the grandest she had ever seen, with two huge chandeliers dripping in shimmering crystal pendants. Vast mirrors on the walls reflected the electric light from the elaborate lamps around the room. But beneath the grandeur, the dancefloor was covered by boxes, paintings leant against the walls, and what looked like statues were under white sheets. Amongst the chaos there were two chairs back-to-back and toppled to the floor so that their occupants were lying on their sides, tied to each other and to the chairs by ropes. Edward, Paul and Wilco took hold of the men and chairs and lifted them upright. Edward and Wilco set to untying them while Paul checked each man. Gags of fabric hung about their necks and the cheeks of each was raw. There were other marks that made Nell want to turn away. Elliot and PC Atkinson had both taken a beating. Both had black eyes, split lips and bruises forming on their faces.

Charlotte and Alice stood to one side, Charlotte with her arm around Bertie and Alice holding Tommy.

'What happened to you?' Paul asked as he checked Elliot's pulse.

'I'm ashamed to say it was one man,' Elliot said. 'He caught us unawares and knocked us both out cold. We woke up like this. We've been here most of the afternoon. We couldn't make you hear us over the storm.'

'Don't say anything more,' PC Atkinson said as he rubbed his wrists having been freed by Wilco. 'I don't mean to be rude,' he added, 'but I think we should wait to give a proper statement.'

'Quite right,' Paul said. He turned to Charlotte. 'I need some iodine; do you have a bottle?'

'Of course,' Charlotte said, stepping forward. She bent to look at Elliot's face. 'You could do with some cold water and some flannels to take that swelling down.'

Nell saw Paul smile when he looked at the side of Charlotte's face as she consulted PC Atkinson's wounds. 'I forgot. You were a nurse. You could tend these wounds with your eyes shut and without me around.'

Charlotte would ordinarily have blushed at any compliment

from Paul. But now, she tucked her hair behind her ear and gently took Elliot's hand to check the welts cutting across his wrists. 'I'll be right back,' she said and ran from the room.

The moment she was gone, Edward, who had untied the final rope from PC Atkinson's wrists, stood and ran his fingers through his fringe.

'You've no call to be ashamed, Elliot. I know you would have fought harder than any man.' He turned to his wife. 'Alice, please take Tommy and Bertie up to the nursery.'

'But Edward,' Alice said. 'What is happening here?'

'Please,' Edward said, 'I'll explain everything later.'

'But Edward—'

'Darling, please,' Edward said with uncharacteristic sharpness. 'Do as I ask. We will talk about it later.'

Alice gave PC Atkinson and Elliot a final look before she placed her arms around the boys and guided them away.

'Well,' Wilco said, as he helped Edward untie the rope securing PC Atkinson's ankles to the legs of the chair. 'There's never a dull moment here at Hill House, is there?'

'No,' Edward laughed nervously, 'although this wasn't planned as part of your visit.'

'Oh, I don't mind,' Wilco said. 'It adds a bit of spice to a week in the country. So, what was it?' he said. 'A spot of breaking and entering?'

'Something like that,' PC Atkinson said, glancing at Edward.

It was clear to everyone else in the room that there was more to this than a chance brick through a window to snatch a candlestick or two. All except Wilco, who, full of bluster and ignorant of whatever had been taking place at the house that day, appeared to be entertained by events. 'I hope you gave as good as you got,' he said, 'but judging by the state of you I suppose you two came off worse. I say,' he said as though the penny had just dropped. 'I wonder if this has anything to do with that chap the young maid spotted lurking around the stairs?'

'Can you hurry up at all?' PC Atkinson said. 'I need to telephone the station.'

'Nell can do that,' Edward said, glancing towards the door as he struggled with the knot. 'The card is on the desk in my father's office, Nell.'

'Me?' Nell said.

'Yes, you,' Edward said, adding, 'Wilco, Paul and I have rather got our hands full.' Nell had never cared for sarcasm, and Edward's words were enough to bring her back to the moment and away from the board in the dining room. 'Who should I ask for? And what should I say?' she asked PC Atkinson.

'Inspector Painter,' he said. 'Try his home telephone number first. Even he doesn't stay at the station all night. Tell him that Mr Elliot and I have been attacked. He'll know what to do.'

Rain lashed against the windows in Sir Charles' office. Nell flicked the light switch. A small card sat on the blotter on the desk. It was the same as the card she had been given. She picked it up and read the words. There was Inspector Painter's name, along with two telephone numbers. The printed number was accompanied by the word *Station*. And then there was the handwritten number with the word *Home*. Nell grabbed the telephone handset and dialled the second number.

The line rang. Once. Twice. She held the telephone receiver between her chin and shoulder and looked about the room. She was drawn to the painting of the view from Primrose Hill and an image of the sullen man she had seen standing there at their first meeting. She became aware of a voice answering the call.

'Hello,' it said.

She pictured a small parlour. Intimate and homely. He was standing in his house, the rain lashing against the windows there too, a table with a cup of tea on a saucer. He had been reading a book.

'Who's there?' he asked.

'Is that Inspector Painter?' Nell asked as though any confirmation were required.

'Miss Potter,' Painter said with no prompting. 'What is it? What's happened?'

'I think you should come,' she said.

THIRTY-ONE

The long-cased clock out in the hall struck midnight and Nell sat with Alice and Charlotte at a small table in the morning room. The billiard room was out of bounds, filled as it was with police officers.

Within twenty minutes of Nell's telephone call, four cars had arrived filled with constables and sergeants, but just the one inspector. Since Paul had finished tending to Elliot and PC Atkinson, he and Wilco had been sent to sit in the library.

'Are you all right?' Charlotte said, reaching for Nell's hands.

'I'm fine, thank you.'

'You look awfully distracted. What with that fright from the spirit board earlier and now poor Elliot and the police constable.' As she held Nell's hand, she craned past her to look at the closed door. 'Just what do you think is going on out there?'

Alice poured two cups of tea from the pot Mrs Randal had been allowed to bring up for them. 'Here,' she said spooning sugar into each cup and pushing them towards Nell and Charlotte. 'We've all had a shock.'

'I should think that Elliot and that poor constable had more of a shock than us,' Charlotte said, letting go of Nell's hand and stirring her tea. 'Do you think Mrs Randal was able to take them some tea. They looked like they needed it.'

'I'm sure she did,' Alice said, and took a sip from her cup. 'And the children and Bertie, and Audrey and Rosemary are safe in the kitchen, with Mrs Randal and Mary.'

'Do they have a police constable with them?' Nell asked.

'Two,' Alice said. 'The children are having a fine time trying on their helmets.'

Nell watched Alice's face as she sipped her tea again. She was putting on a brave face, trying to calm Nell and Charlotte while her eyes constantly flicked from the door to the bell beside the fireplace. No doubt she wanted to run from the room and fly down the stairs to her children or summon them to come to her by pulling the cord. Instead, she sat dutifully with Nell and Charlotte as they had been instructed to do by the police sergeant, separated from the men and the scene in the ballroom so that they might be questioned later about the events of the evening leading up to the discovery of Elliot and PC Atkinson.

Every gesture, every twitch of her muscles screamed that Alice wanted to get to her children. She must be terrified of what could have happened to them, Nell thought, and what might happen in the future with a man on the loose who was prepared to attack a constable.

'I don't know why the police are making us stay in here,' Charlotte said. 'And that spirit board was useless, wasn't it? Rather than try to scare Nell with nonsense, it might have warned us that there were two men tied up in the ballroom!'

'Do you think they will be all right?' Alice asked.

'They'll be fine,' Charlotte said in the pragmatic way she always talked about illness or injury. 'They took a few blows but nothing a cold compress or two won't sort out. Paul is sure they will recover quickly.'

There came a knock at the door. It opened and a police

sergeant in uniform stood in the doorway. 'Is it convenient if I come in and speak to you ladies?' he asked.

Alice nodded. 'Please.'

He entered the room and closed the door behind him.

'You've kept us waiting long enough,' Charlotte said.

Without waiting to be invited, the sergeant took a seat at the table. Alice poured a cup of tea and handed it to him.

'Much obliged,' he said as he spooned in three sugars.

Nell sat with her hands in her lap while Alice and Charlotte answered the sergeant's questions. Every so often, he would lick the tip of his pencil before placing it to his notepad again. Nell did not know what she should say. She could hardly sit there mute. But likewise, she had promised Edward and Painter that she would say nothing to anyone. Did that include the police? To avoid suspicion, she intermittently chucked her two-penn'orth into the responses that Alice and Charlotte gave.

They had all spent the day together, so it was quite easy to simply corroborate their version of events. To explain her two absences, she said that she had gone to sit in the conservatory to listen to the rain. And, when she had really been eavesdropping on Edward's telephone conversation, she said she had gone to powder her nose. The sergeant coughed at that little detail but dutifully added a note to his pad. He raised his eyebrow when they explained the game on the spirit board, although none of them mentioned Nell's funny turn, for which she was grateful.

Charlotte made her joke again that it must be a faulty spirit board since it had failed to alert them to two men in the ballroom. This seemed enough to satisfy the sergeant that he had heard enough about the game.

When it came to the question of how Bertie and Tommy had known to go to the ballroom, Alice was the first to respond.

'They heard a noise,' she said.

Nell looked at Alice and saw her eye twitch.

'What sort of noise?' the sergeant asked.

'A muffled noise.'

'Hmnnn.' The sergeant made another note before moving on to ask what each of them had seen through the open doors.

Nell continued to look at Alice. She had told a lie. To a police sergeant. Alice had been standing next to her at the bottom of the stairs. They had witnessed the same thing at the same time. It had been as if Bertie and Tommy had sensed something rather than heard it. There had been no noise, muffled or otherwise. If there had been, Nell would have heard it, too. Hadn't Tommy told Bertie to 'feel it'? And immediately after that, Bertie had run to the ballroom in search of the key. Hadn't Alice intervened in the dining room just prior, reassuring Bertie that it was not his fault that he had not been there to guide Tommy?

Nell continued to stare at Alice's face. Alice was telling a lie to protect her son and the older boy in her care. But what was the truth? What was it about Bertie and Tommy's behaviour that had to be hidden? Why couldn't Alice simply say that the boys had seemed to sense it? Was Alice in on the attack on Elliot and PC Atkinson? Nell shook her head. Of course, she wasn't. Alice's lying had everything to do with protecting two boys and nothing to do with the crime that had taken place.

'And do you have anything else to add, Miss Potter?' the sergeant asked.

Alice turned to Nell and gave just a little shake of her head.

'No, nothing,' Nell said.

The sergeant closed his notepad and said that the women would need to wait in the morning room until enquiries were complete. Charlotte objected; why should they be held separately to the men? The sergeant responded by closing the door on his way out.

Despite Charlotte's irritation, the three women waited. Every so often Alice looked at Nell. But they could not talk of

her lie in front of Charlotte. If Nell tackled it at all, it would
have to be in private.

Eventually a police constable pushed open the door and
said that they were free to leave the room.

'I should think so, too,' Charlotte said. 'This is our home.
We should be free to go wherever we please, whenever we
please.' She was still full of bluster when they emerged into the
hall where Edward rushed to Alice and Paul to Charlotte.
Wilco and Nell stood slightly apart.

'What has happened?' Alice asked.

'There was a break-in,' Edward said. 'The police said there
have been quite a few burglaries of houses in the area. Unfortunately, poor Elliot and PC Atkinson happened across the
burglar when he was up to no good.'

'Was anything stolen?' Charlotte asked.

Edward rubbed his temple. 'We can discuss that in a
minute,' he said. 'First, is everyone all right? And the children?'

'Everyone is fine,' Alice said, slipping her arm through
Edward's. 'But Elliot and the poor police constable. How are
they?'

Paul stepped in to answer. 'They took a pounding, but they
will be okay. They've got a few bruises and flesh wounds but
nothing that won't heal in a week or so.'

'Do they need me to see to them again?' Charlotte asked,
putting her arm through Paul's.

'No,' Paul smiled and gently patted her hand. 'Your tender
ministrations earlier did the trick. PC Atkinson has gone home
to his mother and Mrs Randal has made up a bed for Elliot in
the old men's quarters so that she and Mary might keep an eye
on him tonight.'

'Rogues and scoundrels,' Wilco said, shaking his head. His
slight amusement of earlier seemed to have morphed into fury,
no doubt fuelled by the police questioning and the realisation of
the seriousness of the situation. 'An Englishman's home is his

castle,' he said, as he paced up and down the hall. 'It should be sacrosanct. Some ne'er do well breaking in and taking what another man has worked so hard for...' He visibly shook as he spoke, and his cheeks turned the colour of claret. He came to a sudden stop. 'Ed, if you want me to, I could telephone my father. We could have an investigator here in the morning to look into this business. I'm sure the police around here are used to catching the odd poacher, but this is on a different level.'

'Thank you, but the investigation is in good hands,' Edward said. 'Inspector Painter was in the Metropolitan Police. He has dealt with some very serious cases in the past.'

'If you're sure,' Wilco said.

'I am. Before he left, Inspector Painter made sure to instruct the six constables on duty to patrol each door to the house. I shall be speaking to him again tomorrow to get an update.'

'But, Edward,' Charlotte said. 'You haven't told us what was stolen.'

Edward ran his fingers through his fringe. 'Why not wait until the morning. We've all had enough excitement for one night.'

Charlotte let her arm fall from Paul's and took a step towards Edward. 'What is it?' she demanded. 'What are you not telling me?

'I'm sure it's nothing—' Alice started. She was silenced when Charlotte took another step towards Edward so that she was practically standing on his shoes.

'What is it?' Charlotte demanded again.

'Inspector Painter thinks that the burglar may have been keeping a watch on the house for some time and they saw us store items in the ballroom while we were moving them to prepare the hallway. He wondered whether someone from the village might have told the wrong person, you know, after they came in to help clean the hallway before we put everything back to surprise Mother.'

'Don't be ridiculous,' Charlotte snapped. 'I would trust them all with my life. Nobody from the village is any part of this. And you can tell your precious Inspector Painter that, too.'

'It was just one line of enquiry—' Edward began.

'Then he can stop that right there,' Charlotte said. 'He's looking in the wrong place. Are there any other "lines of enquiry"?' she added rather sarcastically.

'I'm not sure. Probably. Yes, I should imagine so,' Edward said.

'Good. And now, will you please tell me what has been taken?'

'Really, this can wait to the morning,' Edward laughed awkwardly and ran his fingers through his fringe again. 'We're all tired.'

'Tell me!' Charlotte demanded.

Edward leant forward. His spectacles fell so that he had to push them back up the bridge of his nose. 'They took one or two of the Highland watercolours Mother is fond of...'

'And?'

'The golden eighteenth-century French clock.'

'And?'

'Isn't that enough?' Edward laughed awkwardly again.

'None of those things is important enough for you to try to keep it from me,' Charlotte said, frowning.

'Do you want me to tell Charlotte?' Paul asked.

Edward removed his spectacles and rubbed his eyes before replacing them. 'Thank you, but no. I'll explain. Charlotte, it's... it's...' He took a deep breath. 'They've taken the portrait of Tom.'

Charlotte held her hand to her mouth. She shook her head as though she would not believe it. Tears slipped down her cheeks. Paul put his arms around her.

'But that's all Mother has left of Tom,' Charlotte sobbed.

'It's all any of us has left of him.' She turned and hid her face in Paul's lapel.

'I'm sorry,' Edward said, placing a hand on his sister's shoulder.

'You've no call to apologise,' Wilco said. 'It's hardly your fault that bounder broke in and stole your family's possessions.'

Nell glanced at Edward's face; the guilt was plain to see. To the others, it no doubt looked like sorrow, but, to Nell, the dark circles beneath Edward's eyes and the lines etched into his face screamed just one thing. Guilt. Whatever he had been plotting with Painter had gone horribly wrong, leaving two men injured and that most precious of items stolen.

Alice gently prised Charlotte from Paul. She turned her around and allowed Charlotte to cling to her. 'I'll see her upstairs,' Alice said. 'Will you be all right to make your own way up, Nell?'

'Yes, I'm fine,' Nell said. She wasn't ready for bed yet. There were questions she wanted answers to before she could even contemplate sleep. And the last place she wanted to be, in that moment, was alone with just her thoughts for company.

'Well,' Wilco said, 'I think I'll turn in.'

Paul too made his way up the stairs, having been asked to stay at Hill House for the time being so that everyone involved in the unfortunate affair was in one place, should the police need to speak to them again.

As soon as the two men had departed, Edward said, 'I think I'll do a round of the house to make sure all the doors are locked and there's a police constable at each.' He set off towards the corridor beneath the stairs, walking quickly but not quick enough to escape Nell. She followed him as he checked the outside door in the luggage room. Through the panes of glass, Nell could see a police constable stationed outside.

'May I have a word?' Nell said.

'Can't it wait? I am rather busy,' Edward said.

'No, Edward, it cannot wait.' There was nobody else around to hear but just in case, Nell leant in close. 'I heard you on the telephone to Inspector Painter earlier.'

Edward stopped. His shoulders drew back. He marched past her up the corridor. But Nell was never more than a single footstep behind him.

THIRTY-TWO

Edward paced along the carpet behind Sir Charles' desk. 'What have I done?' he said. 'What have I done?'

'What has been going on here today?' Nell said with a ferocity she had not quite intended.

Edward removed his spectacles and rubbed his face. When he replaced them, Nell could see through the thick glass that his eyes were bloodshot.

'None of this was meant to happen,' he said. 'It had all been arranged.'

On top of the bureau behind Edward was a drinks tray. Nell eased past him and took up a crystal decanter. She removed the stopper, poured large slugs of brandy into two glasses, and placed the decanter on the desk. Making Edward sit in the chair behind the desk, she handed him one of the glasses. She sat in the chair opposite him.

'Drink it,' she commanded.

Edward lifted the glass to his lips. With a swift flick of his head, he knocked the drink back in one. Nell copied him and refilled the glasses as the thick hot liquid coated her throat and set her chest ablaze.

Edward removed his spectacles again and placed them on the blotter. He rested his elbows on the desk and clasped his forehead. 'I'm so sorry,' he said quietly. 'I'm so, so sorry.' He gripped his hair so that his fringe was hidden in his fists.

'You got us out of the house today to flush someone out. Who, Edward? Who is behind these thefts?'

'Nobody knows for sure,' he said, still clutching his fringe, still not looking at Nell.

'But you made sure the house was empty today in the hope that the burglar would target Hill House?'

Edward nodded. 'A telephone call came to say that another house had been burgled, so the police officers left.'

'Except for PC Atkinson.'

Edward nodded.

'And let me guess,' Nell said. 'The other house hadn't been burgled.'

Edward shook his head.

'So it was a trick, and your plan backfired. PC Atkinson and Elliot were left alone. And the burglar attacked them and broke into the house.'

Edward nodded. 'I should never have agreed to such a plan. Did you see them, Nell? PC Atkinson and Elliot. They were beaten black and blue. It's my fault.'

Faced with Edward's painful contrition, Nell softened a touch. 'No, Edward, it's not your fault. Whoever is behind these burglaries is clearly a very clever crook who knew just what to do to best you all.'

Edward laughed sadly. 'If only you knew the half of it.'

'What do you mean?'

Edward looked up. He smiled sadly. 'You can wheedle most things out of me, Nell. But not that.'

'Not what? The identity of who is behind the crimes?'

Edward looked at her with his bloodshot eyes. 'I can say no more.'

'But Edward—'

'No, Nell,' he responded, and Nell was surprised at the force in his voice. 'Too many people have been hurt already. I will not risk you too.'

Nell gave up. She had pushed it as far as she could for one night.

Edward picked up his spectacles and wiped the lenses on his shirt. He hooked the wires over his ears. 'I'm sorry about everything else tonight,' he said. 'I should never have let Wilco bring that stupid bloody game into the house.'

'Don't mention it,' she said. 'It's been a long day and I over-reacted. I'm fine now, really.'

'Are you sure?'

'Yes, Edward, I'm fine. Please don't worry yourself about me. I think I'll go up to bed now. You look like you could do with your sleep. too.'

'I'll just do one more circuit of the downstairs before I turn in,' he said. 'And Nell, I don't want to alarm you but please do be on your guard for the remainder of your visit. I know how you like to wander the grounds but promise me that you will take care and not take any unnecessary risks.'

Nell crossed her fingers in her lap. 'I promise,' she said.

Edward accompanied Nell into the hallway and bid her goodnight at the bottom of the stairs. Nell paused halfway up and looked back at Edward. He was standing in the vestibule with his hand on the lock and his forehead pressed to the great front door. His shoulders rose and fell. If the weight of a single strand of straw were added to that slight frame Nell felt sure it would crumble.

THIRTY-THREE

The rain outside had subsided so that a fresher breeze blew in through the open windows. For the first time in her visit, Nell had to crawl beneath the eiderdown. The weight of the covering on her body was comforting somehow. But there was nothing to provide relief from the maelstrom in her head. It spun around and around like an out-of-control zoetrope. So many unwelcome images leapt and danced before her eyes: the waking dreams; the seaside fortune teller; the pointer flying across the spirit board; Tommy and Bertie in some kind of symbiotic relationship, not only with each other but with this house; Alice's complicity in the boys' strange behaviour; Tommy's message that this house was helping her; poor PC Atkinson and Elliot bruised and beaten in the ballroom.

In the conservatory, Paul had reassured her that she was not mad when she spoke of her waking dreams. But that was before the sprit board. What would he say now if she ran to him and told him everything? Would he still say she was quite sane? The only crumb of hope that she was able to cling to was that these things had not all been hallucinations or dreams. Other people had witnessed at least some of the strange occurrences this evening. Perhaps she had somehow controlled the board; hadn't Paul said that the human brain was capable of far more than it was given credit for?

Nell turned on to her side and pulled the eiderdown to her chin. However inexplicable and terrifying these experiences were – even the prospect that she might be losing her mind – they paled into insignificance when held up against her thoughts of Philip. Because she knew without a doubt that it was his name the spirit board had been intent on spelling out.

Philip.

Nell twisted the eiderdown in her fists. Nobody knew of his existence in her life. Not Charlotte, not her family, not any of her friends. She had tried so hard and for so long to consign her memories of him and their time together to a history, to a version of herself forever lost. In life, Philip had been her secret. In death, she wanted to keep him that way; to hold him close as only hers.

Philip.

He was the beginning, middle and end of everything that plagued her. It was not his fault. He had been innocent and blameless. It was she who was to blame. For everything.

How had that board known his name? And how cruel it had been for someone to tell Tommy to say that the house was bringing him to her to deliver a message that she should be loved again. Nothing and no one would ever bring him to her. She would not and could not be loved again.

Nell buried her face in the pillow to muffle her cries. The rain began to fall again, the wind howled outside the window and a sob wracked Nell's body.

When the clock down in the hall chimed three, Nell pushed away the eiderdown. She had lain there, listening to the chimes mark each hour since midnight. And every quarter and half hour since. When the chimes marked half past three, Nell slipped from the bed. Taking her robe from the bathroom door, she slipped it on, secured it at the waist and quietly let herself out of the bedroom and into the dark corridor.

By the moonlight from the glass dome high in the ceiling above the hall, Nell made her way along the corridor and down the stairs. The inner, wooden doors to the vestibule had been locked and bolted but the doors to the ballroom stood ajar. Nell could see that the curtains at the many doors and windows leading from the ballroom to the garden were pulled back so that the shadow of a police officer pacing outside elongated on the wooden dancefloor and fell on the boxes and furniture still piled in the room.

Nell let herself through the door at the very back of the hallway and felt her way along the walls of the narrow corridor, down the stone steps, her progress helped by the grooves worn into the stone by centuries of footsteps treading the same path. Just enough moonlight inched through the windows high in the wall of the basement kitchen for Nell to find a glass in a cupboard and fill it at the tap. Resting against the sink, she took a sip of the water. Up at ground level, the boots of a constable crunched through the gravel as he kept watch on this part of Hill House. Nell watched his feet disappear and reappear. Only a fool would believe that the police would deploy a presence such as this to protect a handful of vases and paintings.

Nell pushed away from the sink. Retracing her steps in the darkness, she arrived back in the hall. She paused at the foot of the stairs, almost tempted to look over her shoulder into the dining room. Almost, but not quite. Instead, she placed her hand on the banister and was about to ascend the stairs when a movement made her stop and look around. There was nothing and no one to be seen. 'You're hearing things,' she whispered beneath her breath. All was still. The movement would have been the shadow of the police constable outside the ballroom windows. Nell placed her bare foot on the bottom step. But as her sole sank into the carpet, a sound from behind made her look around again. A noise came from beside the fireplace. It sounded like something rolling across the tiled floor, like an upended milk bottle rolling along a front path. Nell peered into the darkness and watched as an object came into view. It was spherical and it rolled towards her before slowing and coming to a to a stop before the fireplace.

Nell looked over her shoulder. It was surely too late for Tommy to be out of bed and playing a trick. She stooped and prodded the object. It rocked but stayed in place. Picking it up, Nell held the object up to the scant moonlight. It was a ball. A glass ball. She twisted it to better take in the detail. The ball was decorated with leaves, berries and holly. It was a Christmas tree bauble. She stared at the bauble in her palms but before she could question why it had rolled across the floor in the middle of summer, a scent made her close her eyes and breathe in deeply. It was oily and rich and brought to mind a forest in the Highlands.

'I'm dreaming,' Nell said softly, her eyes still pressed shut. 'I'm imagining the smell of pine trees.'

A great heat sprang from beside her and an orange-yellow glow warmed her closed eyelids.

'It's not real,' she said, 'this isn't real.'

Her thought was accompanied by a sound like a log cracking as it fell through a grate and the sizzle of berries popping in the heat. Nell prised her eyes open. When she saw that the hall was in darkness, she sighed. But then a reflection materialised in the mirror above the fireplace. Behind her the panelling on the walls altered so that it was no longer shades of grey in the darkness. The very colour of the wood bloomed to a honey hue that shone in the light now blazing from so many electric lights. Paintings appeared on every panel and statues and vases sat on plinths in the alcoves around the hall. As Nell watched, the hall around the mirror itself came to life: a garland of holly unfurled above the fireplace, its lush greenness peppered with the bright red berries she had heard popping in the heat from the blazing fire that she had felt on her closed eyelids. A Christmas tree now stood beside the fireplace, its candles lit and the most exquisite glass baubles adorning its branches. Colour and life spread as though a great brush had been taken up and was painting life into the hall. It happened so quickly that Nell could not keep up. She blinked and, when she opened her eyes, she was in the midst of a throng of people. They were not mere reflections in the mirror; they were all around her. The heat of so many bodies and the heady scent of expensive perfumes and colognes made her take a step back. There was barely an inch of tiled floor visible beneath the feet of the throng of men in tails and women in their finest gowns and tiaras and dripping diamonds. Guests spilled into every room. Through the open dining room door, Nell saw a spectacular swan, carved in ice, in the very centre of the table. Footmen in their finest livery served vast roasts and moved in and out of every room, skilfully navigating the crush as they offered trays of drinks, while guests helped themselves to salads and dainties and ice creams that covered the table. A particularly important looking man at the front door announced each new arrival while maids in black dresses and crisp white aprons waited to take away coats and hats.

All around Nell, voices were raised in merriment, there was laughter and the chink of champagne saucers. But not a single one of the many people in the hall at Hill House paid her any mind. No one appeared to be aware of the presence of a barefoot woman in their midst, dressed in nothing but a bathrobe. Nell secured the robe a little tighter around her waist. They couldn't see her, because there wasn't really a Christmas tree or a sculptured swan or footmen wearing the gold braided livery she had found up in the lumber room. She closed her eyes and squeezed them tight. It did nothing to quiet the chatter and laughter.

The sound of a band struck up and it was all Nell could do to stop from being carried on the wave of people moving from the hall into the ballroom. She pressed against the wall beside the Christmas tree to let them pass. As the music played and the crowd dispersed still further, Nell prised herself away from the wall. A gentleman stood beside the bannister; he took a case from the inside pocket of his jacket. As he removed a cigar, Nell moved towards him. He didn't move. Didn't flinch. She reached to tap him on the shoulder. He didn't acknowledge her presence at all. With the cigar clenched between his teeth, he slipped the case back inside his pocket. Taking out a box of matches, he struck one. Nell blew as hard as she could, trying to extinguish the tiny flame. The man sucked on the cigar, drawing the flame to it until the tip glowed. He threw the spent match into the fire on his way to the ballroom. As he left, he exhaled, leaving a trail of smoke behind. Nell coughed. She tried to touch one of the decorations on the tree. Another glass ball, this time painted silver and decorated with a golden star. As hard as she tried, her hand would not grasp it. How could any of this be? She was affected by what these people did but could not affect them. She was no character from a Dickens story observing a Christmas past. This was not her past. It was a dream summoned from her imagination and there was no helpful ghost to explain what she should make of it. What could she possibly learn from a history that was not hers? Nell turned to run up the stairs to her room, to fall into bed to make this dream go away, but found her path blocked.

Up on the landing, a woman emerged from the door leading to the stone steps. Coming to the head of the stairs, she paused. The look on her face as she descended seemed to Nell to be one of confusion. Nell took in other details of the woman as she

made her way slowly down. She wore a dress of the deepest
blue with a pearl necklace at her throat. To Nell's eyes, the
dress seemed rather old-fashioned, although it fitted the woman
in every way. As she grew closer, Nell saw that she had been
styled to perfection but in an understated way, with the most
delicate of rouge kissing her cheeks and a line of kohl accentu-
ating her eyes. The woman paused at the bottom of the stairs,
with Nell not more than three feet away. Nell stared at the side
of the woman's face. She was familiar. But this finery was not.
Slowly the woman's face began to make sense. Nell had seen
her on a different day. Dressed in outside clothes, her cheeks
ruddy from the cold. She had seen her in the stable, talking to
the man. This woman in the midnight blue dress was the
woman from her waking dreams.

'Please,' Nell tried. 'Who are you. Why am I here?'

The woman did not hear. She turned to the ballroom,
making her way towards someone waving at her through the
doors. Nell followed close behind. The sight that met Nell as
they crossed the threshold made the breath catch in her throat.
Hundreds of candles glistened in the two vast chandeliers above
the couples packing the dancefloor. Light from the crystal
pendants sparkled in the mirrors lining the walls. At the far end
of the room, the band sat before a backdrop painted to resemble
a palace of ice and each of the blue curtains at the windows and
doors had been decorated with lengths of crystal pendants
threaded together, giving the illusion of icicles.

The woman stopped to speak to someone, and Nell realised
she was unable to hear distinct conversation. It was as though
the sound of the band and the general din of the party guests
drowned out any individual noise. She leant in closer to the
conversation. The woman was speaking to an even younger
woman. It took a moment, but Nell recognised the blonde hair,
the wide blue eyes and the upturned nose. It was Charlotte! A
younger version of her friend, at least a decade younger than the

Charlotte Nell now knew, and a version of Charlotte only just past the cusp of womanhood. Charlotte laughed openly and joyfully with the girl beside her, and they spoke to the woman until a horde of young men descended on Charlotte and her friend, grasping for their dance cards.

The band struck up another tune and the woman retreated to the hall with Nell following her. The woman came to a stop and looked up the stairs as though she might leave the party. Any chance of a departure disappeared when a familiar-looking man approached her from behind. Before he spoke, he took a deep breath as though summoning courage. When he spoke, the woman closed her eyes and dipped her head before turning to him. Nell looked from one to the other as the man took a dance card from his breast pocket and secured it with a ribbon at the woman's wrist. He held her hand for longer than was necessary and he pressed his thumb into her palm. The look in their eyes was full of love. But sadness too. The moment between them broke when the approach of another woman made a furrow appear between the man's eyebrows and the woman snatched her hand from his grasp as though his touch had been wrong. Nell had heard not a single word spoken but could tell so much simply from the intimacy of a shared look and physical contact.

She turned to see who had broken such a perfect moment, but found she was no longer in the hall. She was in the ballroom where the band had struck up the Blue Danube. She breathed a sigh of relief to see the man accompany the woman in blue to the dancefloor. He closed his eyes as he took her hand and pressed his palm to the bare skin of her back. They began to dance, the woman constantly stepping on the man's feet as she lost time. He seemed not to notice and held and guided her, so they were equal partners in their waltz. They spoke as they danced. And it seemed that in that moment they were alone in the room. An island of just two. Nell watched the man's fingers move as he pressed them against the woman's skin. She watched the woman close her eyes as she rested against his shoulder. It was as though they were attempting to soak in the essence of each other, as if each second together was as precious as a lifetime. The dance ended. Everyone clapped and Nell lost sight of the couple. When she saw them next, they had parted. The man led another woman in a scarlet dress to the floor. They began to dance to some sort of Scottish jig. The woman in blue stood beside Nell and watched them. The look on her face was one of loss. Of love. Of devastation. Nell wanted to run to the man to tell him that he was needed. The woman began to walk away, and Nell looked desperately to the dancefloor, willing the man to come. With her back to him, the woman could not see how the man stared past his dance partner to her. 'You should be together.' Nell said to the woman. 'Look at him. See how he looks at you.' She reached to touch the woman's arm, but her hand made contact only with the air. The woman took a step away and Nell became aware of another woman. She was older, with an exotically patterned gown, dignified and standing upright. Unlike the other party guests, she was not watching the dancefloor, she was looking directly at Nell. Nell was sure she made eye contact just before she nodded, as though in recognition.

'Mrs Hart!' Nell called, but as she took a step towards the older woman, the sensation of a dark curtain falling stopped her short. All colour, music, and movement evaporated. Nell was no longer in the ballroom in the midst of a party but standing before the mirror in the dark hall, the world around her once again shades of grey. Her reflection stared back at her, and she suddenly knew. The couple she had just watched in their most intimate moment were the woman from the mirror and Mr Townley!

Grabbing the bottom of her robe, Nell ran up the stairs, let herself into her bedroom, and stood with her back to the door. It had all been a dream. Hadn't it? Feeling the weight of something on her hip, she slipped her hand inside the pocket of her robe and pulled out an object. She held it up to the moonlight. It was a Christmas bauble. Not the holly decorated bauble that had rolled across the floor of the dark hall. But the silver bauble with a golden star.

THIRTY-FOUR

28TH JULY 1924

Nell lay in bed, staring up at the ceiling. Somewhere in the distance a cockerel crowed. Outside, the final vestiges of night were on the verge of giving way to the new day. She listened for any other noise. The house was silent.

Lying awake in the wee small hours, she had made up her mind to leave the house at first light. She had to escape, if only for a few hours. Some time alone. No thoughts. No people. No...anything. Paul had said the human brain was capable of more than it was given credit for, including hallucinations. And he should know.

Nell slipped from bed, dressed quickly, and pulled back the curtain to look down at the drive. The police constable guarding the front of the house appeared from beneath the portico and looked like he was setting off for the gates. Letting herself out of the room, Nell crept down the stairs and across the hall. She carefully turned each lock, pushed open the front door and closed it softly behind her. The police constable was halfway to the gates and Nell kept one eye on him as she turned right onto the path before the house, heading for a part of Hill House land she had yet to explore.

Leaving the path, Nell picked her way down the steep dark lane with a ditch on one side and a fence on the other. She pulled her collar a little tighter around her neck as she focused on putting one foot in front of the other on the rough path, carefully stepping from one jagged stone to the next and avoiding the mud, which seemed intent on catching her off guard. The rain overnight had made the stones slippery and the mud wet. The last thing she needed was to go head over heels and end up in a heap at the bottom of the ditch.

She paused to check that she was still alone. The only eyes watching her were those of the songbirds overhead, and those belonging to the sheep in the field running parallel to the lane.

Coming to the end of the lane, Nell passed through a gate in the stone wall and closed it securely behind her. Beyond the gate and wall was a thicket of trees, full of their summer leaves. She turned back to look up at the house. It stood grey against the early morning sky. Not even the slightest hint of movement. She viewed Hill House and its surrounding land through the frame of a perfect square of wire fence sitting atop the wall. A few droplets of early morning dew clung to the wire, glistening in the pale light of the morning that was about to break. Across the valley, a strip of peachy light appeared above the haze of clouds. Nell became aware of a smell. Not unpleasant. More... familiar. It was the smell of summer days after a rain shower, when she would venture to the back of Father's garden to play with the water that had collected in the broken plant pots and hunt for worms tempted out of the ground by the thud of the falling rain. On one of those days, she had decided to climb the tallest tree at the back of the garden, out of sight of the house and to escape her mother telling her friends why she had dismissed Mrs Nevin. Mother had revelled in the fact that she had uncovered the thief who had stolen her silver Apostle spoons. It was impossible to trust anyone these days, wasn't it? Even her daily who had been with her for almost eight years!

Trying to climb to the highest branch, Nell had lost her footing on the slippery bark, tumbled to the ground, and hit her head on the way down. The doctor had been called and Nell cried out for Mrs Nevin. But no attempt was made to contact the disgraced former employee.

Nell rubbed the scar on the side of her face. It had faded with time, but she could still feel it, rising from her skin. It was a permanent reminder that she had taken the spoons from Mother's sideboard to use as tiny spades to dig in the mud in the garden, before they tarnished, and she put them in the rubbish bin. Mother would never have forgiven her if she had found out and would have made her daughter relive the shame of her theft over and over and over. And Mrs Nevin knew that.

Nell picked up a stick and poked some leaves stuck in the wet mud.

Three geese flew overhead, their call honking around the valley. Above the hillside, the sun began to appear. Orange light reflected in the glass of the windows of Hill House. The fields were no longer a dim dark green. They burst out in pale greens, yellows, a ruddy blush like that on a ripe apple. More birds sang as they crossed the now pale blue sky, all hint of the grey of the previous night's storm chased away by the waking day.

Nell became aware of a crack of twigs behind her.

'Good morning, Miss Potter.'

Nell gasped, twisted around, lost her footing in the mud, and fell backwards. Painter was there to catch her before she could tip beyond the point of no return. Catching her from behind, he kept her on her feet. For a moment, they stood there, Nell steadying herself, Painter with his arms around her. Nell looked down at his hands clasping her stomach. Painter coughed. He took a step back and Nell watched his hands slip from her.

'Are you in the habit of going abroad alone at this hour?' he asked, a little officiously. Nell closed her eyes for a moment to both compose herself and form a response. Still facing away from him, she said, 'I'm not a criminal.'

'I didn't say you were.'

'And I am not a suspect?'

'You are not.'

Nell knew that Painter was well within his rights to question anyone who had been in the house last night and to explore the scene of a crime in any way he saw fit.

'It didn't go to plan, did it?' she said.

'What didn't go to plan?'

Nell was on the verge of saying she knew all about the seaside diversion and the plan to flush out the criminal that had gone wrong and had led to the attack on PC Atkinson and Elliot. But she knew that such a revelation would put Edward in a difficult position.

She couldn't help asking him though. 'Who is behind these crimes?'

'We're still investigating that.'

'But you have a suspicion. Is it somebody with a grudge against the Mandevilles?'

The tone of his voice changed ever so slightly. 'What makes you say that?'

'What they chose to steal. The clock and the small paintings would have been easy to carry off and have commercial value. There were plenty of other items that would have been easy to carry away. But the portrait of Edward and Charlotte's brother is life-sized, as I understand. And it's so personal. Why would a criminal take that?'

'We are still following up on lines of enquiry.'

There was something about the slight change of pitch of Painter's voice and his persistence in maintaining a generic response which indicated that she had touched on something.

'The Mandevilles and their home are the targets, aren't they?' Nell spun around to try to catch Painter unawares and to read his true answer in his face. But his face had a story of its own to tell. He was unshaven with the tell-tale shadow of at least a day's stubble. Dark circles made his eyes appear sunken. There was a smudge of dried mud across his right cheek. His clothes were crumpled and creased, his shoes caked in a thick layer of mud and leaves.

'Have you spent the night out here?' Nell asked. 'It was raining nearly all night.'

'Unfortunately, we can't choose the weather.'

'Surely one of your constables in some kind of Mackintosh cape could have watched the house for you.'

'There are some things you have to do yourself.'

If it was possible, he looked even thinner than when she had last seen him, his face gaunt. Nell experienced an over-whelming urge to take Painter to Mrs Randal's kitchen. To make him tea and eggs and bacon. Even to draw a bath to warm him after a night out in the rain.

Realising she had been staring at his face, Nell knew she had to say something. 'You're not going to tell me what you know about who is doing this to the Mandevilles, are you?' she said.

'No,' he said.

It was the answer Nell had wanted. It was confirmation that the Mandevilles were specific targets, but that Painter wouldn't tell her.

'I don't suppose you need the notes I've been keeping,' she said.

'Notes?' Painter said.

'You asked me to keep an eye on anything suspicious and I've been keeping notes.'

Nell was about to ask whether she should consign them to the wastepaper basket when she saw his eyes lock on something past her and up the hill. A muscle twitched in his cheek. Nell turned to see what he could see.

From their position down in the copse, it was possible to see part of the drive where a car was making its way slowly along the gravel. Painter pressed close to the wall and indicated for Nell to do the same. She joined him and looked up at the house. Painter leant in closer and whispered, 'Be very quiet, noise travels at this time of day.'

'It would be a bold burglar who drove up to the house in plain sight for all to see,' Nell said.

Painter put his finger to his lips.

Together, they watched the car come to a stop at the front of Hill House. The driver got out to open the back door. A person emerged from the back seat. They were too far away to tell who it was, other than it was likely to be a woman, since the person wore a dress and a long coat.

'Are the Mandevilles expecting a guest?' Painter asked.

'Not that I know of.'

The police constable guarding the front door approached the car. There appeared to be a small exchange before the constable returned to the front door, opened it, and stood aside to let the woman enter. The driver got back in the car and drove away.

'She must be known to the family,' Painter said. 'Otherwise, the constable wouldn't have let her in.'

'I can go and find out who she is,' Nell said, making to stand. Painter put his hand on her arm and held her.

'Don't always rush in, Miss Potter. You need to be more careful.'

Nell looked down at his hand, clasped around her arm. 'Just how dangerous is the person behind these crimes?' she asked.

For a moment it seemed as though Painter was about to give her another generic answer. Instead, he sighed and said, 'You are persistent, aren't you?'

'I just need to know what I am facing. What we are all facing.'

Painter sighed again. 'This goes no further.'

Nell nodded.

'I won't put a name to them, but the person I suspect is ruthless and powerful. And power in the wrong hands is even more dangerous than a gun or a knife.'

'But why is this person so against the Mandevilles? What could they possibly have done to deserve such treatment?'

'I am more concerned about what this person may do next.'

'What do you think they will do?'

Painter shook his head. 'I've said too much already. But please, Miss Potter, be very, very careful. If you see anything at all that alarms you or seems out of place, telephone me immediately. You still have my card, don't you?'

She nodded. It was tucked safely in her bag. As it had been since the moment he had handed it to her.

THIRTY-FIVE

Making her way back up the lane, Nell could sense Painter's eyes watching her. He had refused her offer of breakfast in the kitchen but had assured her that he would make his way home for a few hours' sleep and something to eat. Leaving him behind, Nell felt a bit vulnerable.

The police constable at the front door was surprised to see someone coming along the path. When Nell explained that she had slipped out when he was taking his turn toward the gate – which she guessed he wasn't supposed to do – he held the door open without question.

Nell wiped her muddy shoes vigorously on the mat in the vestibule. Inside the hall, all was quiet, the only sound the tick of the long-cased clock. Nell became aware of a scent. It was at once familiar and unfamiliar. It was a scent heavy with spice and jasmine. She looked around for a source but found none in the simple sprays of meadow flowers in glass vases on the mantelshelf. Slowly she began to connect the smell with memories. The scent was welcoming with pleasant associations. Then it came to her. It was the perfume of someone she liked very much. And just as she put a face to the scent, a voice said, 'Nell! What a delight it is to see you.'

Nell turned to the morning room to see a woman coming towards her, her arms outstretched.

'Mrs Hart!' Nell said as she found herself clasped in the woman's embrace and smothered in her spicy, warm perfume. Mrs Hart kissed her on both cheeks before stepping away. She kept hold of Nell's hands.

'Let me look at you,' Mrs Hart said, looking Nell up and down. 'Beautiful as always,' she said. 'Inside and out.'

Nell smiled. She was well aware that she must look like she had been dragged through a hedge. But it was Mrs Hart's way to see everyone with a different eye than anyone else. She had a unique way of looking at the world.

'You look wonderful, as always,' Nell said, admiring Mrs Hart's peacock-blue dress and the immaculate scarf at her neck, decorated with green and gold paisley. The only thing slightly amiss was her silver-grey hair. Pulled back from her face, it seemed to be held in place rather roughly, as though she had dressed in a hurry.

'Pish!' Mrs Hart said. 'I simply threw this dress on last night before jumping on the ferry.'

'But why are you here?' Nell asked. 'Aren't you supposed to be on the Isle of Wight?'

'I'd had enough of Cowes,' Mrs Hart said. 'You haven't met my brother's wife, have you? I adore Lady Mandeville but there is only so much holiday I can take in her company. I'm not being unkind, I'm sure she would say the same of me. Anyway, enough of that, tell me how the writing is coming along. Charlotte told me all about it on the telephone. Has Hill House provided any inspiration?'

It took a moment for Nell to realise that she hadn't given Prince Carlos and his femme fatale a thought in at least a day. 'It's going well,' she fibbed.

Mrs Hart's eyebrow lifted. 'Good,' she said, although Nell felt sure Mrs Hart had seen through her and read the truth. Mrs Hart looked into Nell's eyes and smiled. 'There's something else, isn't there?' As Nell tried to look down, Mrs Hart dipped so that she could still see into her eyes. 'There's something taking shape. You have a sparkle about you.' Mrs Hart led Nell to the door at the back of the hall. 'What I need is a cup of tea. I don't know what secret blend it is that Mrs Randal brews up, but I am yet to find another cup of tea to touch it.'

As Nell followed Mrs Hart through the door and down the stone steps, she wondered whether she should alert Mrs Hart to what had been happening at Hill House. But she was so unsure of what she was allowed to say to whom and what she was not to say to anyone, that she decided to keep her own counsel. It wasn't until they were at the kitchen door that it crossed Nell's mind that Mrs Hart hadn't even mentioned the police constable guarding the house. What on Earth did she think he was doing standing sentry beneath the portico?

They entered the kitchen to find Mrs Randal, Mary, Audrey and Rosemary all busy preparing breakfast. There was much curtsying and apologising for the pots still in the sink since they'd all been so tired after the trip to the seaside.

'Think nothing of it, Mrs Randal,' Mrs Hart said, sitting at the table.

Mrs Randal wiped her hands on a towel. 'Wouldn't you be more comfortable upstairs, Mrs Hart?' she asked.

'I'm led to believe that in the absence of Sir Charles and Lady Mandeville, things are a little less formal in the dining and refreshment arrangements.'

Mrs Randal hesitated before adding a little tremulously, 'Well yes, but...'

Mrs Hart smiled. 'My dear Mrs Randal,' she said. 'You are not getting anybody in trouble with your confession. I hear everything from my niece. You know how my darling Charlotte likes to talk. And if I had my way, we would have supper from trays on our laps and tea in the kitchen every morning and afternoon.'

Mrs Randal breathed a sigh of relief. 'Thank you, Mrs Hart.'

Mary placed a teacup and saucer before Mrs Hart.

'Oh, that will never do,' Mrs Hart said. She rose from her chair and began to take teacups and saucers from the shelf and place them on the table. 'We will all take tea together,' she said, retaking her seat. 'And I want to hear everything about these two darling creatures I see before me.'

Audrey and Rosemary cowered beside the dresser. With some gentle coaxing Mrs Hart managed to get the sisters to join her in sitting at the table. Mrs Randal and Mary made a pot of tea and put some bacon on to cook and Mrs Hart asked both girls some questions. She soon had them chatting away. Mrs Hart took the loaf Mrs Randal placed on the table and carved two large slices. She buttered them generously and added blobs of strawberry jam. She pushed the plates towards the girls. They looked from the bread to Mrs Randal. Mrs Randal nodded, and the girls fell on the bread, eating between smiles. Nell decided to help by pouring the tea and passing cups around the table.

In a short space of time, everyone in the kitchen knew all about Audrey and Rosemary's lives and their time in the orphanage following the death of their parents. Rosemary even went so far as to take the postcard of the donkeys from the pocket of her apron. 'Miss Daphne said I should have it for the night since we both loved the donkeys so.'

Rosemary slipped from her chair and stood beside Mrs Hart, who took great interest in Rosemary's story of the donkeys and the seaside and their ride on the train and the wonderful picnic. As she spoke, Mrs Hart put a reassuring arm around the girl's waist and pulled her close.

'And you bought the postcard for Daphne with the penny Mrs Mandeville gave to you?' Mrs Hart asked.

Rosemary nodded.

'What a precious girl you are. A lovely, wonderful generous little girl. I am so proud of you.' Mrs Hart planted a kiss on the girl's face and Rosemary beamed as brightly as the sun that now shone through the windows high in the basement walls.

'When you and Audrey are old enough, I hope you will consider coming to live here at Hill House with us to help a bit with our chores. How does that sound?'

Rosemary nodded enthusiastically.

'And you, Audrey?' Mrs Hart said. 'Would you like to come and live with us?'

'Would that be possible?' the older girl asked, sitting up straight with her hands in her lap. It was clear from the way Audrey behaved that the few years longer she had lived on the Earth had given her more reason than her sister to be suspicious of what the future might hold for them.

'I will make it possible,' Mrs Hart said. 'And if you need a reference from someone who has worked for us – just to be sure that we are not terrible ogres – you can ask Mary here. She has been with us since she was about your age.'

Audrey thought for a while. 'And Mary is now training to be a teacher too?' she asked.

Mrs Hart smiled. 'Indeed, she is. So, you see, special – sometimes even magical – things can happen when you come to stay at Hill House.'

Mrs Hart glanced at Nell. And Nell felt sure that in some way the statement was directed at her. Mrs Hart returned to chatting with the girls, leaving Nell to wonder what Mrs Hart knew. Nell shook her head. Mrs Hart simply wanted to help people. That was her nature. Charlotte had spoken of it many times and now she was witnessing Mrs Hart's generosity for herself. She had experienced it too when Mrs Hart visited

Charlotte in Cambridge and took them both out for the most magnificent teas and always insisted on taking them to a department store to buy them some trinket or other.

The name Leonora Hart had long held magic for Nell. She had heard it many years before she finally met the formidable woman or indeed, Charlotte. Leonora Hart had been a stalwart of the WSPU. While in training, Nell had often heard her revered for using her personal wealth to fund and further the cause. When they first met in a tearoom in Cambridge, Nell had felt too bashful to say to the exotic and marvellous Mrs Hart that she knew of her. But Charlotte had been keen to tell Nell of the direct action Mrs Hart had taken for the cause. Over late-night midnight feasts in their room, Charlotte had told Nell of the window smashing and demonstrations in which her aunt had participated. Mrs Hart had never said as much to her niece, but Charlotte had it on very good authority that her aunt had been in attendance at some of the pivotal meetings and actions.

Nell watched Mrs Hart with Audrey, Rosemary, Mary and Mrs Randal. She was different to so many of her class. She was gracious, with a clear sense of right and wrong and social justice. She didn't only speak about reform and parity between the classes, she lived it.

Mrs Hart was turned away from Nell, deep in a conversation with Audrey about the lessons Audrey favoured at school, when Nell felt something touch her hand. She looked down. Mrs Hart's hand was on hers, giving it a gentle pat.

Out in the hallway, a bell rang.

'The dining room,' Mary said jumping to her feet.

'I'll put the sausages and kippers on,' Mrs Randal said. 'You take up the tea and coffee, Mary. Audrey, Rosemary, wash your hands now, girls, and get that bread sliced and toasted. Be sure it's neat and thin, just like I showed you. We'll be sending no doorsteps upstairs in this house.'

Audrey leapt from her seat and Rosemary left Mrs Hart's

side. Both girls ran to the sink. Audrey turned the tap on and helped her little sister lather her hands.

'Get that soap under them nails,' Mrs Randal said as she pushed the sausages around the pan. 'Good and proper now. You could grow potatoes under there.'

'Is there anything we can do to help?' Mrs Hart asked.

Mrs Randal performed a little curtsy. 'Oh no, Mrs Hart,' she said. 'I shouldn't hear of it.'

'You are a well-oiled machine,' Mrs Hart said, taking in the activity around the kitchen: the boiling of kettles, the warming of tea pots and coffee pots, the spit and sizzle of pans. 'We are spare parts,' she said to Nell. 'In any case, it is time for me to face the music. What a surprise they will all have upstairs when I sit myself down for a plate of kippers with Audrey and Rosemary's toast!'

Together Nell and Mrs Hart took the stone steps up to the network of narrow corridors. As they emerged through the small door into the finery of the hallway, Nell felt she really must prepare Mrs Hart for what was about to come.

'Mrs Hart,' she began, 'you need to know what has been happening here—'

'I already do,' Mrs Hart said as they crossed the hall, heading for the dining room.

'How? You were only outside with the police constable for a few moments. That's not enough time to be told what has happened here over the last few days.'

'How do you know that I spoke to the police constable, Nell? Were you spying on me,' Mrs Hart said, sounding entertained rather than annoyed.

'Well... yes... not you exactly.'

Mrs Hart tapped her arm. 'I'm teasing. But rest easy, my dear, I am aware of everything.'

'How?'

'Ah, now that would be telling,' Mrs Hart said with a wink.

THIRTY-SIX

Mrs Hart swept into the dining room to gasps and much excitement. Nell followed in the wake of the great woman as Charlotte rushed to her aunt and embraced her. 'What are you doing here?' Charlotte all but squealed. 'Oh, how I have missed you, I must tell you everything that has been happening here,' Charlotte began. She was silenced by her aunt holding up her hand.

'Let me say "hello" to everybody first,' Mrs Hart said, making her way around the table as everyone rose from their chairs. 'Anthony,' Mrs Hart said to Wilco, 'it really has been too long. How is your mother?'

'Very well, thank you, Mrs Hart,' he said. For the first time since her arrival, Nell witnessed Wilco treat someone with deference. He even performed a small bow.

Next Mrs Hart took Paul's hands. 'My darling, Paul,' she said as he threw formality to the wind and kissed her on both cheeks. 'I don't think I have ever seen you look as well or as happy,' she said with a glint on her eye. 'Are you here on business or pleasure?'

'Both,' he said.

'My brother returns next week,' Mrs Hart said, 'if it is he that you need to speak to. Perhaps to ask a question?'

Nell saw a knowing glance pass between Paul and Mrs Hart.

Mrs Hart moved around the table to Edward and Nell watched as she gave him an extra-long embrace. He closed his eyes briefly and rested his chin on his aunt's shoulder. He reminded Nell of a small boy in need of consolation. Mrs Hart said something to him, and he nodded before stepping back.

Finally, Mrs Hart embraced Alice. They were closer to Nell than any of the other people around the breakfast table. As Mrs Hart embraced Alice, she said, 'Don't worry, my darling. I am home now. Your boys will be safe with me.'

Alice nodded and Nell thought she looked like she might cry. The dark circles beneath her eyes suggested she had not slept a wink.

'I will sort everything,' Mrs Hart said before kissing Alice on the cheek.

'So, the police came because—' Charlotte began.

Again, her aunt silenced her gently. 'Let me sit down, at least,' Mrs Hart said. Edward pulled out a chair for her. Mrs Hart placed a napkin in her lap and patted the empty chair beside her. Nell dutifully sat down, and everyone sat with her.

'Now, Charlotte,' Mrs Hart said. 'I'm aware of everything that has happened here while we have been away. Nell told me all about the dramas unfolding over tea in the kitchen earlier. She got up early to write and unfortunately for her was disturbed by my arrival. That's right, isn't it?' Mrs Hart said to Nell.

Nell nodded. What else was she to do? Call Mrs Hart a liar?

Despite her aunt saying she knew all, Charlotte took it upon herself to recall every detail of the previous day, from the trip to the seaside and the picnic to the game of cricket. Her story was temporarily broken by the arrival of breakfast, which Mary, Audrey and Rosemary placed on the sideboard. The family and their visitors helped themselves. Nell waited for everyone to finish filling their plates before looking over the food on offer. It all looked delicious, but she had no appetite. She took a scoop of scrambled eggs and a slice of toast and sat back at the table as Mrs Hart poured her a cup of coffee.

After eating a mere mouthful of bacon, Charlotte placed her fork on the plate and picked up the thread of her story. She told of the Punch and Judy show and the trip to Madame Zelda. Much to Nell's relief, Charlotte had so much to say that she raced through the events in that hut on the pier in her hurry to get to the events of the evening. When she finally arrived at the retelling of the spirit board, she slowed her pace. Wilco interjected to embellish the details. They were both so involved in their story that they failed to see Nell's discomfort. To them, they were simply recounting the events before coming to the climax of the story with the discovery of Elliot and PC Atkinson in the ballroom. But as they spoke of the spirit board and its apparent interest in Nell, Nell saw that Mrs Hart sat a little more upright in her chair. She dabbed her mouth with her napkin and placed it beside her plate, although she did not release it. Every so often, Nell noticed Mrs Hart's grip tighten, deepening the creases in the thick white cotton.

Finally, the story came to an end and Charlotte sat back in her chair.

Mrs Hart still held her napkin. 'And Elliot and the police constable are not seriously hurt?' she asked.

'No,' Paul said. 'I checked them over myself. They are bruised and sore, but they will heal quickly.'

'I spoke to Elliot this morning,' Edward said. 'He felt well enough to return to his room above the stable. He would rather not have any fuss.'

'Quite,' Mrs Hart said. Her voice was tight, and she still

gripped the napkin. 'And where is that "board" now?' She said the word "board" with such disdain that Nell felt it was a great effort for her to say it at all.

'In the billiard room,' Wilco said. 'Why, do you fancy a go this evening?'

The napkin tightened still further in Mrs Hart's hand. 'I want it to be burned. Edward, do you understand me,' she said without looking at her nephew.

'I say!' Wilco protested. His mouth moved as though to continue his protest. He was silenced when Mrs Hart slammed down her hand with the precision of an axe slicing through wood.

'I will not have that thing in my home. Am I understood?' Mrs Hart looked up directly at Wilco. He looked chastened and said nothing.

'I'll have Elliot see to it,' Edward said.

'No,' Mrs Hart said. 'I will talk to Elliot. Alice, I would like to see the children. I will join you in the nursery at eleven o'clock this morning.' She released her grip on the napkin, pushed back her chair, and got to her feet. 'If you'll excuse me.' Almost before everyone else could push back their chairs to rise, Mrs Hart left the room.

Everyone sat down. All eyes on the door.

'What was that all about?' Wilco said.

Paul pushed his plate away. 'What did I say last night about that spirit board? Some people are upset by it. We should never have agreed to messing with it.'

'That's all very well to say now,' Wilco said. 'But I'm going to be out of pocket when that thing goes up in flames.'

'I didn't even have the chance to tell her about Tom's portrait,' Charlotte said. 'But I suppose she knows since you told her everything, Nell.'

'Yes,' Nell said uncertainly. If she said anything else, she would reveal Mrs Hart as a liar. There was nothing for it, she would need to seek Mrs Hart out at some point to tell her about the thefts. Why had Mrs Hart told them that she had told her everything of the events of the evening?

'And was she terribly upset?' Charlotte asked.

'She was stoic,' Nell said.

'It's so odd to have police at every door,' Charlotte said. 'Edward, when are we to find out more about the police investigation?'

'I'm meeting Inspector Painter later today. I hope he will have more to tell me.'

'Because we need to get Tom's portrait back before Mother and Father return. I don't think Mother will be able to come to terms with—'

'Yes, Charlotte!' Edward said sharply. 'I do not need you to tell me how Mother will react.'

Charlotte rose to her feet. 'Do not talk to me like that, Edward. You are my brother, not my father. And you can't speak to me in any way you please.'

The chair scraped along the floor as Edward left his seat. He rested his fists on the table and leant forward. 'You think you know everything. You know nothing, little sister.'

Paul dropped his napkin on the table and got to his feet. 'We are all a little overwhelmed with what has happened,' he said calmly. 'Perhaps we all need to return to our rooms to calm down a little.'

Charlotte and Edward stared at each other, the heat of their anger visible in the flush rising in their cheeks.

'I wonder,' Wilco said, also standing, 'whether I shouldn't check the train timetable. It might be time for me to head back to London.'

Nell watched as Edward's head hung forward. 'As you like,' he said with all the energy of a boxer backed onto the ropes. Even Alice didn't jump in to try to smooth things over this time.

She stared at her husband as though willing him to tell her what to do.

Nell looked round the table. Besides Edward, she was the only one with a full picture of what was happening. The thefts and the attack on PC Atkinson and Elliot were part of a vendetta against the Mandevilles. It had begun with the man sneaking down around the stairs and then confronting her in the woods – possibly even before that. Whoever was behind this was escalating their behaviour. More than ever this family and their friends needed to pull together, to close ranks and show a united front so that this person could not come between them. On top of that, they also had that roof to think about.

'Wilco,' Nell said, 'I wonder, have you seen the lake at all while you've been here?'

Wilco shook his head. 'I don't think Edward has included that on any of his tours.'

'Paul, have you seen it? I hear that the trout are rather good.' As she said the words, Nell hoped that Paul would pick up on her subtext.

'Oh yes,' Paul said. 'It's a wonderful spot. Wilco, why don't you and I go and see if we can bag a trout for dinner? It's the perfect spot to spend a sunny afternoon. We could even take a flask of something and shelter beneath the trees down there.'

Wilco appeared to mull it over for a few moments. 'Why the devil not?' he said. 'It's too lovely a day to spend on a train in any case. I need to make a couple of telephone calls. What say we meet in the hall in half an hour?'

'Perfect,' Paul said.

With renewed enthusiasm, Wilco left.

'Is that what you intended?' Paul asked.

Nell smiled. 'It was. Thank you.'

'I may be a Yank,' he smiled, 'but I pride myself on picking up on subtleties sometimes. In any case, I could do with something to occupy the day. I doubt the police inspector will let us leave. There's no need to tell Wilco that; we can let him think that it was his idea to stay.'

Edward sat back in his chair. 'Thank you, Nell. Thank you, Paul. At least you two are keeping the end up. You are better advocates for Hill House than I can be at the moment. I'm just so tired.' He looked over the top of his glasses. 'And I'm sorry, Charlotte, for shouting at you.'

The apology was all Charlotte needed to rush to her brother's side. She slipped her arm around his shoulders and kissed him on the top of his head. 'I'm sorry too, Edward. And don't worry, I'm sure the police will find Tom's portrait. Mother and Father need never know that it was ever missing.'

'I wish I could share your certainty,' Edward said.

'Won't you join us at the lake?' Paul said. 'You could do with a spot of relaxation.'

Edward shook his head. 'I should stay here in case I am needed by the police.'

THIRTY-SEVEN

Nell paced up and down in her bedroom. With every circuit, she passed the desk. Her typewriter had given up calling out to her. The story of Prince Carlos and his femme fatale had slipped from her grasp like sand through the hands of time. The hallucinations featuring Mr Townley and the unknown woman – no doubt brought on by imagining him as the inspiration for her central character – were indulgent flights of fancy.

With everything happening at Hill House, it seemed ridiculous and frivolous to write a story, making up a crime to capture in the pages of a light-hearted novel. Crime was anything but light-hearted. It was terrifying and ended with real people being hurt.

Nell stopped and rested with her back to the wall. As the lives of the Mandevilles had been turned inside out, so had her world. She wasn't simply watching the world through a slit in a child's toy, static images in a zoetrope creating the illusion of movement. She was inside it, with an unseen hand spinning her, making her dance and lurch from one awful or impossible situation to the next. It was a hand she could not see and had no power to plead with to make it all stop so she could catch her breath.

Pulling back the curtain, Nell looked out of the open window. It was still early but already the warmth had returned to the day. The world was drying out. Soon, it would be as though the storm of the previous night had never taken place. Any trace of puddles on the paths would dry to nothing, it would be possible to sit on the wooden benches around the gardens without getting a wet behind and to walk in the grass with no fear of ruining the leather of one's shoes. But there was one place that would take longer to dry out. With no sun breaking through the canopy of trees, the carpet of leaves in the copse would stay damp and mud would suck at the soles of anyone who ventured through the gate.

Was he still down there, watching the house with no regard for his own health and welfare? His only concern that he protect the people up at Hill House from whoever was trying to harm them. What about him? Who in the world was protecting and caring for him?

Nell pictured Painter's face and his manner. Even when he was going about his business, he carried that sadness with him. It was there in his sombre suit, his slim face, his sad eyes. If she had the courage to ask him what had brought the darkness to him, would he answer?

THIRTY-EIGHT

The constable at the front door let Nell pass without question. Inspector Painter had instructed him that the residents of Hill House were free to leave the house, on the condition they stayed within the boundaries of its walls.

Knowing that Paul and Wilco had been directed to the far side of the lake as the best spot to find trout – and not wanting to encounter another living soul – Nell kept to the path and away from the wood. Just short of the boathouse, she slipped down the bank and sat on the sand. Kicking off her shoes, she rested her elbows on her knees, and cupped her head in her hands. The sun warmed the back of her neck, and she focused on the gentle shush of the waves lapping at the shore. Nell had no idea how long she had stayed in that position when she was roused by a soft voice.

'Hello there, Nell.'

She looked up. 'Hello,' she said.

'Do you mind?' Mr Townley pointed to a spot a little way along the shore. Nell nodded. He pinched his trousers just above the knees and sat against the grass on the slight hill, feet flat on the grass, his arms resting on his knees so that his hands hung lose.

Nell clutched her legs tighter and rested her chin on her knees, looking out over the lake.

'Penny for them,' Mr Townley said.

'They really aren't worth it,' Nell said.

There was a pause before Mr Townley said, 'I hear quite a lot happened last night. I saw Elliot this morning.'

'How is he?' Nell asked.

'More embarrassed than anything. He'll be fine.'

'You weren't working here yesterday?'

'No. My services weren't needed.' He paused again. 'And how are you today, Nell?'

It was Nell's turn to pause to think of how to frame what she was about to say. 'Tired,' she said. 'And it's rather your fault.'

'My fault?' Mr Townley said, a laugh in his voice.

'You've been plaguing my dreams.' She turned to look at him.

'I say,' he said with a smile. 'I've never thought of myself as the man of someone's dreams.'

Nell smiled and looked away. Mr Townley really was very handsome. But to her, he felt more like a brother than a lover.

'What role do I play in these dreams of yours?' he asked.

She shrugged. She had no desire to go into the details and it would only sound like gobbledygook. 'Various things. Dreams rarely make sense.'

'I'm glad to hear I'm so memorable!' Mr Townley said with a laugh again.

Nell looked out at the clear water lapping gently at the sand.

'I hear you had quite an evening too last night,' Mr Townley said.

A slim seam of white foam frothed on the ripples as they

moved back and forth over stones on the shore. Nell wanted to say that she was sure she didn't know what he meant. But the energy to say the words was not there.

'It's impossible to keep anything quiet in a house like this,' Mr Townley said.

'It was nothing,' Nell said, digging her chin into her knees.

'As I understand it, you were shaken by what came through on a spirit board.'

'I overreacted. I was tired. I don't believe in it anyway,' she said.

There was a pause. 'Ten years ago,' Mr Townley said, 'I would have called anyone mad if they had tried to convince me that something like a spirit board was anything but a game. But we can all have our minds changed. If you want to talk about what happened last night, I've been told I'm a good listener.'

Talk about it? How could she talk about any of it? She hadn't spoken to anyone of the events that the spirit board and recent events were intent on making her relive. Closing her eyes, Nell shook her head. But try as hard as she might, she could not shake away the image forming on the blank canvas behind her closed eyelids. The image of a man in an officer's uniform that had come to her as the board attempted to spell out his name. He was smiling as he always had whenever he saw her, his nose a little crooked from a schoolboy rugby tackle gone wrong, his habit of absent-mindedly whistling 'The Lark Ascending' so that the world was never silent with him in it. He had been there all day. Waiting for her to close her eyes. And he was there again.

Philip.

Never, in all the time she had known him, and in all the time since, had she uttered his name to anyone but him. Philip, an officer, and a king's messenger who frequently visited the War Office in London to collect orders to deliver to France. Funny. Kind and gentle. Philip, who loved music and dreamt of becoming a concert violinist and who teased her for being tone deaf. But, as he always said, opposites attract.

Tears began to form beneath Nell's closed eyelids.

'He sounds like quite a man,' Mr Townley said softly.

Nell opened her eyes and Philip disappeared. 'How... how did you know what I was thinking?' she said.

He was looking at her intently, kindly. 'I didn't. You were talking under your breath.'

Nell clutched her head. 'Was I? I'm going mad. I don't even know when I'm talking now.' She looked out across the lake.

'You lost him?' Mr Townley said.

Nell nodded.

'In the war?'

Nell nodded again.

'Nell,' Mr Townley said. 'I'm not a clever man, but I believe a Greek philosopher once said that the soul is immortal. It never dies. Imagine this, Nell. Imagine they are with you. Imagine they can see and hear you. Consider if the boot were on the other foot, you would want the object of your affection to live a full and whole life. The greatest gift we can give in the end is the freedom to move on. To give our blessing for the people we love to live again. Any man who loved you would not want you to be so sad.' His voice softened further. 'At the very end of our lives, all arguments and harsh words are forgotten. All we remember is the people we love and who love us.'

Nell wrapped her arms around herself. 'You can't know that,' she said. 'What if the last thing that the dying remember is the hurt we caused them?'

'You're seeing this from your point of view, rather than his,' Mr Townley said. 'Your love would have comforted him. Believe that. Those that leave don't want those left behind to grieve. They want you to remember the happy times. And they want you to live a full and happy life. Don't let grief destroy you, Nell,' Mr Townley said.

Nell bit down on her lip. She didn't want to weep in front of this man she hardly knew.

'If you remember just one thing, let it be that even if this is not the life you expected, it is the life you have. Take all the joy it has to give. It is not disloyal to live again. It's what your life is for.'

Nell looked down, focusing on the sand beneath her legs. 'I'm sorry,' she said and closed her eyes.

THIRTY-NINE

The sun was high in the sky when Nell came to, her head still resting on her knees. She looked around, but Mr Townley had gone. Collecting her shoes, Nell left the shore, climbed up the bank and walked along the path towards the house.

In the vestibule, she scratched the soles of her feet against the harsh mat to remove the grass and gravel clinging to her skin. The hall was uncharacteristically quiet, and she was able to make her way upstairs unseen.

Closing the bedroom door behind her, Nell let her shoes fall to the floor. She sank on to the bed, lay her head on the pillow and clasped her knees to her chest. After only a minute or so, she was disturbed by a knock at the door and sat up. Mary entered and placed a sandwich and glass of lemonade on the nightstand, saying quietly that Alice had arranged for lunch to be brought to her so that Nell could enjoy the peace and quiet and the opportunity to work on her book. Mary closed the door softly behind her and Nell sat up on the edge of the bed.

Outside the window, the scantest of white clouds crossed the pure blue sky. The leaves on the tops of the trees hardly moved at all in the still summer air. Outside, the world was as it should be, as it had always been, while the worlds inside this house and inside her mind were worlds she could not understand. She had spoken more today of her life than she had in years. But not everything. Because as compassionate as Mr Townley was, as kind and as caring, he would judge Nell as harshly as the world would if anybody ever found out her secret.

Nell glanced at her reflection in the mirror, sitting on the bed, her dress creased, her face tanned by the sun. Since she had not attempted to style her hair that morning, rather than sitting poker straight to her chin, it formed a mass of unruly waves. It was the hair that nature intended her to have.

The eyes looking back at her were the eyes she shared with the young woman who had spent too many hours in front of the mirror of a boarding house in West Kensington, preparing for a day of work at the War Office. Her hair had been longer then. Much longer, so that she had to roll it and pin it, before scrutinising it from every angle. They were the eyes that had tried to hide the smile whenever she thought of him and what he might think of her hair, her face, her figure. They were the eyes that recalled every detail of the pub where he had invited her to have a drink and every detail of the room in the hotel where they began to meet when he was in town. The eyes that remembered each detail of his body as he lay beside her – the fine hair in the centre of his chest and running down from his navel. The eyes that had watched his fingertips delicately brush her breasts and stroke her waist so that they longed for him to touch her more. The eyes that saw her fingers trace the line of his body before running through his hair and pulling him to her.

They were also the eyes that had stared at her after their final parting at Waterloo, pleading with the universe that she would be a better person – less vain, less self-absorbed – if only she might receive a letter from him to say that he forgave her for the harsh words she had propelled into the world by the secret she had revealed. She had waited weeks for him to reply to her letters, desperately apologising for how she had spoiled their parting, waiting for his forgiveness and his advice on how they should manage the situation in which they found themselves. She would do whatever he thought best. She just needed to know. She loved him so very much.

Every morning, she had listened for the rattle of the letterbox in the narrow hallway of the three-storey boarding house. Each room was crammed with beds to accommodate the young women answering the call of their country to do their duty. For a modest weekly sum, they had bed and board, taking all meals in the cramped parlour surrounded by their strict landlady's menagerie of birds and creatures, caught, killed and stuffed in the previous century and trapped beneath glass domes in perpetuity. The young women had made a sport of being first to the front door to collect the post, each waiting and praying for a letter from across The Channel. The house in West Kensington might have been a church, it had heard so many whispered words destined for the ears of God.

That morning in early September, Nell was on her way down the stairs when she heard the letterbox rattle. She ran along the hall with its familiar loose tiles and stooped to collect the post from the doormat. She flicked through the various envelopes and when she came to a bundle tied together with string, she dropped every other envelope to the floor. Stamped in black across the top envelope were the words: UNDELIV-ERED. RETURN TO SENDER. Another stamp read: NEXT OF KIN NOTIFIED. And then, written by hand, in red pencil: KILLED IN ACTION 17/8/18.

She was not his next of kin. She had never met his next of kin. She was a stranger to Philip as far as the world had been concerned. He had received none of her letters. He had been killed just a week after that final parting and before the first of her barrage of correspondence arrived. He had never heard her apologies, and she would never have his forgiveness. She had let out a cry which brought all the other young women to the hall. They knew that cry. They had heard it many, many times. And each time Nell had heard it before that day, she'd been wracked with guilt at the thought that she was glad it wasn't coming from her.

Nell's eyes stared back at her still. In the last six years, she had relived the moment she collapsed on the cold tiles in that hallway in West Kensington more times than she could count. She wished so many times that she could change what she had done and what she had said at that final parting as the guard's whistle shrieked and steam filled the air. But each time the outcome was the same. On that day, on the concourse of Waterloo Station, her words had been so harsh. She had watched as the smile in Philip's eyes changed to a look of confusion and uncertainty. Had he even heard her call after him as he sprinted to the platform to board his train to take him to France? Had he heard her call his name in her desperation to grab the final furious words she had said to him and swallow them back down? She had been angry and scared and had spoken from fear. She had sent him to France under an awful cloud. She had never had the chance to put it right. And never would.

Nell gripped the edge of the bed. Their relationship had been short and sudden, and it had always been a secret. Philip had said he would tell his parents after the war, and after their being together would no longer put an end to her important work at the War Office. He had been thrilled at the prospect of telling them; they would be sure to love her as much as he did. In her most desperate days after his death, she had travelled to his parents' house, to see where he had lived as a child. She had taken the train to Durham, to a beautiful house in the countryside. She had walked up the drive. A man came out. She knew he was Philip's father. He was so kind and looked so much like Philip. But when it came to it, she had said she was lost and looking for a different house. She had turned and run away. What would she have said to them? She would have tarnished his memory. Wasn't it enough that they had lost their only child?

Nell gripped the edge of the bed even tighter. All these memories came to her in the blink of an eye. And yet... and yet... she could not bear to recall the secret she had been so desperate to share with Philip, or that other day in the boarding house in West Kensington the month after the unread letters were returned to her. That warm autumnal day in early October, perfect in every way. When people had taken to the parks of London, feeling as though a cloud was lifting from the world. Could it be true that the tide of the war was turning and that it might soon be over? London had been charged with an energy, a sense of anticipation, the expectation of hope. It was in the air and on the lips of everyone who spoke. But for Nell, the events of that afternoon had seen her world reduced to a black pit of solitary pain. Alone in her room in the boarding house, she had been dragged down into the broken half-life that had been hers ever since.

Nell hid her face in her palms. Six years. Six years had passed and still the memory of that October afternoon drained the light from any day. Smashed her into pieces that it took weeks to reassemble. And then, only into the shadow of a person. The shadow of a person with no hope of a future.

Releasing her grip on the eiderdown, Nell curled into a ball on the bed, burying her head in her arms. Birds sang outside the window, voices murmured down on the drive and she lay there until the bread of the sandwich dried and the sun crossed its peak in the sky and slipped down into the afternoon.

FORTY

A knock at the door made Nell sit up slowly. When she didn't answer, there was another knock. 'I'm not decent,' she said.

'Miss, I've been sent to fetch you,' Mary said through the closed door. 'One of the constables says he needs to have a word with you.'

'Thank you, Mary. I'll be down in a minute.'

Nell steadied herself before pushing away from the bed. In the bathroom, she filled the sink with cold water. Wetting a flannel, she pressed it against her face. She watched the water drain down the plughole and glanced at her reflection in the mirror. The water had calmed the pink swell of her cheeks and eyes. She prepared her features in the way she always did to face another person. For the briefest moment she considered running a comb through her hair.

'I believe you want to see me,' Nell said to the constable waiting in the morning room.

The constable held his helmet in the crook of his arm. 'I've been asked to drive you into Northampton,' he said.

'Northampton?' Nell said. 'Why?'

'The order was telephoned through. That's all I know.'

'Where am I to go in Northampton?'

'I'm afraid I'm not at liberty to say. Would you come with me, please?'

Nell followed the constable out to a car. He opened the back door for her before getting in the front, starting the car, and driving away from the house. They drove past St Mary's church and out through the village, with its small pub and post office and houses around the village green, before heading into country lanes.

A few times, Nell pressed the constable on what he knew. Each time he answered that he was simply following orders and refused to reveal where he was taking her. Nell gave up asking. She rested her head against the seat. She hardly knew this version of herself who mutely agreed to accompany a constable to she knew not where. She was too tired to pursue the question and too tired to care.

After twenty minutes or so, the green of the countryside gave way to the redbrick of a town. They drove through the outskirts and gradually came to roads with more houses and businesses lining the pavements. They passed a sign or two, directing the way to the general hospital and the constable took one of the turnings. He slowed the car and drove through a set of gates but, instead of heading for the main hospital with its grand, tall buildings, he drove in the opposite direction until they came to a single storey building tucked away in the grounds. He brought the car to a stop and the door to the building opened. They were too close for Nell to see more than the bottom half of the person who had exited the building, but they wore a dark suit with a gold chain hooked over a button on their waistcoat, connected to the watch in their pocket.

The car door opened. 'Miss Potter,' Painter said. He held his hand out to her.

'I can manage. Thank you,' Nell said.

Painter retracted his hand.

Nell took a deep breath and stepped from the car. 'Why have you brought me here?' she asked.

'It's rather delicate. Please, Miss Potter, won't you follow me.' Painter held open the door for Nell to pass first into the building. Immediately she was hit with a stench so overpowering that it made her clamp her hand over her nose and mouth. The smell of solvent and chemicals cloyed at the air so that Nell could almost taste it.

Painter closed the door to the outside. 'I'm sorry,' he said. 'You get used to it. I didn't think to warn you.'

They were in a small anteroom, with white tiled walls, a striped wooden floor, and a single green painted door leading further into the building. A nurse sat at a desk in the corner and a huge vase of flowers sat on the desk: pink roses, violet buddleia, stems of honeysuckle and sweet peas. The highly perfumed flowers were no doubt intended to mask the harsh chemicals when in fact, they added a sickly overtone.

'I don't think I want to get used to it,' Nell said through closed fingers. 'What is this place?'

'A mortuary,' Painter said, his voice deadpan, no emotion whatsoever.

Nell briefly removed her hand before slamming it back over her mouth. She was instantly very awake. 'Why in heaven's name have you summoned me to a mortuary?'

Painter removed his hat and placed it on the desk. Using the heel of his hand, he forced his hair back from his face. 'There was an accident,' he said. 'Earlier today a man was found beside the railway tracks on the line leading out of Northampton. He died.'

'Oh, how awful,' Nell said. 'But I don't see what that has to do with me.'

'It's a remote part of the line that leads eventually to the station that serves Hill House. At first sight, it appears that he may have fallen from a railway bridge. He has no paperwork on his person or any means of identification. And we've had no reports of anybody missing locally.'

'I'm really sorry,' Nell said. 'But I still don't see how I can help.'

'You were troubled,' Painter said. 'By a stranger in the woods at Hill House a few days ago. That has been the only report of a stranger acting suspiciously in the area recently.'

'You think it might be him? And he might be the person responsible for beating the constable and Elliot?'

Painter rubbed his top lip with his fingertip. 'That would be getting a little ahead of ourselves. I would simply like to rule him out of our enquiries.'

'Or rule him in,' Nell said.

'Quite.' Painter rubbed his top lip again. 'So, would you be happy to help us make an identification?'

'You want me to look at him?' Nell said. 'But... but... I didn't see his face.' Her voice started to shake. 'I told you. I'm sorry, I can't help.'

Painter took a step closer to her. 'People remember more that they realise sometimes. When presented with evidence again it jogs their memory.'

'I'm not... I can't.' Nell backed away, the sickly-sweet scent of the flowers bringing her close to the edge of vomiting.

'He can't hurt you now. If, indeed, he is the man you saw in the wood.' Painter paused and Nell could feel him searching her face as she stared at the floor. 'It would help the investigation if we could make an identification. It could help us bring these crimes to an end.' Painter closed the distance between them again. 'I'll be with you the whole time.'

FORTY-ONE

The room was tiled in white. The floor, white. The walls, white. The only windows were narrow and high up, almost touching the tall, white-painted ceiling. It was cold, so very cold. Nell shivered as she stared at a point where one floor tile ended, and another began. She was aware of the table in the centre of the room. A man in a white coat standing beside the table was speaking to her. She had focused her attention on his face when Painter held the door open to let her into the room. The man in the white coat was short, very slender, with a horseshoe of dark hair and a thin moustache. He explained what would happen. He would pull back the sheet and she would look at the body. She should approach the table so she could see clearly. She should not be shocked by the appearance of the body. It had some bruising to the face but to all intents and purposes would look like it was asleep.

'You let me know when you're ready,' the man in the white coat said.

Nell still stared at the floor.

She felt a warmth beside her. A pair of black shoes stepped into view. 'Miss Potter,' Painter said. 'Are you ready?'

She nodded.

There was movement beside the table. The sound of soft leather soles on a hard surface. The sound of fabric moving.

Nell felt something touch her arm. 'Are you ready?' Painter asked. She nodded again and let him guide her to the table and to the white sheet draped down the sides. Everything inside Nell told her to turn and run from this room, from this building. But the Mandevilles needed her to do this. They were relying on her. She was the only one who might have seen something. Other than Rosemary. And she couldn't very well let a little girl take her place here as she was too scared to face whatever had to be faced.

Slowly Nell lifted her eyes, taking in the length of the sheet and the motionless shape beneath. She looked past the face, to the light brown hair swept to one side. It was rather long and overdue a trip to the barber. The head rested on a block. She looked down the side of the face. The position created by the block made the chin stick up slightly. Slowly she let her eyes travel up and the sight made her want to weep. Terrible purple-black bruises covered the man's face, and his cheeks were hollow, sunken. Scabbed-over wounds criss-crossed his face like so many black scars. She let her eyes travel to his eyes, to the closed lids, unnaturally still, no flutter as there would have been in sleep. Like his cheeks, his eyes were sunken, as though his face was collapsing in on itself. The force that had sustained it and given it shape and form had left. There was nothing. No life. Nell had never seen a body so still. So hollow. Whatever had made this man himself had gone.

'Miss Potter,' Painter said softly, 'do you recognise him?'

Nell let her eyes travel down to the shape beneath the sheet. The body was rather slender and quite short.

'How... how tall is... was... he?'

The man in the white coat consulted a clipboard. 'Five feet six,' he said.

Nell shook her head. 'It's not him.'

'Can you be sure of that?' Painter asked.

She nodded. 'He was taller than me. Much taller. And broader. He was a very big man. It's not him.'

'And his face?' Painter said. 'Do you recognise him?'

She shook her head, stifling the tears that welled in her eyes. 'I'm sorry.'

'You've nothing to be sorry for.' Painter nodded to the table and the man in the white coat lifted the sheet to cover the body. But not before Nell took another look at the bruised and battered face of death.

FORTY-TWO

It was Painter, not the constable who drove Nell back from the hospital. He drove slowly and she stared out through the windscreen, seeing the sallow and sunken face of the dead man everywhere. When they came to a stop, it took Nell a moment to realise. And when she did, she saw that they were not at Hill House but outside the pub on the green.

Painter got out and opened her door. She stepped out of the car, this time accepting Painter's hand by way of help. She followed him as he knocked on the door of the pub. It was opened by a woman wearing an apron and accompanied by the smell of cooking.

'Inspector Painter,' she said with a smile. 'We don't usually see you until much later in the day. I'm in the middle of making steak pie for tonight. Please, come in.'

She stepped aside to let them pass. Painter removed his hat and stooped beneath the low doorway. He went to a table and held out a chair for Nell to sit.

'I'll be just a moment,' he said and placed his hat on the table.

Nell looked around. She was in the snug of a country pub

with low ceilings, dark wooden beams, bare wooden floors, a large fireplace and horse-brasses decorating the walls. It smelled of beer, tobacco, and cooking.

Painter returned. He placed two glasses on the table and took a seat beside Nell.

He pushed one of the glasses towards her. 'Drink this,' he said.

She looked into the amber liquid wetting the bottom of a glass. 'I'm not thirsty,' she said.

'It's for the shock. Here.' Painter picked up the glass and placed it in her hands. She took a sip of the drink. It burned her tongue and her throat on the way down.

'Take another sip,' Painter said.

Nell mutely did as she was told.

'Better?' he asked.

Nell shrugged and placed the glass down on the table.

'You did a good thing back there,' Painter said. 'It's never easy, but it has to be done. I take it that was your first dead body.'

'And hopefully my last,' Nell said. 'I'm sorry,' she said, remembering herself. 'I make quips when I'm nervous.'

'It takes people in different ways,' Painter said, taking a sip of his drink. 'Some get upset. Others try to make light of it. There's nothing unusual in how you are reacting, given the circumstances.'

Nell took another sip of the drink. She waited for it to warm her chest before placing the glass back on the table. She swirled the brandy around and looked into the vortex. 'Have you seen many? Dead bodies?' She directed her question to the glass rather than to Painter.

'Too many,' Painter said.

Still looking into the glass, Nell said. 'Do they always look like that? Peaceful?'

'When they're in the mortuary, yes.'

'But not always?'

'No. Not always.'

Nell stared into the glass. 'Somebody loved him. That man belongs... belonged to someone... How do you ever get used to it?'

When Painter didn't respond, Nell looked up to find him staring into his glass. He picked up his drink and knocked the remainder back in one. 'Another?' he said, collecting both glasses. Without a single glance in her direction and without waiting for her to reply, he got up and made his way through to the bar.

Nell stared at a knot in the dark oak tabletop. A hand appeared and a drink was placed before her.

The feet of the chair beside her scraped across the floor. 'You don't,' Painter said. 'And you never should.' He cupped his glass and spoke to the liquid. 'Each death is a loss to someone. No matter what a person has done – even if he or she is a criminal – there is always an innocent person somewhere who will mourn their loss. A Mother. Father. Sister. Brother. Wife...' Painter's eyelids flickered. He grabbed his glass and took a sharp draught.

Nell watched as he gripped his glass so hard, she feared it may shatter. The dark circles beneath his eyes reminded her of the man she had seen on that first night in Sir Charles' office. The man whose shoulders slumped as he looked at the painting of Primrose Hill. The man she had taken pleasure in goading.

'I'm sorry,' Nell said. 'I can be quite blunt. It's the writer in me. I'm constantly prodding to look for a story.'

'I don't have one to tell,' Painter said. He released his glass and ran his palms down the legs of his trousers, his hands coming to rest on his knees. As a police inspector, Painter's business might be to wheedle the truth from anyone attempting to keep it from him, but he had failed to learn the art of subterfuge himself. There was a story behind those eyes and behind the protestations. Nell's author's intuition had seen it before and saw it again.

Painter picked up his glass and took another sip. 'Has something happened today?' he asked.

'What do you mean?' Nell said.

'You seem like a different person from this morning.'

The sadness in his face once again held a mirror up to Nell's sadness. As much as she couldn't bear it in herself, she could bear it even less in this man who was working so hard to protect the Mandevilles. 'A visit to a mortuary will take the spark from a girl,' she said. She watched Painter's face, waiting for a response. Almost despite himself, it seemed, the corner of his mouth lifted, and his nose twitched slightly.

'You're doing it again,' he said and rubbed his top lip. 'But I'm serious. Has something happened today that I should be aware of?'

It was Nell's turn to consult her drink again. She swirled the thick liquid about so that it coated the inside of the glass. 'I've been thinking about something that I haven't thought about in a while. It's nothing to do with the break in or the strangers.'

Painter nodded. 'As long as you're all right,' he said.

'I am.' Nell crossed her ankles beneath her chair as he would see her crossing her fingers. 'There's absolutely nothing wrong with me.' She paused. 'I'm glad to see you wiped the mud off your face,' she said, before hiding her smile by taking a sip of her drink.

Painter's eyebrows lifted in what looked like mock shock, but he was prevented from responding by the arrival of the landlady. She entered through the door leading to the bar, rubbing her hands on her apron.

'Everything all right in here?' she asked with a wide smile.

'Thank you, yes, Mrs Kendal,' Painter said.

'And will your guest be joining you for dinner later this

evening?' she said, smiling at Nell. 'It'd be no trouble to lay an extra place.'

'No, thank you,' Painter said. 'Miss Potter is a guest at Hill House. I should imagine they will be expecting her.'

Mrs Kendal's smile widened. 'Oh, you must be the author,' she said to Nell. 'We've heard all about you. And what an awful business it is with someone breaking in like that. And poor Mr Elliot and that poor constable being attacked. It makes you feel unsafe in your own bed.'

'You're perfectly safe,' Painter said. 'There's nothing to worry about.' He stood up and positioned himself between Mrs Kendal and Nell. Somehow, he managed to manoeuvre the landlady back through to the bar while she continued to chatter.

When he returned, he picked up his glass and drained the final mouthful. 'I'll walk you back,' he said.

It was a perfect late afternoon. The sun shone. Women sat on benches around the village green. Small children pointed to the ducks on the pond and an older boy set his miniature yacht on the water. A handful of people milled around outside the Post Office.

Painter closed the door of the pub behind them. A key turned in the lock inside.

'Isn't it against the law to serve alcohol out of licensing hours?' Nell asked.

'Not to residents,' Painter said.

'You live here? In the pub?'

'I'm staying here. It's convenient to be close by when I'm working on a case. And they let me have sole use of their telephone.' Painter placed his hat on his head and adjusted the brim. He began to walk away and Nell walked beside him. They walked in silence for a while along the narrow pavement and past a row of cottages with thatched rooves and flowers around their doorways.

'If there had been any other way, I would have spared you that trip into Northampton.' Painter said, looking forward, his hands forced into his trouser pockets.

'I know,' Nell said.

'And I think it would be better if we don't mention the death of this man to the Mandevilles. I don't want to raise concern if it leads to nothing.'

'Understood,' Nell said. She would rather not recall the poor man's face or recount the details of the awful building in the grounds of the hospital. She looked down to the pavement before looking up at the side of Painter's face. They continued in silence towards the spire of St Mary's church. The thatched cottages with their whitewashed walls gave way to a row of redbrick workers' cottages.

'Are you any closer to finding the person you think is behind the crimes?' Nell asked.

'I'm sure we will bring this to an end soon.'

'That will be a relief for everyone,' Nell said.

They came to the gates of Hill House. The constable guarding the front door was halfway down the drive. He stopped and saluted Painter. Painter touched the brim of his hat in reply before turning to face Nell. Removing his hat, he pushed his hair back with the heel of his hand. 'You mustn't worry yourself unduly,' he said. 'We have men looking after you and the Mandevilles. I'm sorry if I've involved you too much already. I shouldn't have asked you to help me by keeping an eye on the goings on at Hill House.'

'I don't mind, really,' Nell said. 'It's given me something to fill my time. I don't seem able to come up with a story worth writing.'

'That's as maybe,' Painter said. 'But I've had time to think about it. It was unfair of me. I'm concerned that I might have worried you more than is necessary.'

Nell smiled up at him. Painter had no need to feel sorry. He had asked for her help with his enquiries. What kind of person would she be if she had refused? And what kind of person would she be to let him feel any guilt or regret? He carried a permanent burden in those sad eyes without the need for her to add to it. 'Even if you hadn't asked for my help, I'm sure you realise I wouldn't have been able to resist sticking my beak in,' she said. 'I'm afraid that before you, you see an incorrigible nosey parker. I make it my business to know everyone's business, whether or not they want me to.'

Nell watched Painter, waiting for his reply. She didn't have to wait long to receive the response she had hoped for. The side of Painter's mouth rose. 'I really have never met anyone quite like you, Miss Potter. Do you ever take anything totally seriously?'

'Rarely,' Nell said. 'And never if I can help it.'

She was rewarded with a proper smile from Painter. He shook his head. 'I think there's more to you than meets the eye, Miss Potter. You are more serious and more sensible than you let on.'

'Me? Never,' Nell said.

Painter laughed. It was a soft laugh, a gentle laugh that creased the skin around his eyes and made him lean forward and shake his head again. There was even a hint of a glimmer in those grey eyes. Painter placed his hat back on his head and ran his fingers along the brim.

'If you don't mind,' he said, 'I will walk you to the house. I've promised to update Mr Mandeville on developments.'

'On one condition,' Nell said.

Painter looked at her and raised an eyebrow.

'That you no longer call me Miss Potter,' Nell said. 'I much prefer Nell.'

'If you insist,' Painter said. 'Nell, it is. But only when we are alone. When we are in the company of others, it will be Miss Potter. I have to maintain my professional standards.'

'Very well,' Nell said.

'After you,' Painter said, holding out his palm for Nell to pass through the gates first. He fell into step beside her.

She looked down at their feet, walking side by side. 'I see you cleaned your shoes after your foray into the woods this morning,' Nell said. 'Is that part of the police handbook? To have clean shoes at all times?'

'It's top of the list,' Painter said. 'They even issue us with regulation boot polish.'

Nell looked up at him. He was smiling at her, still with his hands dug deep into his pockets as he walked.

They reached the front of the house and the constable held the door open for them. On crossing the threshold, Painter removed his hat and used the heel of his hand to smooth his hair. There seemed a kink to it that he was constantly at pains to flatten.

Light flooded the hall and Painter's footsteps made a regular thud on the tiles as he walked beside Nell. The bronze tiles glittered in the late afternoon sunlight, which reflected in the mirror and lit the pale wooden panelling with a warm glow. Just before the fireplace, Nell stopped and turned to face Painter. He held his hat in both hands, turning the brim around between his fingers.

'Thank you.' he said. 'For your help today. I know it wasn't easy.'

'What wasn't easy?'

Both Nell and Painter turned towards the morning room where Mrs Hart stood in the doorway.

Painter pushed his fringe away from his face again. 'Miss Potter helped me with my enquiries today.'

'I see,' Mrs Hart said, approaching them. 'So that's why you called for Miss Potter to be taken to Northampton.'

'That's right,' Nell said, a little too quickly. She slowed to add, 'I had to recount everything I have seen at Hill House since my arrival. I've spent so much time in the grounds that Inspector Painter was interested in hearing about what I might have witnessed.'

'I see,' Mrs Hart said. There was more than a slight smile as she spoke, looking from Nell to Inspector Painter so that Nell felt she was being surveyed by the headmistress after sneaking out of school.

Painter rubbed his top lip. 'Miss Potter has been very helpful.'

'I'm glad to hear it,' Mrs Hart said. 'And Nell, dear, you look a little flushed. Are you quite all right?'

Nell touched her warm cheeks with the back of her fingers. 'I always go red when I have been outside too much.'

'Ah, yes,' Mrs Hart nodded. 'That would explain it. You are positively glowing.' The smile never left her face when she looked again from Nell to Painter.

Painter coughed. 'If you'll excuse me,' he said. 'I was hoping to have a word with Mr Mandeville. Do you know where I might find him, Mrs Hart?'

'In his father's office,' she said, still looking at Nell. Still smiling. 'Would you like me to show you the way?'

'No, thank you,' Painter said. 'I know where it is. If you'll excuse me. Mrs Hart. Miss Potter.' With no further discussion, his footstep echoed away up the hall.

'Well, well, well,' Mrs Hart said. 'Would you like to join me for some tea, Nell. I think you have—'

'No, thank you, Mrs Hart. That's very kind of you.' Nell had heard something in Mrs Hart's voice that meant she wanted to do more than take tea. 'I should go to my room to write,' she said, pointing up the stairs as though Mrs Hart would not know where the guestrooms were in the house in which she lived. 'I'm sorry, you do understand, don't you?'

'Of course,' Mrs Hart said, still with that knowing smile.

Nell turned and ran up the stairs. But as she ran along the landing, she saw through the bannisters that Mrs Hart was still in the hall, looking up at her.

FORTY-THREE

Throwing open the bedroom door, Nell collapsed into the chair at the desk. She took up a sheet of paper, placed it against the roller of the typewriter and wound it into place. She stared at it. If she were to tap the keys now, in an attempt to commit all that had happened in the last day onto paper, nobody in their right mind would believe it.

She pushed the typewriter away, got up from the desk and paced from the bathroom door to the far wall and back again. On the third length of the bedroom, she stopped in front of the mirror. Mrs Hart was right. Her cheeks were flushed to a deep pink. Two brandies and too much time in the sun would do that to a person. Closing her eyes, she saw Painter talking to Mrs Hart, twisting the brim of his hat through his fingers as though he were a naughty schoolboy. Nell had wanted to turn to watch him make his way up the hall, to thank him for his kindness, but Mrs Hart would have misconstrued it. People had the habit of interpreting situations to suit their own desires and motivations.

There came a knock at the door and it opened gently. 'Sorry, Miss,' Mary said. 'I've been sent to see whether you will

be joining everyone for dinner? Mr Edward is making his cocktails on the terrace.'

'Would you mind terribly giving my apologies?' Nell said.
'I've had a busy day and I really do need to write.'

'Very good,' Mary said. She was about to close the door
when Nell called out.

'Sorry, Mary. This isn't very important. But I wondered
whether you might know whether Inspector Painter is still
here?'

'No, Miss. He left not a few minutes since. I saw him
leaving by the front door as I was up on the landing here. Was
there any particular reason? Do you have a message for him?'

'Oh, no, nothing at all. I just wondered, that's all.'

'Very good, miss,' Mary said and closed the door behind her.

Alone once more, Nell began to pace again, this time, to the
window and back to the door. She paused to glance out of the
window then sat down on the edge of the bed.

Kicking off her shoes, Nell threw herself back on the bed.
She placed her head on one pillow and grabbed another and
clasped it to her stomach while she stared up at the ceiling.
Would Painter have told Edward about the poor man who had
died on the train tracks? The image of the battered and
damaged face made her clutch the pillow tighter. It seemed that
all day, she had thought of or been presented with death. Death.
Grief. Mourning. Loss. These things conspired to sap the colour
from life. And they always brought with them a grim wave of
tiredness. As Nell's eyes closed, she saw a pair of highly
polished black brogues. Their owner was the only sensible and
grounded thing she had encountered since arriving at Hill
House. The thought of him brought with it a sense of calm. The
world stopped spinning out of control. The world stopped... the
world... blackness...

· · ·

When Nell woke, the room was in darkness. Outside, stars shone in the velvet blue-black of the night sky. Sitting up, she arched her body from side to side. She reached to switch on the lamp and found a plate and glass covered by a napkin on the nightstand. She lifted the napkin from a neatly arranged salad of cheese with buttered bread, a sliced apple and several stalks of celery. Nell picked up the bread and took a large bite followed by a large chunk of the cheese and a slice of apple. She washed it down with a mouthful of lemonade.

Getting up from the bed, she stood in the window and breathed in the warm summer night-time air, full of the scent of freshly cut grass. What a day of contrasts it had been. What was it about this house and the people who lived here and hereabouts that made the extraordinary seem to happen every day? Philip. She had spoken of Philp. For the first time. And then there had been that poor man at the mortuary. But as she thought of him, another man jostled for position in her thoughts. She breathed in deeply again. This time, behind the warm scent of grass, was the musty scent of damp leaves. She had misjudged him. He was a good man. An honourable man. A man who deserved – and most likely had – a woman who matched his qualities.

Nell picked a pip from a slice of apple. She had spent too much time alone. Too much time thinking. Discarding the pip on the plate, she let herself out of her room.

Nell made her way along the dark corridor towards the landing and the light glowing from the hallway below. She leant over the bannisters. Voices and laughter floated up from the billiard room. The clock down in the hall chimed ten. After three hours asleep on her bed, her dress resembled a crumpled paper bag, and she could only imagine what her hair must look like. She could hardly join the Mandevilles and their guests dressed like this.

A movement further along the landing made Nell turn around. Peering into the gloom she could just make out that the little door leading to the stone stairwell stood ajar. Mary must have left it open when she brought up the plate of food.

The sound of billiard balls cracked below. Somebody laughed. Nell leant over the bannisters. The laugh came again. It was light and rather high pitched. Nell listened carefully, and when she heard it for a third time she realised it was coming not from the billiard room, but from the direction of the door on the landing.

'Tommy,' she said under her breath. Had he left his bed to come to play a trick on her? Well, she would not let him get the better of her this time. Nell let her eyes adjust to the gloom. She looked about. All was clear. She tiptoed towards the door and, since her feet were bare, she made no sound at all on the carpeted landing. She stopped at the door and took hold of the handle. She paused for a second. And then yanked the door open. 'You won't catch me out this time, Thomas Mandeville!' she said, bursting into the stairwell. She slipped her hand inside and felt along the wall until she found a light switch. Flicking the switch, a bare bulb lit the grey stairwell. Nell looked up the stairs and then down, expecting a little face to appear. She hopped from one leg to the other as the stone chilled her feet. There was nobody to be seen. She waited, anticipating a laugh, her sign to be led on a wild goose chase. All was silent. Still. Unlike last time, there were no footsteps for her to follow. Placing her hand on the wooden handrail, Nell took a few steps up. 'Tommy?' she tried again. 'Are you there?' Silence. Still holding the handrail, Nell made her way up the stone steps.

At the top of the house, she stopped. The stairwell might be lit but the narrow corridor leading to the unused bedrooms was in darkness, save for squares of dim moonlight on the floor from the windows in the slanted ceiling. She looked down the stairs and along the corridor. 'Tommy?' she whispered. No response. Nell searched for a light switch but found none. She was tempted to head back down the stairs but hesitated. If Tommy had made his way into the attic, she should really find him to make sure he returned to his bed. It couldn't be safe for a small child to be alone in this remote and lonely part of the house.

Taking a deep breath, Nell plunged into the darkness, along the corridor and past the deserted rooms. She felt the creak of each floorboard in her stomach. It made her pause and reach for the security of the wall. Her illogical brain told her that at any moment something might jump out or materialise before her. As she carefully continued, her logical brain tried to tell her there was no more to fear in this attic than there was down in her bedroom.

When she was almost at the lumber room, Nell saw a shimmer, as though the very air had altered the shape of everything around it. It lasted only a second before everything returned to normal. The half-light was playing tricks on her senses now.

At the lumber room, she reached in through the door and flicked the light switch. The bulb bloomed above and the room looked as it had a few days before: trunks, boxes, valises, rails of clothing.

'Tommy?' she whispered. 'Tommy. You can come out now. You're not in trouble.'

Nothing. No sound. No movement. There was no sense of another presence. Even so, Nell eased past the boxes and trunks, heading for the brightly coloured shawl at the very back. She crouched down on her haunches. The cigar box was open on the floor. Nell peered into the miniature version of Hill House and her breath caught. The downstairs rooms were full of dolls. All dressed in their finery. There was a table full of food in the dining room and the miniature guests were served by footmen. In the ballroom, a band sat before a painted backdrop and men and women were positioned in a dance. And, in the hallway, a Christmas tree was decorated with tiny candles and baubles. Beside the tree stood a woman in a blue dress. With her was a man, touching her hand as though tying a dance card to her wrist. Nell could almost hear the music and smell the perfume and cologne. She moved backwards. This was her waking dream brought to life. Had she somehow seen this before? Had it triggered the dream? She tried to convince herself that she had but knew she hadn't.

'Tommy?' she said, a hint of desperation in her voice. It was then she saw the figures outside the house. A replica of Hill House's gates with its golden lions sat a short way from the house. A man had his hand on one of the gates, holding it open for a woman. It was the doll with the scar on her face, but her hair was wavy rather than straight. The man wore a dark suit with a dark hat.

Nell stood and fell backwards. 'What is this?' she said. Scrambling to her feet she stumbled as she tried to run through the room, crashing into the stacked boxes and furniture. A lamp tumbled to the floor. A chair toppled. And when she was almost at the door, her foot caught a sheet, pulling it from the table it covered. She wrestled it away so that it became a ball of linen on the floor and brought the table crashing down, spilling what had been hidden beneath the sheet. Nell gasped and shook her head. The spirit board and its pointer sat askew on the floorboards, blocking her path to the door. In her mind's eye, Nell saw the pointer begin to move. Swaying backwards and forwards. Backwards and forwards. She wanted to scream out but there was nobody to hear. Desperately, she looked towards the back of the room. As she turned, the atmosphere shifted. The disturbance in her vision returned, but this time, instead of disappearing as quickly as it had appeared, it moved towards her. Nell watched as the shimmering disturbance grew closer. And then came a laugh. Not a laugh, but a giggle. It was sweet, like a small child's. And it was right beside her. Something touched Nell's hand. She looked down but there was nobody there. She ran. Jumping over the board, she sprinted through the door and along the corridor. Without looking back, she ran as fast as she could down the stone stairs, the blood pumping in her ears. She carried on past the door to the first floor and didn't stop until she came to the very bottom. She ran through the stone corridor, down the steps, along the basement corridor and into the kitchen.

FORTY-FOUR

Mary and Mrs Randal jumped from their seats at table. 'Whatever is it?' Mrs Randal said to Nell.

'It's not the burglar returned, is it?' Mary said.

Nell shook her head, gasping for breath.

'You look like you've seen a ghost,' Mrs Randal said. She put an arm around Nell and had her take a seat. 'Mary, get that bottle of sherry from the cupboard.'

A glass was placed before Nell. She took it up and knocked it back. The liquid burned as it hit her throat and then her chest. The glass was filled again. She cupped it and felt Mrs Randal and Mary retake their seats. They wore dressing gowns and Mrs Randal had a hair net over two rollers in her fringe. There was a notepad and pencil on the table, beside two cups and a steaming pan on a trivet. 'I'm sorry to have disturbed your cocoa,' Nell said, when she felt able to speak.

'Nonsense,' Mrs Randal said. 'You're not disturbing anything that can't be reheated.'

The women were both looking at her with such concern, but she couldn't tell them what had happened. 'I had an awful dream,' she said. 'I woke up and was terrified. I didn't feel like I could join everyone in the billiard room dressed as I am. So, I came down here, I hoped you wouldn't mind.'

'Mind!' Mrs Randal said, 'Of course we don't mind.'

'I'm not surprised you had a nightmare,' Mary said. 'With all that's going on here.'

'Inspector Painter said we are all safe,' Nell said. The last thing she wanted to do was alarm Mary and Mrs Randal. This was their home. They should feel safe here.

'Of course,' Mrs Randal said. 'Those robbers got what they came for. They won't be back again, you mark my words. The police are here, just to be on the safe side. Mary, get another cup and warm that pan through. What Miss Potter needs is a nice hot cup of cocoa. That's what settles your nerves after a scare.'

'The children,' Nell said. 'Are they in bed?'

'Many hours since. They are safely tucked up,' Mary said, placing the pan on the stove. 'And fast asleep. I checked on them not long ago. The babies are in the nursery. Bertie is in another room of the nursery wing and Audrey and Rosemary are in the other. They're all keeping an ear out for each other. The inspector said we're all to stay at the house for the time being, rather than going back to the village.' She stirred the cocoa and knocked the wooden spoon against the side of the pan. 'I'm glad we don't have to go up to the old servant quarters in the attic,' she said, placing the pan back on the trivet. 'Those rooms haven't been slept in for years. They're full of spiders. They give me the creeps.'

With a swift flick of the glass, Nell finished the sherry.

'It's like old times.' Mrs Randal smiled. 'Having so many rooms full. So many lives under one roof to do for. So many mouths to feed. Sorry, Miss Potter,' she said, looking at Nell. 'You won't be wanting to hear about this.'

'Please,' Nell said. The longer she could keep them talking, the longer she could stay in the kitchen with company. Mrs Randal took her at her word and fell into a conversation with

Mary about arrangements for the next day's meals, scribbling notes on the notepad.

Nell hooked her feet around the legs of the chair. The room was warm from the heat of the day and the stove. Even so, she shivered. When Mary placed a cup of cocoa before her, she thanked her. Down in the warm kitchen, the events of the attic seemed so far away. All was normal. The talk of food. The arrangements for showing Audrey and Rosemary how to make a bed properly and to the standards of the absent housekeeper, Mrs Moriarty. How Bertie would have the job of sorting out the newspapers in the morning. The smell of bread baking in the ovens. Could she have imagined it all? It was possible. She took a sip of the milky sweet cocoa. She could go back up and see whether the miniature Hill House was still set for Christmas. See whether the air was still disturbed and whether the spirit board still lay on the floor. Nell wrapped her legs tighter around the legs of the chair. She would rather run out of the house and take her chances in the woods than ever set one foot in the attic again.

Soon the time came for Mrs Randal and Mary to head to bed. They didn't seem to mind that Nell joined them on their way up the stone staircase. They all let themselves out through the secret door on the landing on the first floor.

'You're all right now, aren't you, Miss Potter?' Mrs Randal said, her voice soft in the darkness of the landing.

'Yes, thank you. And thank you for the company,' Nell said.

'We'll leave you here, then,' Mrs Randal said. 'I'm in with Audrey and Rosemary. Mary is in the nursery with the babies.'

Nell nodded.

Mary and Mrs Randal wished her a final goodnight and headed in the opposite direction.

Back in her room Nell slipped off her dress and slipped beneath the eiderdown. The atmosphere in the room felt familiar. Safe. Nevertheless, she could recall enough of what had happened in the room above to pull the eiderdown over her head. The warm milky drink mixed with sherry did its job. Her eyelids fluttered. Her brain attempted to replay the events of the day. The final thing she saw before darkness and exhaustion stole her consciousness, was a doll in a hat, holding open a tiny gate.

FORTY-FIVE

29TH JULY 1924

'We missed you last night, Nell,' Charlotte said as she looked over the breakfast things laid out on the sideboard. Settling on a spoonful of scrambled egg, she sat in the chair beside Nell and took a slice of toast from the rack.

Nell sipped at a cup of hot sweet coffee.

'Did you manage to write much?' Mrs Hart asked, scooping a mound of strawberry jam onto her plate.

'A little,' Nell lied.

'We had a fabulous game of bridge,' Charlotte said, scraping butter onto her toast.

'As usual, Nell, Charlotte won,' Mrs Hart said. 'I still say she will make our fortune one day. We just need to find a gambling den and sit her at a table.'

Charlotte laughed. 'I'm not sure there are any gambling dens in Northampton, Aunt Leo.'

'I wouldn't be so sure!' Mrs Hart laughed.

Edward, Paul and Wilco all arrived together. After bidding the women good morning, they looked over the offerings on the sideboard.

'Paul convinced us to take a turn outside before breakfast,'

Wilco said. 'Says it's good for the constitution.' He took up a plate and lifted the lid from a tureen heated from below. 'Ah, kedgeree,' he said. 'My favourite.'

'We called in on Elliot,' Edward said, taking a seat. He thanked his aunt for the coffee she poured for him.

'How is he?' Mrs Hart asked.

'Healing nicely,' Paul said. 'Once the bruises are gone you will never know that anything happened to him.'

Nell sipped her coffee and managed to stay out of most of the conversations. She smiled when it was appropriate, laughed when it was warranted. The men filled their plates and tucked into a hearty breakfast. The atmosphere was in stark contrast to the breakfast of the day before. Nell looked at the faces around the table. How easily people were able to forget. Or was she being ungenerous? Was it more a case of needing to move past something awful? Only Edward gave away his concern every so often with a glance in Nell's direction.

When the men stood, saying they would go to the library to read the morning papers, Nell stood, too. 'I should go and do some writing,' she said and left her companions behind.

Nell sat at her desk, staring at the keys of her typewriter. It seemed that she had spent every morning since her arrival at Hill House attempting to explain the events of the preceding day or night. But this time, any explanation defied her. Try as hard as she might, there was nothing she could say to explain what was happening. Every path to logic was blocked by the illogical. All science blocked by unfathomable events.

There was a sharp rap at the bedroom door. 'Come in,' she called. She waited. The door didn't open. Nobody entered.

'Come in,' she said again. Again, the door didn't open. Nell got up from the chair and crossed the room. She turned the handle and the sharp rap sounded again. As she yanked the door open, she heard a voice. It was faint and she couldn't make out what it said, but she heard it. There hadn't been enough time for whoever had knocked on the door to make their escape but when Nell lurched from the room and looked up and down, the corridor was empty. The secret door at the head of the stairs was closed. She was about to close the bedroom door, when she saw a flash of light. It came from the direction of the landing and moved towards her at great speed. Her vision was disturbed, the movement blurring colours and shapes of everything it crossed as it had in the lumber room the night before. But this time, the light appeared to have more energy, more vividness. And it rushed past her and into her room.

There came another rap, softer, this time from the closed bathroom door. Nell ran to yank it open. Bath. Toilet. Sink. The curtain gently blowing at the open window. Not a person in sight.

'Where are you? Show yourself!' she shouted. Her heart punched at her ribs, but she would not back down.

A crash came from the bedroom. Her bag had fallen from the chair. The contents were all still inside. Except for one item. Nell ran back into the bedroom and stooped to collect the small white card containing Inspector Painter's telephone numbers.

The door to the corridor was still open. Nobody entered yet Nell sensed somebody at her shoulder. She heard a sigh. It was so close that she felt it as a breath against her ear. She froze, still clutching the card. Another breath brushed the fine hair on the back of her neck.

'Love again,' a voice said. It was so soft. So deep but so gentle. It was the voice of whispered promises of a life together. The voice of stolen afternoons in an out-of-the-way hotel. The voice that had given her life meaning before its loss took all meaning from her life.

'I won't believe it,' she said, her voice shaking. 'This isn't real.'

She stood absolutely still. The presence stayed with her, as though looking over her shoulder, at the card in her hand. The room was silent. All was calm. Nell closed her eyes. 'Is it you?' she said quietly. Another breeze whispered on her neck. She raised her hand and cupped her skin, leaning into the breath. Slowly, very slowly, she felt the presence slip away. The bedroom and bathroom doors closed as though moved by a gentle hand.

Nell took in a gulp of air. Everything in the bedroom appeared perfectly normal except for her bag on the floor and the card in her hand.

'It's not true,' she managed to say. 'A house can't do all this. And that wasn't—'

Before she could say his name, a breeze blew the curtains. It wasn't a normal breeze but seemed to have shape and form. The curtain billowed at an unusual angle. It remained in its odd manner for a moment longer than science would have allowed. The fine hairs on Nell's arms stood on end as though stroked by a kind hand.

Every logical thought tumbled from Nell's mind. If this were real then so were the messages from the spirit board, the predictions of Madame Zelda, everything Tommy and Mr Townley had said to her, the fact that this house could talk to her. This version of the world was the South Pole to the North Pole of all she had ever held as true. Twenty-eight years of experience, education, and unshakable belief in the rational fell away, leaving room for an alternative version of the world. And if she listened to it then she had to take notice of the message it seemed determined to send her at every opportunity and through every vessel at its disposal... Nell turned her hand over and looked down at the card in her palm. In the same way she had opened her mind to these impossible thoughts, she opened her heart – just a chink. Instantly it pounded. Blood rushed so it felt that the organ in her chest was new. The blood fresh and full of life.

She slammed the card down on the dressing table and ran from the room, sprinting down the stairs, through the hallway, into the vestibule, and out through the front door. When the police constable patrolling the drive asked where she was going, she called over her shoulder that she was going to the lake.

Running parallel to the boundary wall, she soon passed the church. The trees became denser as she ran deeper into the woods, jumping over exposed roots and dodging the tangle of branches. Once or twice, she ran too close to a bush so that thorns and barbs scratched at her legs. But it was not enough to slow Nell. She ran past a clearing, the thought crossing her mind that the man who had tried to attack her might be lurking in the woods. Let him try it now and she would give him the full force of whatever was powering her on.

Eventually the trees gave way to grass. Just short of the boathouse, Nell ripped off her dress and slip, leaving her clothes strewn across the sand. She only just had the sense to kick off her shoes before running at full pelt into the water in just her underwear. As soon as the water was up to her waist, she submerged her head. She surfaced, coughing, and breathing sharply as the cold water bit her flesh and shocked her nerves. She all but fell into the water again and began to swim, kicking and crawling as fast as she could until she was in the centre of the lake. But as fast as Nell kicked and as fast as she made her arms pull her through the water, she could not outrun the feelings. The cold water and exertion would not make them go away. Because they were in her. In her core.

Nell swam back to shore. When she came to a place where she could stand in the water with her feet on the silty ground, she knew that, as certainly as she could feel the sharp stones digging into her heels, she could feel a sensation she had thought lost to her. The blood rushing into her heart.

She waded towards the bank, dripping water. The wet silk of her underwear clung to every part of her, to every contour and muscle. The thin fabric could no longer conceal the physicality of her beneath. Her nipples bloomed through silk made sheer. The triangle of hair between her legs pressed against the garment that usually hid her. Part of her wanted to hide in the water or hurriedly dress behind the cover of a tree. But there was another part that wanted none of that.

'I am not invisible,' she shouted. She wanted so much for a pair of grey eyes to look upon her, standing there in the water. To *see* her. She wanted those eyes to take her in. To know her as a woman. She wanted him to want her as much as she wanted him. 'There,' she called out. 'Is that what you wanted? I admit it.' Nell looked into the woods but could not see or sense any eyes looking back at her. She put her hand to her chest. Blood pumped inside her, pounding in her throat. It pushed and coursed through her veins and arteries so that every inch of her skin was alive. She felt the presence of her blood warming her cheeks. And she felt it in her breasts and between her legs. She imagined his hands on her stomach as they had been in the copse. His arms around her. Holding her. A fire had been set within her, which the water had not cooled.

FORTY-SIX

'Miss,' the police constable said when he pushed the front door open for her. He delivered the word with a rising intonation as if asking a question. That question being why she was entering the house with no shoes, unbrushed hair and the damp ghost of her brassiere and draws visible through the cotton of her thin dress. It was a question that Nell did not feel compelled to answer.

A commotion at the top of the stairs made Nell look up. Mary held the baby in her arms and Charlotte clutched Daphne's hand while the little girl gripped the bannisters with her other hand.

'Hello there, Nell,' Charlotte said as she approached on her slow journey, as little Daphne was determined to make her own way down.

'Hello,' Nell said as the party reached the step just above her.

'Oh,' Daphne said pointing at Nell. 'Miss Potter is all wet.'

'Indeed, she is,' Charlotte said. She crouched to speak to her niece as though taking her into her confidence. 'The older you get and the more you get to know Miss Potter, the more you will learn that she is rather unconventional. I wouldn't be surprised if Miss Potter hadn't been swimming fully clothed, just as she did at the seaside.'

Daphne wrinkled her nose and laughed. 'Funny Miss Potter,' she said.

Nell smiled at the little girl. 'I am a little odd,' she said.

'We are on our way down to the kitchen to get a spot of elevenses,' Charlotte said standing again as Mary jiggled the restless baby on her hip while he tried to grab her hair. 'We fancy a glass of lemonade and a biscuit or two. Would you like to join us, Nell?'

'Thank you, but I really think I should change out of these wet clothes.' She stepped aside to let the little group pass.

'Join us if you change your mind,' Charlotte said, helping Daphne down the next steps with Mary following, wrestling her hair from the baby's firm grip.

Nell reached the top of the stairs and was on her way to dry off and change when the sound of familiar voices made her stop. She followed the quiet murmur along the landing and away from her room.

'You can talk to us now that Charlotte and Mary are gone and have taken the babies away,' she heard Bertie say. 'You needn't be afraid.'

Nell stopped just short of the room towards the end of the unfamiliar corridor. The door stood ajar. She crept past and looked through the gap between the door and the frame. The room was furnished with a cot, three small beds and a larger bed, the walls decorated with paintings of characters from nursery rhymes. Toys were strewn across a rug: a Noah's Ark with pairs of animals either marching towards a gangway or fallen over; a castle with knights on horseback seemingly attacking the drawbridge; a stack of building bricks with numbers and letters of the alphabet painted on each side.

Inside the nursery, Mrs Hart and Alice sat in two armchairs before the fireplace. Bertie knelt on the floor beside Tommy, who was playing with his box of dolls.

'Who would I be afraid of?' Tommy said.

Mrs Hart and Alice both leant forward, watching Tommy. He had a doll in each hand and manipulated them so that the feet made a gentle tip tap sound on the floorboards. They appeared to be the dolls of two children.

Bertie's fringe had fallen forward. He scooped it away from his eyes when he looked to the women as though seeking confirmation that he should continue. Mrs Hart nodded.

'Do you remember what happened the night before last?' Bertie said to Tommy. 'What you said to me in the hall?'

'I wasn't in the hall,' Tommy said, positioning one of the dolls so that it sat down.

'Do you remember what you said about the police constable and Mr Elliot?' Bertie pressed.

Tommy shook his head. 'I remember being in bed and then being in the kitchen with Mrs Randal, Mary, Audrey and Rosemary and eating biscuits. We really aren't supposed to eat biscuits in the middle of the night, you know. And then Daphne, Charlie and I tried on a police constable's helmet.' He looked up. 'Why are there police constables in the house?'

'They are visiting.' Bertie said.

'Tommy, darling,' Alice said. 'Do you remember coming into the dining room to see Miss Potter that night?'

'No,' he said. He stopped playing with his doll. He looked directly to the door and smiled. Nell retreated, her back pressed to the wall.

'What is it, Tommy, darling? What are you looking at?' Nell heard Mrs Hart say.

The tip-tap of the dolls started up again. 'Nothing,' Tommy said. 'I thought it might be my new friend.'

Mrs Hart and Alice rose from their chairs. There was the

sound of footsteps approaching the door. Nell dipped into an alcove a little further along the corridor. She stood flat against the wall. She had no intention of leaving; not now that her name had been mentioned. And not with the four people in that room who were the only people who seemed to know what was happening to Tommy.

She broke cover briefly to see Mrs Hart and Alice standing outside the nursery.

'Do you think he's telling the truth?' Nell heard Alice whisper, as she retreated to the safety of the alcove. She could hear Bertie keeping Tommy busy in the nursery, chatting about his dolls.

'I do,' Mrs Hart said.

Alice and Mrs Hart were so close that Nell felt sure they would see her if she moved. And all the while they spoke, the sound of the dolls' tip-taps could be heard, punctuated by the two boys talking.

'Who is this friend he is speaking of?' Mrs Hart asked.

'Some person he has conjured up,' Alice said. 'With everything that has been happening here in the last week, he has talked constantly of a new friend visiting him to play. He's overheard so many things and he keeps running off. It's not surprising his poor little mind doesn't know what is real and what is fantasy.'

'Children have imaginary friends,' Mrs Hart said, 'you mustn't be anxious.'

'I'm not anxious,' Alice said, 'I'm terrified. Every day recently I feel odd, Leo. What with Tommy and now the burglary and that poor policeman and Elliot. Things are happening here that can't be explained.' Alice's voice was terribly quiet when she said, 'What if I am slipping away? What if someone else is going to come to take my place? Edward. The children—'

'You know I can't talk to you about such things,' Mrs Hart said, cutting across Alice. 'If we talk of it, your position may be in even greater peril. All I can say is that I haven't sensed anything to say that you will be going.'

'And do you usually sense such things?'

'Alice!'

'Did you feel it when Louisa went away, and I came back?'

'Alice, please, you really must stop,' Mrs Hart said sharply. And then in gentler tone, 'Why don't you take Tommy down to the kitchen for a glass of lemonade?'

'So that you can speak to Bertie alone? I thought he had lost his connection and that it had passed to Tommy. But that night with the spirit board, it was as though Bertie sensed something. He came running just as Tommy came in to speak to Nell in one of his trances.'

'Alice!'

'I'm terrified for my son,' Alice said, sounding on the verge of tears. 'I'm terrified that I might leave. I want this all to stop. I want to go back to normal.'

'My darling, Alice,' Mrs Hart said calmly. 'This *is* our normal. You know I cannot ask how you came to be here or about your life before. And I cannot promise that you won't leave. All I can say is that I don't feel that it will happen.'

'"One in, one out. It's the way it's always been". Isn't that what you all say? It's what Bertie said when I arrived when he was a little boy.'

Nell had to slam her hand across her mouth to stop from calling out that Tommy had said those exact words to her.

Alice's voice sounded almost hysterical when she said, 'I'm only here because Louisa let me in. At least you all belong here. I'm the only outsider. I'm the only one whose presence here is under threat. What if it's someone else's turn to come to Hill House? What if I have to make way for someone else?'

'My darling,' Mrs Hart said. 'What has been happening here is at the hand of man. The thefts. The burglary. These are all the stuff of normal life. Tommy is simply practicing his skills on Nell.'

'What must Nell think of us? What must she think is going on here?'

'I'm sure she simply thinks that Tommy is a little boy who says odd things from time to time. As you thought of little Bertie when you first arrived.'

'I can't even talk to Edward about any of this. Tommy is his son, too. But he doesn't know anything about this side of him. I've never even been able to tell him the truth of who I am. Do you know how hard it is to keep these secrets from your husband?'

There was a pause before Mrs Hart said softly, 'I do. I had to keep this side of me from Fred. Believe me, I know just how hard it is.'

'I'm so sorry, Leo. That was thoughtless of me.'

'No, Alice. It's perfectly understandable. You are concerned for your son. But please be reassured when I say that I feel you are not leaving us. That is all I can say. Now why don't you take Tommy downstairs?'

'All right,' Alice said. The fight had left her voice. 'But please, Leo, you will tell me if you feel anything? I need to know what I am dealing with.'

'I will,' Mrs Hart said. 'I will.'

There were voices in the room: Alice hurrying Tommy to take him to the kitchen, Tommy insisting that he simply must bring his box of dolls with him. Nell held her breath as they made their way down the corridor. At the sound of Alice and Tommy taking the stairs down, Nell crept back to her position just outside the door. Footsteps paced up and down the floorboards inside. Nell risked peeling away from the wall to look through the gap once again.

Bertie stood on the rug before the fireplace, his hands in the pockets of his short trousers, as he looked at a spot before him. Every so often, Mrs Hart was visible crossing the room. Eventually she stopped. She faced Bertie, with her back to the door and to Nell.

'I have never known anything like this,' she said. 'I've been away for just three weeks and it is as though the whole world has gone mad.'

Mrs Hart began to pace again. Bertie scooped his fringe away from his face. 'I came home from school just after you left for the Isle of Wight. Everything was calm and normal. This all began when Miss Potter arrived.'

Mrs Hart stopped pacing. 'So, it is Nell who woke Tommy.' Bertie nodded. 'It would seem so.'

Mrs Hart tapped the toe of her shoe on the floorboard. 'At least we know now that the gift has transferred to Tommy. I had wondered whether it might pass to Daphne. She would have been easier to manage. I adore Tommy but he is rather a handful. It was so easy to guide you through your journey. You were such a good little boy and a willing pupil. It is a shame that the gift has left you. But there are reasons for everything.'

Bertie looked to the rug again. 'I'm sorry that you had to cut your holiday short. I tried to look after Tommy. But I didn't know how.'

'Oh, my darling,' Mrs Hart took Bertie's hands. 'I haven't even asked how you are. It is such a shock when your gift moves to the next person. I remember it well. But you need to be very brave. Together we can help Tommy. We are the only two who can now. We still feel enough to be able to guide him. And you must try to help Alice. She needs to feel reassured. But you also know that you must be very careful. Do not tell her anything she does not already know. We cannot put her time here at risk.'

Bertie nodded. 'I will do my very best,' he said.

'I would expect no less.' Mrs Hart put her hand to the boy's cheek. 'Bertie, were you present when the spirit board communicated with Nell?

Bertie shook his head. 'I was in my grandmother's cottage. I asked Tommy what was said but he remembers none of it. From what I've heard, the board wanted to speak to Nell and would speak to no other, even though she refused to take part. The board appeared to be spelling out a name when Nell ran from the table. That's when Tommy arrived. I arrived shortly afterwards and after that we found the police constable and Mr Elliot in the ballroom.'

Mrs Hart began pacing again. 'Is everything happening here connected?' she said almost to herself. 'If these things are connected, I cannot see how.'

'May I ask a question?' Bertie said.

Mrs Hart stopped. 'Of course, Bertie. You may ask me anything.'

'Why was it Miss Potter who woke Tommy's gift? She is of this time.'

As Mrs Hart was about to respond, Nell heard footsteps on the stairs. She looked to the landing and back to the nursery. If she were found out now, it would be clear that she had been eavesdropping; she had no conceivable reason for lurking around doors, listening to other people's conversations. And if she were found out, Mrs Hart would certainly make sure that she was not around to overhear any future conversation. At the last moment, Nell threw herself into the alcove, missing any reply that Mrs Hart may have given.

The footsteps walked rapidly up the corridor. Nell heard Mary's voice. 'Mrs Randal says will you be joining us for lemonade and biscuits? She says if you are, you may want to come now as Master Tommy may soon have polished them off.'

'Thank you, Mary. Yes, we will join you now. I'm sure Bertie doesn't want to miss out on his morning tea.'

'Very good, Mrs Hart,' Mary said. She left the room and

Nell risked a peek out of the alcove to see Mrs Hart and Bertie walking behind her. Mrs Hart held Bertie's hand.

Nell kicked at the back of the alcove with her heel. Of all the parts of the conversation to have missed, it had to be the part where her involvement in this circus might somehow have been revealed. She bit her lip in an attempt not to scream out.

FORTY-SEVEN

Once the coast was again clear, Nell ran the length of the corridor, past the landing and into her room. She slammed the door and fell against it. Even if she had been able to hear what Mrs Hart and Bertie had said about her, it wouldn't have made any sense. None of this made any sense. Tommy possessed some kind of gift that she had woken? Alice might leave if this Louisa character made an appearance? What did any of it mean? At least Alice's behaviour in lying to the police now made some sort of sense now. She was protecting a secret shared with the boys and Mrs Hart. But why had Mrs Hart and then Bertie spoken of Nell being of this time? Of course, she was of this time. What other time could she be of? And had she imagined Philip's voice earlier?

Nell looked around the room. This was all real at least. She was quite sure that she was standing in this room. It was July 1924. She was Nell Potter, sometimes known as Margot Evangeline.

Opening the door to her room Nell was halfway down the stairs, with the intention of getting some air, when a tremendous scream came from the direction of the kitchens. She looked down and saw people rushing into the hall: Mrs Hart, Mrs Randal, Charlotte, holding Daphne's hand, and Mary, carrying the baby on her hip. At the head of the party was Alice. She was screaming. 'Tommy! Tommy! Where are you?'

Alice disappeared into the morning room. Charlotte scooped little Daphne into her arms and ran into the billiard room. The other women scattered into other rooms, all calling out for Tommy.

'Tommy, darling,' Mrs Hart called. 'Nobody is angry with you. Come out from wherever you are.' She looked up the stairs. 'Nell, dear, have you seen Tommy?'

Nell raced down the remaining stairs. 'No,' she said. 'I haven't seen him.'

'He's gone missing,' Mrs Hart said as Mrs Randal appeared from the ballroom shaking her head. 'We were taking tea in the kitchen. One minute he was under the table eating a biscuit and playing with his dolls and the next he had vanished.'

Nell's blood drained so that she felt faint. Alice ran back into the hall, her eyes flicking frantically all around the space. She rushed to Nell and grabbed her hands. 'Nell, have you seen Tommy? Have you seen my boy? Please say he was with you.'

Nell shook her head. 'I'm sorry.'

Alice released her hands. She gripped her face and let out a cry. The women massed around her. Daphne appeared from the billiard room. She ran as fast as her little legs would carry her towards her mother.

'Daphne, come back,' Charlotte called after her niece.

'Mama,' Daphne wailed. 'Mama, where is Tommy? Why are you crying?'

Alice seemed not to hear her daughter, her eyes wide and staring.

Charlotte caught up with Daphne before she could get to her mother. Charlotte held her briefly, the girl burying her face in her aunt's skirt, before asking Mrs Randal to take the baby and Daphne down to the kitchen.

'Don't worry,' Charlotte called as Mrs Randal led the girl away, crying for her mother, which made her baby brother commence wailing. 'Tommy is just hiding somewhere. He's playing. He will be found soon. Your mother is a little worried, that's all.'

Mrs Hart took Alice in her arms, just in time to stop her from collapsing.

'Where is he?' Alice cried. 'Where is my boy? I want my boy back.'

Edward ran through the door beneath the stairs. 'What is it?' he asked. 'What's happening?'

Charlotte had tears in her eyes when she said. 'It's Tommy, he's missing.'

Edward ran to his wife. Mrs Hart stepped away and Alice collapsed onto her husband. He held her as she wept.

'Missing. What do you mean missing?' Edward asked.

'We were in the kitchen,' Mrs Hart said. 'Tommy was playing under the table one minute and then he was gone.'

'It's a big house,' Edward said. 'He could be hiding.'

'He's gone,' Alice cried. 'I can feel it.'

The front door opened. Alerted by the commotion in the hall, the police constable entered. He was quickly appraised of the situation by Charlotte. He ran back through the front door and blew his whistle. Within less than a minute half a dozen constables stood in the hall.

One who seemed to be in charge sent the other men away in different directions to check the outside. He asked Edward and Alice to stay with him and gave Charlotte, Mary and Mrs Hart instructions on where to search. 'Look in cupboards, under beds, in favourite hiding places. You know the inside of this house best. My men will look outside.'

'What can I do?' Nell asked. 'I don't know the house well, but I want to help.'

'Just look anywhere you think a little boy may be hiding,' the constable said before turning his attention to Edward and Alice.

Nell set off towards the stairs, heading for the nursery. But something stopped her. 'I'll check the basement. Everyone else has gone upstairs.'

'Good idea,' the constable called after her.

Nell raced along the corridor with its stone-flagged floor and whitewashed walls, taking the steps down to the basement. She could hear Mrs Randal in the kitchen, cooing to the children, reassuring them that their mama would be happy again soon and that Tommy was just playing a silly trick on everyone. Nell went from room to room: from a room full of bottles and jars, to a scullery with a sink, to storerooms full of jars and cans, to what was clearly the housekeeper's parlour with a desk stacked with ledgers, an aspidistra in a pot and a pair of blue and white Staffordshire pottery dogs on the mantelshelf.

She came to a room with a heavy metal door leading to what must have been the silver safe. In another wall was a wooden door. Any frantic and cursory inspection and a person could have been forgiven for thinking it was closed. Nell approached the door. A cold breeze rushed around her legs. The door was open, just a crack. And just wide enough for a slight child to slip through. Nell opened the door a little further. A colder blast blew from the absolute blackness within. With it came the chalky scent of stone that had never seen the light of day or warmth of any kind. Nell shivered and looked over her shoulder. Each of her senses sprang to life. She opened the door further still. 'Come on, Nell Potter,' she said. 'You've got to be brave.'

Reaching inside, she felt along the wall. When she couldn't find a light switch, she turned back and looked around the room. On the mantelshelf, she found a candle and a box of matches. She struck a match, lit the wick, and threw the spent match into the fireplace. Holding the candle aloft, she made for the cellar.

The smudge of light was just enough for her to see a steep flight of rough wooden stairs. Nell picked her way carefully down using her free hand to steady herself against the cold, damp wall. Everything beyond the faint light of the candle was in darkness.

By the time she reached the bottom, Nell felt she had left her courage on the top step. 'Come on,' she whispered. If there was a chance a small boy had made his way down here, then she could not turn and run back up the stairs.

Nell moved the candle from side to side. The cellar was carved into thick grey stone with low ceilings. All around archways were stacked with hundreds of bottles of wine covered in a thick layer of dust. Nell held the candle higher. A corridor led away into the darkness. She took a deep breath. 'Tommy,' she said in little more than a whisper as she made her way slowly into the black which seemed to grow darker the further she got from the stairs. She arrived at a junction where the cellar split in two. She looked back. The light from the open door seemed so far away. Whichever way she went, she would be out of sight of the door and the stairs. She took one last look at the patch of daylight and turned left.

'Tommy,' she whispered, 'Tommy, are you hiding? Come out, you're not in any trouble.' Cold seeped from the stone into Nell's palm as she felt her way along the wall. There was debris underfoot. With each step, it cracked beneath Nell's sole. 'Tommy,' she tried again, glad of the company of her own voice. 'Tommy.'

The flame guttered. Nell stared at the small white light. She held her breath. That delicate flame was all that separated her from absolute darkness. The flame guttered again. There was a noise behind her. The candle trembled. Nell took a step forward and tripped over something on the floor. She stumbled into a shelf. A bottle fell. It smashed, splashing its contents up her legs. Nell held up the candle to see what had caused her to trip and then a bright light pierced the darkness. Nell blinked. She saw what was on the floor and the candle fell from her hands.

FORTY-EIGHT

Nell stared at her feet; at the shattered green glass and the wine, splashed up her legs and trickling into the gaps of the stone floor; at the snuffed-out candle rolling around, the claret, turning it from white to red. With the light from many bulbs blazing overhead, she stared at the object that had caused her to fall.

'Miss Potter,' a familiar voice said from the direction she had come. She didn't respond. 'Nell,' the voice said in a gentler tone. A hand touched her arm and Nell spun around.

Painter removed his hat. 'You're hurt,' he said, looking at her legs.

'It's just wine,' she said.

'Why are you down here in the dark?'

'I couldn't find the light switch.' She pointed to the object she had stumbled over. 'There,' was all she could say.

Painter handed his hat to Nell. He pinched the legs of his trousers and lifted them ever so slightly to crouch. He took a pen from the breast pocket of his jacket and moved the two child dolls that were on the floor beside the cigar box.

'Tommy was playing with them before he disappeared,' Nell said.

'Directly before?' Painter asked.

'What do you mean?'

'Could he have come down here, lost his dolls, and then gone missing?'

'It's a possibility,' Nell said.

Painter looked up at her. 'Do you think it likely?'

Nell looked at the dolls. 'I can't believe he would abandon toys of which he is so fond.'

Painter wiped his pen on a handkerchief and placed it back in his pocket. He stepped over the box and dolls. It was then that Nell saw two of the other dolls in the open cigar box: the female with her hair cut short and the male in the dark suit and hat. She looked towards Painter who had taken hold of a metal door halfway up the wall. It looked to Nell like a delivery hatch. When he pulled, the metal hinges creaked and it opened with no resistance. The sudden shock of daylight made Nell wince. The hatch opened at just below ground level to the rear of the house. Painter leant out. Parting tall weeds, he reached onto the gravel path. He retreated into the cellar, holding aloft a small shoe.

Painter sent Nell into the kitchen to ask Mary to step outside for a moment. He hadn't gone in himself as he didn't want to cause alarm. He waited for them in the housekeeper's parlour. Mary took in the details of the small brown shoe. She clasped her hand to her mouth.

'I need to hear you say it,' Painter said.

'It's Tommy's shoe,' Mary whispered.

'And he was wearing it this morning?' Painter said.

She nodded.

'And he was playing with his box of dolls when you last saw him?'

Mary nodded again. 'He was under the table in the kitchen playing with them.'

'These?' he said. He produced the box and opened it to reveal the small dolls, still dripping wine.

'Oh no!' Mary sobbed.

Painter nodded for Nell to join him at the door. 'Keep her in here,' he said. 'I don't want to panic the family. Say nothing to anyone.'

'Do you think Tommy crawled out of the hatch himself?' she asked.

'That would be my preferred version of events.'

'Or someone took him?'

Painter didn't respond. He simply looked down at her.

'Why was there no constable guarding that hatch?' Nell asked.

'Because we didn't know it was there.' Painter frowned. 'Lock the door behind me. I'll come back as soon as I can.'

'But I want to help,' Nell objected.

Painter leant in closer to Nell and spoke quietly. 'The biggest help you can be to me now is to keep this from the family until I have more information.'

Nell watched Painter sprint the length of the corridor to the door opening to the outside. She watched him take the steps up to ground level two at a time, with the cigar box under his arm. It was only when she closed the door of the housekeeper's parlour that she realised she was still holding Painter's hat.

For half an hour at least, Nell had to field Mary's questions. While Mary sat in an armchair beside the fireplace, Nell paced up and down. She did her very best to put Mary's mind at rest. She was sure that Tommy had simply run off somewhere.

Hadn't he run away only days earlier from Mary herself? He had no doubt dropped his dolls in his excitement, intending to collect them on his return. He had lost his shoe in his rush to run out into the grounds. He would be home just as soon as he was hungry.

Since Nell chose not to tell Mary that the shoe and dolls had been found in the cellar before an unguarded entrance to the house, she almost began to believe that the pacifying tale she was spinning might be true. And all the while she tried to calm Mary, she twisted the brim of Painter's hat around in her hands.

Every so often, Nell saw boots run past the window high in the wall. She wanted to be up there, helping, not stuck in this room with Mary sobbing gently, doing her best to stay quiet so that she would not be heard by Mrs Randal and the children in the kitchen.

Nell pictured the dark cellar. Had Tommy been scared? Had he called out for his mother? Where was he? Had someone taken him? She closed her eyes and all she could see was the empty cellar. And the shoe. And the dolls.

There was a knock on the door and Nell rushed to open it. It was a police constable. He had been asked to let her know that she and Mary should stay in the room for a while longer. Nell reluctantly closed the door and recommenced her pacing, falling again into the pattern of reassuring Mary. Talking continually seemed the only way to make the time almost tolerable. She became aware that she was talking drivel, chatting away while Mary sat in her chair, almost mute apart from sobbing.

After what felt like hours there was another knock at the door. Nell again opened it. This time the police constable asked Nell and Mary to follow him. Nell looked down at Painter's hat in her hands. It would look odd if she carried it around the house. She carefully placed it on the desk.

'Everything is going to be all right,' Nell said as she and

Mary followed the constable out of the room. Another constable was outside the kitchen door. From the sound of the children chattering, Nell knew that they were still in the kitchen with Mrs Randal and still oblivious to what had passed.

Nell and Mary followed the constable up the stairs, through the long corridor, past the bells and through the doorway at the back of the hall. The constable stopped outside the morning room and held the door open.

Inside, the Mandevilles and their visitors had been assembled. Alice, Charlotte and Mrs Hart sat in chairs while Edward stood behind Alice, his hands on her shoulders. She held a handkerchief to her face. Paul and Wilco stood before the fireplace. The constable ushered Nell and Mary into chairs beside the other women. Within moments Painter entered, accompanied by the uniformed police constable who had seemed to be in charge in his absence.

'Thank you for your time,' Painter said to everyone. 'I know this is a very difficult situation for all of you.'

'What is happening, Inspector?' Mrs Hart said. 'Where is my great-nephew? Have you found him?'

Painter pushed his hands into his pockets. He stood firm, his feet planted to the rose-covered rug beneath his shoes.

'In my experience it is preferable in these situations to be candid.' He spoke in a tone so grave that Nell felt the collected anxiety in the room. 'We believe that young master Mandeville is no longer in the house.'

'Has he been kidnapped?' Wilco said.

Alice screamed. Charlotte, Mrs Hart and Mary cried out. Paul left the fireplace. He stood beside Charlotte and took her hand.

'Please,' Painter said, still calm, still rooted to the rug. 'Let us not jump to conclusions. We have evidence to suggest that Thomas left the house in an unorthodox manner. At this point we don't know whether he left of his own accord. Due to the manner of his departure, we think he may have left with some-body else. What we are certain of is that he is no longer in the house.'

'How can he have left the house without one of your consta-bles seeing him?' Paul asked.

'I can't go into the specific details,' Painter said.

'But you have constables at every door,' Charlotte cried. 'How can he have got away without being spotted?'

'As I say,' Painter said calmly, 'I cannot go into specific details at this point.'

'This is ludicrous,' Wilco said. 'A young chap has either escaped from this house or you have let someone snatch him from right under your nose.'

Alice cried out but Wilco was on a path from which he would not deviate. 'Ed,' Wilco said, turning to Edward. 'Will you let me telephone my father now to get a professional inves-tigator here?'

Edward stared ahead, his eyes fixed on the closed door. He had the look of a man who would not be out of place in the hospital where Nell's friend worked in Hanwell.

'Ed?' Wilco said.

'I'm sure that Inspector Painter has this in hand,' Paul inter-vened, his soft American accent like balm to the rough edge of Wilco's anger. 'We must give the police the chance to find Tommy.'

'Find him,' Wilco said, his face growing redder with each word. 'They are the ones that bloody well lost him.'

'We all need to try to stay calm,' Paul said.

'Calm?' Wilco scoffed. 'How can anyone stay calm in this situation?'

'Please, Wilco,' Paul said.

Wilco took a step towards the door.

'Please, Mr Wilkinson, stay where you are,' Inspector Painter said. His calm was matched by Wilco's fury.

Wilco made for the door, but Painter put himself between him and the exit, showing no fear in blocking the path of the much larger man.

'What are you going to do?' Wilco said. 'Arrest me?'

'If you give me reason to,' Painter said. 'But Mr Wilkinson, believe me when I say, I am doing everything in my power to locate young Thomas. You have my word on that.'

Wilco backed away slightly.

'We have tracker dogs coming from London,' Painter said. 'They should be here within the next two hours. We'll be able to search the grounds thoroughly then.'

Nell watched as Wilco retreated still further. On any other day she would have taken notes on this fascinating display of masculine bravado and strength. How the power of words and presence was able to best overwhelming physical strength. But today, all she could think was how she wished that Tommy were here, in this room, with the people who loved him.

'You'll let me know if you need any assistance,' Wilco said. 'You will have my father's connections at your disposal.'

'Thank you,' Painter said, taking a step back.

Wilco reached inside his pocket and took out a silver case. He removed, then lit a cigarette.

'What can we do until the dogs arrive?' Mrs Hart asked. 'We can't just sit here, doing nothing.'

'I'd rather none of you left the house,' Painter said. 'We need to keep the land as undisturbed as possible for the dogs. And I'd like all of you to be available should I need to ask any questions.'

'Very well,' Mrs Hart said. 'Perhaps we can make some lunch for you and your men.'

'That would be very much appreciated, Mrs Hart,' Painter said.

'How can you think of making food,' Alice said suddenly. 'My boy is missing. We should all be out looking for him.'

Mrs Hart rose quickly from her chair. 'Alice, darling, we need to be occupied while the search is conducted by those who know best what to do. The least we can do is prepare them some refreshments. They cannot be expected to work without sustenance. Come,' she said and held out her hand.

Almost instinctively, Nell thought, Alice took Mrs Hart's hand, still clutching her handkerchief.

Charlotte got up, too. 'You don't think that it has anything to do with that man who was seen hiding by the stairs a few nights ago, do you? And is he something to do with the attacks on the constable and Elliot?' It was clear from the look on her face that she had given this great thought. Nell turned to Painter. He didn't so much as glance at Edward.

'We are pursuing all lines of enquiry,' Painter said.

Mrs Hart led Alice away with Charlotte following behind. When Nell made to follow them, Painter gave a discreet shake of his head. With everything going on, none of the women seemed to notice Nell's absence from their party and once they were out of earshot, Painter approached Edward. 'Mr Mandeville,' he said. 'Please would you come with me.'

Like a man desperate for an instruction on how to behave in such an unfamiliar situation, Edward followed. As they passed Nell, Painter said, 'Miss Potter, if you wouldn't mind coming, too.'

'What about us?' Wilco called after them.

The other police constable stepped forward. As Nell followed Painter and Edward from the room, she heard the constable tell Wilco and Paul that they should feel free to go where they wished as long as they remained inside the house. She did not hear any reply since Painter held the door beneath the stairs open for her and Edward to pass through.

FORTY-NINE

Painter followed Edward and Nell into Sir Charles' office and closed the door behind them. Edward stopped just inside the door. He stood absolutely still, staring at the floor until Painter guided him from behind to sit in the chair at the desk. Even then, Edward sat with his shoulders rolled, staring so hard at the blotter that he seemed to be looking through it to the wood of the desk below.

Nell hovered in the doorway and Painter stood at the desk. 'Mr Mandeville,' he said. Edward failed to respond.

'Edward!' Painter said, sharply. Even Nell felt herself jump to attention. 'You have to snap out of this,' Painter said, placing his palms on the desk, leaning towards Edward. 'What use are you to me or to your family in this state?'

Edward looked up at Painter, his eyes watery. Nell wanted to look away but couldn't. Painter stood up straight. As he brushed his hand across his hair, Nell realised she had abandoned his hat in the room downstairs. She looked at the side of his face and his altered profile with no hat. His jaw was firm. He stared at Edward. He seemed at once kind and determined.

'It's my fault,' Edward said.

'No. It is not,' Painter said firmly. 'You have done everything in your power to protect your family. That is all that can be asked of any man.' He paused. For the first time in the exchange, he faltered. His jaw clenched. He quickly regained his composure. 'I have brought Miss Potter here as she found the evidence that led to us discovering that your son had left the house.'

Edward shook his head. 'It's him, isn't it? He has taken my boy. We all know what he is capable of. We all know—'

'That's enough for now,' Painter said. He glanced over his shoulder at Nell. 'I need to talk to Mr Mandeville,' he said. 'Would you mind going to your room?'

'Who is Edward talking about?' Nell said, wondering why she had been summoned and then told to go away. 'Do you know who has taken Tommy?'

'There's only one person who would have taken my brother's portrait. And now he has taken the child I named for him. It's—'

'That's enough!' Painter said, silencing Edward.

'Who is it?' Nell asked, taking a step towards the desk. Painter stepped forward so that Nell had to take a step back or have him walk into her. He reached past her and opened the door. In a movement that Nell couldn't quite fathom and without touching her, he managed to make her leave the room. He joined her in the corridor and pulled the door to behind them.

'Who is it?' she demanded. 'And don't play me for a fool. Don't say that you don't know.'

Painter sighed and ran his hand over his hair again. 'I can't tell you because it may put you in danger. Now, will you go to your room so that I know where to find you when I'm finished with Edward?'

'I'm not a child,' she said, folding her arms across her chest.

'I'm a grown woman and I don't need to be sent to my room like a naughty girl.'

Painter looked down at her, the line of a frown cutting his eyebrows. 'I am very well aware that you are a grown woman,' he said. The intensity in his eyes made Nell turn her eyes to the floor. 'But I would not be doing my duty if I did not protect you.'

'How exactly is this protecting me?'

He took a step closer and said more quietly. 'Because I know you now. And I know that you will not be able to resist running into danger. If I told you who I suspect of taking Tommy, I know you would go after him.'

'You don't know that,' she said.

'Please,' Painter said softly. 'Go to your room. I will come to you. And when I am able, I will tell you everything I know. I'm sure I don't need to remind you, but please, talk to nobody of any suspicions you may have. And I mean *nobody*. Other than me.'

Nell climbed the stairs in a daze. If she succumbed to all that she had seen and heard in the past few days, then she would believe that events within this house were being directed by some unseen force. Surely, a benevolent presence would not play fast and loose with the Mandeville heir. She pushed open the door to her room and came to an abrupt stop.

FIFTY

Huddled in the corner of Nell's bedroom were Bertie and Rosemary, their backs to the wall, legs clutched to their chests, faces buried in their knees, each sobbing. Audrey was crouching before them, attempting to console them.

'Audrey?' Nell said.

'Oh, Miss,' Audrey said jumping to her feet. 'I'm so sorry. They ran in here and I can't get them out. They won't stand. All they will do is sit there and cry.'

Nell knelt before Bertie and Rosemary. 'There, there,' she said. Some innate instinct told her to put her hand to the hair of each child. They both leant into her touch. She stroked Bertie's soft blonde hair and Rosemary's long dark hair.

Nell turned to Audrey who was standing beside her. 'What has happened to them?' she asked.

'I don't know, Miss,' Audrey said. 'Rosemary was playing under the table in the kitchen with Master Tommy and his dolls. Bertie went to give them another biscuit but they were gone. I don't think anybody knew that Rosemary was gone, too. I didn't like to say anything in case it got us into trouble. We're not in trouble are we, Miss?' There was such fear in her eyes that Nell got to her feet and held Audrey close. Beneath the working dress, she was slight, like a bird, and she trembled like a sparrow caught in a net.

'No, Audrey, you're not in trouble at all. Go on.'

'When all the grown-ups ran out of the kitchen, me and Bertie searched all the rooms. We found Rosemary in Mr Bainbridge's room – he's the butler. She was shaking and staring.'

Bertie started to tremble. 'Bertie,' Nell said softly. 'What is it?'

He shook his head and sobbed. 'I can see him, but I don't know where he is. He is scared. He is so very scared. He is crying for his mother.'

A chill swept through Nell. 'And you, Rosemary,' she said gently. 'What did you see?'

Rosemary shook her head, her face still buried in her knees.

'Tell Miss Potter,' Audrey said. 'Tell her what you saw. If you don't, we may not get Master Tommy back.'

These words made Bertie cry out. As though in response to his pain, Rosemary finally whispered. 'The man.'

'The man?' Nell said.

Rosemary looked up and nodded. 'The man. He came in through that door in the wall. In the cellar. That's how he has been visiting Tommy.'

'He's been here before?' Nell said, trying to keep her voice calm so as not to alarm the girl still further.

Rosemary nodded. 'Tommy said for me to go to the cellar with him. The man brings him toffees. Sometimes they meet in a den in the woods. Tommy said that if I went with him, I might get some toffees too.'

'And you know this man?'

Rosemary nodded. Her bottom lip trembled.

'You can tell me,' Nell said kindly. 'Who was the man?'

'Go on, Rosemary,' Audrey said. 'Tell Miss Potter.'

'He... he... he was the man from that night.'

'By the stairs?' Nell said.

Rosemary nodded.

'And he took Tommy out through the hatch in the cellar?'

Rosemary nodded again. 'I was so scared. I was all alone in the dark after they went.'

Nell knelt again and took the girl's hand in hers. 'You have been so incredibly brave telling me this, Rosemary. You have helped Tommy no end. You can be sure of that.' She indicated for Audrey to kneel beside her. 'Look after these two. Don't let them go anywhere. You can do that, can't you Audrey?' Nell transferred the younger girl's hand into the care of her sister.

'As though my life depends on it, miss,' Audrey said.

Closing the door softly behind her, Nell ran. She ran as fast her legs would carry her along the corridor and down the stairs.

In the hall, she came across a group of police constables. 'Inspector Painter?' she said holding her sides and catching her breath.

'He was heading down to the kitchens last I saw,' one of them ventured.

Nell hurried to the back of the hall, through the doorway, along the cool corridor and down the stone steps. She charged into the kitchen. Mrs Randal was there with Mary; Mrs Randal was in the process of carving generous slices from a large ham sat on a wooden board on the table, and Mary was at the sink, shaking excess water from a colander of lettuce leaves. They had been joined by Mrs Hart, Charlotte and Alice. At Nell's arrival, Mrs Hart and Charlotte paused in buttering a mountain of bread. Alice didn't register her presence. She sat at the table clutching the two smallest Mandevilles to her.

'Inspector Painter?' Nell said.

'What is it?' Mrs Hart said, her knife paused midway to the butter.

'Nothing,' Nell said, trying to still the shake in her voice.

Mrs Hart placed the knife in the butter dish. She untied her apron, folded it neatly and placed it over the back of a chair. 'You carry on, ladies. There's a horde of hungry mouths to feed. People work best when their bellies are full.' She glanced at Alice before taking Nell's elbow, guiding her from the room and walking in silence to the stairs.

Mrs Hart waited until they were at the top of the stairs before speaking and then only in a controlled whisper.

'What is it, Nell? What has happened?'

Nell thought back to her promise to Inspector Painter. The promise that she would not discuss the crimes with anyone but him. But there could be no harm in telling Mrs Hart. She would help, not hinder the investigation. 'It's Bertie and young Rosemary,' she said. 'I think they know what happened to Tommy.'

Mrs Hart came to an abrupt halt. 'Where are they?'

Forgoing the hall and any questioning by the police constables, Nell followed Mrs Hart up the stone stairs and through the hidden door on the first floor. Mrs Hart threw open the door to Nell's bedroom.

'Bertie!' she said. 'And you Rosemary and Audrey. Have you had a nasty shock, my darling creatures?' She knelt before the children and gathered them all to her. 'Now girls,' she said. 'Why don't you go along with Miss Potter? I need to have a quick talk with Bertie.'

Audrey stood and helped her sister to her feet.

'You go and wait outside on the landing for me,' Nell said.

When the girls had left, she said quietly to Mrs Hart, 'Had we not ought to tell the police what the children have seen?'

Mrs Hart rose and said quietly. 'There are some things that must be dealt with within the family. And you are part of our extended Hill House family. Only once we know what we are dealing with should we involve the police.'

As much as Nell respected Mrs Hart, she couldn't just

accept what she was saying. 'But Bertie and Rosemary said a man took Tommy and he is the man that has been making a nuisance of himself and probably the man behind the burglary. What if Tommy is in danger?'

'Nell,' Mrs Hart said sternly, 'I fear that my great-nephew may be in even more danger if we do not find him first. We must try to establish what is happening before bringing in the police. They serve their purpose, but sometimes more subtle approaches are needed. Bertie will tell me all I need to know.'

'But—'

Mrs Hart held up her hand. 'I know that it is a challenge for you to keep this from Inspector Painter, but please, Nell. Do this for me, for now. I beg you. Take the girls downstairs. Do not let them speak to anyone of what they have seen but please ask Alice to come to me. You can do that. Can't you?'

'I don't seem to have much choice,' Nell said.

'There is always a choice. I just hope you can see your way clear to making the right choice for this family.'

Outside, the two girls waited. Nell led them down to the housekeeper's parlour. Rosemary sat close to her big sister on the sofa and Audrey placed a protective arm around her.

'Will you be all right if I leave you?' Nell asked. 'You'll be safe in here.'

'We'll be all right. Thank you, miss,' Audrey said.

'And you will stay here until I get back and tell nobody what you saw. It's really very important that we say nothing until Mrs Hart has had the chance to decide what to do. We can trust Mrs Hart, can't we?'

Audrey nodded. 'She seems like a very kind lady.'

'She certainly took a shine to you and Rosemary. I think she likes you and trusts you.'

Audrey's cheeks flushed.

Closing the door behind her, Nell paused in the long corridor. She would not tell the police of the events Rosemary had witnessed in the cellar. Not because Mrs Hart had asked her to keep quiet, but because Painter had asked her not to speak to anyone of the crimes. She had already gone against what he had asked of her by not staying in her room and involving Mrs Hart.

She had to find him. And Mrs Hart had until she could track Painter down to do whatever it was she felt she had to.

FIFTY-ONE

In the kitchen, Nell found Mrs Randal and Charlotte busy making sandwiches. Mary was showing Daphne and Charlie how to cut shapes from biscuit dough.

'That's it,' Mary cooed. 'You are being ever such good children, aren't they, Miss Charlotte?'

'They are,' Charlotte said. There was an unfamiliar shake to her voice and Mrs Randal wiped away a tear. The disappearance of one small boy was already tearing this family apart. Nell couldn't bear to think what would happen to them if Tommy couldn't be found.

Alice sat at the table with a knife in her hand, staring at a slice of bread.

'Alice,' Nell said from the doorway.

Alice's hand stayed above the bread, holding the knife perfectly still as though she were a marble statue. Her pale skin had taken on the pallor of alabaster. The contrast in her skin and hair colour was startling, giving her an otherworldly appearance. 'Alice,' Nell tried again.

Charlotte placed a slice of bread on top of a slice of ham.

She wiped her hands on her apron before gently touching Alice's shoulder.

'Alice, darling,' Charlotte said. Alice moved her head slowly as though in a dream. 'Nell is here to see you.'

This time, and quite without warning, Alice leapt from her chair. She gripped Nell's hands. 'Have they found him?' she said. 'Have they found my boy?'

Alice's eyes were wide, the whites shot through with red lines. Her hair fell loose, as the clip barely holding it in place gave up and fell to the floor. She searched Nell's eyes, looking for an answer. Nell wished so much that she could provide the balm to ease the suffering of this woman who had shown her so much kindness.

'No,' Nell said. 'Not yet. But Mrs Hart wants to see you. I think she has an idea that might help find Tommy.'

With Alice's mute compliance, Nell was able to direct her through the house and up to the landing. Alice's body walked beside her, but Nell knew that her thoughts were somewhere else entirely.

'Thank you, Nell,' Mrs Hart said when Alice entered the bedroom. Mrs Hart had managed to move Bertie so that he sat on the bed. Nell helped Alice sit beside him.

'I hope you don't mind that we have commandeered your bedroom, Nell,' Mrs Hart said. 'And I hope it's not an imposition too far, but I rather need to speak to Alice and Bertie alone. I'm certain that Audrey and Rosemary would be pleased with some company.'

'Of course. I'll go and see them now.'

Nell pulled the door to behind her but had no intention of going anywhere near the basement. Instead, she pressed her ear to the closed door. It was Alice's voice she heard first.

'I need to go to see Louisa,' Alice said. 'She'll know what to do and if she doesn't, she can find out.'

'Alice,' Mrs Hart soothed. 'You are confused. She was

special and dear to us. But what you're suggesting comes with incredible risk. You don't even know that you will be able to find her.'

'We're from the same time.'

'That's just the problem; you don't know that if you leave you will go to wherever she is. The world may have moved on.'

'What else can I do? My son is missing. Nobody else can help.'

'Alice, please, this is all going too far, you know Bertie and I shouldn't be talking to you about this. Even saying what we have is putting your position here at risk.'

'What else am I to do?' Alice cried.

'Oh, my darling,' Mrs Hart said.

There was a pause before a new voice joined the conversation. 'It is true, Mrs Hart,' Nell heard Bertie say. 'Alice must go to find her.'

'Bertie,' Mrs Hart said. 'Can you be sure?'

'I feel it,' he said. 'That is all I know. She is the only one who can help. One in, one out.'

Alice cried out again and Mrs Hart gently soothed her.

'The time is now,' Bertie said. 'Alice must go now.'

The sound of movement made Nell run to the far end of the corridor. She opened a door and dipped inside, finding herself in a small store cupboard amongst brooms and pails and cleaning supplies. When she felt the coast should be clear, she looked out to see Mrs Hart, Alice and Bertie emerge from her bedroom. She waited for them to go downstairs before making her way to the landing and peering over the bannisters.

'We simply must go outside,' Mrs Hart said to the two constables in the hallway. 'As you can see, Mrs Mandeville needs some restorative air. It just won't do to keep her cooped up in the house all day.'

The constables looked at each other. 'I'm not sure,' one of them said. 'We should really ask you to stay inside the house.'

'I think that's a slight over-reaction,' Mrs Hart said. 'We will simply take a turn to the gates and back again. You can even watch us from here, should you feel you need.'

The constables looked at each other again. 'Very well,' the taller of the two constables said. 'But please stay on the path. We need to keep the land free of contamination for when the dogs arrive.'

Alice stifled a cry.

'Thank you, gentlemen,' Mrs Hart said. 'I am very grateful for your understanding.'

The shorter of the two constables opened the front door. He had closed it before Nell came rushing down the stairs. 'Sorry,' she said. 'I was powdering my nose! I'm with them.'

The constable opened the door and Nell ran out.

She came to a stop beneath the portico. Mrs Hart, Alice and Bertie were just a short way down the path. Nell hid behind one of the pillars. She stooped to remove her shoe, shaking it as though to shake out a piece of gravel, creating a plausible reason for her delay in joining the others, should the constables in the house be watching her.

Leaving the safety of the pillar, Nell watched the small party walk down the drive. Sheep bleated in the fields. Crows cawed up in the trees. But none of this would be loud enough to mask the crunch of her shoes in the gravel if she followed in their footsteps. If they saw her, it would surely put paid to the secret plan they were carrying out to find Tommy. Crossing the gravel to the grass bordering the drive, Nell followed with as much confidence as she could.

Soon, Nell was parallel with the copse at the end of the lane. Where was Painter when he was needed? And what would he make of the group heading for the gates? She may have grown used to the peculiar events in Hill House but Painter, surely, he would not tolerate this. She wished he were here. He would know what to do.

By the time the small party reached the gates, Nell was just a few feet behind. She dipped behind a tree.

'Alice,' Mrs Hart said. 'Are you sure you should be doing this? It is such a risk.'

'If it brings my boy back, I'll do anything.'

'Bertie,' Mrs Hart said. 'Are you sure this is the right thing for Alice to do?'

'I can only say what I sense,' Bertie said. 'And this feels like what Alice must do.'

'It is such a leap of faith,' Mrs Hart said. Her voice was soft and uncertain in a way Nell had never before heard. 'I trust in us. But I have to say I am fearful.'

'This is my decision,' Alice said. 'Whatever happens, remember that I did this for Tommy. If I don't come back, please tell Edward, Daphne and Charlie that I love them so much. Tell them that I love them more than life itself.'

'Oh, Alice,' Mrs Hart said.

'People can build new lives if they have to,' Alice said. 'I know that better than anyone. Hill House saved me. But my future is nothing compared to the future of my boy. If I don't do this and Tommy never comes home, I will never forgive myself for not trying. We don't know where he is or if someone is hurting him... I can't wait any longer. I know you understand that.'

'Very well,' Mrs Hart said softly. 'I do understand.'

Nell heard kisses and sobs before Alice said, 'Everything is going to be all right. I will see you soon. Louisa will know what to do.'

There were footsteps in the gravel. Then silence.

'Bertie,' Mrs Hart said, 'please go and look.'

Footsteps ran through the gravel. There was a pause. Footsteps ran back through the gravel.

'She is gone,' he said. 'The path outside the gate is empty.'

Once again, the only sound was the caw of crows and the

bleat of sheep. Nell waited and listened. She wanted to show herself and have Mrs Hart and Bertie explain what was happening. Why did Alice have to leave to allow this Louisa person to come to Hill House? Why did it carry such risk? And where was she going?

A cry came from the other side of the tree. 'Oh, my heavens,' Mrs Hart said. 'Oh, my good Lord. It is you returned. Oh, my darling, darling girl.'

Nell waited for Alice's response. Instead, a woman's voice unfamiliar to her spoke. 'Oh, I've missed you all. Bertie, look how grown up you are!'

Nell could resist no longer. With great care, she looked around the trunk. Both Mrs Hart and Bertie had their backs to her. Before them stood a woman. It was not possible to see her face as she and Bertie were deep in an embrace, Bertie clinging to the woman and weeping so that his shoulders shook.

'I thought I would never see you again,' he said through sobs.

Finally, he pulled away from the woman. She smiled as she brushed the blonde hair back from his face and kissed him on both cheeks. 'Well, here I am,' she said.

Mrs Hart moved in to embrace the woman, who closed her eyes and rested her chin on Mrs Hart's shoulder, giving Nell the opportunity to look at her face. She was an attractive woman. Nell guessed her to be a decade or so older than herself. She smiled as she received Mrs Hart's enthusiastic embrace.

Mrs Hart released the woman and said, 'Has life been kind to you, Louisa?'

The woman smiled. 'Very kind.'

'But we mustn't say too much,' Mrs Hart added.

'No, we mustn't. But what I will say is that everything is fine. Everyone is fine. Please don't worry. I know what needs to be done and I am best placed to do it. It was best that I came back. For now, at least. Beyond that I can't say anything.'

There was something about how she spoke that reminded Nell of Alice. A bit of an accent that wasn't quite like the Mandevilles. There was also something familiar about her that Nell couldn't quite place. She was a woman in her middle years. She reminded her of someone. Although in Nell's mind she should be younger.

'Come,' Mrs Hart said. 'We must go before we raise suspicion.'

From behind the tree, Nell watched the three of them pass. She was about to follow but sensed a presence. There, watching the progress of the visitor from the other side of the path, was Mr Townley. He was in full sight of anyone passing but had somehow escaped the attention of the small party. There was a look in his eyes as he watched the newly arrived woman that Nell had not seen before. She felt it, felt what he was feeling. And her heart at once flooded, then broke. When the little party disappeared around the side of the house, he let his head fall and turned and walked away through the trees.

FIFTY-TWO

Nell paused behind the tree closest to the house. The grief and hopelessness beyond that grand front door mixed with the sensation of loss and longing she had just seen in Mr Townley's face.

What if the Mandevilles and this Louisa didn't hold the answer to finding Tommy? Was she really going to step aside to let events play out without intervention? Painter. The Mandevilles needed Painter. They needed his grounded, pragmatic approach. He needed to be told what Rosemary had seen so that he could find a rational route to an explanation for Tommy's disappearance. Mrs Hart may have been emphatic in her refusal of police intervention at this stage, but she was hardly impartial. And she might not know what was for the best.

The police constable at the door to the conservatory raised a quizzical eyebrow when Nell approached. She reassured him that a fellow constable had said she could leave the house to take the air. She asked whether he had seen Inspector Painter, he said he hadn't. She received the same response from the constables stationed at the back of the house, outside the dining room doors and at the top of the stairs leading down to the kitchen. Finally, when Nell came to the constable stationed outside the hatch leading down to the wine cellar, she received a different response. 'He had his car parked round by the stables,' the constable said. 'But I saw him drive away a while back. I'd say at least an hour ago.'

Nell hurried to the stable yard. Elliot may have seen Painter and may know where he had gone.

Pushing open the door to the stables, Nell was met with the smell of leather and hay. A dappled grey horse snuffled at a net suspended from the wall. She had never stepped foot in this place but, with sudden clarity, she realised she knew it. It was the stables where she had watched the man and woman; strangers she had assumed summoned to her daydream from the depths of her imagination. Until she realised one was Mr Townley. And here, and now, in this place growing more familiar by the second, she realised the woman in her dream was anything but a stranger to Hill House. *One in, one out...*

The door she had entered through opened. 'Hello, Nell.'

Nell turned to see the newly arrived woman. 'It is you,' she said. 'You're Louisa. I've seen you in my dreams.' She took in the fine lines around Louisa's kind eyes. 'But you were younger.' As soon as the words left her mouth, Nell knew how ludicrous they sounded. 'What is happening here?' she said. 'What is happening to me? Because I think I'm going mad. I see things. I hear things. I experience things. And you are part of it. Where is Alice now? And why did she have to leave to let you in?'

'You need to listen to me,' Louisa said. 'I'm sure from what you've seen and heard that you know so much of what happens here can't be spoken about. For now, you need to do what I ask. I'll try to help you understand what is happening to you later.'

Taken aback, Nell said, 'Aren't you in the least surprised that I told you I had seen you here before when you were younger? Especially since I had never set foot inside Hill House before this week.'

'No, Nell. I'm not at all surprised,' Louisa said. 'I think you know I have returned for a particular reason. And you know that I have to be careful what I say.'

'I know that you are protecting Alice. That Alice can only come back if you leave. And that if you and she aren't careful she may not be able to return at all. I know it because I have heard people say it. But knowing it doesn't mean I understand it.'

'For now, don't try to understand it. Just know that houses can be more than bricks and mortar.'

'Are you asking me to believe that Hill House is controlling all of this?' Nell asked with a laugh in her voice. 'Where have you come from, Louisa? And where is it that Alice has gone to?'

The smile left Louisa's eyes. She took Nell's hands in hers. 'You need to listen to me,' she said. 'I know who has taken Tommy.'

'What?'

'The man behind all this is George Caxton. The break-ins, the thefts, all that has happened to Tommy. Caxton blames the Mandevilles for everything bad that has happened in his life, when the only person to blame is himself. He's evil, Nell. Pure evil. Taking Tommy is just his latest way of getting some kind of twisted revenge. You need to go to Caxton Hall. You need to find Caxton and stop him.'

'Me? Why me?'

'Just trust me when I say it has to be you.' Louisa paused. 'The Mandevilles don't even know half of what Caxton is capable of. What he has done and what he will do.'

'And how do you know?' Nell asked, exasperated at the turns in the conversation. 'How can you possibly know what he will do in the future?'

'There's no time to explain now. The police have been

alerted but they are travelling by road to Caxton Hall and won't be there for some time.'

It was clear to Nell that she wasn't going to get the answers she wanted yet. All she knew was that Tommy needed her. 'How will I get there?' she asked.

Louisa nodded to the room at the end of the stables. 'Elliot will help you. He has always been loyal to the Mandevilles.' Louisa let Nell's hands slip from hers and opened the door to leave. 'I'll see you again later. And I'll try to help you understand all this before I leave. But please, you have to be the one to help Tommy.'

FIFTY-THREE

Nell entered the small room with a fireplace, a table and shelves stacked with saddles and blankets. Ben looked up from his position on a rug before the fire. He wagged his tail as a figure appeared from between the shelves at the far end of the room. But it wasn't the person Nell was expecting.

'Hello, Nell,' Mr Townley said.

'Were you eavesdropping?' Nell said.

Elliot entered the room. He looked surprised to see Mr Townley. He removed his cap and stood up absolutely straight. 'Cap—' he started. But after a look from Mr Townley, he glanced at Nell and quickly said. 'Mr Townley. I wasn't expecting you today. I've been sent to saddle up Ambrose to take Miss Potter to Caxton Hall. That bastard Caxton has taken Master Tommy.'

'I heard,' Mr Townley said, his hands balling into fists.

'Mister Edward and I suspected it was him behind all this,' Elliot said. 'He must have escaped that prison in India.' He glanced at Nell and rubbed the black scab splitting his top lip. 'If it is Caxton then it's not safe. I could go.'

'Miss Potter is more than up to the task,' Mr Townley said. 'Would you saddle up Samson, please?'

'Samson? Can she handle him?'

'He'll look after her.'

Nell looked from one man to the other. The dynamics of power seemed all wrong. Shouldn't it be Elliot giving instructions to Mr Townley? He was his employee, after all. Elliot marched into the stable with a saddle. He placed it on the back of the large black horse and tied a strap around its belly. He led the horse out of a door further along.

In the yard, Elliot came to a stop at a set of stone steps and placed the bit between the horse's teeth. Nell climbed the steps and looked at the mountain of black horse. 'I'm not sure this is such a good idea. Why don't you go, Mr Townley?'

'It's not possible,' he said. 'You know you have to do this.'

He was right; she could sense that it had to be her. Why, she didn't know.

She took a breath, placed her foot in the stirrup and somehow managed to clamber into the saddle. The horse didn't flinch. Elliot handed the reins to her and adjusted the stirrups, tightening the straps and yanking her feet higher.

'Thank you, Elliot,' Mr Townley said.

Elliot touched the peak of his cap. 'I'll follow the police in the Rolls,' he said.

With Elliot gone, Nell looked down at Mr Townley. 'You know Louisa, don't you?' she said. She couldn't leave without at least some explanation for why she saw them in her dreams and his behaviour in the trees. 'Why didn't you speak to her? I saw you watching her when she arrived earlier.'

The look of loss and longing returned to Mr Townley's face. He turned his eyes to the ground. 'She can't know I am here,' he said. 'She has a life, and I can't do anything to jeopardise the happiness she has found.' He looked up at Nell again. 'You'll understand what I'm saying when you need to. But she can know that I loved her. That I will love her forever.'

Nell nodded. There was no more time for questions.

Mr Townley walked out of the yard and Samson followed, his metal shoes clopping on the cobbles. Nell swayed on Samson's back. They stopped on the path outside the stable gates.

'Samson will look after you,' Mr Townley said. 'He knows the way. Keep the reins loose and he will go ahead. Pull on them if you want him to change direction. Keep your feet tight to his flank. He might be old now but he can fly when he gets the scent of fresh air. Are you ready?'

'I think so,' Nell said. She gripped the reins.

'Go boy!' Mr Townley called.

Almost before the command had left his mouth, Nell felt herself thrown back, her head jerking so that she had to fight to right herself. Samson's hooves thudded on the grass. Nell tucked her chin into her chest. The wind rushed past her face. She closed her eyes and clung on for dear life, rising and falling in the saddle, the leather reins twisted twice around her wrists. She leant forward and pressed her forehead into the horse's neck, his mane whipping about her face. She knew they must be racing past familiar landmarks – the woods, the lake, the boathouse – but she saw none of them. With what sense she could muster, Nell knew she should be frightened. On the contrary, she felt oddly safe. She was in the care of a creature who knew and understood its business. In spite of his size and power, Samson was taking care of her. And the knowledge that they were racing to help Tommy stopped Nell pulling on the reins to bring him to a stop.

Soon, Nell felt Samson's gait alter. He slowed ever so slightly, giving Nell the chance to prise her face from his neck and sit up. They were ascending the hill. She leant forward. It took a fraction of the time for Samson to reach the peak that it had taken her to ascend on the bicycle. If anything, Samson seemed to pick up speed up as they neared the peak, facing the challenge as though it were no more taxing than trotting about the flat paddock behind Hill House.

Samson began the descent. Nell sat back; her spine almost parallel with his. She forced her shoes against the stirrups and braced as he powered down the hill. Descending into the bowl of the valley, Samson gathered momentum and it was all Nell could do to keep hold of the reins and stay in the saddle. Samson's mane whipped about them, his hooves thundering on the ground. Nell felt they were no longer bound by the laws of gravity but were flying in the moments when all four of Samson's hooves were in the air.

As the detail of Caxton Hall came into view, so did the sight of a car parked on the drive outside the house. A black car. A black car that Nell had sat in only days earlier.

When they reached level ground, Nell pulled on the reins. But her attempt to bring Samson to a stop outside the house failed. Caxton Hall flashed beside them, the windows and doors and architecture a blur. Nell's stomach leapt into her mouth. What if she was unable to stop him?

'Woah,' she tried and pulled on the reins, but Samson seemed oblivious to her request. He left the lawn and galloped past the house until his path was blocked by the wall. Nell pulled hard on the reins and Samson slowed and finally stopped. Nell yanked her feet from the stirrups and dropped to the ground. She looked about, unsure of where to look or what she was supposed to do. It occurred to her that she was looking for an escaped convict. She should be scared, but the sight of Painter's car and the thought that somebody might be preparing to harm Tommy made the blood rush to her head and chest.

The sound of raised voices reached her. She opened the gate in the wall and ran into the gardens. A small rowing boat was on the lake, moving away from the shore. There were two men onboard. Nell looked harder. Oh God. Oh no. The hair. The red curls. Tommy was in the boat, too.

Nell ran across the lawn and down the steps. When she reached the lake, she half ran, half waded through the water. The boat moved further from the land. Nell kicked off her shoes, tore off her dress and launched into the lake. She swam; swam harder than she had ever swam in her life. Her arms split through the water as she crawled and kicked beneath the surface. She turned her head to draw in breath only when she had to. She swam until her lungs burned and she had to stop to gasp down air.

Treading water, Nell looked around. The boat was as far away as ever. She looked towards the shore and to Caxton Hall. There was nobody to be seen. Nobody she could call on to help her. Where was Painter?

She twisted in the water, looking back to the boat. Rather than moving away, it had come to a stop, rocking from side to side. The sound of gruff voices raised in argument split the air. Nell was unable to hear distinct words. She eased beneath the surface and swam towards the boat in a breaststroke rather than the more obvious crawl. The water was clear, and the keel of the boat grew larger as she approached. She slowed. The occupants were too concerned with shouting at each other to notice her. She began to tread water and pressed her cheek to the side of the boat.

'I don't want any part of this,' one of the men said. His voice was rough and his accent unfamiliar. Nell continued to tread water, keeping as close as she could to the waterline, bobbing as the boat rose and fell with the movement of the people onboard.

'You'll do as I say,' another voice said. It was more refined. It had to be Caxton. Nell's hands instinctively balled into fists, mirroring Mr Townley's reaction to the name. 'You've had enough money from me,' Caxton said. 'And for what? You couldn't even bring yourself to deal with that fool, Barnes.'

'That was never part of the deal.'

'The deal is what I tell you it is. Would you have preferred him to go to the police as he threatened to? I don't pay you to then have to do my own dirty work.'

'You can keep your blood money.'

'Oh, no. You don't get to back out now.'

'I'll not hurt a hair on that bairn's head.'

Nell slammed her hand across her mouth. Tommy. They were talking about Tommy.

Caxton laughed. 'Barnes did make rather a mess when he fell onto the train tracks. You should have seen the look of surprise when he went over the edge of the bridge. It was quite something.'

The man in the mortuary. Caxton had killed him. Nell looked desperately around. What was she to do? Against two men and in the water, she would be overpowered. But she had to get Tommy away from them. The boat moved suddenly, lurching to one side. The oar closest to her left the water. It rose into the air. The boat lurched again.

'I want my mummy,' a small voice cried. Nell looked desperately around again.

'Shut him up!' Caxton hissed. The oar flailed through the air as though someone was about to use it as a weapon.

'Do it yourself,' the other man said.

'How dare you speak to me like that?'

'I dare because you're not right in the head. You said this was about getting even with relatives who owed you money. Taking some things to get back at them. Not harming a bairn. And not killing Barnes. I should never have got him involved.'

Caxton laughed. 'You weren't so squeamish when it came to keeping that police constable and groom quiet.'

'A bit of a beating and tying someone up isn't the same as murder. What you did to that man back there. There was no call for that.'

Caxton laughed again. 'It's a bit late to get squeamish. You're in this up to your neck. You do what I say, or you'll find yourself back in that prison cell where I found you.'

'I'll take my chances. I'll not hurt this child and I want no part in what you did to Barnes or that police inspector. For all you know, he might be dead, too.'

'Let's hope so.'

Nell momentarily forgot to move. She slipped beneath the water before instinct kicked in and her legs remembered what to do.

The boat rocked violently. There was a loud splash. A man emerged from the other side of the boat, swimming towards the far bank. He was struggling to make progress with his long black coat weighing him down. Nell could see enough of him to know he was the man who had threatened to attack her in the woods.

'Get back here,' Caxton shouted. 'I said get back here!'

The man in the water didn't break his stroke as he swam away.

Caxton yelled and swore. The boat rocked wildly.

'Mummy!' Tommy called.

'Shut up,' Caxton said.

'I won't,' Tommy yelled. The boat rocked.

'Sit down, you brat,' Caxton shouted. 'Sit down before I wring your bloody neck!'

Nell could wait no longer, she reached up, and with every ounce of strength she could muster she grabbed the side of the boat and hauled herself up so that she could see inside. Caxton sat on the bench seat, gripping the sides. He wore a pale suit, and his back was to her. Past him, she saw Tommy standing at the bow end.

'Nell,' Tommy yelled. He tried to run to her, but his path was blocked by the man.

'Stop making the boat move!' Caxton shouted to Tommy. He kicked out his legs to keep the boy away. Tommy fell, landing on his backside. The man's head whipped round. He glared at Nell. His face was wide with eyes too close together. But it was the meanness that made Nell want to turn away. The look in his eyes was a mixture of fury and terror. If she was reading this correctly, then he was holding onto the boat because he couldn't swim. But his fear would make him unpredictable.

'You let him go,' she said, putting all her fury into her demand. 'I know who you are! You're George Caxton. You won't get away with this. Too many people know.'

Caxton laughed. 'I'll let him go all right. I'll let him go to sink to the bottom of this lake. Once I've wrung his neck.'

Tommy cowered, curling into the point of the bow.

'It's all right Tommy,' Nell said.

'Don't fool yourself,' Caxton said.

'Why do you want to hurt him?' she said. 'He's just a child. He can have done nothing to you.'

'His family are the stain on my family's history,' Caxton said, turning away from Nell and directing his words to Tommy. 'If it weren't for them, this house would be mine. I will see to it that the Mandeville line is stopped. Beginning with this one, named for that idiot uncle of his. He turned my father against me, and I will not stop until I have wiped the name of Mandeville from the face of the Earth.'

It had been Nell's intention to keep him talking and it had worked. Nell swam along the side. If she was going to face an adversary, she would do it looking him in the eye. She emerged beside Tommy, hauling herself back up so that she could see inside the boat again. Caxton seemed genuinely shocked.

'You will not harm a hair on this boy's head,' she said.

Tommy reached for her. The boat rocked.

'Stay still,' Caxton yelled.

Tommy had his arm about Nell's neck. She whispered to him, 'Jump into the water Tommy. I'm going to get one of the oars. Hold onto it and swim to the shore. You remember how I showed you at the seaside. Kick your legs. Kick them as hard as you can.'

He nodded.

'What are you saying?' Caxton demanded.

In a single movement, and with all her strength, Nell grabbed one of the oars and pulled it overboard. It smashed into the water. 'Now!' she shouted.

Tommy jumped into the water. He doggy paddled to her. 'You're so brave,' she said as she took his hands and placed them on the oar. 'Go,' she said. 'As fast as you can to the shore.' The oar acted as a buoyancy aid. Tommy nodded and kicked his little legs, the water frothing in white peaks behind him.

'You bitch!' Caxton yelled.

Nell spun around to face Caxton. She stared up into his eyes, at the horrible, sneering mouth. 'You should be in prison in India.'

He laughed. 'Yet clearly, I am not, *Miss Potter*. Oh, don't look so surprised. I've seen you creeping here about.'

'I knew I saw movement up at the window that day,' she said, treading water and flicking her wet hair from her eyes.

'There's nothing I don't know about what goes on here and at that wretched hovel across the valley.'

Nell wanted to yell and gouge his eyes out and demand to be told what he had done with Painter. She wanted to taunt him that it was his sister, not he who had inherited Caxton Hall. But she couldn't; she had to give Tommy the chance to get away. She looked over her shoulder and saw that he was making good progress.

'You seem quite taken with that police inspector,' Caxton said when she didn't respond. 'I saw you both here. All this time I have been under your noses and you are all so stupid that you have not seen it. And now, let's just say that he is... *indisposed*. Permanently, with any luck.'

Nell dug her fingernails deep into her palms. She stole a glance toward the shore and saw that Samson had followed her through the gate and was in the water.

'Look at you, all but naked,' Caxton leered. 'A nice girl wouldn't be seen in such disarray. Are you a nice girl, Miss Potter? I don't think so. I've seen you. Gallivanting around. Swimming in that fetid lake across the valley. Do you make a habit of taking off your clothes in public? If we were on solid ground, I would show you what a man does with a woman like you.'

Nell glanced towards the shore again. Samson had swum out. Tommy had abandoned the oar and taken hold of the reins and Samson was swimming them back to shore. They were within a few feet of safety.

'Don't think the brat has got away,' Caxton said. 'You may have won this skirmish, but I will win the war.'

With Tommy safe in Samson's care, the anger Nell had contained burst red hot through every fibre of her body. She grabbed the side of the boat and pulled as hard as she could. It rocked violently.

Caxton gripped the sides, his smirk replaced by wide-eyed terror.

'What's wrong?' Nell said. 'Scared, are we?' She may be near naked, and Caxton may be able to see every curve and contour of her body beneath her sodden silk, but for the first time in her life, she *felt* more than a physical equal of a man.

She rocked the boat again.

'What do you want?' Caxton said, staring at the bottom of the boat, a tremor in his voice. 'Money? Is that it?'

'I want you to leave Tommy and his family alone.'

For the briefest of seconds, Nell let her guard down. Caxton lurched forward. He made a grab for throat. She raised her arm to defend her neck with the hard bone of her forearm and pushed away from the boat with her feet.

'Do you want to drown?' Nell said.

'I can swim,' Caxton cried, on his knees in the bottom of the boat.

'A man who can swim does not cling to a boat as though his life depends on it.'

Nell's heart raced. She thought about Painter and what Caxton might have done to him. She looked to the shore. Tommy was standing in the shallows, holding Samson's reins. He was safe. She looked at Caxton again.

'You have no idea what you have done,' he said, his face scarlet. 'Do you realise what I can do to you?'

He continued his rant, but Nell didn't wait to hear it. She submerged beneath the water. Using the bottom of the boat as a guide, she felt her way beneath and resurfaced on the other side so that Caxton couldn't see her. He was still ranting. She inched along the side of the boat, grabbed the oar that sat on the water and pulled it free. Caxton made a grab for it, but too late. It smashed into the water and Nell pushed it away. Still on his knees, Caxton leant over the side of the boat, desperately scrabbling at the water. His eyes filled with fear. He was so badly balanced that she could grab his arm and pull him overboard. But could she be responsible for the death of a person?

Nell shook her head. She would leave him for the police to find. So what if he came after her when this was over to get his revenge. Tommy was safe, and his family and the police would know who was behind the crimes and the kidnapping and the murder of the man on the railway tracks. She took a final look at Caxton on his knees, leaning over the side of the boat, scooping at the water in an effort to reach the oar.

He wasn't worth a single second more of her time. There was another man she had to get to.

'You bitch!' Caxton bellowed as Nell swam away, his furious insults pursuing her. A single thought rushed through Nell's head as she swam, keeping her head beneath the surface to better cut through the water. She pictured Painter's face and gasped for a breath. When she finally surfaced, she found she was only a few feet from shore.

'Nell!' Tommy shouted, waving wildly.

Nell let her feet find the bottom of the lake, her toes slipping in silt and weeds. 'Stay there, Tommy. I'm coming.' She waded through the water towards him. Tommy released Samson's reins and when Nell reached him, she sank to her knees in the shallow water and scooped him into her arms.

'Oh, you brave boy,' she said, kissing his face and holding him tight. 'You brave, brave boy.'

Tommy's arms were around her neck, his wet curls on her cheek.

She pulled away, holding him at arm's length. 'Are you hurt?' she asked, searching his face, checking his arms and legs sticking from his sopping shirt and shorts.

'I'm not hurt,' he said. 'But Nell, one of the bad men hurt another man.'

'Where, Tommy?' Nell said, trying to keep the shake from her voice. 'Where is Inspector Painter? Where is the man the bad man hurt?'

Tommy pointed up the garden to the orangery. 'There,' he said. 'The man thumped him. I was outside with the other bad man, but I saw through the window. He fell on the floor.'

Nell pushed Tommy's curls from his face. 'Tommy, can you be a really brave boy again. Can you go to the building next to the house? Knock on the door and keep knocking until someone comes. Tell them I need help. Tell them to telephone your father and send Doctor Kenmore right away.'

He nodded. 'Will I take Samson?'

'Yes, Tommy. Take Samson.'

Nell knew that should anyone try to approach Tommy, Samson would make such a fuss that she would be alerted.

'Go,' Nell said. 'As quickly as you can.'

She waited just a moment to see Tommy run with Samson trotting by his side, before she took off up the garden, past the fountain, across the lawn, up the steps and through the parterre. She glanced towards the kitchen wing and saw Tommy and Samson not far away.

The door to the orangery stood open. She didn't slow as she ran towards the humidity, the green scent of foliage and the heady perfume. But the sight that met her amongst the dense flowers and fruits stopped Nell in her tracks.

FIFTY-FOUR

Slumped, with his back to a huge terracotta pot containing a fern so vast that its fronds reached to the high ceiling, was the lifeless form of a slim man in a dark suit. His head hung limply to one side and he clutched his stomach. His waistcoat had ridden up. Blood leeched through his white shirt between his fingers and bloomed in the moisture on the floor around his outstretched legs.

Nell ran across the warm tiles. 'Painter!' she called. He didn't respond. She sank to the floor beside him.

'Oh my God. Oh my God,' Nell said.

Painter's chin had sunk to his chest and his skin was so very pale. She put her hand out to touch him. It trembled.

'James,' she managed to say. She put her fingertips to his cheek. 'What has he done to you?' She cupped his face in her palm and a hot, fat tear slid down her cheek.

There came a moan.

A slight movement.

'James,' Nell said. 'James, can you hear me?'

He moaned again.

'I'm going to look,' she said. 'I'll try not to hurt you.' She prised back his hands. Thick blood oozed from a wound in his stomach. She replaced his hands. 'Help is coming, James. The police are on their way.'

Painter's eyes parted just barely. 'Nell,' he said quietly. He coughed and tried to sit up.

'Don't move,' Nell said. 'Save your strength.' She used these words, these platitudes. She had nothing else to give. She knew nothing of how to help an injured person.

'Pressure,' Painter said so quietly that the words were no louder than the soft *pit-pat* of condensation as it dripped from the glass ceiling to the floor tiles. 'Must stop the blood.'

Nell looked around desperately for any piece of fabric that might do. She could try to remove his jacket and use that but to move him might injure him still further. There was nothing. She looked down at herself. With no more thought than she might give to removing her gloves at a dance, she crossed her arms over her body and lifted her slip over her head. Carefully, she prised Painter's fingers away. She placed the pink silk over his stomach.

'Harder,' he said. 'Press harder.'

Nell did as he asked. But as she pressed, he cried out in pain.

'I'm sorry,' she said.

'Harder.'

She pressed down again. Painter coughed. His back arched.

'Help is coming,' Nell said. She glanced over her shoulder towards the house. When she looked at Painter, his eyes were closed, his head resting back against the terracotta pot. 'You're going to be all right, I promise.'

Nell was aware of her closeness to him, her bare chest pressing against the fabric of his jacket.

'If I die—' he said.

'Don't say it,' Nell said. Not now. He couldn't leave her alone now.

Painter took a shallow breath. 'Inside pocket.' He nodded towards his chest.

Maintaining the pressure on Painter's stomach with one hand, Nell slipped her other hand inside his breast pocket. She pulled her hand free and was holding a photograph. A photograph of an attractive woman and a young girl. Six or perhaps seven years of age. They were in a studio, standing before the painted backdrop of a country garden. They smiled for the camera and looked so happy as they posed either side of a man; the woman with her hand on his shoulder and the little girl holding his hand with her head resting against his arm. The man's face was fuller, his eyes free of dark circles. He smiled proudly. In a way Nell had never seen him smile.

'Your wife and daughter?' Nell said.

'Miriam and Dorothy.'

'They're beautiful.' Nell turned the photograph so that Painter could see it. 'Where are they?' she asked.

She watched Painter's pupils flick over the image from beneath his half-closed eyelids. His face crumpled. On a laboured breath, he said, 'Dead.'

'Oh, James,' Nell said. 'I am so very sorry.'

A tear slipped down his cheek. 'I'm the only person left to remember them.'

Nell felt the sob as she pressed down on Painter's stomach. She slipped the photograph back inside his pocket and with her free hand, circled his neck. She pressed her face to his as he wept.

'It was me,' Painter said, his body shaking. 'I killed them.'

Nell pulled away and stared down at him. The sorrow in his face, in his voice and in his tears told her that it simply was not possible. This honourable man was not capable of killing his family. If... if he were to speak his last words, she could not let it be those words. 'Was it an accident?' she said. 'Did Miriam and Dorothy die in an accident?'

Painter took a stilted breath. 'I came home from the Front.' His eyes closed. 'I brought influenza into our home.'

'They died of the Spanish flu. After the War?' Nell said.

Painter's tears fell on Nell's arms. She held him, pressing her cheek to his. 'You're not to blame. You're a brave, brave man who did his duty. They could have caught it from anyone. Miriam and Dorothy won't be forgotten,' Nell whispered. 'I promise.'

There came the sound of footsteps through gravel, and voices – the voices of many men. From amongst them came the voice of a woman.

'Nell,' she heard someone say gently. 'Nell.' A face appeared beside her. An arm around her shoulders. 'You can come away now,' Charlotte said. 'Paul is here, he knows what to do. Elliot told the police you were coming here so we came too. In case we were needed.'

Paul knelt beside Painter. He placed his hand over Nell's hand. 'I'll take it from here,' he said. 'You've done a great job, Nell.'

She felt herself helped to her feet. 'Tommy,' she said. 'Have you seen Tommy?'

'He's safe. He told us what you did,' Charlotte said, placing a jacket around Nell's shoulders. 'My family will never be able to thank you enough for saving him.'

Nell was passed into the care of a Caxton Hall maid and guided from the orangery and out into the sunshine. She looked back. Charlotte knelt beside Paul, quickly removing items from the surgeon's bag he had brought with him. Police constables crowded the entrance to the door, all of them had removed their helmets and watched as Paul looked beneath her blood-soaked slip covering Painter's stomach. The last thing she heard was Paul shout. 'Get the ambulance from Northampton General here. Now!'

FIFTY-FIVE

Nell sat alone in the matron's office. They had finally found her somewhere to wait when she refused to leave. A nurse had placed a hospital gown over her before clothes were sent from Hill House for her to dress in. A police sergeant and a constable had taken her account of the events of the afternoon beginning with her arrival at Caxton Hall, every detail about Tommy and Caxton, and ending with her arrival at the hospital. They had even wanted to hear about the journey when Elliot drove her in the Rolls Royce at full speed, following the ambulance. She had been able to give them the account they wanted. The facts were there. There was no call to think about how to respond to their questions. But when she asked whether Caxton had been arrested, they said that investigations were continuing.

Every now and then a nurse would enter to place a cup of tea down and remove the previous cup which had gone cold. As the day turned to early evening, a nurse arrived and turned on the lamp. She knelt before Nell and bathed her arms and legs. Nell had watched the water in the bowl at her feet bloom red. When she held herself and rocked, the nurse placed a reassuring hand on her knee.

Alone, Nell sat on the armchair in the corner of the room, her knees curled beneath her. The window had been slid open a crack. A grasshopper chirruped in the small courtyard outside. Nell focused on a swirl in the rug before the unlit fireplace. She had stared at the same point all afternoon. Every knock at the door had sent a stab through her body. Each person had left without delivering news and each time, Nell allowed herself a moment of relief before focusing on the swirl again.

And then there came a different knock. Sure and firm. The door opened.

'Can I come in?'

Nell nodded.

Paul took a chair from beside the desk. He sat before her, a doctor's white coat over his normal day clothes.

'How are you, Nell?'

She looked up from the swirl. 'How is he?' she asked.

'No sugar-coating?'

Nell shook her head. She stared into Paul's face. 'The knife missed all the vital organs,' he said. 'The surgery went as expected. But Inspector Painter lost a lot of blood.'

Nell looked back to the swirl. 'Will he live?'

'He has a fighting chance. But we need to prepare ourselves for any outcome.'

'Can I see him?' Nell asked.

'Technically, no. But since he's my patient, yes.'

Paul held Nell's arm and guided her down a long corridor. She watched her bare feet. One in front of the other. One in front of the other, following the direction of the herringbone pattern of the floor.

They turned into another corridor. Paul stopped at a door. 'Are you sure you want to see him now?' Paul asked. 'You wouldn't rather get some sleep and come back in the morning?'

'Now,' Nell said. 'I want to see him now.'

'Okay. But just five minutes. You need your rest after today, just as much as Inspector Painter does.'

He opened the door to a small room. A nurse turned to them.

'I've said Miss Potter can sit with Inspector Painter for five minutes, Nurse Hughes,' Paul said.

'Very good,' the nurse said. 'He is comfortable for now. And sleeping.'

The nurse walked toward them, her crisply starched apron rustling. She carried with her a bowl covered with a towel. Nell's view of the room was blocked. She stood aside to let the nurse pass.

'He's been anaesthetised so he's out for the count.' Paul said and held the door open. 'I'll be waiting right out here.'

Nell entered alone. The door closed behind her. The light was bright in this room with its pale walls and the air hung heavy with the tang of iodine. Painter lay motionless beneath a white sheet tucked to his waist. He wore a pair of blue striped pyjamas and his hair had been parted neatly to one side in a way Nell had not seen before. She sat in a chair beside the bed.

A metal bowl sat on the table next to the bed. Beside it was a pile of neatly wound bandages. 'They're taking such good care of you,' Nell said. 'Paul is looking after you.' She moved her hand over Painter's and placed it gently on top, feeling his warmth. The fear that had occupied her during every second of every minute of every hour in the matron's office rose to the surface, sitting like oil on water. The fear that Painter would feel that he had nothing to live for. The fear that he would give up.

'You have to fight,' she whispered. 'You have to stay alive.'

She removed her hand and gripped the seat of the chair, moving it as close as she was able to the bed. She placed her hand over his again and moved her lips close to his ear. 'I have a confession of my own,' she whispered. 'A secret I have never told another living soul.' She looked over her shoulder. The door was still closed. She turned back to Painter. 'I want you to know you are not the only one who carries a burden from that War. I...'

She faltered. She had convinced herself that she would be able to do this. Now the words sat like rocks in her mouth. But she had to do it. And she had only minutes.

'I... I knew a man. In the War. I was in love with him. But we had to keep it secret so that I could carry on in my job. He was an officer. I met him when I worked in the War Office. We were together only a handful of times. But we felt like we had known each other forever. And then... and then...'

There was a noise in the corridor, but the door stayed closed.

'He volunteered,' Nell said, 'to join his regiment on the Front. He felt it was his duty to fight rather than stay behind the lines just because his father had been able to pull some strings. But I had found out... I... I was pregnant. I went to the station. He hoped I had gone to see him off. He was so happy. And then I told him... about the baby. That I wanted him to stay. He was so confused. I was angry with him for going, for putting his life in danger. We parted so badly, and I was distraught. I sent the man I loved to his death believing that I hated him. After I lost him, I stopped taking care of myself. I had nobody to confide in. And then... And then... And then, I lost it... I lost my baby.' Tears streamed down Nell's cheeks and onto the sheets. 'I've blamed myself for so long because I thought it was my fault that I lost my child. But perhaps neither of us are to blame for what happened to us. That war... there was so much damage. It's not your fault your family got ill. And now you need to stay alive so you can remember Miriam and Dorothy. They need you to do that.' She faltered. 'I need you to do that.'

Nell cupped Painter's face in her palm. She leant forward

and kissed him softly on the cheek. She sat back and took his hand in hers.

'Paul and the nurse will be back soon,' she said. 'And I'll have to go. But I'll come back tomorrow.' She managed a little laugh though the tears stuck in her voice. 'I have made myself rather a nuisance around you, haven't I?'

It was then that she felt it. A pressure on her fingers. Slight at first. And then firmer. She looked at Painter's face. His eyelids fluttered, and then opened. Painter's grey eyes looked at her.

Nell sighed. She leant to press her lips to the back of his hand and Painter squeezed her fingers again.

FIFTY-SIX

30TH JULY 1924

Nell turned onto her side. The sun broke through the gap in the curtains as she attempted to piece together the fragments of the evening before.

She remembered arriving back at Hill House. Elliot had driven her from Northampton. She had spent the journey with her forehead pressed to the car window, watching the stars and the moon. There had been no fuss when Elliot brought the car to a stop and held the door open. Police officers silently patrolled the grounds and Mrs Hart and Charlotte waited beneath the portico to welcome her. The house was quiet when they helped her upstairs. They removed her clothes and slipped a fresh cotton nightdress over her head. When she asked whether Caxton had been captured, Mrs Hart told her not to worry about that. In hushed tones they had assured her that Tommy was well. He had eaten a supper fit for a king and had gone to bed in the nursery beside his sister and brother, safe and seemingly none the worse for his ordeal. The Mandevilles had Nell and Inspector Painter to thank for the return of their precious boy. She realised that she couldn't ask whether Alice had returned, not when Charlotte was there.

'Good morning,' a voice said.

Nell sat up. Mrs Hart was sitting in a chair beside the bed.

'Did you sleep well?' Mrs Hart asked.

'Yes, but why...'

'I wanted to be here in case you woke in the night. And I wanted to be here when you woke this morning. Nobody who has been through what you went through yesterday should be alone.'

'I'm sorry you had the bother.'

'Bother?' Mrs Hart smiled. 'You could never be a bother. And this is a particularly comfortable chair. I spent many a night sitting beside beds in this house during the War. Watching over young men in need of care. And yesterday you brought our boy back. You can have no idea how special you are to us.'

'I only did what anybody would have done.'

'No, Nell. You had choices to make yesterday. Difficult choices. The choices you made saved Thomas. And you showed incredible courage.'

Nell recalled the confrontation on the boat. 'George Caxton?' she said. 'What has happened to him?'

Mrs Hart's nose twitched as though a salmon on the turn had been placed in her lap. 'He fled. He managed to reach the shore and made off.'

'But he can't swim. And I left no oar in the boat.'

'Men like George Caxton will always find a way. Apparently, there were some men on the other side of the lake waiting to help him should he get into trouble.'

'And where is he now?' Nell asked. 'He will come after Tommy.'

'The dogs they brought in to look for Tommy lost George's scent,' Mrs Hart said. 'It would seem that someone was waiting in a car to whisk him away. The police gave chase, but he managed to escape. They are still looking for him but if I

know George, he has probably made it to the Continent by
now.'

'But he won't give up. He is capable of murder.'

'I know. Which is why we will be ready next time. George
holds the Mandevilles responsible for everything that has
happened to him, ever since he tried to destroy my brother's
reputation and was punished for it by his father. I don't like to
say this about a person, but if George is not sick, then I believe
he is truly evil. He is without compassion or kindness of any
kind.'

'Aren't you frightened?' Nell asked, picturing the near-rabid
man she had faced on the boat.

'We have had to live with his threat hanging over us for
many years. But we will protect ourselves more diligently from
now on. And you will have our protection, too.' Mrs Hart
paused. 'You were so brave to have tackled him alone. As was
your Inspector Painter.'

Nell looked at the white ribbon running down the front of
her nightdress. 'Inspector Painter is brave. But he is not mine.'

There was a pause before Mrs Hart said, 'Would you have
him be?'

Nell lifted her head. Mrs Hart was looking at her kindly. 'I
won't pry,' Mrs Hart said. 'But I see your sadness, Nell. And it
breaks my heart. And I see how you look at James Painter. If
you had the chance to put right what clearly troubles you and
stands in the way of your happiness, would you?'

'In a heartbeat,' Nell said. 'But I can never put right what I
have done.'

There came a knock at the door. Mrs Hart rose to open it.
Mary entered with a tray, which Mrs Hart took from her. Mary
smiled at Nell and closed the door behind her.

Mrs Hart placed the tray in Nell's lap. She poured a cup of
tea and stirred in two lumps of sugar. She scooped two mounds

of jam onto the hot buttered toast and sat back in her chair. 'You need to build your strength,' Mrs Hart said.

Nell picked up a slice of the toast and took a bite from the corner. She took a sip of the tea.

'Better?' Mrs Hart said.

Nell nodded. When there were only crumbs left, Mrs Hart took the tray and placed it on the dressing table. She retook her seat.

'Nell,' she said. 'I know you spoke to our visitor yesterday.'

Nell swallowed her final mouthful of tea.

'I won't insult your intelligence, Nell. I know you are aware that not everything that has been happening here is easily explainable.' Mrs Hart looked directly at Nell. 'I cannot say too much. There are people whose position here is at risk.'

Alice, Nell thought. Though she dared not say the name.

Mrs Hart crossed the room and opened the door of the wardrobe. 'I want you to take a walk with me.'

'I have to go back to the hospital,' Nell said, looking at the dress Mrs Hart was laying out on the bed.

'It's been arranged. Elliot will drive you later today,' Mrs Hart said. 'Paul telephoned earlier. Inspector Painter passed a comfortable night and is stable. So now I need you to get dressed and come with me.'

Mrs Hart was not a woman to be argued with, so Nell pushed back the sheets and took the dress into the bathroom. When she emerged, Mrs Hart was waiting for her. She led the way from the room and down the stairs with Nell following.

'Where are we going?' Nell asked as they reached the hall and passed the fireplace with the fauns silently playing their instruments.

'We are taking a walk,' Mrs Hart said to the police constable guarding the hall.

Mrs Hart walked quickly, emerging from the portico, heading

down the drive. She walked with purpose, her back straight and her eyes forward. 'You must steel yourself,' she said, still looking straight ahead, still walking with her back upright and clasping her hands.

'For what?' Nell said to the side of Mrs Hart's face.

'Sometimes, in order for us to recover, we must face greater pain.'

Nell felt a chill run through her. 'Has something happened to James? To Inspector Painter? Is his condition worse than you have said?'

Mrs Hart shook her head. 'I have told you what Paul has told me.' She carried on, leaving Nell to stare at the back of her head. She quickly followed and when Mrs Hart came to a stop at the gates, so did Nell.

Mrs Hart turned to her. The familiar compassion had returned to her eyes. She took Nell's hands in hers. 'Choices, Nell. We all have choices of what we do, or do not do. Choices of what we say, or do not say. And what might cause you pain might ease the suffering of another. But all of this is a choice.'

Nell tried to read what Mrs Hart meant in her face. She was about to say that she did not understand when Mrs Hart filled the silence. She held out her open palm. 'After you,' she said, indicating that Nell should lead the way.

Nell stepped through the gates.

And froze.

FIFTY-SEVEN
10TH AUGUST 1918

Nell stared at her feet, unable to take another step.

Where there should have been her flat tan pumps, were a pair of patent black shoes with a strap and a darling heel. They were the shoes she had so admired for months in a shop in Bond Street. The shoes she had saved for and bought so that she had been the envy of the other girls at the boarding house.

She should have stepped onto the pavement outside Hill House. Just along the road should be the church with the weathervane and a small row of workers' cottages. But instead there were people. Everywhere, people. Hurrying. Jostling. The shrill shriek of whistles. A newspaper seller calling out. A flower stall at the entrance to a platform. A man shining shoes outside the teashop, with its window steamed by condensation.

It was... but it couldn't be. Nell knew this place. She had travelled from here many times. Often catching a train to Clapham Junction for a connection to Cheam. How could she have stepped through the gates of a house in Northamptonshire onto the concourse of Waterloo Station?

Buffeted by people rushing past, Nell stood and stared. A man in a bowler hat apologised when he bumped into her. Two young women, arm in arm, ran past her towards a platform and a departing train. And everywhere, everywhere was khaki. Men in khaki with canvas kit bags slung across their backs moved in waves around the station like a green sea filling every gap and space.

'Germans suffer humiliating reverse!' The newspaper seller called. 'Victory for the British at Amiens! Read all about it!'

A sensation rose in Nell. She pushed through the crowds towards the newsstand. Stumbling.

She fished a coin from the handbag balanced in the crook of her arm and saw that she wore a brown suit. The suit she had worn for her work in the War Office. She handed the coin to the boy and took the newspaper. She read the date – 10th August 1918. The newspaper fell from her grip and was immediately trampled under so many feet. Nell wrapped her arm around her waist.

She looked up and through the crowd. Pushing against the direction of travel, she saw a man, wearing not khaki, but an officer's uniform. His cap was knocked askew to reveal his dark brown hair. A man paused to apologise but the officer smiled and waved away the apology.

Nell stared. She began to shake.

'Nell,' the man called, waving as though she had not seen him. Her ears would have picked his voice out over the din of a thousand more people. It was the voice that had whispered to her of his love. His lips so close to Nell's ear that she could feel his breath. They were lips that had known her. The only lips that had ever known all of her.

'Nell!' he said as he made his final push through the crowd. He dropped his kitbag to the ground. He put his arms around her and picked her up so that her feet were off the ground.

'What are you doing here?' he said as he let her down. His smile was so wide. His brown eyes shone. He looked into her face, smiling all the while.

'It is you, Philip?' Nell said, her eyes taking him in.

'Of course, it's me. Who else were you hoping to meet? Do you have a fancy man hiding hereabouts? Where is he? Let me at him,' Philip said with a laugh. He was so sure of her. So certain of her love for him that he could make a joke of the prospect of a secret adversary for her affection.

'There is only you, Philip,' Nell said. 'There has only ever been you.'

He kissed her full on the lips and pulled away. 'Now, you're not going all soppy on me, are you?' he said. 'We'll have no tears.'

She tipped her face to the floor and he dipped to look at her.

This was the point. Here. The moment she had lived over and over and over again. His ability to seem permanently happy had given her so much joy. It was one of the reasons she had fallen in love with him. But in that moment, his ability to be jolly in the face of tragedy had set her mood on edge. Didn't he know? Couldn't he see her torment? Well, if he couldn't see it, she would tell him. She would point out the newspaper headline and ask how he could be so reckless as to go to the Front when he didn't have to. The war was being won, what good would his presence do? She would say that a telephone call to his father and surely, he could return to his old job. He would say that he had to do his duty. How could he live with himself if he were so cowardly that he didn't fight alongside the other men of his regiment? She would ask what use a dead martyr would be to their unborn child. He would be so shocked, so anxious that he just stared at her. She would ask if he had nothing to say and the whistle would blow, signalling that his train was about to leave. She would ask him sarcastically if he was not happy. He would say that he didn't know how to feel. He loved her but they would need to talk about it when he could. And she would tell him not to bother. If he loved her, he would stay. He would try to kiss her, and she would turn away. He would have to run for his train. Again, he would tell her that he loved her. But she would not look at him. Until it was too late, when she called out his name, but he had already disappeared into the crowd.

'A penny for them,' Philip said.

'I love you so much,' Nell said. 'I love you so very, very much.'

'And that's why you came to see me off?' he said.

Nell nodded.

'No secret affair going on behind my back then?' he laughed.

'Never,' Nell said.

Philip smiled and kissed her. He took a step back, still holding her hands. The whistle blew.

'That's me,' Philip said.

'May I come to the platform with you?' Nell asked.

'I thought you'd never ask.' Philip picked up his kitbag and slung it over his shoulder. The whistle shrieked again. 'We'll have to run,' he said and grabbed Nell's hand. He set off, Nell running as fast as she could to keep up with him. With his free hand, he held his cap in place. His hand holding hers was so firm. So sure. So alive.

As they ran past the guard, he called after them, 'One minute. Time enough to say your goodbyes.'

Philip's bag bounced up and down on his back as Nell gripped his hand, refusing to let go even if it he could have made quicker progress without her.

Philip stopped at the first carriage and threw his bag through the open door. He took Nell in his arms. She pressed into him.

'What have you done to me, Nell Potter?' Philip said into her hair. 'I am under your spell. You have bewitched me.'

Nell's heart ached. 'Then can I cast a spell now?' she said. 'If I ask you to stay, will you?'

'I can't do that,' he said into her hair again.

She looked up into his brown eyes. She rose onto her toes and kissed him. Kissed him until she could not breathe.

The whistle shrieked again. Philip rested his head against hers so that the peak of his cap rested on the top of her head.

'If anything happens to me—' he started.

'Don't,' Nell said. 'Please don't.'

'You have my blessing – no, my instruction – to live life for me. You were made to be loved. You must always be loved.'

'I can't...' Nell faltered as the first tear fell.

Philip wiped it away with his thumb.

'I love you, Nell Potter. I love you with every beat of my heart. I love you more with every sunrise and every sunset. Every time the moon rises in the night sky while I'm away, I will be there with you. But if I don't come back, I will make it my mission to find a way to make sure you love again.' She felt a warmth on her cheek.

She pressed her lip to Philip's cheek and kissed his tear away.

'Promise me,' he said.

'I promise.'

He held her again and grinned. 'But I have every intention of coming back. You won't be rid of me so easily.'

The whistle shrieked. Philip boarded the train, still holding Nell's hand. He released her to close the door but leant through the window and took her hand again. He kissed it and pressed it to his heart.

The wheels of the train began to churn. The train moved. And still Nell held Philip's hands through the open window.

'Stand away!' the guard shouted.

Steam hissed from beneath the train. Their grip on each other slipped. For a moment they were fingertip to fingertip, before Philip slipped from Nell's grasp.

He leant through the window, removed his cap and waved

it. The beautiful smile lit his face. The train turned a bend in the track, and he was gone. Philip was gone.

The sob Nell had been holding inside came. Steam swirled about her. She clutched her stomach. 'I am so sorry,' she said, looking down between her parted fingers. 'I have lost Philip, and I will lose you too.'

She lurched blindly in the direction of the concourse. She stumbled and hands reached out to catch her.

The steam cleared.

There was no longer a station.

Sunlight flooded the drive beyond the gates with the two lions holding aloft their globe. Nell choked on sobs. She collapsed and was caught by strong arms.

'There now, lass,' Elliot said as he picked her up. She pressed her face into his shoulder. The tears came unchecked.

'You're safe now,' Mrs Hart said and stroked Nell's hair. 'Come, Elliot, let us get Nell back to the house.'

Footsteps crunched in gravel. Nell had her arms about Elliot's neck. He held her and carried her like a father might carry an ailing child. She muffled her cries in his shoulder. He seemed not to notice. If he did, he did not mind.

She heard voices. Mrs Hart explaining to the constable on the door that something had upset Miss Potter. With no more ceremony, she felt herself carried up the stairs and along a corridor. Mrs Hart remained by Elliot's side the whole time, cooing soft words to Nell.

When she was placed on a bed, Nell curled into a ball, covering her head with her hands.

Eventually the tears dried on her cheeks. She shook; trembling replacing the cries. In the distance she heard the door close. She felt the bed dip. 'I'm so sorry,' a voice said softly.

FIFTY-EIGHT

The weight on the bed shifted. Nell opened her eyes. Louisa was smiling down at her. 'I don't have long left,' she said. 'I need to show you something. I promised to explain as far as I can.'

Louisa took a small framed photograph from her pocket.

Nell sat up to better see the face of the man saved for eternity in the silver frame. She looked and then moved in closer still. For a moment, she forgot to breathe, her eyes unable to convince her brain that they were conveying the correct information.

'Who is this?' she said, staring into the eyes looking back at her from beneath the peak of an officer's cap.

She received no reply.

'Louisa?' Nell tried again.

'I'm so sorry,' Louisa said. 'I was asked to come here to help you. And I did it gladly.' She gripped the edge of the bedspread. 'I thought I could cope with being here again. In Hill House.'

Nell looked again at the face in the photograph. This man was a mixture of Charlotte and Edward. He had the kind eyes of both, as well as a nose that turned up ever so slightly at the tip. This was a ruddy and healthy face. The face of a man who spent time out of doors, in gardens and on the land about the house. How had she not seen the similarities before?' Because this was not the first time she had come face to face with this man.

'Is this Thomas Mandeville?' she asked.

Louisa nodded.

Everything tumbled into place. Why he had appeared in her dreams with Louisa. Why he had been arguing with her in the stables. Why he had danced with her at the Christmas Eve Ball. The man she knew as Mr Townley was not Mr Townley at all. He was Thomas Mandeville. The seemingly living, breathing man who had appeared to her, hiding his true identity, had been a decade dead, buried in a grave across The Channel. How was it possible?

'Ten years,' Louisa said softly. 'It's been more than ten years since I was last here.' She twisted the bedspread through her fingers. 'Next month is the anniversary of his death. I've recently had signs that I would be called to come here again. I ignored them. I thought surely my mind was playing tricks, with the anniversary coming up. Then Alice came to see me. I knew there was no way she could have come to me unless it was a matter of life and death.'

Nell heard the words Louisa said but she had her own words that she needed to share. She might never get the chance again. 'I saw you,' she said. 'I saw you and Thomas together.'

Louisa turned and searched Nell's face, as though trying to find the truth in it. 'You did?'

Nell nodded. 'He loved you so very much.'

Louisa searched her face again. 'How can you be sure?'

'The way you looked at each other,' Nell said. 'The way he looked at you in the stable. And sought you out when he was dancing with another woman at the Christmas Eve Ball. He was dancing with her but wanted to be with you. You had your back to him so never saw how he looked at you.'

Louisa still searched Nell's face, as though waiting for more proof.

'I saw him tie the dance card around your wrist,' Nell added. 'I saw how he pressed his thumb into your palm. And I saw his hand on the base of your spine when you danced.'

'You really were there,' Louisa said. 'I hardly dare to remember some of these things you are telling me. But they are all true.'

'I thought I was losing my mind,' Nell said. 'That I was hallucinating or somehow experiencing waking dreams. But I now know I was there. I don't know how. But I was. Even if you couldn't see me. Where are you from, Louisa?' Nell asked. 'And who is Alice?'

With a sad smile, Louisa said, 'That, I can't tell you. Just know that this is where Alice belongs. One in, one out. It's the way it's always been. It's the way it always will be.'

'What does that mean? Tommy said it to me too, but I didn't understand.'

'It means, Nell, that some of us are lucky enough to be chosen to visit Hill House. Some stay for a few days. Others for years. And then there are others, like you, who belong in this time and are fortunate to fall into the path of the Mandevilles and their home. I think you know now that the unexplainable happens here. And once you are chosen, you become a part of this house and its history.' She paused. 'I'm sorry that I forced you to be the one to go to Caxton Hall today. Just know that you had to.'

'I'm glad I was there.' Nell said. 'I don't have many skills but at least I'm a decent swimmer.'

'There are even more reasons that it had to be you.' Louisa said. 'But someone else will explain why. I can't.' She paused again. 'May I ask you a question?

Nell nodded.

'Before you came here, were you without hope?'

Nell stared at her.

'You don't have to answer,' Louisa said. 'It's just the only explanation I can give you for why you have been chosen to be one of Hill House's special visitors. It was the reason given to me. It seems to be the way things work.'

'How what works, Louisa? I don't understand any of this. Do you know what happened to me this morning? Just before you sat on the bed? I went back. I went—'

'Stop, Nell, please. We can't talk about these things; about the experiences you have had that are out of the ordinary. It may put the presence of other people here at risk. I know this is all so hard to understand. But please, Nell. Please be careful what you say.'

'Why?' Nell said. As hard as she was trying to grasp what Louisa was telling her, was she really to believe that Hill House had the ability to control the events she had experienced and witnessed since stepping foot inside its grand front door?

'I know something happened to you today,' Louisa said softly. 'I don't know what and you mustn't tell me the details. But I do know that sometimes there is a way the world was destined to play out. An intervention might alter the course of the future that was once supposed to be. A terrible future.'

A tear slipped down Nell's cheek. For a moment she was not in the bedroom but on the platform at Waterloo. She heard again the new words Philip had said to her.

'I can't love again,' she said. 'I just can't. I barely know how to live. He was the first person to love me. But I have never spoken of him. No living soul knows anything about us. I was alone then, and I am alone again now.'

'You are not alone,' Louisa said, placing her arms around Nell. 'And you will love again.'

'How do you know?' Nell cried.

Louisa pulled away. She collected the framed photograph and placed it on the nightstand. She looked into Nell's eyes.

'Because I was once you. This place was where I found love. And I had to learn to let that love go so I could live again.'

'And did you? After Thomas? Did you live again?'

Louisa looked into the face in the photograph. 'Eventually. I'm married now to a kind and gentle man. I have two daughters. But not a day goes by that I don't miss the man in that photograph.'

'Isn't it a betrayal to find someone new?' Nell said.

'A life well lived is greater thanks to them than a half-formed existence. Breathe, Nell. Smell the air. Walk in the rain. Let someone who loves you hold you. It will be different. But it will feel good. It's been ten years and I still feel the loss of Tom. But he will always be in my heart. I will miss Thomas Mandeville every day of my life.' Tears hovered in Louisa's eyelashes. They broke free and fell down her cheeks.

It was on the tip of Nell's tongue to say that she had met Thomas. But the words stopped in her mouth at the thought of Thomas' words. He was gone and Louisa had to live her life without him.

Nell pulled Louisa close. She could feel Louisa's body heave as she sobbed.

'It's been so long that I'd forgotten,' Louisa said. 'Sometimes I feel I imagined how he looked at me. How he held me.'

'I have never seen a man look at a woman as he looked at you,' Nell said. 'He loved you. He will love you forever.'

Nell held Louisa closer. With their arms around each other they wept. They cried for a grief so deep there were no more words. They were near strangers but shared a longing in their souls that would never again have its home.

Eventually Louisa pulled away. 'Thank you,' she whispered. 'But I have to go.' She wiped at her red-rimmed eyes with the heels of her hands.

'To let Alice return,' Nell said.

Louisa smiled though she still had tears in her eyes. She got to her feet, straightened her dress and brushed damp strands of hair from her cheeks. 'You have a huge heart, Nell Potter,' she said. 'Keep that, and keep your spark and spirit.'

Louisa took Nell's hand. Nell got up and walked with her to the door.

Out in the corridor, Louisa paused. She kissed Nell on the cheek. 'You will love again. Trust me,' Louisa whispered. 'There are things that I know for sure. And that is one of them.' When Nell made to speak, Louisa pressed her finger to her lips. She winked at Nell before heading for the stairs, stopping only to wave as she took the first step down.

FIFTY-NINE

Nell stood with her back to the closed bedroom door for a moment before walking the short distance to the desk before the window. The typewriter sat waiting, its keys untouched in days. Her bag lay open on the floor, beside the leg of the desk. Inside was her notebook, half-filled with the fledgling story of the Olympian and the femme fatale and half-filled with her observations and amateur sleuthing. There was nothing in those scribbled pages that came anywhere close to the story she had lived out in the last few days. If she could write it down, surely it would be so far-fetched that any reader would consider it to be fantasy.

Nell ran her fingers down the curtain that had taken on a form when she heard the voice speak to her. Philip. It had been Philip. Of that, she now had no doubt.

'You said you would make it your mission to come to me, if I didn't do what you said,' Nell whispered. 'You made me make you a promise.'

The curtain billowed. The scent of freshly cut grass reached her on the air coming in through the open window. Nell sensed something at her side. The air brushed her legs. She looked down. It was not air. She released the curtains to stroke the red curls of the child who had entered the room without her noticing.

She knelt down and took him in her arms.

'Thank you,' Tommy said. 'Thank you for saving me.'

'It was my pleasure,' Nell said. 'I think you and your family may have saved me, too.'

Tommy pulled away. He had the faraway look in his eyes. 'The things you have seen,' he said. 'You have saved us. Here, you will be looked after. Here, people care for you. Here, you will never be alone. It is not just your future you have changed.'

There was a knock on the open door. The sound seemed to break whatever spell had been cast over Tommy. He blinked and looked into Nell's face as though it was a bit of surprise to see her. In his ordinary, playful voice, he said, 'That man was horrible yesterday, wasn't he, Nell? Thank you for bringing me home. It's a good job you taught me how to swim. Otherwise I might have drowned with the eels!' He shivered and turned his nose up.

The door opened a little further. 'Is it all right if I come in?' Alice asked.

Nell got to her feet. She nodded. 'Of course.'

Tommy slipped away. 'Bye, Nell,' he called as he ran for the open door. 'Mrs Randal is making ALL of my favourite food today and I want to see what is ready!'

Before he could make his escape, his mother knelt in the doorway and scooped him into her arms. She dusted his face with kisses until he squirmed free of her grasp.

'I am all right, Mama,' he said. 'There's no call to cry again!'

Tommy ran away along the corridor and Alice closed the door behind him. She fairly flew across the room. She threw her arms around Nell and pulled her so close.

'Thank you, thank you, thank you,' she whispered as though sharing a secret. 'You brought my boy back to me.'

Nell put her arms around Alice, the sensation of holding a member of the Mandeville household becoming almost as familiar as passing the time of day. 'I only did what anyone would have done.'

'No,' Alice said. 'You did far more. He wasn't supposed to... In another lifetime, he...' Alice cried and held her face. Nell held her tighter.

'I'm glad I was there to help,' Nell said. 'And I'm glad you came back.'

'So am I,' Alice nodded. 'So am I.'

'But that's all I'll say,' Nell said.

Alice released her and Nell was once again presented with a woman with tear-damp cheeks. Alice looked on her and smiled. 'I have been sent to collect you, Nell,' she said. 'You are wanted.'

SIXTY

Nell sat in the back of the Rolls Royce, between Mrs Hart and Alice, the green of the Northamptonshire countryside passing by at a sedate pace. Paul had telephoned again to say that he would allow one visitor to sit beside Painter's bed for a few minutes. He was very weak and needed to recuperate with the minimum of fuss and excitement. Mrs Hart had decided that she, Alice, and Nell would visit. Paul would allow it, she was sure. He was hardly likely to refuse a trustee of the hospital now, was he?

Outside the car, the countryside gradually gave way to town. If Paul allowed it, Nell would visit Painter to see for herself that he was on the road to recovery. Then she would travel back to Hill House to pack her case and return to London. The last thing Painter needed was her unwanted attention.

She could no longer delay facing the music that would accompany her into her future. Tomorrow, she would travel to Cheam to throw herself on her mother's mercy. She would weather her mother's reaction and retreat to her childhood bedroom. The prospect of returning to the tenuous existence of her London life in Bloomsbury made her want to crawl beneath a rock to hide. All she wanted now was a place to stop. And to think. And to let all that had happened sink in. It felt like an eon had passed since rushing for the train at Euston. And that she had lived a lifetime in just six days.

Paul was waiting at the hospital door to welcome the car. He watched as the three women emerged.

'I thought I said one visitor?' he said, raising his good eyebrow.

Mrs Hart patted his hand. 'You are a dark horse,' she said. 'Taking up the role of surgeon here and telling nobody.'

'I wanted it to be a surprise.'

'It was certainly that,' Alice said and kissed him on both cheeks.

'As I said yesterday,' Mrs Hart said. 'My brother returns from the Isle of Wight next week. I take it this new role of yours has something to do with the question you have to ask Sir Charles. And the fact that the result of that question will mean you have to be close to Hill House.'

Paul tapped the side of his nose. 'You'll get nothing from me.'

'Hmnnn,' Mrs Hart said. 'Well, all I'll say is I haven't seen Charlotte so happy as she was when she heard the news of your new position.' She smiled and then added. 'I know the way.'

Nell followed them into the hospital. She realised that it hadn't even occurred to her to ask why Paul had operated on Painter. She was just glad that he had.

Paul hung back to let Mrs Hart and Alice go ahead. He fell into step beside Nell. 'And you, Nell?' he asked. 'How are you?'

For the second time in two days, Nell walked with him in the direction of the herringbone floor. 'I'm fine,' she said.

She could feel him looking at her. 'You went through a lot

yesterday. If you feel numb, it could be shock. We can talk about it after your visit if you'd like to.'

Nell stared at her feet for a moment. 'If I ever feel I want to talk about it, it will be to you,' she said. She glanced at Paul. He gave her one of his half-smiles.

'I can't wait to get to know you better, Nell,' he said. 'I can see now why Charlotte is so fond of you. You have a good heart.'

'Will you invite me to stay when you are living at Hill House with Charlotte?'

Paul pressed his finger to his lips, but the smile radiated from his eyes.

'Don't worry,' Nell said. 'I'll not tell a soul. I'm good at keeping secrets.'

Nell waited outside the room with Mrs Hart and Alice while Paul went inside to check that Painter was well enough to receive visitors.

Paul emerged, followed by a nurse. 'Mrs Hart and Alice, you can go in first. I don't think he's up to three visitors at once.' He held the door open. 'But two minutes only.'

Mrs Hart and Alice entered. Paul closed the door. From inside, came the sound of tears and 'thank yous'. Paul stood to one side with the nurse, consulting a chart. Directed by Paul, Nell sat in a chair in the corridor, gripping the edge of the seat. All the while, she could hear the voices of the women in the room. If Painter said anything, it wasn't much, and it was too quiet for Nell to hear.

Paul consulted his watch. He pushed open the door and leant inside. 'Time's up,' he said. Mrs Hart and Alice emerged, both holding handkerchiefs to their faces.

'Such a good man,' Mrs Hart said, dabbing her eyes. 'Such a brave man.'

The nurse led Mrs Hart and Alice away, saying that she

wanted to show Mrs Hart some new rose bushes in the garden where the patients convalesced.

Paul smiled at Nell. 'Your turn,' he said. 'And I'll give you five minutes.'

He held the door wider. Nell prised her fingers from the seat. Taking a steadying breath, she entered the room.

It was as she had left it. White walls, white tiles, the smell of iodine. For a moment she couldn't look at the bed. And then a voice said, 'Nell.'

She lifted her eyes to him. Painter had been propped up on pillows. His hair was still parted oddly but his skin had more colour.

'Inspector Painter,' she said.

He shook his head. 'James,' he said. 'Call me James.' He nodded to the chair beside the bed and Nell took a seat. She placed her bag on the floor.

'How are you feeling?' she said.

'I've been better.' He tried to shift and winced.

Nell leant forward but stopped short of trying to help him. 'Shall I call for Paul?' she said quickly.

He shook his head. 'No. It'll settle.' His voice was hoarse and strained.

Nell sat with her hands in her lap. Yesterday and last night, she had said so much to him. But that's when he had been unable to hear. She looked at him and tried to smile.

'Thank you,' he said. 'For saving my life.'

'I did what anybody would have done. I'm sure it was Paul who—'

'No,' Painter said. 'It was you.'

Nell looked at her lap again.

'I hear Caxton has made his escape,' Painter said.

Nell nodded.

'You didn't listen to me then,' Painter said.

'What?'

'I hear you went after him.' He shifted and winced again.

'I had to. He had Tommy.'

'Promise me something,' he said, his voice strained. 'If he comes back, you'll run the other way.'

'I—'

'Promise me,' he said.

Nell looked at the crease between his eyebrows. 'I promise.'

He leant back. 'Thank you.' He closed his eyes and swallowed.

'I brought you something,' Nell said. She reached into her bag and pulled out an item. She placed it on the bed. 'You left it behind in the housekeeper's parlour,' she said, 'so I went and got it.'

Nell still had her hand on the brim of Painter's homburg. She was about to pull it away when Painter placed his hand on her hand. His fingers wrapped around hers. Nell shifted her focus to the sheet, turned back and tucked in tightly. 'Did you hear?' she said. 'What I said to you last night?'

He squeezed her fingers. 'Not really. I just knew you were here.'

She turned her hand over to grasp his. 'Promise me you'll get better,' she said.

'I promise,' he said.

SIXTY-ONE

'I won't hear of it,' Mrs Hart said when Nell tried to explain that she would pack to return to London as soon as they arrived back at Hill House. 'You'll stay for another night, at least,' she insisted as Elliot drove them on their return journey.

Nell's thoughts turned to Robert Amos, her publisher. She was going to have to find the courage to visit him to tell him that there were no chapters, despite what she had promised. The image of his face disappeared, replaced by the house in Cheam. 'One more night,' she said, 'and then I really must go back.'

'Very well,' Mrs Hart said. 'Then I will accompany you. I need to pay a visit to my solicitor in town and I do so hate to travel alone.'

Mrs Hart and Alice fell into a conversation about how best to ensure that Tommy wasn't so trusting of strangers and the extra security measures Edward was already planning. It was all so practical.

Nell looked out of the window at the trees passing by. She touched the back of her hand. She could still feel the imprint of fingers there.

'What did Inspector Painter have to say?' Mrs Hart asked. 'I wager he thanked you.'

'Yes,' Nell said. 'He did.'

'And did you make arrangements to see him when he leaves hospital?' Alice asked.

'I said I would come back to visit once I have spoken to my publisher. And when he is discharged.'

'Quite right,' Mrs Hart said and patted Nell's knee.

When Elliot turned the car through the gates of Hill House, an unexpected sight met them. The police were still there, standing guard outside the front door, but they had been joined by a green delivery van.

'Why on Earth is there a van outside the house?' Mrs Hart said. 'Elliot, do you know?'

'I'm sure I don't, Mrs Hart,' Elliot said. He brought the Rolls Royce to a stop behind the van and just short of the portico. The back of the van was open, and two deliverymen made their way carefully down the ramp at the back, moving a large rectangular item covered by a sheet.

Elliot got out of the car and opened the back doors for the women. The deliverymen passed through the vestibule as Nell followed Mrs Hart and Alice into the house. They were met by many voices coming from the hall, Nell craned to see past her companions and the deliverymen to find every Mandeville and all their guests assembled in the hall. Even the children were sitting on the bottom stair, watching the activity.

The deliverymen stopped before the fireplace. Slowly, they lowered the covered object and rested it against the fauns. Edward signed their clipboard and the men left.

'Edward, what is going on?' Mrs Hart asked her nephew.

For the first time in so many days, Nell saw Edward smile. He ran his fingers through his fringe.

'Would you like the good news? Or the even better news?' he said.

'Edward, stop toying with us,' his aunt said.

'I shall burst if I don't tell them,' Charlotte said, rushing to the Nell, Alice and Mrs Hart. 'George Caxton has been caught!' she said. 'He telephoned the house where Cousin Emma and her family are staying in France in an attempt to throw himself on his sister's mercy. But Emma would have none of it. Oh, she played along but then contacted the French police. George was arrested trying to board a train in Paris. So, you see! We can all sleep soundly in our beds again.'

'Oh, that is wonderful news,' Mrs Hart said.

'We are all safe,' Alice sighed.

Nell looked from Alice to Mrs Hart. George Caxton had escaped from a prison in India and made his way halfway across the world to get to the Mandevilles. Would the authorities in France have a better cell in which to hold him?

'Are we not to tell them the other news?' Wilco said. He slapped Edward on the back.

Edward smiled again.

Tommy ran to his father. 'May I?' he asked, pointing up to the sheet draped over the object before the fireplace.

Edward swept his son into his arms. 'Of course, you may,' he said and kissed Tommy's red curls. He held the boy up so that Tommy could clasp the sheet.

'Are you all ready?' Tommy said, turning back to look at his audience.

There was a collective call of 'Yes!' With one hard yank from Tommy, the sheet fell from the object.

'Oh, Edward,' Mrs Hart said. 'He is home. He is returned to us!'

Nell looked at the gilt frame holding the portrait of a handsome young man in a blue uniform. The red plume of his gold helmet appeared to blow in the wind. He sat astride a fine black stallion. Nell would have recognised that most wonderful of beasts anywhere. Just as she would have recognised that man on Samson's back. He was the man who had sat beside her on the bank of the lake and on the bench in the gardens, imparting his wisdom with an infectious smile. He was the man from her dreams. And the man of Louisa's dreams.

'The police conducted a search of Caxton Hall,' Wilco said. 'They found that Caxton and his accomplices had been hiding out in a room on the upper floor. Everything stolen from here was found. One of Caxton's accomplices is still on the run, but the police think he is long gone. The other met a sticky end on the railway tracks.'

'What's a "sticky end"?' Tommy asked, his arms still about his father's neck.

'Nothing to worry yourself about,' Mrs Hart added quickly and shook her head at Wilco, who nodded in return. 'What we need is a celebration.'

The conversation moved on. It bubbled around Nell. There was so much excitement and joy. Edward called for three bottles of champagne to be brought up from the cellar, insisting that each police constable must have a glass too. The children were asked what they would like to eat as a treat. Anything, they could have anything their little hearts desired. The happy group began to make their way through to the billiard room and out into the garden.

Nell hung back in the hall. 'I'll join you in a moment,' she said when Charlotte tried to take her hand.

Alone, Nell took a step closer to the portrait. She stared into the eyes of Thomas Mandeville. 'I know you're still here and can hear me,' she whispered. 'Louisa loved you. She always will. She will never forget you but she is living her life again. Just as you wanted her to. Your soul found hers.'

Nell felt something nudge her feet. She looked down. A bauble sat rocking gently on the bronze and white tiled floor, decorated with a gold star. Stooping, she collected the ornament. A shadow crossed the floor. It was a shadow with the shape and form of a man crossing the light from the open front door. Nell looked up. There was nobody there. A breeze blew into the hall carrying with it the scent of cigarette smoke, although the air outside was perfectly still.

With her typewriter and small suitcase, Nell boarded the mid-morning train to Euston with Mrs Hart and Tommy, who had been allowed to accompany them. Mrs Hart had promised that, once her business was complete, she would take him to Hamleys so that he might chose a gift for being an incredibly plucky young chap.

Nell had said her goodbyes to the Mandevilles at the door of Hill House with promises of coming back again very soon. But, as Elliot had driven them away from Hill House, the reality of the impending visit to her parents and to see Robert Amos had elbowed any fanciful ideas of a return visit out of the way.

Mrs Hart had paid for them to travel first class and to take tea in the restaurant car. Tommy kept his great aunt occupied while Nell watched the world pass by the window. She felt sure that Mrs Hart looked at her every so often, smiling at her in the way that someone who knew a secret might smile. But each time she turned to Mrs Hart, Nell failed to catch her eye.

At Euston, Nell helped Tommy down from the carriage before collecting her typewriter and suitcase from the luggage rack.

'Are you in a particular hurry?' Mrs Hart asked as other travellers rushed past them on the platform.

'Not a very great hurry,' Nell said.

'Would you mind, in that case, accompanying Tommy and I on a quick errand. I need to check on a tenant of a house I own and could do with someone to keep an eye on Tommy.'

Nell looked at her wristwatch. There was nobody waiting for her. The unceremonious return to her real life could be delayed by an hour or two.

'Of course,' she said. 'I'd be pleased to help.'

Mrs Hart had a porter hail them a taxicab and they travelled through London. Tommy sat close to Nell, pointing out the sights as they went – the tall buildings on the Euston Road, the newspaper sellers calling out the headlines, horses and carts and taxicabs and draymen and people taking up so much space that it was hard to see the grey of the pavement or road. It all seemed so loud, so busy, compared to the green and quiet of the Northamptonshire countryside.

'What a thing it is to see things for the first time,' Mrs Hart said, smiling at Tommy with his nose pressed to the glass. 'The newness of a world. Should you like that, Nell?'

'A new world?' Nell said. She thought to her empty flat. 'I suppose it would be interesting. But I'm a bit too long in the tooth to see the world for the first time.'

Mrs Hart smiled at her again. That smile that seemed to tell of a secret. Nell shook her head. She saw the unexplained everywhere now, even when there was nothing to see.

Tommy pointed to Big Ben as they crossed Westminster Bridge. 'See, Nell,' he said. 'Isn't it marvellous.'

'It is, Tommy,' she said and pulled him close as they crossed the dark water of the Thames, remembering the water of the lake and this precious soul swimming as his life depended on it.

'Where is the house that you rent?' she asked Mrs Hart, for want of a diversion.

'Putney,' Mrs Hart said. 'It was the home I shared with my husband before he passed. Now I rent it to a very dear friend.'

They soon arrived in a residential area and the taxicab pulled up to the pavement. Mrs Hart paid the driver and pushed open the gate of a neat house with roses in the front garden. Using a key she took from her bag, she opened the door. Nell followed her inside. Tommy raced ahead as though he were entitled to be there.

'Should he be running about?' Nell asked as Mrs Hart closed the door behind them. 'Won't your tenant mind?'

Mrs Hart smiled. 'No, she won't mind. She's very understanding. You can put those things down,' she said, pointing to Nell's typewriter and suitcase. Nell did as Mrs Hart said and placed them on the floor at the bottom of the stairs. It seemed presumptuous to make herself so at home, but Mrs Hart clearly knew her tenant.

Nell was prepared to wait in the hall, but Mrs Hart ushered her into a room at the front of the house. As soon as she crossed the threshold, Nell stopped abruptly. She looked around the comfortable parlour, at the floral wallpaper, the furniture, the cushions, even the plant in a tall stand in the window.

'What is it?' Mrs Hart asked.

'I don't know,' Nell said. 'I think I must have been in a house like this before.' And there was a smell. A smell of cooking that reminded her of an aroma of baking that had come from the kitchen when she was a very small child. But many people baked. It was hardly an unusual pastime.

'I see,' Mrs Hart said. She folded back the doors separating the parlour from a dining room. Tommy ran to a set of double doors opening onto the back garden. He slid the catch across and raced outside.

Nell saw a standard lamp beside the dining table. 'I have that very lamp,' she said. 'My great aunt left it to me.'

'I know,' Mrs Hart said.

'How do you know?' Nell said. She turned to Mrs Hart and was met with a benign smile. 'Where is your tenant?' Nell asked, a strange sensation blooming in her stomach.

Before Mrs Hart could answer, there was a sound out in the hall. It was the sound of a key in the lock and the front door opening. There were voices. A woman and a child. Nell smoothed down her skirt, ready to introduce herself and feeling more than a little embarrassed that she was part of this intrusion. She certainly wouldn't have taken kindly to her landlord parading all and sundry through her flat and having strangers making themselves at home when she was away.

'Mama!' the child's voice said. 'Mama!'

Assuming that the child was chivvying her mother along, Nell looked toward the hallway. There was the sound of little footsteps coming at a rapid pace.

'Miss Lilian! Miss Lilian! We should have arranged your clip before you see your mother,' the woman out in the hall said.

A child appeared in the doorway. From the brief glimpse Nell got of her, she would have put her at a year or so younger than Tommy. She wore a pale blue dress and had the darkest brown hair. The waves sat on her shoulders and her fringe was held back in a clip that sat askew.

Nell saw only these scant details. Because before she could see anything else, the child ran across the room, in the process, dropping a violin case to the floor.

The child threw her arms about Nell's waist. 'Did you have a good time in the country?'

Nell looked down at the child, unable to talk. The child turned its face up to her. And Nell saw it. The smile. The brown eyes.

'Well, Mama?' the child smiled at her.

Nell stumbled back.

'Mama? Mama?' the girl said, her voice full of concern.

The woman from the hallway appeared in the doorway. 'I am sorry, Miss Helen,' she said. 'But Miss Lilian was so excited to see you. You know she won't be told when she has her mind set on something.'

'Mrs Nevin?' Nell said, her hand to her mouth.

'Are you quite well?' Mrs Nevin said, taking a step into the room.

'Miss Helen is quite well,' Mrs Hart said. 'It was awfully hot on the train. I think we could all do with a glass of lemonade.'

Mrs Nevin smiled. 'Very good,' she said. 'Will I leave Miss Lilian with you?'

Mrs Hart nodded. 'Thank you, Mrs Nevin.'

Mrs Hart stooped to speak to the child. 'Mama is a bit tired. She has been extraordinarily busy writing for a whole week,' she said. 'Tommy is in the garden. Why don't you go and play with him? He's been so excited to see you. We'll call you in when the lemonade arrives.'

The child loosened its grip on Nell. She turned to Mrs Hart and threw her arms about her neck. 'Very well, Aunt Leo,' she said. She looked up at Nell. 'Lemonade *always* makes us feel better, Mama, doesn't it?' The child smiled at her before charging toward the back door.

Even though the child had turned its back to Nell, she could still picture her smile. She had pictured it a thousand times. It was Philip's smile.

'Calm yourself,' Mrs Hart said, taking Nell's elbow and guiding her to a small sofa. She helped her sit. Through the open back doors, Nell watched the child race to Tommy, her heels kicking up and her hair loose behind her. Tommy and the girl laughed as they embraced.

'She's mistaken,' Nell said. 'The child is mistaken. There can be no other explanation.'

'Lilian is not mistaken,' Mrs Hart said softly. 'Nell, I know you understand. Lilian is your daughter. You are her mother.'

'I am dreaming. It's another of those hallucinations. What cruel trick is this to play?' Nell clutched her waist and held herself.

'You are very much awake. Be calm, and I will explain what I can.'

'Calm?' Nell half-laughed. 'Calm? How can I be calm when you tell me that child is my daughter? I am nobody's mother. I lost Philip. I lost my baby. This is all too cruel.'

Mrs Hart took a handkerchief from her handbag. She used it to dab at Nell's eyes. So gently. So calmly. 'You know I have to be careful, but I will tell you this. Hill House is a very special place. Not all houses are simply bricks and mortar.'

'That's what Louisa said. Oh, this is ludicrous,' Nell said. 'A house can't change history. It's not possible. None of this is possible.'

'You have seen things at Hill House,' Mrs Hart said. 'You now know the impossible to be possible. Sometimes. Especially when we show love and compassion. And when we sacrifice something precious.'

Mrs Nevin knocked on the door. Mrs Hart called for her to come in. She entered and placed a tray with four glasses and a jug on the table. 'Thank you,' Mrs Hart said.

'Just ring if you'll be wanting anything else,' Mrs Nevin said. 'I shall be in the kitchen. I'm making jam tarts. They are Miss Lilian's favourites,' she smiled. 'As they were Miss Helen's.'

She left and Nell looked at Mrs Hart. 'How?' it was all she could say.

'Sometimes words aren't enough to explain something. Sometimes you need to feel it.' Mrs Hart stood. She smoothed down her skirt and made her way to the back door. 'Tommy. Lilian,' she called. 'Come in now, for your lemonade.'

There was such a commotion from the backdoor and across the room, both children jostling to be the first to the tray. They each helped themselves to a glass. They gulped down the cloudy green liquid and had to gasp for air. The little girl wiped her mouth on the back of her hand and Tommy copied her.

Nell couldn't take her eyes from the child.

Mrs Hart held out her hand. 'Come, Tommy,' she said. 'Show me where you saw the frog last time we visited. Lilian,' she said to the little girl. 'I think your mama would like a hug.'

Mrs Hart led Tommy away as he chatted about the frog at the end of the garden. He was sure there might be a newt, too. The girl placed her glass on the tray. With no further ceremony, she ran to the small sofa. Nell scooped her into her lap. The movement felt as natural as breathing. The girl held Nell tight, her arms about her neck.

'I have missed you, Mama,' she said.

Nell pulled the girl to her and held her. Her brown hair smelled of rosewater and buttery pastry. Her small body fit to Nell's as though it had always been there. As Nell rocked the life in her arms, memories, moments, every minute and every second of this precious girl's existence, knitted into her as though it had always been there.

Lilian Philippa Potter Johnson.

She had been born in the front bedroom of this house on a glorious early summer's day in May 1919. Nell had been attended by Mrs Hart and Charlotte, who Nell had befriended on her trips to visit Mrs Hart at Hill House. The Mandeville children always came to the house in Putney when Mrs Hart visited and were Lilian's playmates. Nell had met Mrs Hart the day the unopened letters had landed on the doormat. Mrs Hart had found a young woman crying by the banks of the Thames. She had taken her for tea and had somehow managed to get her to tell her story. She was the first person Nell had spoken to of her pregnancy. Mrs Hart had taken Nell back to the boarding house, collected her things and taken her to the house in Putney, hiring a nurse to see Nell through her confinement. She hadn't gone to Cambridge, but Mrs Hart had encouraged her to follow her dream to become a writer. Mrs Hart had managed to track down Mrs Nevin to help with the house. And with the baby.

The baby.

Her baby. Who she nicknamed Lilypip so that she would remember her father every time she heard her name.

Lilypip. With her father's eyes, his hair, and his talent for music. And Nell's terrible tendency to get into mischief.

All this Nell knew. It had always been there. Every birthday party and Christmas and every scraped knee. Lilian's first word, spoken in this parlour. 'Dada', she had said, as she looked at the photograph Nell kept of Philip and which Lilian now kept beside her bed to kiss every night.

Lilypip. Who adored animals and books and jigsaw puzzles. And who, if ever she was asked how she would like to pass a day, would say she wanted to visit the animals at the zoo. It was where her father's parents always took her when they visited from Durham. Mrs Hart was acquainted with the Johnsons through friends of friends and brokered that first meeting when Nell still carried their son's child. Philip's parents had fallen deeply in love with their granddaughter, who was the very image of their beloved boy. Nell's own mother had been, and still was, a harder nut to crack, but her father took every opportunity to visit Putney to tend the gardens and to train his granddaughter in the art of pinching out leaves from tomato plants, so they grew straight and true.

Lilian loosened her grip on Nell. 'Mama,' she said, looking up at Nell, her eyes such a deep brown and her voice full of childish concern. 'Do you feel better now?'

'Oh, Lilypip,' Nell said, pulling her close. 'I have never felt better.'

'Was it the lemonade? Mrs Nevin makes the best lemonade, doesn't she?'

'I think so, darling. I really do think so.'

Lilian dug her hand into her pocket and brought out a crushed buttercup. 'I picked this in the park for you, but it got a bit squashed.' She smoothed out the petals. Lifting her chin, she held the tiny flower to her throat. 'Do I like butter, Mama?'

Nell looked at the little spot of yellow sunshine beneath Lilian's chin. 'You love it so much you would spread half a pound on your toast if you were allowed.' The words just came, Nell knew not from where.

Lilian giggled and leant into Nell. 'You always say that, Mama.'

'I do, don't I?' Nell said.

There was a commotion in the doorway to the garden. 'Lilian. Lilian. Won't you ever come out to play?' Tommy called.

'May I?' Lilian asked.

Nell looked into the brown eyes looking back at her. She wanted to hold her and keep her and never release her. But the words that came to her mouth said, 'Of course, darling.'

Lilian slipped from Nell's lap and skipped to the back door where Tommy was waiting. Together they ran into the garden.

Nell stared after them. Her daughter – *her daughter* – was playing in the garden with Tommy Mandeville. She was flesh and blood.

Mrs Hart re-entered the house. She crossed the room and took a seat beside Nell.

'Is this real?' Nell said, still looking to the doors. 'Is she real?'

'Very real,' Mrs Hart said.

When Lilian and Tommy disappeared further up the garden, Nell turned to Mrs Hart. 'I hardly dare take my eyes from her,' she said.

'She won't disappear. You have my word on it,' Mrs Hart said.

'How?' Nell said. 'How... I feel like I have known her for her whole life.'

'You have.'

'But everything else is the same? I came to Hill House looking for inspiration for my next book.'

'Any part of your life touched by Lilian has changed, but everything else is as it was.'

'Everything with Caxton still happened,' Nell said feeling her way through the memories in her mind like a person feeling their way in a darkened room.

'I'm afraid to say it did,' Mrs Hart said.

'And Wilco was there?'

'He was.'

'And Paul is still the new surgeon and he is going to propose to Charlotte?'

Mrs Hart smiled. 'Everything, Nell. Everything is as you remember it. All you did was leave your daughter in the care of Mrs Nevin for a week so that you could work on your next book. Others' memories of some of the conversations you had will be altered slightly. But that is all. And let me ask, Nell, did you find inspiration this week?'

'Excuse me?' Nell said. What a question to ask. What did it matter whether she had found inspiration to write a book when her whole life had been unstitched and stitched back together in a pattern she could not comprehend?

'I think it goes without saying,' Mrs Hart said. 'That we do not talk of the... more unusual happenings at Hill House.'

Nell could hardly hold back a laugh. 'Who would I tell? Nobody would believe me.'

'And of course,' Mrs Hart said. 'There would be no corroboration if you did. But people draw inspiration from Hill House in all manner of ways.'

Nell shook her head. Mrs Hart was talking in riddles. 'I won't tell anybody, if that is what you want to hear me say.'

'I know,' Mrs Hart said. 'But I must thank you before we draw our conversation to a close.' Mrs Hart looked towards the back door. 'Had you not been a guest at Hill House this week, the outcome for Tommy with Caxton could have been different. Had it not been for you and Louisa, it would have been very different. One good turn...'

Nell let Mrs Hart's words sink in. If the last week had taught her anything, it was that it was not so ridiculous to give voice to the most far-fetched of thoughts in her head. 'I saved Tommy for you. So, you saved her for me? Hill House made Lilian come to me?'

Mrs Hart touched Nell's hand.

'But how, I don't—'

Mrs Hart held up her hand. 'Some things just are. That is all you need to know.' She picked up her glass to take a sip. 'Ah, your Mrs Nevin does make the most delicious lemonade.' She placed the glass back on the table. 'As to this quarter's rent, let us defer it for six months. You know, I don't know why you won't take the Johnsons' offer of an annual allowance to help towards raising Lilian.'

'Because I'm not a charity. I have told them many times that I am grateful for their consideration, but I am independent. I will raise Lilian on my own. All they need to give her is love.'

While Nell tried to work out where the words had come from, Mrs Hart smiled. 'I'll have a word with my accountant and let him know not to expect the rent until the New Year.'

Nell stared at Mrs Hart. She spoke so matter-of-factly, as though she had just indeed paid a visit to the house in Putney to discuss the rent. Nell thought despondently that even with six months' grace, it was unlikely that her bank account would yield more than a few pennies.

'I have a feeling your money worries will soon be a thing of the past,' Mrs Hart said. Brushing down her skirt, she added. 'We should be on our way. I have an appointment with my solicitor.' She stood and called to the back door. 'Thomas, it is time to go. Say goodbye to Lilian, please.'

Miraculously, Tommy responded to an instruction from an adult. He was soon back in the parlour with Lilian, their cheeks red from playing in the sun.

'Lilian,' Mrs Hart said, 'Please come with me to thank Mrs Nevin for the lemonade. Thomas, say goodbye to Nell, please.'

Lilian accompanied Mrs Hart out into the hall, chatting as they went.

When Tommy made his way, he didn't run or skip. He walked slowly to Nell. He sat on the sofa beside her and took her hand in his.

A laugh came from the direction of the kitchen. Nell's ears tuned to it. It was a laugh full of light. She had heard it before.

'She was waiting for you,' Tommy said. 'She has always been with you. But recently you have heard her.'

'The dolls' house...' Nell said, looking to the kitchen. 'The running in the attic and the laughing and the stroking my hair in the night. It was Lilypip.'

Tommy gently squeezed her hands. 'It is time for us to leave. At least for a while. But,' he said, squeezing her hands again. 'There is a heart that is broken. In a body in pain. Sometimes a patched-up heart can fit the broken pieces of another. Two halves may make one whole.'

Even with everything that was happening to her, something so deep inside Nell pulled towards that man in a hospital bed in Northamptonshire.

Tommy smiled, his faraway smile. He reached to kiss Nell on the cheek. She held the precious boy close. But as she held him, his behaviour altered. He squirmed to be freed and sat back. He shook his head and sniffed the air. 'Those jam tarts

smell jolly good,' he said. 'Do you think Mrs Nevin will let me
have one?'

'I should think so,' Nell said.

Slipping down from the sofa, Tommy ran to the kitchen.

Alone, Nell looked around the room. Being here felt as
natural as drawing breath. This was home, where she lived with
her daughter. Where she worked and where her life was. Pieces
of that life were slotting into place, replacing the pieces of
another life. The memories of that other life did not disappear,
but moved away, fading into the background. But one piece was
still there. A piece which held the darkness and the sadness.
Philip had never known his daughter. His daughter would
never know him. Never know the love of a father who would
have adored her.

Nell looked to the mantelshelf. To a photograph she knew
would be there as she had placed the frame there herself. The
young man in that photograph in his officer's uniform would
always be young. His smile would always be true, his
complexion fresh. His hair would never grey with age and his
shoulders would never sag with the weight of the burden life
had placed on him. She closed her eyes and heard the words she
had heard in the bedroom at Hill House. And the promise she
had made to Philip.

'I don't know if I can,' she whispered. A breeze blew
through the open window, disturbing the curtain. It blew the
hairs on Nell's arm. She closed her eyes and nodded.

SIXTY-THREE

SATURDAY 20TH DECEMBER 1924

On a crisp, chill December day, three figures look from the frost-covered grass of Primrose Hill, across Regent's Park, and towards the city below.

A man and a woman stand on either side of a child, a small girl, who is excited that she can hear the lions at the zoo roar from here. The man kneels, to talk to the child. He explains that it was his daughter's favourite spot, too, when she was very small. He and her mother would bring her here to look over London. They lived in Camden, so it was very close.

Did his daughter like animals? the girl asks.

She did, the man replies. Giraffes were her favourite.

The girl squeals. They are her favourite too.

The woman looks at him and smiles.

As one, they decide to walk through the park and into town; it is too nice a day to take a bus or the crowded Underground with the Christmas shoppers packed in for their final Saturday of shopping. As they walk, the small child reaches her mittened hands up to hold the hands of both the man and the woman.

When they reach the West End, they brave the crowds to look in the window of Foyle's on Charing Cross Road. There is a display in the window, of a book that has been rushed out for Christmas. It is the story of a house that comes alive. The story of a family who welcome wayward souls to help them find the right path. It is a work of pure fiction, the author explains when *The Times* asks where she found her inspiration. It is a departure from her usual books. It was written in just a month and has been rushed out for Christmas. It is predicted to be a huge success.

The three decide to celebrate with iced buns and sweet tea in a small teashop where the windows drip with condensation. They watch the shoppers hurry by, attempting to guess what gifts they have in their parcels and bags.

Afterwards, the man hails a taxicab to take them back to the house on a neat street in Putney.

A roaring fire in the hearth awaits them and a warm welcome from a woman who is roasting a joint of beef for their dinner. She tries to hide a smile at the sight of the man and woman together. She is more like family than a member of staff.

Over dinner, the man asks the girl what she might like Father Christmas to bring her. She would like a puppy, she says. When he says that it might squirm too much to stay in a stocking hanging on the mantelshelf, the woman says that it might also make a mess that the girl might not want to clear away. The girl says she will. She promises and promises. What the girl doesn't know is that the puppy is being collected at midday on Christmas Eve by her grandfather. There are plans to keep it from her until Christmas Morning when the intention is that it springs from a box to surprise her, just after she has placed her new favourite decoration on the Christmas tree. It is a silver bauble decorated with a gold star that her mother brought back from her trip in the summer.

After dinner they sit in the parlour, the man in the armchair before the fire and the woman and the child on the small sofa. The girl asks if they would like to hear her play her violin. They say they would like it very much. She plays Good King Wenceslas and then Amazing Grace. She is talented beyond her years. When she notices a tear in the woman's eye, she is concerned. But it is nothing, just a smut from the fire, the woman says.

The girl takes a book down from the shelf. She sits on the rug before the fire to read. Soon, she is standing beside the arm of the chair to ask the man to help with a tricky word. And then she has crawled into the chair beside him, resting her head on his shoulder so that he might read to her.

The woman watches them and her heart fills. It is only the third time he has visited. He lives some way away and is busy with his work. She hasn't wanted his presence to disrupt the child's life. She needn't have worried. Two more contented people she has not seen.

When the girl yawns, the woman carries her to bed. She tucks her in and kisses her goodnight.

Before returning to the parlour, she watches the man through a gap in the open door. The man is standing, looking out of the window.

She still has her dark days. What happened to her, still happened to her. And what happened to him, still happened to him. They have each spoken to a good doctor who has helped them understand and begin to live with their experiences, and the repercussions.

She pushes open the door and he turns to look at her. She thanks him for the kindness he has shown the child. He says that it is a pleasure. His trips to see them have become the highlight of his life.

They stand and look at each other. Each watches the reflection of the fire in the other's eyes. And then they lean into each other and kiss for the first time.

They kiss again.

He holds her close, and she feels safe and wanted in his arms.

It is not as it was with another man. It is different. But it is good.

A piece of the jigsaw falls into place.

She closes her eyes and kisses him again.

A LETTER FROM THE AUTHOR

Dear reader,

I'd like to say a huge thank you for reading *The Mandeville Secret*.

I hope you enjoyed spending time with Nell and continuing the journey of the Mandevilles and their home, Hill House.

If you want to join other readers in hearing about my new releases and bonus content, you can sign up here:

www.stormpublishing.co/callie-langridge

If you enjoyed this book and could spare a few moments to leave a review, I would hugely appreciate it. Even a short review can make all the difference in encouraging a reader to discover my books for the first time. Thank you so much!

History has always been my passion. Exploring old houses and imagining the lives that have lived within their walls has fascinated me for as long as I can remember. Bringing this to life with the Mandevilles and their special guests at Hill House is a constant joy.

Thanks again for being part of this amazing journey with me. I love to hear from my readers through my social media channels, so please feel free to find me for a chat. I hope you'll stay in touch as I have so many more stories and ideas to share with you!

All the very best,

Callie Langridge

facebook.com/CallieLangridgeAuthor

twitter.com/CLangridgeWrite

instagram.com/CallieLangridge

ACKNOWLEDGEMENTS

I would like to thank everyone at Storm for getting the Mandeville series into the world. Special thanks to Kathryn and Vicky and all the readers for being wonderful and helping me make this book the best it can be. And thank you to Oliver for establishing a marvellous publisher that's friendly, warm and supportive.

I am so fortunate to be surrounded by a fantastic group of fellow authors who have kept me company on the path of writing this book. Thank you to my marvellous writing pals who have been there from the very first line, written many years ago – Zoe Antoniades, Sam Hanson, Susie Lynes and John Rogers. I'm also lucky to have collected many other writing pals along the way who have provided encouragement with this book – Clarissa Angus, Claire McGlasson, Emilie Olsson, Kate Riordan, Emma Robinson, Bev Thomas and Lisa Timoney. Thank you (and perhaps apologies) to those of you who have spent nights at writing retreats with me in creaky old manor houses that might have been haunted...

A woman cannot live by writing friends alone. I will forever be grateful to Kim, Val and Virginia for their ongoing encouragement and never-ending patience and enthusiasm for my writing. And a very special thanks to Pete, always my cheerleader in chief.

Printed in Great Britain
by Amazon